Mr. Darcy's Brides

A Pride and Prejudice Vagary

by Regina Jeffers

Regency Solutions

Mr. Darcy's Brides

A Pride and Prejudice Vagary

Regency Solutions

Chapter 1

"ARE YOU WELL?" his cousin, Colonel Fitzwilliam, whispered. "You appear as if you were going to the guillotine. You can still call off this madness."

Darcy closed his eyes and swallowed hard against the panic filling his chest. "It was my mother's dearest wish," he said in lame explanation, but in his heart he knew it could not be so. He sincerely believed that Lady Anne Darcy would want him to be happy, and without a question in his mind, marrying his cousin Anne would never bring anything but loneliness and misery. However, each time his Aunt Catherine repeated the tale of how she and Lady Anne had looked upon the newborn Anne and had made a pact that he and Anne would marry, the story took precedence over his hopes for a marriage where his wife would assist him in shouldering the burdens of Pemberley and of his name. Marrying to secure bloodlines was a common practice among the aristocracy, but Darcy had never thought he would be called upon to make such a sacrifice. "I am of an age where I require a wife. Pemberley requires a mistress. And with what occurred with Georgiana at Ramsgate, as you know more than anyone, my sister requires a confidante and an advisor."

The colonel pressed. "No one can say that I do not adore Anne, but this is not the marriage either you or she deserves. And as to Georgiana, thanks to our aunt's overbearing nature, Anne possesses no experience in society. She could not assist Georgiana now or in the future. It is more likely that it would be Georgie who would offer the advice. I beg you not to permit Lady Catherine to destroy your life or Anne's simply to support her ladyship's consequence."

Darcy shot a hurried look around the church. "It is too late. There are too many witnesses for me to call off now. Such would destroy Anne's reputation."

Elizabeth knew she would not be able to see much from behind the veil draping the curve of her bonnet, and she held no doubt that her head would itch from the scraps of a cut up wig she had attached to the straw bonnet. Before she left her childhood home, she had discovered the wig in the attic at Longbourn. Mr. Hill, her father's manservant, seemed to think it had belonged to her paternal grandfather, a man of "peculiar tendencies," Mr. Hill had said with diplomacy.

"It does not matter if the wig were nicer," she had assured her sister. "It will be enough to provide the impression that my hair is blonde, and the veil will cover my face until it is too late for Mama to realize it is not you who has married Mr. Collins. The morning shadows in the church will do the rest. If we are fortunate, it will be cloudy on the day of the ceremony."

"Are you certain this is best?" Jane pleaded with tears forming in her eyes. "As much as I have no desire to marry the man, neither do I wish you to be attached to Papa's cousin."

The fact that Jane had participated willingly in this charade spoke a great deal of her sister's dismay at their mother's ultimatum that Jane marry Mr. Bennet's heir, Mr. Collins, a man none of them knew by countenance.

"I am certain." Elizabeth squeezed the back of Jane's hand to comfort her sister's growing anxiousness. "Even if Mr. Collins would suddenly switch his promise to marry one of the Bennet sisters from you to me, grounds for an annulment would still remain, for I shall take my vows as *Jane Bennet*. The marriage will be void. You must simply escape to Aunt Gardiner's relations in Derbyshire. I will stall as long as possible, so you may be several hours upon the road before anyone discovers our deception. As only you and I and Aunt Gardiner know of your whereabouts, you should be safe until Mama's vengeance has waned."

"More likely, the devil's disciples will be wearing nothing but their unmentionables before our mother's ire dissipates."

Elizabeth agreed, but she would not give voice to her concerns. Jane's agreement to escape to the northern shires was uncharacteristic enough. "The only thing that worries me is that you will travel so far and alone."

"I assure you, in these circumstances, I can be as strong as is required, but do not fret of my traveling unchaperoned, for Aunt Gardiner will send a maid with me. But what of Papa? How shall Mr. Bennet react when he discovers what we have done to thwart Mama's plans?"

After his horse had thrown him during a thunderstorm, their father had experienced a long bout of consumption, which had turned into lung fever. Such was the reason Mrs. Bennet had decided that Jane must marry their father's heir presumptive in order to save the family. It was almost as if their mother had decided that Mr. Bennet would leave them at the mercy of the "odious" Mr. Collins, as Mrs. Bennet was fond of calling the man. As Jane was considered one of the prettiest ladies in Hertfordshire, their mother had thought that Mr. Collins would accept a comely wife immediately. Their mother assumed that if Mr. Bennet passed from his afflictions, Collins could drive the Bennet family from Longbourn. Therefore, Mrs. Bennet meant to secure Mr. Collins's patronage by marrying off her eldest daughter to the man.

"Papa is improving, but he is not yet well enough to bring a halt to Mama's manipulations, and, in truth, I feared speaking to him of this matter. He would insist upon leaving his bed before

Doctor French says it is safe. However, I have recruited Mary to watch over him, and I have made some bit of explanation to our sister. She has promised her silence unless we meet difficulties."

"You realize our mother will be enraged by our actions?" Jane asked in tentative tones.

"I shall be viewed as the architect of this plan," Elizabeth said with a shrug of resignation. She often knew her mother's disfavor. Fanny Bennet rarely had a kind word for her second daughter. "But better Mrs. Bennet's temper than a lifetime of drudgery with Mr. Collins in a cottage in Kent, bowing and scraping to know the pleasure of his benefactor. Papa calls the man an obvious twit. I am not certain that Mr. Bennet has ever met the man, but Papa considered Mr. Collins's father a candidate for Bedlam. Naturally, he would transfer his opinion of the late Mr. Collins to his son."

That conversation had occurred four days prior. Jane and Mrs. Bennet had traveled to Cheapside two days later, and Elizabeth had followed the day after. While her mother and sister had known the comfort of Mr. Bennet's coach, Elizabeth had braved the mail coach, riding on top all the way to London. If all had gone as she planned, Jane had boarded a northbound coach at half past nine of the clock this morning. The wedding was to take place at eleven. Fortunately, another ceremony was to follow at half past eleven, so everything had to run efficiently.

Aunt Gardiner had assisted her two favorite nieces with what others would call a "hare-brained" scheme, as foolish as a March hare. Their aunt had made arrangements for Jane to stay with Aunt Gardiner's relations outside of Derby. This morning, she was to insist that Mrs. Bennet view the church prior to the ceremony to make certain all was done properly. After all, Mr. Collins was a man of the cloth and would not approve if things were performed in a slip-shod manner. As quickly as they departed the house, Jane was to be on her way to the posting inn and the coach north.

Perhaps things would have been different if her family had known anything of Mr. Collins prior to the news that he

4

was willing to marry Jane, but they knew nothing of the man's countenance or of his disposition or of his mind. All they knew was that Collins was the son of her father's cousin, a man with whom Mr. Bennet had experienced a falling out more than two decades prior. "He could have moles all over his face," Jane had declared with a dramatic shiver, and Elizabeth had fought the urge to say something more repugnant. Even so, Mrs. Bennet had corresponded with the man and had made all the arrangements for the wedding.

Mr. Gardiner, on the other hand, had sworn to have no portion in bamming his sister. The only part in which he had participated was securing a safe place for Elizabeth to stay and the hiring of a hackney for Elizabeth before he departed for his warehouses. Her uncle knew the driver personally. At half past ten on the day of the wedding, the carriage arrived at the back door of Uncle Gardiner's office on Milk Street.

"Where to, miss?" the driver asked before she climbed into the coach. She carried her bonnet in a stiff paper bandbox.

The question caught her off guard. She had only arrived in London the previous evening and had spent the night "hiding" in her uncle's office, a necessity, for Mrs. Bennet thought Elizabeth still at home in Hertfordshire. She wished she knew London better. "The *saints* church upon the Thames. It is not supposed to be far. Do you know of the one I speak?"

"Aye, miss, I believe I do. The Thames forms the south boundary for St. George."

When she spent time with the Gardiners in London, they attended St. Mary-le-Bow. She knew St. Mary was not the church her mother had selected, but for the life of her, she could not recall the exact name of the church hosting the Collins's wedding, and, needless to say, she could not ask anyone the appropriate directions. She had not seen the name written down and had only heard it when she had eavesdropped on a conversation between Mrs. Bennet and Jane. *I should have asked Jane,* she admonished her forgetfulness. *But there were so many details to remember.* In false confidence, Elizabeth smiled up at the man. "I will trust your instincts. Now, we cannot be late. This is my wedding day." She laughed at her private amusement.

"Have you no servant, miss?"

Her Grandmother Gardiner always said one could tell a liar by how often he smiled, but instinctively, to disguise her nervousness, Elizabeth's smile widened. "They have all gone ahead, and my uncle was called away before he could assist me." She tossed a coin to the man to end his questioning. "Not too much jostling, sir."

Once inside the coach, she lowered the window shade while she set the wigged bonnet upon her head. It was truly an ugly creation. Once the bonnet was set and pinned in place, Elizabeth turned her concentration to mimicking Jane's mannerisms. "Stand tall," she told herself.

Her aunt had instructed her, "When entering the church itself, stay close to the pews: For there is a groove in the aisle's center from so many people's steps, which will make you appear shorter. The sides are an inch or so higher."

The carriage ride had ended quicker than what Elizabeth had expected, for she had been engrossed in all the little details she and Jane had discussed at Longbourn, but in the distance she could hear the various clocks in the City chiming eleven. When she alighted before the majestic-looking church, a young gentleman rushed forward to greet her. "Your groom and your mother are becoming anxious. Please follow me. I will lead you to the anteroom." He glanced to the departing coach. "You are the bride, are you not?"

Elizabeth prayed the man did not look upon her too closely. Knowing her mother, Mrs. Bennet had told all involved of Jane's beauty. "Yes, sir." She glanced about her, impressed by the imposing cut of the houses and the open space surrounding the church. She imagined that Mr. Collins's benefactor had instructed him as to which church was proper for a man she employed.

The man's tone held suspicion. "Why the public coach?"

"My uncle's coach experienced difficulty. He sent me ahead so I would not be late." Elizabeth prayed that God was not keeping a tally of all the lies she had spoken of late.

The man's expression did not soften, but he said, "Then we should not keep your future husband waiting. I certainly would not wish to know the disfavor of a man of his consequence."

Elizabeth wished to know something of Mr. Collins's *consequence,* but she could not ask without betraying her ignorance of her groom; instead, she scrambled to keep up with the man, who pointed to an open door before saying, "Wait there. I will inform the vicar of your arrival."

Elizabeth did as the man indicated. Inside the shadowy anteroom, she took a few steadying breaths before lowering the veil. She could see her feet, but little else.

The man returned within a few minutes. "As you have no male relative to present you, one of the vicar's assistants will escort you. As you are of age, there is no need for your father's permission during the service."

Elizabeth held her tongue. Although she was but twenty, Jane was two years her senior. "I am prepared, sir."

"You are a fortunate young lady," the man announced without preamble. "You shall claim an exalted position."

Exalted? How was being the wife of a country clergyman an exalted position? Elizabeth wondered of the man's meaning, but the rector's assistant appeared in the small room before she could ask her question. The man offered a brief introduction and then caught her arm to lead her toward the main aisle. "I apologize for not providing you a moment to acclimate yourself to your surroundings," he whispered, "but your mother is most insistent that the marriage should occur in a timely manner."

"I understand, sir," Elizabeth spoke from the corner of her mouth.

There were shafts of light from what she assumed were clerestory windows that marked the way, but even so, she clung to Mr. Fredrich's arm so as not to stumble. Evidently, she had received her wish. It was cloudy outside, and the church was filled with shadows. Her stomach churned in anticipation of the upcoming confrontation with her mother. Elizabeth was certain to be locked in her room with only the barest of meals for weeks upon end for the impudence she practiced, perhaps, even a beating, but, at least, Jane would be free to find a proper husband and mayhap a taste of love. As for her, if she survived Mrs. Bennet's punishment, a man who would treat her with respect would be to Elizabeth's liking. Anything beyond that would be a blessing.

About her, Elizabeth became aware of a variety of whispers. There were more people in attendance than she would have predicted. Mr. Collins must have invited several of his university chums or members of his congregation or even relations. Did the man have other relations of which her father remained unaware? Was it possible that his patron had come to view the woman he intended to marry? Then again, those viewing her procession up the aisle could be early attendees for the ceremony which was to follow this one. Did the clouds promise rain? Had the people watching her sought shelter in the church? As she took another step closer to her grand plan, she prayed that Aunt Gardiner could remove Mrs. Bennet from the chamber before the next couple arrived to speak their vows. She thought it unusual for a ceremony on the half hour, but she supposed it was a matter of urgency — a compromised woman or a man near his death or even a mercenary vicar who meant to squeeze every dollar from those willing to pay. Customarily, weddings were only available during the week days between ten and noon.

At length, her hand was placed in Mr. Collins's, and she was surprised by the warmth of his and by the zap of heat shooting up her arm, even through her glove. Elizabeth resisted the urge to shake the sizzle from her hand. As the vicar cleared his throat to begin the ceremony, she gave thanks that Jane had escaped this forced marriage and that their mother had not yet noted it was she rather than Jane standing before the clergyman.

Mr. Collins's hand caught her elbow to turn her toward the robed incumbent. Again, heat rushed up her arm. She convinced herself it was fear that she had experienced, but her heart pronounced it as something more. She wished she had known more of the man standing beside her. He was tall--that much she could discern by glancing down to his feet, which were encased in polished high boots. His feet were large, meaning he was tall. Grandmother Gardiner always said a tall man had much turned under for foundation. The thought of the cackle that would have accompanied her grandmother's pronouncement brought a smile to Elizabeth's lips.

Darcy noted the smile on Anne's lips and wondered why she suddenly appeared content with their marriage. Certainly, he was not. He considered it torture. And why did she attempt to hide her face with the heavy veil? He could barely make out her familiar features. The "mystery" would not make her more beautiful to him. Anne was fair of countenance, but, when exposed to the sunlight, her skin had always appeared extremely pale. Meanwhile, her movements indicated fragility. On her approach to the raised dais upon which the wedding party stood, she had clung to Mr. Fredrich's arm just to navigate the aisle. Darcy wondered if he would be called upon to spend a lifetime of assisting her across the room or up and down the long staircase at Pemberley.

And what of the bonnet she wore? Certainly, the air had a chill on this particular day, but the fur trim upon a straw bonnet was ridiculous. He resisted the urge to look upon his aunt's features. He was certain a look of triumph marked Lady Catherine's expression. He supposed both the fur trim and the heavy veil were her ladyship's idea of what was proper. He had heard tales of how Lady Catherine had insisted upon a veil when she married Sir Lewis De Bourgh, despite his mother, Lady Anne, decrying the necessity. He strained to view something of Anne's expression beneath the layers of lace. He wished he could see her expression to know what she thought of this farce in which they participated. Surprisingly, he knew some comfort in the fact that her hair was tightly constrained beneath the bonnet. If there were curls framing her face or something less strict, he would be crying foul, for he would know that, for once, Anne had broken with her mother's strictures. Instead, looking down upon her, he could view the dark strains of her hair at the edge of the rabbit fur. Her garb was symbolic of how she hid herself from the world. The pretense continued. Such a charade would be his life.

More of immediate importance, he wondered upon the feeling of awareness he had experienced when he had accepted his cousin's hand from the cleric's assistant. The shock had brought a momentary frown to his forehead before he recovered his expression. His cousin, the colonel, must have noted Darcy's expression, for Fitzwilliam cleared his throat in obvious warning. With a heavy sigh, Darcy attempted to concentrate on the vicar's words, but his heart spoke to how wrong this marriage would be.

To his surprise, the ceremony progressed quickly, quicker than he would like, but with a second prompting from the clergy, Darcy repeated his vows. Then it was Anne's turn. He prayed she might have the courage to defy her mother and set them both free, but he knew Lady Catherine's will to be absolute. Anne's nerves must have gotten in his cousin's way, for she broke into a coughing fit, which was mixed in with her promises of marriage. A sip of water permitted her to finish, but there was an unusual rasp to her voice.

Finally, the vicar instructed him to place his ring upon her hand. Dutifully, she removed her glove, and he took her hand in his. Again, cognizance wove its way up his arm, and he found himself leaning into her. The scent of lavender filled his nostrils. Odd. Did Anne not always rinse her hair in rose water?

"I now pronounce you man and wife," the vicar declared.

Elizabeth listened carefully to Mr. Collins's voice. It was a very nice voice — one she could envision listening to with interest as he read to her in the evenings. It was mature and deep and tantalizing. She was beginning to wonder if she had made a mistake. Was it possible that Jane could have known happiness with Mr. Collins? Although she could not make out his features, his bearing and the educated accents of his speech spoke of a gentleman and not the *loathsome toad* he was suspected of being. She shook her head to clear her thinking when she realized the vicar had finished his welcome and the preface.

The incumbent continued, "I am required by church law to ask if anyone present knows just reason why these persons may not lawfully marry. If so, declare it now."

Most assuredly she knew a reason, but Elizabeth bit her lip rather than to confess her misrepresentation before it became common knowledge.

"The vows you are about to take are to be made in the presence of God, who is judge of us all and knows all the secrets of our hearts; therefore, if either of you knows a reason you may not lawfully marry, you must declare it."

Again, Elizabeth prayed that God would forgive her for her silence. She wondered if Mr. Collins could hear how loudly her heart pounded. It seemed to explode in her ears. Not fully listening to the clergy's admonishments to her and the gentleman regarding the need to love and to honor and to forsake all others, she managed to mumble the required "I will" upon cue. The vicar's inflection told her when she should be responding; otherwise, she barely listened to the man, for he spoke in a monotone, as if he were as bored as those listening to him.

The deeper into the ceremony they progressed, the more nausea her stomach knew. She had not eaten this morning, for she was too busy pacing the length of her uncle's office to think upon eating. *Please God, do not allow me to be sick before those who are gathered here.* Her insides lurched, and she pressed her hand to her lips before swallowing the bile that threatened to choke her. A coughing fit claimed her just as the vicar instructed her to speak her vows.

"I take you William (cough) to be my husband (cough... cough) from this day (cough) in sickness and in health (cough... cough...cough) till death do us part (cough...cough) in the presence of (cough) I make this vow." Her coughs hid part of the sacred pledge. For that, she was thankful. Such could prove useful in voiding the marriage later. She was not certain, however, whether she had pronounced Jane's name or not. *It does not signify,* she told herself. *Neither Jane nor I will marry William Collins today.*

The gentleman held out the ring, and she removed the glove from her left hand. He spoke the necessary words. "I give you this ring as a sign of our marriage. With my body, I honor you, all that I am I give to you, and all that I have, I share with you, within the love of God, Father, Son, and the Holy Spirit."

Mr. Collins turned her to face those in attendance, and Elizabeth prepared herself for the *great unveiling.* Behind her, the vicar proclaimed them to be husband and wife, but her mind was on the accusations she would endure from her mother when her face was revealed to those in attendance.

The moment of truth arrived. Mr. Collins reached for the lace covering her eyes and cheeks to expose her to one and all. Unsurprisingly, tears filled Elizabeth's eyes. She had perpetrated a lie upon all she held most dear, and the idea that she would embarrass her family, as well as Mr. Collins, grieved her. She doubted her mother would ever forgive her. Moreover, she had likely sealed her fate: God would never grant her a happy marriage, for she had taken his holy ceremony and had made a mockery of it.

Mr. Collins lifted the veil. Just for a moment she looked into the most compelling eyes she had ever encountered. Then shock sent a variety of emotions crisscrossing his features. Anger. Confusion. Irritation. As well as an expression she could not identify. It appeared to be something close to relief.

But then, he regarded her with narrowed eyes. His mouth tightened; yet, for a moment she half-expected him to catch her to him. *Silly.* She chided herself for her foolishness. *The man does not even know your real name.*

He glared at her boldly. He was undoubtedly a man full of self-assurance. *Where was the self-ingratiating toad her father had described?* There was no question that the man before her could leave servants and underlings quaking in their boots and foolish young women swooning at his feet if he so desired it.

His hair was dark brown with a lock falling across his forehead. As he studied her, one of his equally dark brows remained quirked high. Elizabeth found herself wetting her suddenly dry lips. A flush of color flooded her cheeks. She must appear a fool with her matted bonnet still upon her head, and for some unexplained reason, she did not wish to be viewed as a dullard before this man.

A shriek filled the church, and Elizabeth turned, expecting to discover her mother charging up the aisle to ring a peal over her head. Instead, the caterwaul had come from a handsome, but elderly woman, clad in rich finery and sporting several tall plumes in her hair.

"Where is Anne?" she yelled while raising her fist as if to strike someone. "What have you done with my daughter, you... you...?"

Mr. Collins placed Elizabeth behind him. "We will not learn the truth of Anne's whereabouts if you do not calm down, Aunt Catherine." He shoved Elizabeth in the direction of a military officer, who caught her and dragged her toward a small door behind the altar.

"I do not know who you are," the man said with a backward glance to the commotion erupting in the church, "but you have saved my cousin from the greatest mistake of his life."

Chapter 2

SHOCK STRUMMED THROUGH Elizabeth's veins. Her perfect plan to save Jane had met an unexpected bump in the road and been turned upon its head. Tears filled her eyes at the knowledge of not only failing Jane, but also of the havoc created by her actions. "I am grieved. I am grieved," she repeated as the military officer dragged her from the chapel. She glanced behind her where the groom physically restrained the woman who spewed accusations regarding Elizabeth's character, as well as her upbringing and her birthright.

The officer pointedly closed the door to silence the chaos. He captured her shoulders and shoved her into a straight-backed chair along the wall of the narrow passageway. It was then that she realized her hands were trembling.

The man knelt before her. She noticed that he was a colonel with a very nice countenance. Not exactly handsome, but he possessed welcoming eyes and an expression of true concern. "Are you well, miss? Would you like me to secure you something to drink to settle your composure?"

Despite her misery, Elizabeth offered the man a small smile. "I doubt there is more than sacrificial wine. We are in a *church.* Moreover, I believe I have defamed the church enough for one day."

The colonel's eyes twinkled in mischief. "I am certain the vicar could spare a bit of port if you wish it." She shook off his offer, and he placed his hand upon Elizabeth's and gave it a gentle squeeze of encouragement. "Might you share your side of what occurred in the church?"

She sucked in a steadying breath. "I was to take the bride's place to prevent the marriage."

"Did someone pay you to perform this burlesque?"

Elizabeth wished she knew exactly what occurred so she could explain it to the man. "Most assuredly not. My disguise was my idea."

"Your idea?" he questioned.

"It was meant to save my sister from a forced marriage."

Curiosity crossed the gentleman's features. "Your sister? Not my cousin Miss De Bourgh?"

Elizabeth's shoulders stiffened. "I assure you, sir, I hold no acquaintance with anyone of the surname De Bourgh. My sister was to marry a distant cousin and heir to my father's estate in Hertfordshire. Mr. Collins resides at Hunsford Cottage in Kent. That is all I know of the gentleman except my father deems the man a dimwit."

The colonel barked a laugh, which surprised her. "Your father sounds quite astute." He glanced to the door leading to the chapel. The din had again increased in volume. "It sounds as if my cousin requires my assistance. I will return in a few moments. Do not fret. All will be well. Your *groom* is accustomed to dealing with our aunt when the *grand lady* is in one of her fits."

With that, he stood to leave. As he opened the door, Elizabeth could hear the woman screech, "I want the magistrate summoned immediately." Elizabeth did not wait to discover if the colonel's cousin could calm the woman's ire. When the gentleman closed the door behind him, she followed the passageway to the back of the church, where she took off at a run. She needed to reach her Uncle Gardiner. He was her only hope of not knowing a London magistrate's justice.

Darcy wished his aunt would be quiet for one minute, so he might make sense of what had occurred. He would not openly admit to his present company that he had never desired a marriage to his Cousin Anne, but he knew his duty to his name and his estate and had placed those desires aside. After all, bloodlines were important in the society in which he operated. He shot a quick glance over his aunt's shoulder to see Lady Matlock take his sister Georgiana into her arms and direct his sister from the church.

"Where is Anne?" His aunt stomped her foot in frustration.

"Do I appear to know of my cousin's whereabouts?" Darcy countered.

"I would not have put it past you, Darcy, to have arranged this show to discredit my daughter and to be rid of your duty to your family," she accused.

Darcy's temper snapped into place. "I advise you, your ladyship, to keep such disparagements on my family name to yourself. You will not garner my support by speaking such of the Darcys."

Lord Matlock caught his sister to him. "We must act with more decorum, Catherine," he cautioned.

Not surprisingly, Lady Catherine's dramatics were not so easily dissuaded. "I want Anne found at once." His aunt caught at her chest as if she were in true distress. "Oh, Heavens! What if my darling girl has been kidnapped? What if a ransom letter is being delivered at this moment to Matlock's Town house?"

Darcy's uncle attempted to restrain his sister's hysterics. "I am certain there is another explanation, Catherine."

"Do not cry, Mother!" They all turned to discover Anne rushing up the aisle. A yet untied and heavily veiled bonnet precariously bouncing upon her head. "I am grieved to be late!"

Lady Catherine broke free of Matlock's grasp and caught her daughter to her. "Thank the Heavens you are safe," she said as she cupped Anne's cheeks in a rare show of tenderness. But Anne's profession of apology must have registered with his aunt, for her hold on Anne's jaws tightened until his cousin's mouth appeared that of a floundering fish. His Aunt Catherine hissed, "You are late and not importuned?" Anne attempted to nod her answer, but Lady Catherine tightened her grip once again. Darcy wondered if he would be called upon to save his cousin's life. "You were late upon the most important day of your life?"

Anne mumbled through restrictive breaths. "I was nervous...took a draught...fell asleep."

Darcy thought it apropos that his cousin had turned to the sleeping draughts so readily available in her home for comfort. Lady Catherine had spent a lifetime "calming" her daughter with medicinals.

Lord Matlock pried his sister's fingers from Anne's neck, as her ladyship spoke in deathlike tones. "You were asleep while Darcy was here waiting for you?" Lady Catherine turned to him. "You will marry Anne now," she instructed in the no-nonsense tone his aunt often used with her cottagers. "The vicar will repeat the service."

It would be a cold day at the Devil's workshop before Darcy repeated his vows to another. He did not know why the woman had pretended to be Anne, but he was not sorry for the deception. "I fear that will be impossible, your ladyship. There is the small matter of determining whether I am married to another."

Anne asked in what sounded of delightful surprise, "You married another, Darcy?"

"It would appear so," he said with a silly grin that he could not quite wipe from his lips. He had escaped a fate worse than the great Hercules's trials. The Nemean Lion or even the nine-headed Lernaean Hydra were nothing compared to naming Lady Catherine as his mother in marriage. He would find a means to void his marriage to the stranger and walk away from this disaster with only a few "social" bruises.

"I will not have it!" his aunt's voice again rose in

indignation. "I want the magistrate summoned immediately! That little deceiver will not know success. I will see to it!"

Darcy was thankful his cousin, Colonel Fitzwilliam, reappeared at his side. "The woman?" he asked under his breath.

"In the passageway," Fitzwilliam whispered.

"Would you assist your father in clearing the church? I imagine the vicar would prefer to see our backsides. I will deal with the woman. Did she provide an explanation for what occurred?"

"Yes, but you should hear it for yourself." His cousin's smile grew wider, and Darcy wondered upon the true mirth fully displayed in the colonel's features.

"Does the woman have a name?" Darcy inquired with a lift of his eyebrow.

"In truth, I did not ask. I was too enticed by the twinkle in her eyes."

"You are a scoundrel." Darcy shook his head in disbelief.

"Trust me, Darcy. Look into the lady's eyes, and you will agree," Fitzwilliam warned.

Instead, Darcy looked upon the chaos still going on in the church aisles. This spectacle would be the talk of London tomorrow. The *ton* would relish the tale of how Fitzwilliam Darcy found himself married to a complete stranger. Darcy had no doubt his revered father was turning over in his grave at this very moment, but he held a suspicion that his free-spirited mother would be laughing in delight. He could weather this madness. True he would feel the brunt of several jokes from those at his clubs, but that would be nothing. He was quite familiar with the idea of how a stern upper lip and a scowl could quiet even his strongest critics. He had perfected those looks. It was his gentle side—the "gentle" part of being a gentleman—that he rarely showed anyone other than his closest friends and relations.

First things first, he told himself. He must determine the woman's identity and then discover a means to void his marriage. A tidy sum donated to the bishop should do well in moving this issue through the church courts. But for now, he would have an explanation from a woman whose countenance he would never forget, for, in truth, like his cousin, the colonel, he had looked for a few brief seconds into her eyes after he lifted her veil to discover a certain mystique he could not name.

He tapped lightly on the door so as not to frighten her before opening it slowly. He stepped into the shadowy passageway, but there was no one about. His cousin had not said where the woman awaited him so Darcy moved along the length of the passage, trying the doors as he went. He discovered two storage closets and one small office, but not the female who had disrupted his well-planned day. However, a turn to the left answered his question about her whereabouts. A door stood open to the outside. "Demme!" he cursed, and then recalled he was in a church.

His pace quickened as he burst through the opening, which led to a small enclosed garden. "I may kill her," he groused. "Or better yet, permit my aunt to do so. Where could she have gone?"

"Mr. Darcy?"

He turned to find Mr. Fredrich, the man's face flushed with color. "Your cousin, the colonel, thought the young lady might require her reticule. She left it in the anteroom."

In frustration, Darcy snatched the woman's cloth purse from the man's hand. "Thank you. I will see it is returned to her." If he ever saw her again. "Is there a means from this place? I suspect my return to the chapel will only enflame my aunt's posturing. I am not of the persuasion to tolerate her ire at this moment."

Mr. Fredrich looked to the way he had come. "I understand, sir." He pointed to the far corner of the wall. "There is a latched opening on the other side of the hedges."

Darcy nodded his gratitude and turned toward the opening. Squeezing through it, he crossed to the front of the main church, rather than the chapel his family had employed for his nuptials. "Now where?" he mumbled as he searched the busy street. There was no sign of her. It would be his task to search for a woman whose name he did not know and whose countenance he would never forget, in a city the size of London.

He thought back to his first glimpse of her. He found himself unwittingly amused. This day was not what he had planned.

Heaven above! He had certainly found the woman from the church appealing. Despite the situation in which they found themselves, he doubted she was a silly debutante out to snare him as her husband. If he thought her that devious, he would see her arrested himself. Her expression had said she was as surprised by his appearance as he was with her God-awful disguise. She obviously possessed no vanity, although he could ascribe it to her. Her eyes changed colors as she stared up at him. Her face was naturally clean, with no adornments or creams to enhance her beauty. The lady had made no effort to conceal the sprinkle of freckles across her nose or the slight browning of her skin from being out of doors. Something inside him tightened as he recalled that brief interlude. The woman was beautiful, but not possessing the *perfection* demanded by the *ton*, and, somehow, he preferred her that way.

"Mr. Darcy, sir, do you require my assistance?'

He turned his head to find his footman hustling forward to attend him. "I must find someone," he admitted reluctantly. "Did either you or Mr. Farrin observe a young woman in a pale yellow dress enter the street from the path leading to the back of the church?" He wondered how he had not considered that Anne would never wear a yellow dress, for it would make her appear paler, but why had not Lady Catherine taken note of her daughter's dress? True, Anne wore a light bronzed colored gown, but it was more brown than yellow.

"Dark hair, sir? Small stature?"

"Yes," Darcy pressed.

"The young lady sprinted away, sir."

Darcy raised an eyebrow in disbelief. "Sprinted?"

"Yes, sir. *Sprinted.* She was at a near run."

Despite the travesty going on within the church, Darcy chuckled. "At a run? Through Mayfair? The gossips will enjoy the sight of her." The image brought a smile to his lips. If it proved that she were his wife, the irony of the stranger's escape would not be lost on the matrons of the *ton*, who had taught their daughters never to be more than demure. They would have missed their chance for lack of exercise. The idea amused him thoroughly. He scanned the street again. "Do we know the direction of the young lady's *sprint*?"

"Toward Hyde Park, sir."

Darcy glanced to the ever-darkening clouds. Rain was imminent. "I will follow the lady on foot. You and Mr. Farrin will circle the streets leading to the park. Do not accost the woman if you spot her. Simply follow her until I catch up with you or until she takes shelter somewhere. If so, send me word, but do not permit her from your sight."

Elizabeth had thought for a moment that she was trapped, but she had thankfully discovered the opening in the wall behind the hedges lining the garden. When the ribbon upon her hat had caught on a branch of a low hanging tree, she had ripped the bonnet from her head, which caused some of the pins holding her hair in place to dislodge, but her upsweep stayed in place. She was in too much of a rush to care if her locks all fell down about her shoulders.

Finally bursting upon the street from the church path, she had bumped into an elderly gentleman who had taken great umbrage at her actions and her appearance. "A lady does not go about Mayfair without a bonnet!" he had admonished.

Elizabeth had ignored his harsh words. "Mayfair?" she asked in astonishment.

"Are you inebriated? A doxy? One of those women flaunting their wares? And upon a public street! To think of how brazen you are. Get your person back to Covent Garden before I summon a magistrate!"

Elizabeth did not respond. To be threatened twice with a magistrate in less than ten minutes was more than she could tolerate. All she wanted was to find her uncle and return to Hertfordshire as quickly as possible. Even her mother's foul admonishments would be welcome at this time. Spinning away from the man, she hiked her skirts and took off at a country clip, lengthening her stride beyond what was acceptable in the City. People gawked and huffed as she pushed past them or around them. She wished for her half boots, rather than the slippers she had worn for the *wedding*, and she wished she had had the opportunity to retrieve her reticule, where she had stored away a few extra coins for a hackney when she was in London with her relations, for she always feared becoming separated from her aunt when they went about the shops.

At length, she slowed to catch her breath, but she did not stop. She was accustomed to long walks; yet never with the urgency with which she had traversed the well-kept streets of Mayfair. Elizabeth became conscious of those who crossed the street to avoid her. She must appear to be an escapee from Bedlam to those orderly and stately gentlemen and ladies staring dumbfounded at her. With regret, she glanced to the bonnet she still carried. It was crumpled and misshapen. Tears formed in her eyes as the reality of her "crimes" weighed down upon her. In anger, she tugged a clump of the false hair away from the straw, where it dangled by a few threads. Catching a second piece of the wig, she violently ripped at it. The more of the "falseness" that she tore away, the harder her tears fell. "Even Papa will not forgive me," she mumbled.

"Miss!"

Elizabeth looked up as the man's voice penetrated her misery. It was a voice she recognized: the man from the church. In a swivet, she hitched her skirt again and rushed forward.

Darcy stumbled to a momentary halt as the young woman scampered into the street and right into the path of a gentleman's coach and four. "No...o!" he bellowed, as the horses knocked the woman to the ground. One of them struck her with his hoof before the coachman could rein in the animals. With long strides, Darcy covered the ground between him and the place where the woman lay crumpled upon the street.

"Pardon. Pardon," he murmured as he pushed his way through the crowd who had gathered to look down upon her. He heard people attesting to her appearance upon a quiet Mayfair street.

"She was running. No one runs through Mayfair!" said one matron.

"I thought her mad!" another exclaimed.

"She obviously does not recognize good manners!"

Reaching her, Darcy knelt and surreptitiously tugged the lady's skirt down to cover her exposed ankle and shin to prevent some lecherous gentleman from viewing her limbs. Turning to look upon her countenance again, he realized she was as beautiful as he had assumed from their brief look upon each other at the church. As he rushed to discover her, he had begun to believe his memory faulty, but her features again stole his breath away. Cautiously, he examined her head for injuries. She had yet to open her eyes. "Miss," he encouraged in soft tones, so others could not hear him. "Answer me. Where are you injured?"

"Darcy?" He looked up to view Lord Haverton's troubled face. "My man did not see her."

"I observed it all," Darcy admitted. "But might I impose upon you for the use of your carriage. I cannot leave her lying upon the street. I will take her around to Darcy House."

Haverton knelt beside Darcy to say, "Darcy House? Do you think that is wise, sir? If you bring an injured lady into your home, the Society matrons will shame you into marrying her. She will be compromised. You must think of the lady's future. Why do we not see her to the nearest physician's office instead?"

Darcy leaned over the woman to lift her into his arms. "Nevertheless, I will see the lady to Darcy House where a skilled physician will treat her. Now, will you share your coach or not, sir?"

Haverton caught Darcy's arm to stay him. "You do not

even know the woman's name."

"You err, Haverton. The lady's name is Mrs. Darcy."

Chapter 3

DARCY'S PRONOUNCEMENT HAD certainly stunned Haverton, but not nearly so much as it had astounded Darcy. What had the woman in his arms done to him? And why had he told his lordship, a gossip who would spread the word of Darcy's marriage to all at the various gentlemen's clubs, the stranger was his wife? With the assistance of Haverton's footman, Darcy managed to climb into his lordship's coach and then reclaim the woman into his embrace. Those few short seconds without her had left him feeling bereft of her presence, another fact that shook his customary reserve. He nestled her upon his lap and waited for Haverton's questions. The gentleman did not disappoint.

"I pray you will pardon my curiosity, Darcy, but when did you marry?"

Darcy adjusted his hold upon the woman so her head gently rested against his shoulder before brushing her hair from her cheek. He had thought it chestnut, but it was more mahogany than that. In the sunlight, it would dance with strands of fire. "We married today." He gazed down upon her fine-boned features and nearly sighed with contentment. She was one of the most handsome women of his acquaintance, although "acquaintance" was certainly not the proper word for their relationship.

"Today?" Haverton gushed. "Then why are you not at the wedding breakfast? By God, she was in the street!"

Darcy caressed her chin with his fingertip, and without looking to his lordship, he created a tale that would have made him happier than a stodgy wedding breakfast at Lord Matlock's house. "My lady wished to walk."

"On such a day?" Haverton frowned his disbelief. "Rain will be upon our doorsteps soon."

"But Mrs. Darcy is not so fastidious as women of the *ton*. It is one of the reasons she claimed my notice. She takes pleasure even in a less than perfect day."

Haverton had no time for further questions, for his carriage edged its way to the curb before Darcy House. "Thank you for the use of your carriage, sir. I am in your debt, Haverton." He slid across the coach in preparation of handing the woman down. Darcy knew he should be worried for her recovery, but despite her not responding to being jostled about like a large sack of flour, he had not considered that she would not again know health. Somehow, he figured if God had thrust them together that the Lord would not snatch her from him until they had played their roles in the lampoon they practiced.

"I will take her, sir."

Darcy looked to the open door to find Jasper replacing Haverton's man. He handed the woman to his trusted servant before reaching out a hand of farewell to Haverton.

"You will keep me informed of the lady's well-being, Darcy?"

"Certainly, my lord." Then he scampered down from the carriage to follow Jasper into Darcy House. Inside, he barked, "Mr. Thacker, send for Doctor Nott immediately." Darcy reached for the woman. Although he would not admit it even to himself, she had become essential to his sanity. "Ask Mrs. Guthrie to send up clean rags and water."

"Yes, sir."

As he again adjusted her into his embrace, he remarked, "I

did not expect to see you at Darcy House."

"A man on the street told Mr. Farrin of your rescuing an injured lady," his servant said discreetly.

Darcy nodded his understanding. He would undoubtedly be the talk of London, what with first his aborted marriage and now carrying an unconscious lady into his house, but, for a change, he did not care. As he climbed the steps, he spoke softly to the lady's ear. "Come now. I must have some conversation."

Her eyes fluttered open and closed several times before she sighed, "William."

"Yes," he said with a smile.

"Good," she murmured.

And that was all. Unconsciousness reclaimed her. Darcy wondered what she considered to be *good*. Was it the fact that he was *William* or the fact that she knew with whom she spoke or was it something more sinister?

Elizabeth turned her head slowly to view her surroundings. She could hear someone moving about the room, but she did not wish to disturb the person. Instead, she examined the room. It was a luxurious room, one she had never beheld previously. Pale yellow walls. Dark teak trim. Yellow and white and satin and lace draped the bed and the pillows. The screen beyond displayed a Chinese pattern, but in greens and whites and yellows rather than the reds and blues she had observed in other homes.

"You are awake," a gruff female voice acknowledged.

"Yes, ma'am," Elizabeth said as she turned to look upon the woman. Unfortunately, a shooting pain through her head had her wincing.

"You struck your head upon a paving stone," the woman explained. "And then one of Lord Haverton's carriage horses grazed your shoulder. Doctor Nott has reset it. Much easier to do with your being unconscious and all."

Elizabeth recalled her attempt to escape the man from the church. "I appreciate the physician's care," she said in cautious tones as she assessed her situation.

"Rest. I shall inform the master that you are awake."

"Please do not." She reached to halt the woman's exit, but an excruciating pain ripped through her. She bit her tongue to keep from crying out. The room spun before her eyes, and she sank back against the pillow.

"Easy," the woman instructed. "Doctor Nott says you are not to use your shoulder for several days. I will prepare you some laudanum. This time, do as I say and rest."

He had placed her in his mother's room, the one meant for his wife. It had not been a conscious decision, a fact that scared him more than anything he had experienced previously. That had been three hours earlier. Doctor Nott had come and gone, offering assurances that the lady would heal.

The colonel had also made an appearance to warn Darcy of the family's reaction to his pursuit of the lady. "I assume you located the woman," his cousin had asked as he slipped into the chair opposite Darcy.

"One might say we found each other." His insides heaved, but Darcy swallowed the rush of panic at the unknown. He had not been this out of sorts since he was a youth going off to school for the first time. Although his mother and father had both explained what to expect when he reached the school, the idea that his world was about to change had frightened him more than words could explain. The fact that the woman being tended upstairs in his mother's quarters equally alarmed him was unnerving. He had been sitting for hours replaying every detail of the day and chastising himself for not recognizing the woman's ploy before the vicar had pronounced them man and wife. In other moments, he privately celebrated her interruption. "The lady ran from me and was struck by Lord Haverton's coach."

"My Heavens, Darcy! Please say she survived," his cousin gasped.

"Nott pronounced her on the mend, remarking upon her

hardheadedness."

Edward sat back in his chair. "So, she is here?"

Darcy shrugged his response. "Above stairs. In Lady Anne's room. And what of my sister?"

For the moment, the colonel accepted Darcy's change of subject. "With Mrs. Annesley. And although you did not ask of Anne, please know that I sent our cousin to stay with Roland and his viscountess until this disaster knows an end. My brother will escort Anne to Lincolnshire for the time being. I did not think either Georgiana or Anne should stand witness to the aspersions Lady Catherine presented you. If our aunt learns that the woman in question is at Darcy House, she will claim some charge against the lady and have the magistrate at your door."

"Thank you for seeing to both my sister and Anne. I shall send a note around to Georgiana. I think it best if she is at Pemberley until this situation knows an end. You are a better man than I in this matter to consider the innocents who will be damaged by the gossips. And as to Lady Catherine's threats, when you return to Matlock's household, you should remind her ladyship that I am not accustomed to others dictating my actions."

With a smirk, Edward reminded, "Since you permitted Lady Catherine to dictate to whom you should be married, I doubt if our aunt will heed my advice."

Darcy shot his cousin a quelling look. "Tell me what you know of the woman who chose this particular day to disrupt my life."

There was a glint of amusement in his cousin's eyes. "Not much, except the deception was her idea. Personally, I thought it quite ingenious."

Darcy shook his head in wonder. "I do not even know the lady. Why would she choose to disrupt my nuptials?"

"Do you *wish to know more* of her?" His cousin sat forward to press his point.

Darcy would not admit that he found her ploy both ridiculous and inventive at the same time. He growled his

31

response, "Simply answer my question."

The colonel's lips lifted in a smile. "I did not say the lady meant to prevent you from marrying Anne. I said her disguise was a point of her own making."

"Then whose wedding did she mean to disrupt?" Darcy demanded.

His cousin's teasing came to an end. He spoke with a directness Darcy appreciated. "It seems her sister was to marry a man whose acquaintance we have both had the pleasure, or should I say the displeasure, of knowing something of his character."

A cynical tone marked Darcy's words. "She meant to replace her sister? Does the lady hold an affection for the man?" He was not certain he would approve of another claiming the lady's loyalty, especially if their marriage proved to be legal.

Edward thrummed his fingers upon the chair arm. "I suppose anything is possible. Neither of us has taken the man's measure in person, but, although my acquaintance with the lady was brief, I thought her too sensible to marry a man who would extol our aunt's excellence and be at her ladyship's beck and call. I am speaking of Lady Catherine's new rector."

Shock claimed Darcy's features. "Mr. Collins?"

Edward emphasized his words. "Mr. *William* Collins. Do you recall her ladyship going on and on only two evenings prior on how she had instructed the man to marry the daughter of the man to whom he serves as heir?"

A grim smile touched Darcy's lips. Instead of attending to his cousin's question, he was considering how he had thought the woman had recognized his name from the ceremony and used it when he carried her to his mother's former quarters when, in reality, she had been thinking of Lady Catherine's latest conquest in servants.

"Did you hear me, Darcy?"

"I was not attending," he admitted reluctantly.

The colonel's brow furrowed in displeasure. "I was prompting your recall of her ladyship's pleasure in ordering her cleric to marry." Darcy waved off Fitzwilliam's question with a flick of his wrist and a nod of affirmation. "What will you do with the lady?"

Some dark, inexplicable emotion slipped over him. "What any husband would do with a wife he did not choose and one who might carry affections for another. I plan to keep her upon a short leading string."

Darcy knocked upon her door but did not wait for her to bid his entrance. His housekeeper had informed him of the lady's condition, and he was well-aware of her need for rest. However, he was set upon keeping her from step until he had answers regarding the validity of their marriage and the odd emotions he found tied to her appearance in his life. "Are you well enough for a visitor?" he asked when he opened the door.

At the sound of his voice she scooted up in the bed. He noted her wince of pain, but that was not what stole his breath. Mrs. Guthrie had provided the woman with a gown and wrapper belonging to Georgiana. Although the woman's hair was a bit messy, it was down and draped about her shoulders. Despite being far from a bounder, Darcy had known his share of women, but never had he felt such lust as he did at that moment. He wanted to crawl into bed beside her and never come out again. A small voice in his head repeated the word *mine*.

"As I owe you an apology, I would welcome the opportunity to extend both my regrets for setting your day upon its head and my gratitude for saving me. I will see that my father reimburses you for the expenses of my care."

Darcy pointedly left the door open before crossing the room to sit upon a chair beside her bed. "My cousin, the gentleman who assisted you at the church, related some of what you shared with him. Even so, I am a man who makes no decision without all the facts. If you hold no objections, I have questions for you."

The woman slanted him the beginnings of a watery smile. "I believe you are entitled to an explanation."

He accorded her a faint nod of his head. "First might we begin with your name."

"Elizabeth. Elizabeth Bennet." He rolled her name about in his head. And so he had not been mistaken. When he reviewed the goings on involved in the disaster of his wedding, he would have sworn that she had used the name *Elizabeth*, but her words had been covered by her coughing fit, and he had remained uncertain until this moment. Hers was a name he had always favored. In fact, he had suggested it to his mother for his sister when Georgiana was born.

"And your family?" he asked.

"My father is a gentleman from Hertfordshire. We reside at Longbourn. I am the second of five daughters."

Ah, he thought. *The reason Mr. Collins was Mr. Bennet's heir becomes clear. At least if it proved we are legally joined, she is a gentleman's daughter.* "And your mother?"

"My mother's brother is Mr. Gardiner. He is the owner of Mayo's Imports-Exports. He resides in Cheapside."

Cheapside was not ideal, but Darcy knew something of the warehouses owned by Mayo's. The company and its owner had a reputation for sound business practices. He could not be friends with Charles Bingley without learning something of those who kept London and all of England supplied with essentials. "And the farce at the church was your device?" He presented her a long, slow look.

Meanwhile, she flushed with color after his question. Unfortunately for him, the color added to her appeal, and he adjusted his seat to hide the effect that looking upon her in a nightgown and wrapper and propped in one of his beds had on him. "My father, of late, has suffered from a case of consumption and lung fever. Although he is generally hardy, Mr. Bennet's health has been brought into question." She glanced away before continuing. He noted the tears welling in her eyes when she spoke of her father's possible demise and the effort she made to swallow her fears. "My mother, sir, is often prone to fits of nerves. Fearing my father could pass from his condition, she corresponded with the clergyman, who is Mr. Bennet's heir presumptive, to arrange a marriage between the man and my eldest sister. Miss Bennet is by far the handsomest woman in our neighborhood, but, moreover, she possesses a kind heart. She permitted our mother's cleverness, for Jane never supposed the man would accept Mrs. Bennet's offer."

From what Darcy knew of Mr. Collins, the fact that any woman would choose him appeared inconceivable. For a moment, he wondered why Mrs. Bennet did not offer Miss Elizabeth as Mr. Collins's wife, for he thought hers the most compelling countenance he had ever encountered. "I assume Miss Bennet convinced you to marry the clergyman in her place."

"Not at all. If you held the acquaintance of my sister, you would know she possesses no guile." A true smile broke Elizabeth's lips. "I, on the other hand, have presented my mother more than one gray hair. My sister was miserable with Mrs. Bennet's decision, but Mr. Bennet was too ill to address her concerns. Therefore, I created a switch. Jane has traveled north to spend time with our Aunt Gardiner's relations. I was to pronounce my vows as Jane, thus voiding the marriage. Such was the reason for my disguise. Miss Bennet is fair of head."

In hindsight, Darcy admired her creativity. "The bonnet was an abominable costume piece." He winked at her.

She playfully pouted. "But it fooled you," she teased.

"In my defense, I questioned my cousin's appearance, but when her mother did not object, I brushed my doubts aside."

"Is your lady much put out by my actions?" she asked in concern.

Darcy controlled the flinch of revulsion from her words. The idea of Anne being *his lady* was not to be considered. He had performed in a shameful manner by permitting Lady Catherine to rule him. Darcy knew his father likely frowned down from Heaven. Darcy would not act without purpose ever again. "Although I am certain that Anne could do without my aunt's hysterics, I believe my cousin was relieved by the knowledge that I had wed another."

"We could place my mother and your aunt in the same room and see whose hysterics are more powerful," she said with a teasing tone and then dropped her eyes in what appeared to be embarrassment. For nearly a minute they sat in silence before she said, "And you, sir? Was a marriage to your cousin your dearest wish?" Sincere sorrow laced her words.

"I thought doing so was my duty to my family," he admitted.

Thankfully, she did not question him further. Instead she shouldered his blame along with hers. It was an act which surprised him, for it was customarily his role in his family. "I pray my mother's *nerves* do not have her sending me to my father's Scottish relations. Not that they are not wonderful people," she was quick to add. "But I would miss my sisters terribly. That being said, I fear my cheekiness may prove my undoing this time. You see, I have never been Mrs. Bennet's favorite. She may choose to send me to the American wilderness to fend for myself."

Darcy thought it peculiar that any parent would discourage Miss Elizabeth's smiles or her sense of obligation to her family. He held no doubt that George Darcy would have held the lady up as an example to one and all. Darcy had spent much of his adult life looking for a woman who displayed such loyalty to others. This one had, literally, *fallen* into his embrace, and although he was sore to admit it, he was not prepared to part from her anytime soon.

Not knowing how to respond, he did not address her last statement. Rather, he said, "There is something you should know. I believe my aunt, Lady Catherine De Bourgh, is the benefactor for your father's heir."

"For Mr. Collins?" she gasped. She buried her face in her hands. "I have created a crow's nest of this, have I not? Are the Fates so set against me?"

Darcy smiled at her. The lady appeared genuinely grieved, and he appreciated her sincerity. While waiting for her to wake, more than once, he had wondered if she were some sort of fortune hunter who meant to blackmail him to be rid of her. "I doubt you are cursed." He stood to stare down upon her. "I should permit you to rest. Your injuries remain problematic."

She reached to take his hand, and again a spark of recognition flared in his veins. It took root this time. "I am blessed by your kindness, sir, but I cannot remain in your household without a chaperone."

He squeezed her fingers in reassurance, while watching the realization of her hand in his skitter across her features. "As your mother is unaware of your presence in London and your part in setting aside her plans, I think it ill-advisable to send you to her. I doubt she would hold sympathy for what you have suffered. Am I correct?"

Reluctantly, she nodded her agreement.

"Moreover, neither the wife of a country squire nor a reputable businessman would be able to withstand my aunt's revenge. I fear Lady Catherine is set against you. She means to see you to the magistrate, and she will use her brother's influence to know her way. Fortunately, the Earl of Matlock would never tolerate his sister's manipulations to be directed upon me, for my mother was Lady Anne Fitzwilliam, his youngest sister, a favorite in the Fitzwilliam family."

The woman's expression turned to one of awe. "I have disrupted a marriage in an earl's family! I am doomed!"

Again, he smiled upon her. "The earl is my maternal uncle, but even though he possessed no title, my own father, a man from a noble family of long ancestry, was equally as powerful. And until we hold a definitive answer to the legitimacy of our marriage, you are under the protection of the Darcy family name."

"You are a Darcy?" she asked. Another flush of color claimed her cheeks when she realized she had not asked of his name earlier.

"I am."

"May I know your Christian name? It seems we should, at least, hold an acquaintance."

"Fitzwilliam. After my mother's surname. My cousin, the

colonel, as well as the earl and my cousin Roland, the heir to the earldom, are all *Fitzwilliams*. It becomes a bit confusing at family gatherings and such. Therefore, when my relations and I are together, I am customarily *Darcy* or *William*, depending upon the situation."

Shock marked the woman's features, as she whispered, "I, Elizabeth, take thee William." She squeezed her eyes shut, as if to block out the truth. "Please tell me I did not use my name in the exchange of vows."

"I fear so," he rasped. She appeared so vulnerable that he was tempted to gather her into his arms to comfort her. Swallowing hard against feelings for which he had no name, he added, "When I learned of your connection to Mr. Collins, I thought perhaps you preferred the man. After all, he is *William Collins*."

Her eyes sprang open in alarm. "I assure you, Mr. Darcy, I hold no affections for any man."

Chapter 4

MR. DARCY LEFT her with assurances that he would see to her welfare, as well as with another dose of laudanum, and although she believed him to be a man accustomed to organizing everyone else's lives, Elizabeth could not shake the idea that permitting him to see to her recovery would only complicate the situation in which she found herself. She thought if she could make her way to her uncle's office that someone would fetch Uncle Gardiner, and he would make certain that she was safe.

She wished she could recall what had occurred after she had darted into the street to escape Mr. Darcy. At the time, she had known nothing of his benevolence; all she knew was that she had ruined his nuptials and that a crazed woman was threatening to place her under arrest. She recalled being without funds to reach her uncle, and she had thought Mr. Darcy meant to exact justice when he caught up to her. She had, therefore, fled without looking. The remembrance of his kind eyes when he looked upon her a few moments prior mixed with her need for survival, which brought a shiver of defenselessness crawling up her spine. Mr. Darcy was certainly a man of many moods and a staunch sense of justice, but was there more to him than that? She wished she knew what was her best action, but the achy stiffness of her injuries, along with the still groggy sense of inaction, kept her indecisive. She thought that if not for her injuries, she might be able to walk to Cheapside. She was not certain where Mr. Darcy resided, but she assumed from the quality of the furnishings in the room in which she rested that his house was not within an easy walk to Milk Street.

"Are my clothes about?" she asked the matronly woman who attended her.

"I have set the maids to removing the stains caused by the horse and by the paving stones when you fell. You are wearing a gown belonging to Miss Darcy."

Elizabeth glanced to the now familiar garment. "Mr. Darcy has a sister?" she inquired with interest. "I am one of five daughters."

The woman raised an eyebrow of disapproval. "I am not accustomed to gossiping about my employer's relations."

Elizabeth wished to roll her eyes, but rolling her eyes would take more effort than she could muster, considering her vision was blurry. "I did not mean to intrude." Despite her best efforts, she slurred her words. "I am naturally curious."

Mr. Darcy's servant adjusted the blanket across Elizabeth's chest. "If Mr. Darcy wishes you to know more of his person, he will share it. Now rest. You will require your strength to recover."

"Mr. Darcy?" his butler said tentatively. "There is a gentleman below who requests a few minutes of your time."

With a frown marking his brow, Darcy looked up from his book. "At this hour?" He wondered if his aunt had sent a magistrate for Miss Elizabeth. "Does the gentleman have a name, Thacker?"

"A Mr. Gardiner, sir."

Not the magistrate, he thought, *but someone to remove her from my protection, nevertheless. Miss Elizabeth's family has come for her.* The idea did not please Darcy half so much as it should, but it was only proper to speak to the man. He had set several barristers to work today in pursuit of whether he was married to the woman or not. One of the men mentioned the possibility of Darcy's pursuing a Promissory Estoppel case where one person makes a promise to another, but there is no enforceable contract. However, Darcy had no desire to sue the woman for the promise to "love, honor, and obey." He simply wished to know whether he needed to approach the church courts to void his marriage. "See him up, Thacker," he instructed.

Within a few minutes, a well-dressed gentleman appeared in the open door. He presented Darcy a bow of respect. "Please pardon the lateness of my call, Mr. Darcy."

Darcy's bow was less formal. "I suspect I am aware of your purpose." He gestured to a nearby chair. "Come join me. Would you care for a drink?"

"No, thank you, sir."

Gardiner claimed the chair to which Darcy directed him. "That will be all, Thacker." His butler bowed from the room, and Darcy resumed his seat. "You have come for Miss Elizabeth."

Mr. Gardiner's tense shoulders sagged in what appeared to be relief. "She is here? Thank our dearest Lord. When Elizabeth did not return to my office, I began to search for her. It was only by accident that I overheard a tale of how you and Lord Haverton had rescued a girl in the street. Did she step into the way of his lordship's coach? I told Lizzy that her plan would prove dangerous."

Ah, Mr. Gardiner is not aware of all that has occurred. "I fear your niece ran into the street when she noted my pursuit."

"Your pursuit?" Gardiner's eyebrows drew together in confusion. "Why would a man of your consequence chase after a young woman of little notice? Did our Lizzy offer you an offense?"

"Not unless one would consider her taking the place of my bride during my wedding an offense," Darcy said in droll tones.

"But she was supposed to be at the wedding of her..."

41

Gardiner's words slid to a halt as the truth found root. "Oh, my..."

A hint of sympathy touched Darcy's countenance. "Your niece appears to act before she thinks."

Gardiner ruefully acknowledged, "You have no idea the half of it." The gentleman smiled mirthlessly. "Elizabeth meant to disrupt the wedding of her sister to Mr. Bennet's heir."

"Mr. Collins?" A wry grimace twisted briefly at Darcy's lips as Mr. Gardiner's features again registered his surprise. "Miss Elizabeth has explained her purpose in preventing her sister's marriage to my aunt's rector."

Gardiner's tone was singularly ironic. "Your *aunt* is Lady Catherine De Bourgh?"

Darcy nodded his affirmation. "Needless to say, her ladyship was in attendance at my nuptials, as I was to marry her daughter." The gentleman did not disguise his groan of despair as he buried his face in his hands. "Lady Catherine means to have Miss Elizabeth turned over to the magistrate once she learns of your niece's whereabouts. Such is the reason I brought Miss Elizabeth here, so a physician could attend her, and I could protect her from my aunt's wrath. Moreover, it is important that I determine whether the vows we spoke are legal or not. Fraud must be in place prior to the nuptials. As Miss Elizabeth and I held no acquaintance until I called in upon her earlier today, fraud may not be applicable to annul the marriage."

"But did not Elizabeth use her sister's name in the exchange of vows? That was her intent in foiling Collins's marriage." Gardiner contested.

Darcy drawled with cold formality. "She said, 'I, Elizabeth, take thee William.' I am *Fitzwilliam Darcy*, but am known to family and close associates as *William*. Although we did not sign the registry, I am not certain whether a shortened name is grounds for annulment or to have the marriage declared void. When I spoke my vows, I did so to 'Anne,' my cousin."

Gardiner shared in ironic tones, "*Anne* is one of Elizabeth's middle names. She rarely uses it, only when my children run her ragged by calling for 'Lizzy' all day, then my niece will tease them and say that her name is 'Anne' or 'Lily' or some made-up name." Studying Darcy carefully, the gentleman cleared his throat. "I am certain your legal advisors have already discussed this issue: the marriage is valid as long as those who marry by license marry whom they think they are marrying, no matter what names are used. Elizabeth should have objected to the joining when the vicar asked if she took you as her husband. The fact that she did not could indicate her intent to marry you or her intent to practice fraud. The church courts could rule either way. As to the signing of the register, it is commonplace practice in the church, and I know some bishops have issued warning to clergymen about keeping careful records, but it does not mean the register must be signed immediately after the ceremony. I know a gentleman, a client of mine, who signed the register more than a week following his nuptials, which were conducted by special license and at his betrothed's home. The clergyman had to call upon the gentleman to secure the man's signature."

It was Darcy's turn to know surprise. "I was unaware of your niece's full given name, and as to the other information, I was aware of some, but not all of what you have shared."

"What I do not understand is how Elizabeth appeared at your wedding. She was to be at All Saints at Kingston upon Thames. Where were your nuptials held?"

"A chapel at St. George."

"Admittedly, Lizzy knows little of London. Mr. Bennet despises the place and comes to Town only when necessary. She and Jane visit often, but not enough to understand the city's diverse populations and the neighborhoods harboring each or how there are hundreds of churches with 'Saint' in their names." He smiled sadly. "Why did she not hail a cab to return to my office?"

"Miss Elizabeth left her reticule at the church," Darcy explained.

"But someone would have paid the fare," the gentleman began in explanation, but halted his protest. "It does not signify to second-guess Elizabeth's frightened state." Gardiner sighed heavily. "What do you wish me to do with Elizabeth? It is you whom my niece has offended."

Darcy counted to ten before he responded. What he wished to do and what was proper were in sharp contrast. "Miss Elizabeth should not be moved this evening. Doctor Nott reset her shoulder, and she struck her head upon the paving stones when Haverton's team knocked her down. Such an injury must be handled carefully. Moreover, your niece has expressed concern at having disappointed her mother's aspirations. Miss Elizabeth believes her punishment could be extensive. I know from my cousin that Lady Catherine's ire has yet to abate. If you are agreeable, I think it is best if Miss Elizabeth remain with me until she is well enough to face her accusers or until we have a definitive answer as to whether ours is a legal joining. The vicar did pronounce us man and wife."

"But yours is a bachelor household," Gardiner protested. "If you and Lizzy are not married, her reputation will be ruined."

"As there were several witnesses to the fiasco at the church today, I would venture to say her reputation is already in tatters. No one else knows her name, but society gossips will not stop until they can place a name on the villain in Lady Catherine's shame. In truth, I am a bit surprised that my aunt has not forced her daughter to launch a breach of promise suit against me. Although I doubt the family would stand for her to bring more trouble to their doorstep, my aunt is not accustomed to taking orders from anyone. I am certain the only thing preventing her actions is that my relations have assured her that I am actively attempting to annul or void my vows to your niece. Lady Catherine assumes that my cousin and I will return to the altar."

The gentleman's eyebrow rose in disbelief. "Pardon my curiosity, but it does not sound as if you will comply with her ladyship's wishes."

"I will not," Darcy announced. "I mean to learn of the validity of my marriage to your niece. Afterwards, I will be either sending her home to Hertfordshire or escorting her to my ancestral home in Derbyshire."

Gardiner's chest expanded in a show of bravery. "All that is fine and well, but I cannot permit you to injure Elizabeth in a manner from which she cannot heal."

Darcy leaned forward to press his point. "I am not the type of man who places a woman in danger of any kind. However, the truth remains that Miss Elizabeth has been a guest in my house for some eight hours already. Several of my neighbors observed my carrying her into my home. My suggestion is that you speak to the lady's father. Apprise him of the situation. Control your household, so no one there speaks of these actions. Assure Mr. Bennet that I will do all I can to minimize the damage to his daughter's reputation. In my opinion, Miss Elizabeth's future should be in her father's hands. However, if you think otherwise, I will have my servants bring her down. Mrs. Guthrie, who sits with her, reports to me upon the hour regarding your niece's progress. Miss Elizabeth consumed another dose of laudanum some two hours past."

"And who is Mrs. Guthrie?" Gardiner asked.

"My housekeeper. A lady in service to my family since I was first in breeches. I have ordered her to remain at Miss Elizabeth's side until your niece recovers enough to tend herself. When we finish our conversation, I will ask Mr. Thacker to escort you to your niece's quarters, so you can observe for yourself that she is receiving the best of care. From what Miss Elizabeth confided, I imagine your household is on sixes and sevens. Does Mrs. Bennet understand what occurred?"

"My wife assures me that my sister still places the blame on Miss Bennet's shoulders, but I expect a letter from my brother Bennet announcing Elizabeth's absence from Longbourn. I hope to intercept it. It is essential to Elizabeth's reputation that we contain Mrs. Bennet's 'enthusiasm.'"

Darcy chose his words carefully. "As I see it, at the moment your niece is Mrs. Darcy. Until it is proven otherwise, I mean to see to her health and her well-being." He would not mention that he had called Miss Elizabeth his wife before Lord Haverton or the fact he found himself fascinated by her compelling countenance.

"Why do you not call upon Miss Elizabeth above stairs and then join me in a drink afterwards? I suspect there are a few details remaining that we should address."

Gardiner reluctantly agreed. When the gentleman returned, Darcy meant to learn more of Miss Elizabeth Bennet's character. If she were his wife, he wished no surprises.

Although the clock downstairs had struck two, Darcy had yet to close his eyes. He stared at the familiar draped posts marking the corners of his bed, but his mind was on the lady resting in the adjoining room and on the conversation he had had with Miss Elizabeth's uncle.

"Mrs. Bennet never understood Elizabeth's nature. If my sister had her way, Elizabeth would be another Jane. In truth, I am surprised Miss Bennet agreed to Elizabeth's ploy."

"Did you not know of Miss Elizabeth's plan?" Darcy asked in skepticism.

Gardiner shrugged. "Not initially. The girls regularly correspond with my wife. We are excessively fond of both Jane and Lizzy, as are our children. One or the other often stays with us for a month or two. Mrs. Gardiner agreed to assist them in foiling Mrs. Bennet's plans. My dear wife says she could not stand to see either of the girls attached to a man they did not love."

Darcy swallowed hard against the internal flinch of his stomach. If Miss Elizabeth proved to be his wife, she would not know love in their joining. Dare he attempt to earn her affection?

"Everything was arranged without my knowledge. I returned from business in Portsmouth late on the day Elizabeth set out from Longbourn. My sister and Miss Bennet were in residence at my home when I arrived there. I had no means to stop Lizzy's journey at that time, and so I did the next best thing. I met the mail coach and permitted her to stay in my office. She could not be at my Town house, nor could she stay alone at an inn." The man shrugged his lack of choices. "I refused to take part in the girls' farce beyond allowing Elizabeth a safe place to stay.

I purposely claimed my presence necessary upon the docks the day the nuptials were to take place, so I would not be required to explain myself to Mr. Bennet. It was only after Mrs. Gardiner sent one of our servants to find me that I learned that neither Jane nor Elizabeth made an appearance at Collins's nuptials. Only after I spent the time consoling Mrs. Bennet and her claiming a bed and a sleeping draught, did I set out to discover Elizabeth's whereabouts. I made the assumption that she returned to my office on Milk Street, and I was quite distraught not to find her or a note there."

Darcy asked in curious tones, "What is your opinion of your niece's spontaneous response to her sister's plight?"

Gardiner chuckled softly. "Elizabeth is her great-grandmother made over. She has the look and the temperament of Lily Mae Gardiner. She would storm castles to protect those she loves. Lizzy is the incomparable of Mr. Bennet's daughters. She would stand against any who meant harm to those she affects."

Darcy knew something of protection and the great responsibility that it held.

Gardiner continued, "Elizabeth possesses opinions on a variety of subjects, but, other than Mr. Bennet, whose thoughts are sometimes quite jaded, she has no one upon whom to test her conjectures. My Brother Bennet takes his amusements in noting the foibles of others." Darcy frowned internally, but kept his expression blank. "Our Lizzy enjoys debating the merits of a political pamphlet or a scientific abstract, but she is equally comfortable conversing upon a dance floor. Simply said, she enjoys long walks in the country and the pleasure of good company.

"But only those who know her intimately realize Elizabeth understands what it is to be set adrift. To be alone, even in a crowd. Lizzy is the *odd* one in a family as diverse as society itself. She places walls between herself and those that she fears mean her harm. She will challenge any man brave enough to scale her battlements. Elizabeth will never make it easy for a man to love her, for her emotions always waver against her natural fears of rejection. That emotion comes from the hand of my *dear* sister, who never could understand our grandmother's wit and her zest for life, and so Mrs. Bennet cannot grasp the pure beauty and intelligence simmering below the surface in Elizabeth's character. I pray a man worth his salt will some day take her on, for her love will be the greatest gift he will ever know."

Darcy wondered why Gardiner had chosen to describe his niece thusly. It was not as if Darcy meant to give the woman his heart, only his name, if that proved necessary. Yet, although he was sore to admit it, he, too, was lonely. He often thought if he would have been born a female, he could easily become a spinster. A recluse, never wishing to leave his home. Without the responsibility of his estate, he would gladly remain at Pemberley, ignorant of the way of the world.

"Mr. Darcy?"

"Yes, Sheffield." He sat up in bed.

His valet set a lit candle on the table beside Darcy's bed. He explained, "Colonel Fitzwilliam's man delivered this personally. He said the colonel considered the message urgent and thought you should know of its contents." He extended a note in Darcy's direction.

Darcy took the single page and unfolded it. Leaning toward the candle so he might see better, he read his cousin's hastily written message. "So her ladyship means to foist her will upon mine, does she? We will see about that." He threw back the blanket. "Sheffield, send a message to the mews. I wish my carriage waiting behind my house at five. Then return here. You may assist me in packing. I mean to be gone before light."

Chapter 5

ELIZABETH'S EYES SLOWLY hatched open to take in her surroundings. She was no longer resting in the plush bed at Mr. Darcy's house. "Where am I?" her lips attempted to form the words, but they were too dry to part. She ran her tongue along her teeth. Her mouth tasted as if the British Army had marched through it. A grimace claimed her expression when she forced dampness into her mouth. "Water," she murmured.

An unfamiliar face appeared above hers. "Oh, ma'am, I be ever so glad you are awake. I be worrying on it."

"Water," Elizabeth repeated.

The woman's mouth screwed up in disapproval. "The water not be so good for a soul. Mayhap a bit of ale or wine."

Elizabeth knew some did not boil the water they drank, as her papa had insisted they do at Longbourn, and many suffered a variety of illnesses lurking from their inaction. The thought of her home sent tears pooling in her eyes. When the woman's features turned to concern, Elizabeth mouthed the word "wine," for she had never cared for the taste of ale. The woman, who was likely Charlotte Lucas's age or thereabouts, disappeared for a few brief seconds. The sound of liquid being poured filled the small space, but Elizabeth did not turn her head to view the woman's efforts. She had learned her lesson regarding her head injury.

The woman returned with a china cup, which she set upon a table. Elizabeth thought the cup an odd choice, but she offered no complaint. "Permit me to support you, ma'am." She lifted Elizabeth's shoulders to a sitting position. "Sip this, ma'am. Small sips."

The cup's handle allowed Elizabeth to hold it, and the woman's wisdom now made perfect sense. She did as her companion instructed. After dampness had been restored to her mouth, she carefully handed the cup back to the woman. Slowly, she looked about her. The room was small and cramped, but neat and clean. She wondered for a moment if her mother had imprisoned her in some sort of cellar, but she quickly changed her mind. The cup and the blankets and carpet runner upon the floor were all first quality. When she turned her head more quickly in the opposite direction, surprisingly, the room did not spin before her eyes, but she still had the feeling of movement. "Where am I?" Panic shivered up her spine.

The woman lowered Elizabeth's shoulders to the pillow. "We be on the master's yacht."

Elizabeth made to bolt upright, but her companion pressed her down. "Yacht?" Elizabeth demanded. "Mr. Darcy's yacht? I am aboard Mr. Darcy's yacht?"

"Yes, ma'am. I know not what occurred prior to your arrival upon board, so don't be asking me about it. I was to attend the new Mrs. Darcy. The master asked for someone not afeared of the water, and I's volunteered. I came with you when the master bring'ed you onto the ship."

"Mr. Darcy carried me on board?" Elizabeth looked down at her clothing. She wore what only could be called a man's banyan over the gown she recalled from her stay at Darcy House. Elizabeth felt the heat rush to her cheeks as a half memory flashed before her eyes.

"Come, Miss Elizabeth," the gentleman whispered close to her ear while he gently worked her injured arm into the sleeve of a red and

black satin garment. The same red and black cover up that she now wore.

"*You mean to ruin me,*" she recalled saying in what she intended to be a tease.

"*No, my dear.*" *He lowered her to the bed.* "*I mean to protect you.*"

The woman must have noted Elizabeth's embarrassment. "Mr. Darcy not be permitting others to view you. We's leave London before the morning sun rose in the sky. He covered you with the only garment large enough to disguise yer undress and to protect yer arm. Then he placed a blanket over you."

"How long have we been aboard?"

"This be the second day. That be why I were a worryin'. You've been asleep since you were at Darcy House." Elizabeth wished to scream her objections so all could hear, but she knew what occurred at Mr. Darcy's house was not this woman's fault. She infused her voice with a calmness she did not possess. "Do you think you might assist me to a chair and then fetch Mr. Darcy? The gentleman and I must speak."

When he entered her cabin a quarter hour later, he was impeccably dressed and still as handsome as she recalled. He was tall and imposing, and Elizabeth knew instinctively to cross him would be a mistake. She wished that she were stronger, so she could stand and confront him, but, for now, she would perform as best she could.

"I am pleased to find you from your bed," he said politely while eyeing her with interest.

Elizabeth did not address his attempt at consideration. Instead, she asked, "Could you explain to me, sir, how you thought it acceptable to remove my person from your home to your yacht without my permission?" She watched as a muscle along his jawline twitched, but otherwise, his expression of indifference remained in place.

"It was necessary for you to depart Darcy House, and

as you were in no condition to make that decision, I made it for you. As part of my wedding plans, I was set to sail on the day of our departure; therefore, I took advantage of the ship's preparedness."

"And why was it necessary for me to leave Darcy House? Could you not have sailed alone? I would have been up and moving about in a day or two, and then I could be gone from your society. No one would have known the difference."

Other than a slight lift of his eyebrow, he displayed no reaction to her tight-lipped accusations. "My aunt learned of your presence under my roof. She planned to send a magistrate to my home to arrest you. I thought it best if we were removed from England until this matter can be settled."

"Arrest me?" Elizabeth demanded. "Upon what charges? Certainly what I did was unconventional, but it was not a crime. It was a mistake. I have no desire to remain with you, and you, sir, should be glad to observe my exit. I have caused you nothing but grief and inconvenience. Needless to say, Miss De Bourgh would still accept a man of your consequence. Marry your cousin. Lady Catherine will be mollified, and I will return to my life in the country. All will be forgiven."

"If you think my aunt will forgive or forget your perceived insult, you are sadly mistaken. Lady Catherine will make your life and the lives of your loved ones miserable. Only with my protection will you remain safe," he argued.

Elizabeth swallowed hard against the trepidation filling her chest. "I shall...I shall assume my chances, sir. Surely a woman of Lady Catherine's stature will extend her forgiveness once I explain the situation." She lifted her chin in defiance.

"More likely she will force Anne to sue you for criminal conversation. I know my aunt: She will not be happy until she leaves you and your family in penury. Not only did you forestall her aspirations of having Anne at Pemberley, but you treated her cleric as if he were insignificant. She sees Mr. Collins's character as a reflection of her condescension."

Elizabeth fought the anxiety rising in her stomach.

"Nevertheless, I insist that you set me down in the next port and provide me enough coins to claim passage home. I will have Mr. Bennet reimburse you as quickly as I make my way to Hertfordshire."

"That might be difficult," he said with a wry twist of his lips, "for you to make your way to Mr. Bennet's estate in what you are wearing."

Despite her best efforts, despair pooled in her eyes. "So, you mean to keep me a prisoner by refusing me proper dress?" she accused. "I demand the return of the dress I wore for the wedding!"

He shrugged in indifference. "On the morning of our departure, Mrs. Guthrie and a maid dressed in your gown made a great show of leaving Darcy House. I am certain my neighbors will have taken notice of your exodus. My servants have been instructed that if anyone asks after me to tell them that I was so upset after the wedding that I departed for my estate. The servants will also inform those who wish to be apprised of my comings and goings that the poor soul I saw into my house was a distant relation who had been injured at the wedding and that I instructed my staff to tend the young lady in my absence. When the magistrate calls upon Darcy House he will learn of *your* leave-taking from more than Mrs. Guthrie, who is to explain that *you* fell into the street before Lord Haverton's coach and were treated by Doctor Nott. Both my housekeeper and the good physician will confirm the story of your departure. They will tell the official that you asked to be returned to your home in Bath, and before I left Town upon personal business, I made the necessary arrangements."

"No one will believe such a convoluted tale," she argued.

"On the contrary, my dear. The *ton* is quite gullible. They will believe any tale that smacks of gossip, and they will add their own tidbits to it to make it more outrageous."

"Then what am I to wear?" she insisted, although she wished her voice had not cracked upon the word "wear." She suddenly felt like Mr. Darcy's mistress, for she was dressed for the role.

His expression softened, as if he could read her thoughts. "We had little time to prepare, but Hannah, the maid you met earlier, has altered several of my sister's gowns. Miss Darcy has sprouted up in the last year, but some of her former gowns will do nicely until we can have something specifically designed for you. Mrs. Guthrie suggested those items ordered as part of Anne's trousseau, but I rejected the idea, for my Aunt Catherine could then label you a thief. It is best to do over some of my sister's gowns, rather than to provide her ladyship with a reason to see you behind bars."

Elizabeth wished to acknowledge his sensible actions, but it was her life in which he dabbled, and all his decisions were simply too personal. She gritted out the words, "As I am at your disposal, how are we to proceed?"

"If you are agreeable, I thought we might have supper. I tire of eating alone."

Echoes of wariness rang in her head. "Mr. Darcy, I do not think it advisable for us to spend more time together than necessary." She despised his high-handedness.

"Miss Bennet, we will be aboard this ship for another two days," he reasoned.

"And then what?" Her insecurity spiked.

"And then we will disembark in Scotland where I have business to conduct," he responded in matter-of-fact tones. He was so calm and calculating that Elizabeth thought to throw the cup at him.

She huffed, "Hannah says she was to attend Miss De Bourgh. Did you plan to escort your bride to Scotland, so you might conduct business while upon your wedding journey? Do you hold no affection for your cousin?"

"I saw no reason my marriage should interfere with a business prospect I have courted for well over a year. Moreover, my marriage to Anne was to be one of convenience. On this journey, I had faint hopes that she could enjoy the company of Mr. Allard's wife while the lady's husband and I came to an amicable agreement."

Elizabeth sighed heavily. "Men are the worst creatures on earth."

Mr. Darcy's voice was low and suggestive when he responded, "You hold numerous experiences with men, Miss Elizabeth? How might you prove your opinion?"

Elizabeth blushed thoroughly. "Do not purposely misunderstand me, sir." She clenched her eyes shut to drive her embarrassment away. "What if I do not wish to spend time in Scotland?"

"That might be problematic," he admitted. "As I have already sent Mr. Gardiner details of our journey."

"Uncle Gardiner is aware of our destination?" she gasped.

"The gentleman called upon me late on the evening of your first day with me," he explained.

Elizabeth's lips trembled, but there was little she could do to disguise her emotions. It shook her to the core to realize that she had been beholden to Mr. Darcy for three days. Alone with Mr. Darcy for three days! Her reputation was royally soiled. "Uncle Gardiner was at Darcy House? Why did he not take me with him?" She had thought that of all her family, it would be Uncle Gardiner who would stand against Mr. Darcy.

"Your uncle sat with you for a half hour, but according to him, your responses were unintelligible. I suggested he might speak to Doctor Nott to garner more information on your condition if he wished. Mr. Gardiner was aware of Nott's reputation, but said he would speak to the man in case there were concerns I did not relay. Afterwards, we discussed the options for your care. Your uncle agreed that it was not wise to move you if you had a head injury. He agreed that until you were healthy, you should remain with me. I suggested that Mr. Gardiner apprise your father of the situation and then inform me of Mr. Bennet's desire."

"But Papa has been so ill," she protested. She would not wish to cause her father a setback.

"It is better for your father to learn of your safety from Mr.

Gardiner than to fret over your whereabouts," he countered.

"But..." she began; however, a dismissive gesture from Mr. Darcy cut her short.

"Miss Elizabeth, Lady Catherine is the daughter and the sister of an earl. An influential earl, I might add. She was married to Sir Lewis De Bourgh, and as his widow commands one of the most prestigious estates in southern England. If she tells a magistrate that you stole a shilling from her, no one will question the authenticity of her claim. You will be arrested and placed in prison for a crime you did not commit. Neither your father nor your uncle will be able to protect you. Just because you are innocent will not matter to the courts. I can protect you, for my mother, Lady Anne Fitzwilliam, was also the daughter and sister of the same influential earl, and although my father held no title, he was descended from the nobility. Rosings Park in Kent is considered a showcase in the Southern shires, but Pemberley is among the most admired in all of England. My word will stifle any of my aunt's protests."

When she entered his quarters a quarter hour later, she had straightened the nightgown and robe she wore, using a damp cloth to wet the material to make it appear less wrinkled. Although the garment was soft against her overheated skin, Elizabeth felt like a player in a medieval drama: The damsel being held against her will by the evil lord as in the tales from "A Gest of Robyn Hoyd." She barely reached Mr. Darcy's shoulders; therefore, when she walked, the robe trailed along behind her, like a train, and the sleeves were so long that Hannah had tied them about Elizabeth's upper arms, to keep them in place, giving them the look of a puffed sleeve. The maid had also run a brush through Elizabeth's tangled locks and quickly pinned it in place in a tight knot. She noted what appeared to be disappointment upon Mr. Darcy's features when he observed the change.

Unfortunately for their acquaintance, the previous attraction she had felt for him was tarnished by the manner in which he had arbitrarily decided her future.

He came around the small table to hold the chair for her. "I am pleased your health is improving. The movement of the boat does not appear to affect you. Many do not take well to the sea." He sat opposite her. "My cousin, Colonel Fitzwilliam, despises sailing. In his service to the British Army, he has been twice to the Continent and back. Although he does not elaborate upon the experience, I doubt he left his quarters during either journey." She noted the satisfied smile upon his lips when the servant knocked lightly before entering. The man placed wine glasses and fine china upon the table.

"Although I have never been aboard a ship before, I customarily possess a healthy constitution," she explained as she spread the serviette across her lap. She was a bit self-conscious of her appearance, but after Mr. Darcy's exit from her quarters, she had decided she must "play" the game by his rules if she were to escape this debacle with a shred of her reputation still in place. "The movement caught me off guard when I first stood, but I am certain the laudanum had something to do with the feeling of falling. I managed to reach your quarters with little difficulty."

"Undoubtedly," he remarked. They remained silent while the servant served the first course and departed.

Elizabeth sipped the soup—a creamy broth. Her stomach growled, and she shot a tentative glance to her supper mate. "I apologize," she said. She averted her eyes in embarrassment.

Although she did not look upon him, she heard the amusement in his tone. "I would imagine your *healthy constitution* is simply thankful you have chosen to feed it." His tone turned serious. "Eat slowly. I would not wish for the food to upset your return to wellness. I specifically asked my cook to keep the meal simple and to avoid too many sauces. After your not eating for three days, I assumed you would require something hearty, but plain."

"I am grateful for your forethought, sir." And that was the truth. She was grateful for his tender care of her person, but she could not reason why he had spent so much of his time and his money to protect her. Surely the man had business with which to attend. If his estate was half as grand as he claimed, his obligations were many. He had no need of her. Although she knew it reckless to offend him, she asked, "What do you expect of me, Mr. Darcy? If it is financial compensation you expect, I must warn you that despite my father being a gentleman, he is far from wealthy."

"I have no need of more pounds in my bank accounts," he said with a casual gesture of his hand.

"Then please explain what reason you give for bringing me aboard this ship? I can be nothing to you. Again, I ask what requirement I may fill for a man of your consequence?" Elizabeth prayed he would not ask her to be his mistress, for she did not think she had enough strength to slap him without injuring her arm again or to swim to safety when he dumped her overboard for the insult she had delivered upon his person.

"My response should be evident," he said flatly. "I require a bride."

Chapter 6

"A BR — IDE?" SHE stammered. A flush of color claimed her cheeks.

He worked hard to keep the smile from his lips, turning his attention to the last of his soup instead. "What did you expect me to say?" he asked without looking at her. "That I wished you to be my mistress? I assure you, Miss Bennet, that I do not require you to satisfy my lust." Although, if he would admit it, he secretly would enjoy initiating her in the pleasures of the flesh. Yet, he was too much of a gentleman to claim her virginity without the rites of marriage, and the legality of their marriage remained in question.

Before she could respond, his servants brought in the second course, providing her time to compose her expression. When the food had been set before them and his man left them alone again, she asked, "If you require a bride, then why did you not exchange your vows with your cousin rather than seeking me out?"

"You know the answer," he insisted. "I realize our encounter was from the norm, but I must know the truth of our connection before I could possibly consider marrying another.

As to my cousin, I am of the persuasion that I erred in agreeing to marry Miss De Bourgh. While at the altar, I prayed for God's intervention, and He provided me another path in the form of a beautiful young lady from Hertfordshire."

Despite his attempt at flattery, anxiousness remained upon her features. "My father always says one should beware of the prayers that the Devil answers," she pronounced in righteous tones.

He shrugged in nonchalance. "Mayhap."

"What if I insist that you permit me to leave when the yacht docks?"

"I do not hold you prisoner," he declared.

"Then I will take my leave of you at that time," she confirmed.

He smiled at her. "I am assuming that you will hold no objection if I attempt to change your mind."

"Do you mean to blackmail me, sir?"

Although he was not certain that he wished to keep a woman of Elizabeth Bennet's tempting appearance so close, Darcy permitted her words of disdain without censure. Though he was far from claiming the experience of either of his Fitzwilliam cousins, he had managed to deflect the machination of the *ton*'s most insistent mamas since he came into his majority. A woman of Miss Elizabeth's features, as well as what he was discovering of her sharp wit, would be a tempting morsel, but still no match for his resolve.

"How would I blackmail you?" he asked in even tones. "By your own admission, your father is not a rich man and could provide me little in compensation. Moreover, by now, my trusted servants have explained to the magistrate that I have sent you upon your way. As far as the world knows, you and I are together." He sighed heavily. "Before we negotiate a compromise, permit me to explain what I require of *my bride*."

She nodded her consent, but she did not appear appeased.

"As I explained earlier, I have a business meeting with a Mr. Allard. Thinking I would be married when I arrived upon the gentleman's doorstep, I informed him that my wife would accompany me. As the man has a reputation for outspoken opinions of the sanctity of marriage, I did not wish to offend him by appearing without said wife."

"Then you only agreed to marry your cousin because doing so would serve you financially?" she accused.

Darcy could not force the frown from his forehead. "My marriage to Miss De Bourgh was designed to meet an obligation."

"And what became of that *obligation* that you think to set it aside so easily?" she demanded.

"My cousin, the colonel, convinced me that no one in the family, other than Lady Catherine, ever heard my mother speak of her desire that I make Miss De Bourgh my wife."

Stubbornness marked her features. "Then why would Lady Catherine insist upon this line of thinking? Surely her ladyship must know she could not bring you to heel."

"Miss De Bourgh will soon reach the age when she will inherit Rosings Park. When she turns five and twenty, all of Sir Lewis De Bourgh's holdings become hers. My aunt will be removed to the dower house, unless Anne permits her mother to continue to reside at Rosings." His companion's expression displayed what he had yet to say. "If Anne is with me at Darcy House and Pemberley, Lady Catherine may continue to oversee Rosings Park and her little section of Kent."

"'Oh, what a tangled web we weave when first we practice to deceive,'" she murmured. "Nevertheless, I cannot pretend to be your wife simply because you wish it."

"Who says we are not married?" he countered.

"We did not sign the register," she argued. "I ran from the church before we signed our names."

He shrugged off her rationalization. "Many men and women cannot sign their names. If they are married with a mark of an 'X,' why are we not equally married? The vicar pronounced us as such. Moreover, the church sometimes permits the couple to leave without signing the register. The vicar calls upon the household several days to weeks later for the signatures. I had this conversation with your Mr. Gardiner. He related the tale of a friend of who wed by special license and so the registry was not signed for nearly a month—not until the man returned to London from his holiday with his wife."

"Yet, we did not wed by special license!" she hissed. "Furthermore, I distinctly recall the cleric saying *Anne*."

Darcy smiled smugly. "Which according to your uncle is part of your Christian name."

Frustrated, she stood and tossed her serviette upon the table. "This is madness, sir. We are not now nor will we ever be married. Moreover, I will not play the role of your wife simply so you can broker a business arrangement. Good evening, sir!" With that, she stormed from the room.

"Demme magnificent," he said with a silly grin, as he watched the sway of her hips made more prominent by her need not to swing her injured arm. "Demme magnificent, indeed!"

Elizabeth burst into her quarters, the need to put distance between herself and Mr. Darcy's controlling ways making every step she took more aggravating than ever. She would give anything if she could simply jump over the ship's railing and swim for shore. "Hannah, I wish to dress so I might go on deck," she snapped.

"This evening, ma'am?" The woman appeared shocked by Elizabeth's tones.

She squeezed her eyes shut in vexation. She was never sharp with the servants at Longbourn, and she would not permit the despicable Mr. Darcy to alter her disposition. Sighing heavily, she steadied her breathing before she spoke again. "As much as I would adore a breath of fresh sea air, I do not imagine it would be safe to do so this evening. By the clock in Mr. Darcy's quarters, it is well past seven."

The maid's stiff shoulders relaxed. "Yes, ma'am. My father always say one must be about his wits when sailing at night."

Elizabeth edged the door closed. "Your father was a

sailor?"

"Oh, no, ma'am. Nothin' so fancy. Jist a fisherman. That be the reason I's not bothered by the rockin' of the ship. As the oldest of seven, it be my providence to assist him until me brothers grew into their bodies and could take my place."

Elizabeth sat on the edge of the narrow bed. "How long have you been in service?"

"Since I be ten, ma'am. Mrs. Reynolds, the housekeeper at Pemberley, gave me a position in the estate's kitchen. It was a Godsend, for my mama took ill, and my father needed to stay home many days with her. My brothers were six, eight, and nine at the time and too young to earn money at sea alone."

At Longbourn, the Hills had been her family's long-time servants. Elizabeth thought she knew all there was to know of them, but listening to Hannah, she questioned how much she could recall of the pair's private life. She knew something of Mr. Hill's sister-in-marriage, for the woman, who was a widow, was employed by Mr. Bennet's second cousin, Mrs. Myrtle Flynn. She knew a bit of several of the Hills' nieces and nephews, for she played with them when her parents visited the Flynns, but Elizabeth was ashamed of her lack of condescension in dealing with the couple. She made a silent promise that when she returned to her father's household to listen to what was important in the lives of their servants.

"You must have been quite frightened," she said in sympathetic tones.

"Mrs. Reynolds was kind to me. I even spent some of my time in the nursery with the new Miss Darcy. I assisted the nurse."

"How old is Mr. Darcy's sister?" she asked in curiosity.

"Oh, Miss Darcy be sixteen. She be as pretty as a young princess," Hannah gushed as she set out a brush and a clean cloth upon a tray.

"I possess a sister about the same age," Elizabeth said with a sigh of longing. As much as her youngest sister often irritated her, Elizabeth missed Lydia's natural exuberance more than she thought possible.

"It be hard on the young master," Hannah confided. "Miss Darcy be not quite twelve when the old master passed. Her mama passed within a year of giving birth to the young miss. The present Mr. Darcy became his sister's guardian and the master of Pemberley in the blink of an owl's eye. He be barely beyond his majority when he became responsible for not only his sister, but also the lives of hundreds of cottagers and servants. He has never faltered — not when he lost his mother at twelve or at the loss of his revered father at three and twenty. Certainly, he sometimes appears a bit stiff in company, but that be because of the burdens he carries."

Elizabeth listened intently, but made no remarks.

Hannah continued, "I tended Miss Darcy so long at Pemberley that Mr. Darcy brings me up from Derbyshire to assist in tending to his sister when she was young, for the child afeared the City. I be familiar company and be some ten years her senior and could serve as a chaperone when she went about Town. I learned something of dressing the young miss from her maid. But now that she be a proper young lady, I be hoping the master permits me to remain in me home shire. I surely miss what remains of me family. Such be the reason I made it known to Mr. Darcy that I'd hold no qualms in tending you and being on this ship."

Elizabeth smiled at the woman. "I shall speak to Mr. Darcy of my gratitude and of your desire to remain in your home shire. If the gentleman is kind enough to consider his younger sister's needs by bringing along a familiar countenance to soothe her, surely he will recognize the depth of your devotion to his family and permit you to remain nearer your relations."

"Thank you, ma'am," Hannah said as a blush claimed her cheeks. "It would be a blessing to see my father again before he meets his Heavenly rewards."

Elizabeth was not certain that she could convince Mr. Darcy of anything after her speedy exit from his quarters only moments prior, but she would attempt to do so. In the morning, she would dress and venture above deck to assess the situation in which she found herself. Then she would decide how best she might escape Mr. Darcy's "kindness."

Despite it being impossible for him to be so aware of her, before he turned to look upon her, he had known when Elizabeth Bennet stepped upon the deck. He sucked in a breath. His sister's virginal gown had taken on something more inviting — not that he doubted that his traveling companion held any experience with men beyond a saucy remark now and then. The gown displayed the roundness of her breasts and nothing of the cleft between them. Yet, even so, she was more than tempting. The sea breezes whipped her skirt to reveal muscular legs and a pair of slightly rounded hips. Her head was turned in the opposite direction, and he studied the fragile length of her neck. His fingers itched to touch her.

Looking upon her, he wondered again upon the wisdom to bring her with him. When her uncle called at Darcy House, he should have sent her to the Gardiners in Cheapside. His aunt would not think of searching for her there, but he told himself that when Mr. Collins reported his disastrous wedding to his patroness, then Lady Catherine might place the "twos" together and come up with "four." In truth, he knew enough of Miss Elizabeth Bennet to find her again *if* she proved to be his wife. Against his better judgment, he had made a commitment to her, and that commitment was tantamount. Since he had lifted her into his arms upon a London street, she had been constantly upon his mind. He should have discreetly hired a woman to sate his growing desires, but he knew, unconditionally, that another, even an experienced lady of the evening, could not satisfy him.

A familiar tightness gathered low in his belly as he turned to follow her at a pace that likely resembled a wild animal stalking another. Darcy attempted to ignore the eyes of his servants and crew upon him. He knew he acted from character; however, he needed to be near her.

She caught the rail with one hand, while shading her eyes with the other. She looked to the right and the left as if she expected to observe the English coastline, but they were not skimming the coast. He noted how her shoulders tensed when she realized there would be no immediate escape.

"I pray you do not mean to jump overboard and swim for shore," he said softly as he stepped up behind her. Her spine stiffened when she recognized his closeness. "I imagine it would be difficult to determine if the English coast is near or far and in what direction you must swim to reach it." He breathed his words into her hair. Her skin took on a blush of color, and he wondered why he had failed to notice at the ceremony how her arms and neck were sun-kissed while Anne's were always so pale that one would think his cousin had stepped from a deadly dream.

"I was not thinking of swimming ashore," she contested.

Darcy chuckled knowingly. "You were, but I do not take your desire to escape me personally."

"And why is that, Mr. Darcy?" she accused. "Why would any man not be offended by a woman's desertion?" She had yet to turn to look at him.

However, before he could respond, the yacht's captain called "Ready about!" Instinctively, Darcy caught her about the waist to brace her weight while he forced her forward to lean over the railing. She squirmed against him as he spooned her body with his while the boom swung over their heads.

"Mr. Darcy!" she screeched; yet, he hushed her by lifting her slightly from her feet and setting her down again.

"The ship's tack changes because of the wind," he hissed into her ear. "To stay the course, the sails must be swung around at the end of each tack. Should I permit the boom to remove your pretty head from your shoulders?"

She turned her head to glare over her shoulder at him, and he realized how easy it would be to kiss her in that moment. "Release me!" she growled.

"Hard alee!" the captain sang out.

"Not yet." Despite her grinding her hips against him in her efforts for freedom, he pressed her forward again as the boom made another sweep over their heads. The ship heeled and set upon a new course. "Now." He stood stiffly and brought her up with him.

She swirled around in his arms. "How dare you!" she accused in tones that he was certain more than half his crew heard. She remained pressed between him and the railing, and Darcy wondered if she had any idea of all he dared.

"I thought your head striking the paving brick was punishment enough for your folly," he said in even tones, although his heartbeat should have told her he was anything but calm. "If you mean to be above deck, you must listen to the captain's orders." He stepped back to provide her her dignity. Perhaps he had taken too much pleasure in holding her to him, but who could blame him? She was fine-boned and full of fire. Darcy realized that he liked *fire*. His lips twisted in amusement at the thought.

"You cad!" she snarled. "I thought you a gentleman!"

Angry at his lack of control when in her presence, he snapped, "I am a gentleman. If I were not, you might still be lying unconscious in a London street or at this very moment be attempting to swim in the wake of my ship."

Something resembling annoyance flashed across her features. "No one asked for your assistance, sir!"

"And no one asked you to interrupt my nuptials!" he countered.

"How many times must I apologize for my mistake?" she pleaded. "What must I do to satisfy my debt for your protection from your aunt's outrage?"

Darcy could think of a dozen or more ways she could *satisfy* the debt, but he said, "I require your participation in another farce. Afterwards, I will send you and your eldest sister home to Hertfordshire. It may have slipped your notice, but my family estate is in Derbyshire. Remain with me until my business with Allard is complete, then we will travel to Derbyshire, where you may reunite with Miss Bennet to return home in a private coach to your mother's *retribution."*

Chapter 7

DARCY KNEW THE moment they shared while staring deeply into each other's eyes would forever change them, but he pretended he still had control over his life. He should have permitted her to return to her family, a family she loved so deeply that she would risk her life in order to protect her sister. Yet, from the first time he had taken her hand in his, her presence had become vital to his existence. What was it about Elizabeth Bennet that had him acting the fool?

In his mind's eye, he saw her. The occasional glint of gold strands in her hair gave life to her locks. Dark lashes—so long they rested upon her cheeks when she slept. Eyes that turned from brown to green, depending upon her mood.

How had she breached his personal battlements so quickly? More than one woman had attempted to entice him, but he had withstood them all until he had lifted her into his arms.

It should have surprised him that when they discussed their arrangement that she would be an astute bargainer, but it did not. From what her uncle had shared and from what he had observed personally, Darcy knew her to be intelligent. What did surprise him during their negotiations was the fact that she asked for nothing for herself. It was as if she accepted the fact that their relationship would bring about her complete ruin, but she meant to protect her family. Her resolve only increased his admiration for her.

"When she marries, each of my sisters will receive her share of five thousand pounds, but only upon the death of both of my parents. If others learn of my presence at your side, my parents will have no choice but to send me away," she stated matter-of-factly. "My absence from Longbourn will be noted, and I doubt my father will be able to rein in my mother's lamentations. She will bemoan my downfall to all who will listen, and the servants will talk. I do not wish my sisters to suffer because of my indiscretion. I implore you to agree to support them so they might claim a husband."

Darcy nodded his understanding He had already assumed that he would do all he could to save her family. Clearly, he could simply send her home and be done with her, but he had continued to tell himself that his aunt would leave no stone unturned in seeking out the woman who had ruined her ladyship's aspirations; however, there was the nagging thought that his reasons were more personal, that he actually fancied Elizabeth Bennet, actually preferred her to any woman of his acquaintance. "I will present each sister an additional five hundred pounds."

Her eyes grew wide in disbelief. "That is two thousand pounds!"

Darcy's lips twitched in amusement. "Do you think the sum is not enough?"

"That is my father's annual income." Her tone grew low and gritty.

For a moment, Darcy considered how far below him she truly was, but immediately, he shoved his criticisms aside. Despite her often being testy with him, he enjoyed her company. She did not mince words, nor did she flatter him with silly observations of his consequence and his intelligence. "Then I suppose the additional funds will serve the necessary purpose well." Their eyes tangled. "Is there nothing you wish for yourself?" He noted that Miss Elizabeth was clearly struggling to hold back tears.

"Not unless you have the ability to alter time." She was obviously greatly moved by her situation.

Darcy studied her in earnest. "I fear not, but if God granted me such a wish, it would not be my wedding that I would reset."

She swallowed hard against what appeared to be a swell of emotions. "I beg your pardon, sir. Most assuredly, you would choose something more personal: the death of your parents, perhaps."

Darcy answered dryly, "As much as I would cherish even one additional day with either or both of my parents, I was thinking upon a more recent event, where a former friend once again betrayed me."

Her head came around sharply. "Although we do not know each other well, please know I am considered an excellent listener. I have found the sharing of such woes a step toward healing."

For a moment, Darcy wavered over the decision to tell her of George Wickham's attempted seduction of Georgiana and how that event had him considering marriage more seriously than he had in the past. It would be good to share his ire and his loneliness and his desolation with another, but he had promised his sister that he would never speak of it again. And he had not broken his promise. Although he did not think Elizabeth would carry the tale to others, he truly knew nothing of her character. They had known each other less than a week. How could he trust his sister's reputation to a near stranger? "I appreciate your willingness to take on my tale of woe." He shifted his shoulders to indicate his resolve. "Yet, we both realize that as we cannot change the past, we must face the future with a brave face."

"I thought you might wish the return of your reticule," he said tentatively as he extended the item in her direction. They had exchanged less than two dozen bits of conversations since they had come to their agreement, and Darcy suspected she had second-guessed her decision more than once over the past two days.

The let coach lurched just as she reached for the item, and he moved quickly to steady her before she fell upon the floor. "Thank you," she murmured as she readjusted her seat. Without looking at him, she pulled the string upon the purse and dumped her few belongings into her lap. A frown marked her brows. She gathered the extra coins he had slipped into the bag and held them out to him. "These are not mine, sir."

Darcy shrugged his response. "A lady should always carry a means to secure her safety. When I explained to your uncle that you were on foot when your accident occurred, he mentioned that you always carried enough coins to purchase a hackney's service if you were in need of escape or in danger. Your few coins would not permit you to return to your father's house if you so wished. I thought to provide you the means of doing so if it is still your desire."

"You would permit me to leave?" she asked in surprise.

"You are not my property, Elizabeth. Even if you prove to be my wife, I will permit you to choose your own path. I would only exercise my will over yours if you placed yourself or, if we were to be so blessed, our children in danger. If you wish to return to Hertfordshire when we reach Edinburgh, then you may use the coins in your hand to secure passage and lodging. I will permit Hannah to accompany you. She can return to Darcy House afterwards."

"Hannah wishes to remain in Derbyshire," she argued. She turned the coins over in her hand as she returned them to her lap. "I promised I would speak to you upon it. It would do her and her family well to be closer."

It impressed him that his servant had confided in Elizabeth so quickly. "If that is her desire, I would arrange for her return north," he assured her. "With Miss Darcy now from the schoolroom, my sister no longer requires Hannah's familiarity to find her way in the world."

They sat in silence for several minutes before Elizabeth

remarked, "I am always amazed at the difference in the terrain in Scotland."

He noted she slid the coins into her purse. Darcy was not certain whether she had made the decision to remain with him or not, but he would learn soon enough. As odd as it would sound to another, the idea of not waking in the morning to greet her during her day was as foreign an idea as his forgetting to breathe. "Derbyshire will appear wild in comparison to the shires surrounding London."

"The few times my parents traveled to Scotland to visit Mr. Bennet's family, my mother complained of the uncivilized nature of the land."

Darcy studied her carefully. Although the idea was foolish of him to employ, he wanted her to enjoy the idea of mountains and lakes, as opposed to rolling hills. She had become essential to his daily happiness, for she now occupied too much of his mind for his reason to triumph. Although he had provided her the funds to leave him, Darcy secretly meant for her to remain with him, whether she liked the idea or not. And whether he preferred it or not, he meant to protect her from whatever scheme his aunt concocted. "And you?" he asked. "Did the mountain ridges turn you against the area?"

"Not in the least," she admitted. "I am the adventuress in my family."

Darcy smiled upon her. "Why does that not surprise me?"

She laughed, and he found the sound delightfully comforting. "You, sir, speak as if I committed some horrid act."

"Such as false pretenses," he said with a tease.

"I am grieved, sir," she remarked in good-natured tones. "Your opinion of me is so low."

Darcy straightened and leveled a particular look at her. "I assure you, Miss Elizabeth, that I have never known a more captivating woman."

Mr. Darcy assessed her with unflinching regard, and it was all Elizabeth could do not to squirm under his steady gaze. Her chin instinctively came up, but despite her returning his observational stance, she noted the slight twitch of his lips. *The gentleman thinks me less than a worthy adversary,* she thought. *He shall learn otherwise.*

She returned her gaze to the passing landscape, but even so, Elizabeth wondered upon Mr. Darcy's last remark. Did he truly consider her *captivating*? She had never been the sort to be easily intimidated, but how was that fact attractive to Mr. Darcy? The gentleman appeared to find her handsome enough, but handsome enough to serve what purpose in his life?

What would it be to marry such a man? she wondered. Certainly, he was rich enough to impress her mother — his clothes and Town house and yacht would have Mrs. Bennet in a serious dither, but beyond the basic requirements of life, Elizabeth had never sought a wealthy suitor. She turned her head to peek at the gentleman. His obvious confidence sometimes grated her. How could any man be so self-assured that he placed himself as judge and jury over another's future — over her future? How could she justify staying with him when he was often so high-handed that she considered soundly boxing his ears? Silently, she admitted, if only to herself, there was little missing from his countenance. He had called her *captivating,* while she would mark him among the handsomest men of her acquaintance, especially when he smiled. He did not smile often enough, and she wondered why he appeared so profoundly sad at times. Even though she felt sympathy for the man, she held no doubt that Mr. Darcy would act upon his instincts whether she agreed or not. He was certain of his decisions, and he controlled all within his reach. Hannah had spoken of the responsibilities thrust upon him at an early age. Surely that explained his aplomb. Dare she challenge his authority over her? Moreover, dare she agree to remain by his side? Which would be the more dangerous choice?

"Mr. Darcy, welcome to my home," Allard called as the man and his lady met them in the entrance foyer at Webster Hall. Darcy assisted Elizabeth with her new cloak.

They had spent three days in Edinburgh where he had hired a highly-recommended modiste to create a number of dresses for Elizabeth. He had no idea how many seamstresses the woman had hired to complete the seven gowns delivered to Elizabeth's quarters in such a short time. Nor did he care. In truth, Elizabeth's transformation was well worth every penny he paid to view her displayed to the fullest in a proper dress and bonnet. He had thought her handsome, but he had erred: She was stunning.

"Mr. Darcy, this is too much," she had protested when the modiste had personally delivered the first three of her creations. However, he had noticed the longing in Elizabeth's eyes when she fingered the soft yellow and green confection.

"The Allards will expect my wife to be properly attired," he had argued, but it was he who wished to view her in something other than his sister's made-over gowns. He was surely losing his wits. He had discovered that he enjoyed having Elizabeth on his arm and that he walked with more confidence when other gentlemen turned their heads to look upon her. It was truly loathsome behavior on his part, but he cared not what the world might think.

While in the city, they had spent their time walking in several of the parks, had enjoyed an evening out at the opera, and had visited some of the shops. Each day, he had expected her to announce that she would leave him. His bold move to provide her the means to escape his company and to return to her family in Hertfordshire had proven successful. He was correct in providing her a choice. She would never be governed by him. He had gambled that she was a woman of her word, and so far, Darcy had known delight at having her close. He had also learned something else that he admired about her — several things, in fact — when they visited a local bookstore.

As if the books called to her, immediately, Elizabeth had left his side to search the shelves. He espied how her fingers reverently drifted over the bindings and the gold embossed titles. She was mesmerized by the experience, and looking at her, he was enchanted by her perfection. Ironically, although he had told her to choose as many books as she would like, when they came together before the clerk, she carried only one book in her hands, and it was an historical tome on the war between England and America that had separated the nations.

"For my father," she explained with that challenging lift of her eyebrows, with which he had become familiar.

Darcy had not argued with her at the time, but after their return to their hotel, he had sent Sheffield to the shop to purchase two of the books he had noted her lingering over. With Darcy's instructions, the books were delivered into Hannah's hands to present to Elizabeth. As he expected, Elizabeth did not abuse his servant, although she had privately lodged her objections with him. From that simple interaction, Darcy had learned three things that marked her character: she practiced frugality, despite his telling her to choose as many books as she would like, she had chosen but one title; she placed her father's needs before her own, which meant family was important to her, and she remained cognizant of Hannah's position in his household. Darcy approved heartily of all these observations.

"Allard." He extended his hand to the man with whom he hoped to conduct business. "Thank you for your kind welcome, sir."

"Always glad to have a man of your reputation under my roof." Allard pumped Darcy's hand in greeting. "With your permission, sir," he continued in good-natured tones, "may I give you the acquaintance of my wife?"

From the man's words, Darcy assumed Allard was a Scotsman who had spent many years in England, for although the man's speech retained its Scottish accents, the enunciation of certain syllables had English overtones that softened the man's burr. Darcy bowed stiffly. "We are blessed by your graciousness, ma'am." He noted that Mrs. Allard did not extend her hand to him, and he wondered for a moment if she had approved of her husband's inviting them to her home.

Instinctively, in a silent expression of protection, he reached for Elizabeth's hand and placed it upon his arm. "And this is my wife." Although Elizabeth had curtsied to their hosts, Darcy noted the slight flinch of her shoulders when he had declared her to be his wife. She did not approve of lies, and, normally, neither did he, but these circumstances were far from normal. Despite his knowing otherwise, he had half-convinced himself that Elizabeth was truly his wife.

"Newly married, I understand," Allard smiled knowingly upon Elizabeth.

"We are, sir," she murmured in the softest voice Darcy had ever heard her use. At that instant, he knew true regret. He should have sent her home when he departed for Scotland. He had operated under the assumption that he was what was best for her, but that was not the reason he had brought her with him. In truth, whenever he looked upon Elizabeth, he felt oddly short of breath. He had hoped that this new fascination with the woman would run its course if he simply kept her near him.

But his deception had cost her greatly. He wished he could introduce her by her real name, for Darcy held no doubt that she could charm the Allards without the use of his surname, but a bachelor and an unmarried woman did not travel together unless they held an intimate acquaintance. If he introduced her as 'Miss Elizabeth Bennet,' then her name would be associated with a woman of low morals. Although her hand upon his arm was the only intimacy they had shared in the eight days of their acquaintance, no one who knew her by her Christian name would believe that they had acted as "brother and sister" rather than as lovers.

"A bit bashful," Allard teased. "Do not fear, ma'am," he said with an amiable smile. "Mrs. Allard and I believe that a man and woman can know contentment in marriage."

However, before either he or Elizabeth could respond to Allard's remark, a servant descending the stairs halted her progress with a gasp. "Miss Elizabeth, be that you? Imagine encountering you in Scotland!"

Chapter 8

"JOSIE!" MRS. ALLARD'S disapproval laced her tone. "You cannot think this outburst appropriate!"

Elizabeth left Darcy's side to step between the maid and their hostess. "Forgive her, ma'am," she begged. She shot a tentative look to him and he nodded his encouragement to act upon her instincts. "I am acquainted with Josephine. Her aunt and uncle oversee my father's household, and her mother serves as the housekeeper for a distant cousin. Mr...." She paused, realizing she should not use Mr. Bennet's name. "My parents' household," she corrected, "and that of the Flynns have often spent time together."

"You are related to the Flynns?" Mrs. Allard asked with a slight snarl of distaste.

Elizabeth's shoulders stiffened; however, she admirably kept a smile upon her lips and any derision from her tone. "I am, ma'am, and like my dear father, I hold his connections in affection."

"Certainly," Allard said quickly. "The Flynns are a respectable family. Well situated. I understand their estate is quite profitable."

"But we move in different circles," Mrs. Allard corrected her husband while placing Elizabeth below her. Darcy's glare did little to soften the woman's tones. He had met overbearing women such as Mrs. Allard previously, but rarely had he known one, other than his Aunt Catherine, who was oblivious to the need for politeness. "Josie, you may be excused," the lady continued. "We will speak later."

Elizabeth appeared as displeased by the woman's unforgiving tone as was he, but Darcy would not permit her to appear anything but the perfect guest. He recovered her hand before she could speak the words obviously rushing to her lips. Instead, he said, "Although she acted from form, I do not believe the maid meant to be disrespectful, ma'am, and I assure you neither Mrs. Darcy nor I took offense. In fact, I am certain that viewing a familiar face among your household brings Mrs. Darcy comfort. I would take it as a favor to my wife if you not only extended your assurances to your maid, but perhaps permit the girl to speak to Mrs. Darcy of what she knows of the Flynn household since my wife's last visit. Mrs. Darcy is quite devoted to her family, a fact I must say I admired in her from our first meeting."

Allard stammered, "Most...most assuredly, Darcy. I see no harm in Josie calling upon Mrs. Darcy's quarters once the girl has completed her duties. You will see to it, Colette." He motioned to the staircase. "Now, you and Mrs. Darcy must join Mrs. Allard and me in my wife's favorite drawing room. I wish to learn how Mrs. Darcy took to arriving in Scotland upon a yacht."

As they followed their host and hostess to the drawing room, Elizabeth wound her arm through his. She leaned into Darcy's shoulder and murmured, "Thank you for understanding, William."

It was all he could do not to turn her into his embrace and kiss her properly. He was not certain whether she realized she had called him by his Christian name or not, but he was delighted by the gesture, for until that exact moment, he had been always *Mr. Darcy* when she spoke to him. They were becoming friends. *It is a beginning,* he thought as he led her to a seat upon a settee in what he could only call a stiflingly ornate room. He prayed he would not be required to spend many hours in Mrs. Allard's presence. As to the woman beside him, each day they were together, Darcy found himself more taken with Miss Elizabeth Bennet. In truth, he did not quite understand his fascination with her, but by heaven, she intrigued him.

The evening held the earlier tension involving the maid, and Elizabeth had regretted her quick defense of Josie, for her impulsive act had obviously created a quagmire for Mr. Darcy, who was most desirous of conducting business with Allard. As much as she despised the presumptuous manner in which Mr. Darcy had handled their encounter, his kindness upon her behalf had not gone unnoticed.

"Ma'am?" Hannah tapped lightly upon the servant entrance to Elizabeth's quarters.

"Enter," Elizabeth called. She was already dressed for bed.

Hannah opened the door slowly. "Pardon, ma'am. The mistress of the house be permitting her maid to call upon you if'n you're willing to speak to the girl."

Elizabeth set aside the book Mr. Darcy had presented her in Edinburgh. It was one she had not read previously, and she had been both embarrassed by the gift and delighted by his thoughtfulness. "See her in, Hannah."

The girl entered with her head hanging low in submission. "I beg your forgiveness, ma'am," Josie began without looking up. "I be impertinent to speak to you from turn."

Elizabeth rose from her seat. "I did not consider your enthusiasm *impertinence,*" she said in calm tones, "but each mistress possesses different standards. I understand that our exchange likely challenged Mrs. Allard's authority. It was wrong of you to speak out, but it was as equally wrong of me to encourage your doing so."

"Yes, ma'am."

Elizabeth's arm encircled the girl's waist to lead Josie to one of the chairs. Gently shoving the young woman into the seat, she added, "Your apology is accepted. Now, let us enjoy the bit of freedom for which Mr. Darcy bargained. Tell me how long you have been with the Allards."

The girl she had known since her childhood had yet to look upon Elizabeth's countenance, a fact that bothered Elizabeth more than she could express. She wondered where the high-spirited girl she knew had gone. She possessed fond memories of Josie spending hours leading Elizabeth and Jane on adventures upon the Flynns' estate.

"Came to the Allard household when Lachlan came to work in the master's growing mill. Thought to follow him there, but mama would hear none of it." The girl sighed heavily. "I think I could be of more use if I could stand beside Lachlan than being underfoot here."

Elizabeth politely ignored the girl's pronouncement of her worth or the lack thereof. She had faulted Mrs. Allard's "rules" enough for now, but she made a mental note to discover what had broken the girl's spirits. Instead, she asked quietly, "And what does Lachlan think of Mr. Allard's 'growing mill'?" She should be asking of the Flynns, but she was curious about the business venture Mr. Darcy was preparing to make.

"I only see me brother on Sundays at services, but he 'ppears satisfied. Says he's in a better situation than most, for the master keeps a clean work place. Although he thinks some of what occurs not normal practice."

Again, Elizabeth wished to ask the maid to expound on what she had shared, but she did not want to appear gossipy before Hannah, who waited nearby. Therefore, she changed the subject. "What of my father's cousin, Mrs. Flynn? Is she in health?"

Josie shot a quick glance to Elizabeth before speaking of the Flynn household. The recitation was informative, but it lacked the interaction for which Elizabeth craved. She was in need of news from "home," even if *home* was an estate she had not viewed for some five years.

The girl grew silent after her quick report of the Flynns and their adult children. With a swallowed sigh, Elizabeth rose to excuse her. Without thinking beyond the fact that the maid was her connection to her family, she reached to give the girl a hug in parting, but when Elizabeth placed her hands on the girl's back, Josie jerked away from her. Tears filled the girl's eyes, and a grimace marked her features. "Are you injured?" Elizabeth demanded.

"It be nothin', ma'am," Josie pleaded.

Elizabeth's fury rose quickly. "I wish to know what has occurred, Josie," she hissed through tight lips.

"Please, ma'am," Josie beseeched her. "It go bad for Lachlan if the mistress learns that you know."

"Permit me to view what is amiss," Elizabeth ordered, but she made herself speak in calmer tones. "I shan't confront Mrs. Allard," she assured the girl. "I simply wish to know of your safety. You always treated my sister Jane and me well. Permit me to return the favor."

Reluctantly, Josie turned her back to Elizabeth and untied her apron before lifting the lose-fitting dress over her head to expose her back. It was all Elizabeth could do not to cry out against the injustice. Instead, she infused quietness into her words. "Hannah, fetch me some water and a cloth, as well as that ointment from your bag. The one you used on my shoulder."

Josie whimpered, "The mistress will learn that you treated me back."

"Neither Hannah nor I will speak of it," Elizabeth promised. "But several of these cuts require treatment so they do not fester. We will hurry so you may return below stairs in a timely manner."

Tears formed in the maid's eyes, but she nodded her agreement. Without considering the consequences, Elizabeth set about cleaning the girl's wounds. As she placed a clean cloth over the wounds, she asked in false casualness. "These marks appear to be the work of someone taller and stronger than Mrs. Allard.

Is this the work of the lady's husband?"

Josie lifted the shift-like dress over her head to drop it over her form. "No, ma'am. It not be the master's work. It be Mr. Bradburn."

Elizabeth did not ask who Mr. Bradburn might be or what role the man played in the Allard household. She would discover the man's identity in her own way. Instead, she instructed Hannah to see Josie below stairs and to make certain the girl received no censure for her time away. "If anyone asks, tell them your mistress kept Josie longer than intended."

As quickly as the pair left her quarters, Elizabeth instinctively turned to the one person who could assist her. A vague sense of unreality drove her. Barely aware of her actions, she rushed into his arms.

Assuming the noise of the door opening indicated Sheffield's return, Darcy ignored the sound from the adjoining dressing rooms, but he could not ignore the tearful catch in her breath as she burst through the opening. Immediately, he was on his feet to reach her. Three long strides had him gathering her into his embrace. She was distraught, and that was all he needed to know.

Elizabeth's tears dampened his dressing gown, as ragged rasps tore from her throat, but still he held her and cooed words of comfort in her ear. She nestled deeper into his embrace, and he tightened his hold. His heart raced in tempo to hers. It was amazing how much had changed in his life since he had lifted her veil to expose her to those attending his wedding to Anne.

"Come," he coaxed when her tears slackened. He led her to a nearby chair. "Sit." Kneeling before her, he caught Elizabeth's hand to stroke each of her knuckles with the tip of his finger. He encouraged, "Can you tell me what is amiss?" He prayed she had not known abuse in Allard's household, for he would be forced to tear the house apart board by board if any had harmed her. He watched as bitter guilt took up residence upon her features.

"She was lashed," Elizabeth sobbed through trembling lips.

"Who?" He thought of Hannah and immediately rejected the idea. "The maid from earlier today? Is that of whom you speak?"

"It is my fault," she wailed through another round of tears. Darcy retrieved one of his handkerchiefs and pressed it into her palm before returning to his seat on the floor at her feet.

Although he did not announce his thoughts aloud, he knew without a doubt that what happened to the maid was not an isolated incident. A benevolent master did not punish a servant for something that an apology from the maid could resolve. "It is most assuredly not your fault."

Her brows arched high in disdain. "My mother always says I am too impulsive. Too brash. I challenged Mrs. Allard's authority in her own house, and Josie paid the price for my sharp tongue."

"I admired the fact that you chose to protect the innocent," he admitted. In fact, when she stood against the woman he esteemed Elizabeth for her compassion.

"But Mrs. Allard did not," she argued. Her tears had dried, and Elizabeth's ire had returned.

Darcy captured her hand. "Forgive what may appear to be foolish questions, but I wish to understand you fully." With a deep shuddering sigh, she nodded for him to continue. "First, have you seen the maid's wounds?" Again, she nodded in the affirmative. "How many times was she struck?"

She seriously considered his question before responding. "Some of the marks overlapped," she confessed, "but there were three distinct marks, so we can safely say three."

"Did Josie willingly show you her punishment?"

"No, I insisted upon knowing what occurred." She unconsciously interlaced their fingers. "I meant to embrace her when she set to leave my room, and Josie recoiled from what proved to be my firm touch."

Darcy cupped Elizabeth's hand with his free one. "Did

Josie say that Mrs. Allard was the one who administered the punishment?" Although Darcy had taken an instant dislike of the woman, he did not think her capable of such medieval tactics.

"I specifically asked if our hostess was at fault," she confessed. "And Josie denied my accusation."

"Was it Allard?" If so, Darcy would be on the road to Pemberley tomorrow. He would not associate his name with a severe taskmaster.

"Josie says it was a man called Bradburn," Elizabeth confided.

"Bradburn?" Darcy questioned. "Is that the butler? I thought his name was Roberts, but if such a punishment were to be handed out, in most households the butler would be the one charged with carrying out the act."

She avidly surveyed his expression, and, at length, she accepted what she saw. "I do not know Mr. Bradburn's connection to the Allards. I thought perhaps you might know something of the man."

Darcy said quietly, "I do not not, but I promise I will discover the man's character." He squeezed her hand hard enough to force her to focus upon his words. "I must issue a caution, Elizabeth. A man cannot enter another man's household and expect to execute his will upon those within. Even if I learn Bradburn is at fault..."

"Most assuredly, he is at fault," she interrupted. Her expression hardened.

In response, disapproval claimed Darcy's brow. "Even if I learn Bradburn is at fault," he repeated. "My hands in the matter may be tied. Josie accepted the punishment—likely not willingly, but accepted, nonetheless. Legal action would be null."

She jerked her hand free of his. "I thought you a man of honor!" she accused.

"It is convenient that you now think me honorable, when only two days past you thought me without principles," he countered.

"I had the right of it then!" she quipped.

"Elizabeth, please be reasonable. I simply cautioned you not to expect the world will bend to your will. If Allard were a guest at Pemberley, I would politely listen to his questioning of my treatment of my servants, but the decision would still be mine. Such it will be with Allard." He tentatively rested his hand upon her knee. "In fact, I cannot guarantee that Allard will welcome my questions. He may choose to drive me from his home, but ask them, I will. That is a promise."

"How can I depend upon your acting against your interests in order to protect a mere maid? By your own admission, you have spent more than a year courting Allard's cooperation."

"Trust me," he said simply. "For I have pledged myself to your service."

"I trust no one," she said as she stood to leave. "For all who have asked it of me have betrayed it."

Chapter 9

"TRUST," SHE MURMURED as she stared into the darkness. Elizabeth had returned to her quarters some two hours earlier, but her mind had yet to permit her to sleep. Mr. Darcy had asked her to trust him to act upon her behalf, but how could she? "Betrayal and compromise are the foretokens of tragedy, forcing one to set aside one's integrity. I have only to look to my mother and father as examples of the true meaning of failed promises."

As much as she adored her father's wit and his intelligence, over the years she had come to the truth of her parent's relationship: Her father's emotional betrayal was more damaging than if he were physically abusive to her mother. Not that Fanny Bennet was incapable of driving a sane man to Bedlam, for she surely was, but Elizabeth had decided some time back that Lydia was their mother made over. They were the same side of the coin. Both mother and youngest child simply desired the adoration of those about them. Mrs. Bennet, for all her *nerves*, had proven to be an excellent mistress for Longbourn. She ran the estate with efficiency, a fact upon which Elizabeth had never heard her father remark—had never heard him present his wife even one compliment. Had her father, when Mr. Bennet first met his wife, been as shallow as those who favor Lydia's silliness? How could a man of his intelligence choose a wife he had learned to disrespect? Elizabeth sometimes thought that Thomas and Fanny Bennet used their mistrust for each other as a defense against possible betrayal. It was all so convoluted, and, like it or not, their model for marriage had fueled Elizabeth's innate fear of being found wanting.

"My parents have known each other for nearly five and twenty years. If they cannot discover a means to understanding, how can I trust a man I have known for a mere nine days?"

She rolled to her side and punched the pillow in frustration. "I cannot," she decided. "The gentleman has provided me the funds to return to Hertfordshire. I will leave and take Josie with me. Such is not ideal, but the Hills will welcome their niece. Tomorrow, I shall make a point of learning something of the coaching schedules, and then I will approach Josie regarding our departure."

Darcy wished he had asked Elizabeth to accompany him. He worried over leaving her alone with Mrs. Allard as her only company—not because he thought Elizabeth would shame him by abusing the woman, but because he knew it would be difficult for her to curb her temper when she recognized an injustice. Moreover, he would value her opinion of Allard's operation. There was much of the man's enterprise that Darcy found admirable, but if he were to invest in Allard's business prospect, he would insist upon several improvements of which he had learned when he had hired a British-born American to oversee the rebuilding of the water mill supplying the north pasture on Pemberley estate.

"Ah, here is the man who can answer all your questions regarding the actual running of this labor," Allard said as he motioned a man to join them.

The man might be considered handsome in some circles, but Darcy thought he was almost too perfect. The fellow reminded

Darcy of George Wickham in the way he moved — self-assured and with conceit, smooth, but reprehensible, and a zing of warning skittered up Darcy's spine. Instinctively, his shoulders stiffened, as if in preparation for battle. The man wore an easy smile upon his lips, but he appeared dangerous, nevertheless. His dark smoky-colored eyes, marked by thick black lashes, did not waver as he looked down his patrician nose at Darcy and Allard. He certainly did not respect either of them, which was more than a bit circumspect from a hired employee.

His host shook hands with the man before making the introductions. "I was just telling Mr. Darcy about how well you have everything under your control. A man could not ask for a better person to oversee his prospects," Allard said with what sounded of pride. "This is Mr. Cooper Bradburn. Bradburn, this is Mr. Darcy." The fact that Allard thought it proper to introduce a man of Darcy's consequence to a hired employee rather than to ask Darcy's permission to make the presentation showed how lax Allard was in the rules of proper society, which meant the man could also be a poor taskmaster when it came to business. Darcy made a mental note to explore Allard's prospects with a quizzing glass to discover if it contained flaws.

"Bradburn, is it?" Darcy infused his words with casualness. "I heard your name mentioned, sir, when I first inquired of Allard, but somehow I had the impression that you served as Allard's land steward or some such position upon the estate. You will forgive me if I appeared surprised at discovering your playing an integral role in this venture."

The man's smile never left his lips, but Darcy noted the slight tightening of Bradburn's jaw. "I pray those who spoke of me did not disparage my efforts upon Mr. Allard's behalf."

"Nothing of the negative," Darcy assured the man. "I simply made the assumption you were part of the estate staff, rather than part of the business end of Allard's holdings. Purely the fault rests with me. I suppose it is because my focus for many years has been the growth of the home cottages and the farms found on my estate."

"One could not ask for a better overseer," Allard insisted.

"Then I would be most appreciative of Bradburn's sharing his knowledge of the innovations you have included that makes this a model for all of us to emulate." Darcy schooled his features to reflect his anticipation.

Allard good-humoredly slapped Bradburn upon the back. "Bring Mr. Darcy to the office when you have finished showing him about. Mr. Dredge has some papers for me to sign."

"Certainly."

For the next half hour, Darcy followed Bradburn through a large facility that processed wool, from shearing the sheep to the finished product. He approved of the efficiency with which Allard's workers sheared the fat sheep, using a combination of hand shears and a blade to take the wool in one piece. The wool was then handed off to several women, who separated the belly wool and the tags from the rest of the fleece, where it was then hustled along the line to men, who cut away the tags around the breach, the matted knots, and the off-colored spots.

Children swept the wooden slats of the shearing stalls, removing the loose strands and matted pieces before more sheep were brought in. Meanwhile, on the other end of the line, workers rolled the two sides of the cleaned pelts toward the middle before tying the fleece with paper lengths. The rolled skins were bagged in burlap sacks, turned inside out, and sent to another of the barn-like buildings upon the estate for transportation to markets.

"What occurs to these pens when it is no longer sheep shearing season?" Darcy asked in curious tones. "Does this facility stand empty?"

"The stalls can be easily adjusted," Bradburn explained. "We can slaughter pigs and tan the hides. We have another building where we mill corn and soy."

Darcy studied the layout of the various buildings. "This is a large undertaking. It is admirable that Allard has found a means to employ a large number of people from the neighborhood, but such an operation must take away from the land available for the home farms."

"I do not believe Allard is much concerned about the loss of his land to the expansion of this endeavor. He is paid a pretty penny to provide a service to his neighbors. All in the area profit by having shearing and slaughtering and milling in one place. Those on the surrounding farms no longer need to miss days of work by traveling to another village to sell their wares nor must they attend to all these occupations on their own. Our workers can easily move from one task to another."

"Sounds ideal," Darcy remarked, but he was becoming less enthralled with the idea with each passing minute. He could not, for example, consider charging his cottagers for the cost of slaughtering their pigs for them, which was a point Bradburn had shared with pride. He knew many of his tenants regularly slaughtered their animals, not just to sell the pork to those in Lambton and the surrounding areas, but also to feed their families for the winter.

Bradburn directed Darcy's steps toward an open building — no walls — but covered by a thatched roof to keep out the rain. "Our workers receive a midday meal. We discovered we can work them an extra hour each day if we feed them. It is much more efficient than permitting them to bring something from home. Where would we store a variety of handkerchief-wrapped meals? And as our workers do not all eat at the same time, how would we insure that another did not eat what was carried from home? We would be having arguments to moderate each day."

"Do you employ many from the village?" Darcy had assumed the workers were from Allard's estate, but perhaps he had made another faulty supposition. He eyed the watery soup being dispensed to each man and woman in line. The meal did not appear adequate for a full day's work.

"Perhaps half of our workers come from the estate farms and the village," Bradburn explained. "But we employ others, some as far removed as Edinburgh. We have two small buildings with mattresses for those who cannot travel home each day. Needless to say, the women are housed separate from the men. The workers who sleep and eat upon the estate are garnished a fee for their breakfast and evening meals and their housing."

Before Darcy could ask Bradburn about the wages paid, the clatter of a tin bowl drew their attention to the serving line. Bradburn instantly stormed toward the offender. "Enough, Annie," he growled as he whipped a short cat o'nine tails from the satchel over his shoulder. Bradburn cracked the leather straps down hard on the table. "There will be no food for you today! That is the second time this week you have wasted your share of the meal!"

"She be ill, sir," the man behind the girl informed Bradburn.

"And what am I to do, Hill? Permit her to return to her bed while the others perform her share of today's work?" Bradburn argued.

Darcy watched as the man placed the girl behind him. "I will do Annie's share today, sir. Permit her to return to her quarters."

Bradburn edged closer to the man who stood silent and foreboding. "And what if I believe she requires a taste of my whip? Will you also stand her punishment?"

"If necessary, sir."

Darcy stepped up beside Bradburn to speak quietly to the man. "Should not we permit the line to finish their meal? I assume another group will be excused soon. Mr. Hill has accepted the additional responsibility. Whipping the girl will only weaken her further, and using the leather against Mr. Hill will prevent him from executing the extra duties. The punishment does not merit the situation, in my opinion."

Bradburn turned a steely gaze upon Darcy before recalling himself and placing a smile upon his lips. "Certainly, Mr. Darcy. We should return you to Allard's office." He turned to the onlookers. "Finish up here and be quick about it!" To the girl, he said, "Hill has earned you a day of rest, but do not think I will be so generous in the future. If you cannot perform the necessary work, I will discover someone more worthy."

"There you are, Matthew," Mrs. Allard pronounced in disapproving tones. "I did not expect you so long from home."

Allard bent to kiss his wife's upturned cheek. "Darcy viewed several of the buildings while I called in at the office," he explained before he joined her upon the settee.

Darcy remained standing. As Elizabeth was not in the room, he meant to find her as quickly as he could extricate himself from the Allards' company. Although they had argued last evening, his desire to be with her—to look upon her—had not waned.

"I pray you did not leave Mr. Darcy upon his own?" Mrs. Allard asked suspiciously.

"Certainly not," Allard assured his wife. "Bradburn did the pretty."

Darcy interrupted their exchange. "May I ask of Mrs. Darcy's whereabouts?"

Mrs. Allard's expression displayed her continuing disdain. Darcy had yet to understand why the woman was so set against Elizabeth, but there was true animosity in the lady's attitude toward Elizabeth. Moreover, he would bet several gold coins that the situation with the maid was not the source of Mrs. Allard's contempt. "Mrs. Darcy excused herself to write a letter to her sister. Odd. I did not realize Lady Catherine De Bourgh bore more children than the one daughter."

Ah, there is the rub! he thought. Although he was certain that he included no information regarding his plans to marry Anne in his correspondence with Allard, somehow the man's wife had learned of his intended.

"I must apologize, ma'am. Evidently, you are under the impression that I would marry my cousin Anne. Most assuredly, over the years, there has been some talk of our joining; however, that was never my intention. From the first moment I laid eyes upon Elizabeth, I was a man changed for the better."

"See, Colette. I told you there was a logical explanation." Allard's features took on a sheepish appearance. "My wife assumed you had brought your mistress into our house. I told her you were an honorable man and would not mark us with your deception."

Although he recognized that Allard spoke the truth, Darcy remained uneasy regarding Allard's lady. "I beg your pardon, ma'am," he said in stiffly contrite tones. "I did not think to make an explanation, for I held no knowledge of your hearing of Lady Catherine's aspirations of joining her household with mine. Please know that my aunt's hopes were set in sharp contrast to her brother's, the Earl of Matlock's, plans for my future." Darcy rarely used his uncle's position in society, but in this instance, his doing so appeared necessary. "My wife is the daughter of a gentleman from the southern shires. We exchanged our vows in London some ten days removed. And to allay any other questions, my wife is one of five sisters. Her father's estate is entailed upon his cousin, who currently serves as Lady Catherine's rector. The connections between my family and Elizabeth's are numerous. Now, if you will excuse me, I will seek out my bride."

He did not wait for Allard's apology nor one from the man's lady. He had already experienced second thoughts regarding any association with Allard, but Mrs. Allard's open disparagement of Elizabeth was beyond the pale. He would give the woman one more day to right the snub executed in the name of good manners; if not, he would make his apologies before turning his back upon the bargain he had made with Allard. *Ironic,* he thought as he climbed the stairs toward their guest quarters, *to object to a slight delivered to a woman to whom I am not actually attached.*

Reaching her quarters, he knocked quietly and waited for her to answer. Instead, it was Hannah's countenance peeking out at him. "I wish to speak to your mistress."

"Permit him admittance," Elizabeth instructed.

Hannah stepped aside, and Darcy closed the door behind him. Elizabeth rose to her feet to greet him. With a flick of his wrist he motioned Hannah from the room. From Elizabeth's expression, he could view her strong objections to his presence in her room. She thoroughly disliked him, and he wished he knew what he had done to set her against him, for he most assuredly did not dislike her. He could not explain why every pore of his body remained aware of her, but they did.

Even as she set her disapproving gaze upon him, the faint scent of lavender filled his nostrils, and it was all he could do not to close his eyes and relish the thoughts of her in his arms. Her eyes darkened with her obvious displeasure. "Did you speak to Mr. Allard regarding Josie's punishment?" She claimed the offensive.

"I did not," he said stubbornly. If he had his choice he would back her into the bed behind her, and they could settle their disagreement in a more pleasurable manner.

"Then you leave me no choice, sir," she announced. "I will take Josie with me and depart for Hertfordshire tomorrow."

"You cannot," he stated simply.

"You specifically said that I am not your prisoner, Mr. Darcy," she declared.

"But if I am correct, Josie will not wish to leave with you. I suspect the young man I encountered today is a relation, and your childhood playmate will not wish to leave him behind."

Chapter 10

IT WAS ALL Elizabeth could do not to groan aloud. She squeezed her eyes shut in frustration and concentrated on her breathing. At length, she suggested through tight lips, "There are moments, Mr. Darcy, when I openly rue the day I mistakenly entered the church where you awaited your bride."

The gentleman tipped his head to the side as if in sympathy. "I am well aware of your disdain, Miss Elizabeth, but I pray some of our interactions have proven less contentious. I cannot claim the same fault in you to which you assign to me." He gestured to the two chairs gathered before the hearth. "Perhaps we should discuss what I discovered today, and then we can address your plans to leave Scotland. If you insist upon departing, permit me to make the proper arrangements. I would see to your safety."

"If I leave," she demanded, "what shall you say to the Allards."

"More than likely, I will extend my farewells," he said evenly as he assisted her to a chair before sitting.

"Because I will have ruined your opportunity to conduct business with the man?" she accused.

"No." Mr. Darcy had deliberately stressed the word. "In

business, men typically do not respond to emotions. When I extend my farewells, it will be because the plan Allard purports does not fit my vision for Pemberley and because the man's wife has offered a slight to someone under my protection."

Elizabeth sat as correctly erect as he. His control and his habit of saying the unexpected was maddening to her ability to argue her points. Through tight lips, she ordered, "Explain." Unfortunately, her tone lost some of its previous resolve when Mr. Darcy's steady gaze sent a jolt of heat skittering through her belly.

"I should preface my statements by telling you that before arriving upon Allard's threshold, all my interactions with the man have been in written correspondence. What I viewed today does not correspond to the written descriptions provided me."

Despite her best efforts to remain set against Mr. Darcy, Elizabeth's curiosity won out. "How so?"

His tone wavered unevenly as he explained, "First, from my few brief conversations with Allard today, I do not believe the man is cognizant of what occurs in his name. When we arrived at the site, Allard quickly turned me over to Mr. Bradburn."

"Bradburn?" she gasped. "What role does Bradburn play in the mill?"

"Bradburn is Allard's overseer, although I would not necessarily term Allard's operation a mill."

"An overseer?" she questioned. "Then why was he involved in Josie's punishment?"

Some dark, inexplicable emotion crossed Mr. Darcy's expression. "That is the first question to which we must discover an answer."

Elizabeth sat forward in interest. "How many questions do you possess, Mr. Darcy?'

"More than you truly care to know," he admitted.

"Would you mind sharing your other concerns with me?" she offered.

He appeared relieved. "Such was my purpose in seeking you out."

"Then proceed," she said in sympathetic tones.

For the next half hour, Mr. Darcy described his observations regarding Allard's gathering all the "business" of the home farms in one place, his questioning of Bradburn, and the situation he noted with what proved to be Lachlan Hill.

"It would seem that creating a central facility for shearing sheep would be equally important as having a mill for grinding corn," she remarked.

He nodded his agreement. "Such is the reason I considered Allard's offer, but I did not approve of the collection of fees from the man's cottagers for his providing the service. Instead, I had thought Allard's plan was to open new markets for the produced grain and wool. There is no means to cure meat, for example, to reach much further than a ten-mile radius of Allard's estate. Edinburgh would be ideal, but it is some thirty miles removed.

"Why hire people from as far away as the Flynns' estate when surely there are competent workers in the village, which happens to depend upon the prospects of this estate? Is it because Allard and Bradburn do not wish the locals fully to understand what they execute upon the property?"

"More questions," she repeated senselessly. Once again, Mr. Darcy had Elizabeth's emotions hanging by a thread. He reached for her hand, and she instinctively slipped hers into his. It was comforting to feel his warm flesh resting against hers.

"I warned you this situation was not what I expected. I thought perhaps tomorrow that you might take a walk with me, if you do not think it too far, that is. Allard's buildings are a little over a mile in distance. We could make an impromptu call upon the works. Catch Bradburn going about his business, without the warning I assume Allard sent ahead on this particular day. I would value your opinions."

"I am known as an excellent walker in my family," she explained. "I would be pleased to join you."

"If we casually appear, I expect we will discover less polish upon Bradburn's part," he warned. "However, I must warn you that the man will likely be less welcoming."

"I understand."

As expected, Bradburn had been most displeased to view their approach. Because Elizabeth proved to be a most competent walker, they had circled the various buildings to avoid an encounter with the man until they had taken a better measure of what went on in the numerous buildings upon the property.

"I did not expect there to be so many empty buildings," Elizabeth said as she peered through the smoked glass window.

"This is the third one," Darcy observed. "Does Allard plan an expansion? If so, for what purpose? When we first began our negotiations, it was with the understanding that my people would ship wool to him for sale in the Scottish midlands. I was of the understanding that Allard possessed a facility to turn the wool into cloth. I see nothing on this property that would serve as such."

Elizabeth wound her hand through his arm as they walked on. "Mayhap the gentleman requires your investment in order to build the mill."

"Such was not in the papers Allard's man of business detailed." He nudged her closer to avoid a raised tree root. "I already possess a shearing facility upon Pemberley. I could expand it, and my tenants can continue to send the cured pelts to Manchester."

"They why did you think to expand into Scotland?" she inquired.

He sighed heavily, hoping she would understand. "My father entrusted Pemberley's future into my hands. As such, I struggle daily to keep the property viable for those who call it home, which means I keep an eye on the future—to learn something of the latest innovations and trends in the market. Better roads. Larger crop yields. Stronger construction materials. If one is not prepared for the changes, he fails. My father charged me to care for Pemberley, and each day, I remind myself of his trust. I looked to Scotland, for the Scots have made strides with railroads and with crop rotations. I believe, in the future, we will require both to open new markets. I am sorry to say I have been sadly misinformed of Allard's forward-thinking." It felt good to share his hopes for Pemberley's future with another. His responsibilities often had Darcy feeling alone. He realized he desperately wished to share his vision with someone he trusted, and, whether he thought it possible or not, he did trust Elizabeth Bennet.

"Mr. Darcy!" Darcy looked up to observe Bradburn's approach. The man had a smile upon his lips, but the man's tone spoke of censure. "What brings you to this part of Allard's property again so soon?"

Darcy smiled down upon Elizabeth's upturned face. It was as if she anticipated his response. "Just enjoying the countryside with a beautiful lady upon my arm."

"So far from the manor?" Bradburn asked skeptically.

Darcy noted how Elizabeth's lips twitched in amusement. She meant to dissuade Bradburn with her sharp wit. "I assure you, sir, any day upon Mr. Darcy's arm is a delight, and unlike those of lesser stock, I prefer a hardy stretch of the leg, especially in such agreeable company."

For a moment, Darcy wished she truly thought of him in such terms, for he had begun to think that they would do well together.

"Your wife, I assume." Bradburn's nose notched higher in disapproval.

Darcy wished to reprimand the man, but he knew Allard's man was no match for either him or Elizabeth. Therefore, he ignored Bradburn's displeasure, for Elizabeth still looked upon him with interest. "The woman to whom I spoke my vows," he said, knowing she would understand his veiled truth.

"Is there something you require of me?" Bradburn appeared impatient to return to his work, but then Darcy noted the light blue of a woman's dress as a female ducked behind the first of the empty buildings. *So Bradburn has an assignation planned,* Darcy thought.

Darcy arched an eyebrow, and Elizabeth smiled. She recognized her role in this improvised drama. "I believe I have everything I require." To Bradburn, he said, "I was simply explaining to my lady what improvements I envision when I invest in Allard's occupation."

"Improvements?" Bradburn spoke in suspicious tones. "At your estate?"

Darcy presented the man a steely gaze. "Oh, no. Before I establish any improvements at Pemberley, I will insist that Allard make major changes here. As I view it, this scheme is not successful. It is small in range. The future requires a man willing to look beyond the obvious. It saddens me to say, I have found little beyond the ordinary at Webster Hall."

"Small?" Bradburn's scowl thickened.

Again, Darcy pretended not to take umbrage. "Yes, small. I mean to speak to Allard when we return to the manor. My Heavens! The man has three buildings standing empty! Just think what nefarious practices could go on under Allard's nose if the buildings are not put to good use. Can he not hire people to perform the work or does he possess no plans for expansion? I cannot abide aligning myself with those without ambition," he said pompously. "And do not ask me what I think of the lack of a good road leading to the various marketplaces. There is much in short supply that must be corrected before we can conduct proper business."

Bradburn sputtered, "You are asking Allard for a larger output?"

Darcy tucked Elizabeth closer. "I should not be discussing business with one of Allard's hirelings," he said with a dismissal of his hand. "Come along, my dear. It is time I see your return to the manor house."

Bradburn trailed them as Darcy led Elizabeth on a direct path leading to the dining tent. Darcy wished her to view the service for the midday meal. In truth, feeding the workers was one of Allard's ideas of which Darcy approved, with some obvious modifications. However, before he could point out how he might incorporate the concept at Pemberley, several people rushed to support a slumped over figure. Bradburn picked his way past them to storm the scene, as Darcy whispered, "Annie," in Elizabeth's direction.

Elizabeth immediately released his arm, hiked her skirt, and rushed after Bradburn. Darcy reached to catch her before she placed herself in danger, but she was too quick. Aware of Bradburn's nature to reach for his whip, Darcy lengthened his stride so he might prevent the man from striking the girl or Elizabeth.

"Annie! I warned you!" Bradburn bellowed as he shoved his way through the throng gathered about the girl. Elizabeth followed in the man's wake. Darcy knew instinctively she meant to place herself between Bradburn and the girl. "I told you I would not coddle you. You will pack your belongings and be gone by morning!"

Elizabeth elbowed her way past the man to kneel beside the girl. Darcy reached Bradburn in time to place a staying hand on the man's arm.

"Annie, is it?" Elizabeth asked softly as she pulled a handkerchief from her sleeve to press against the girl's forehead. "What ails you?"

"Feel weak, ma'am," Annie moaned. "Stumach ever so frail."

Without releasing the girl's hand, Elizabeth glanced up to him. "Mr. Darcy, might you ask everyone to step back and permit Annie some air. And ask someone to fetch her something to drink."

Darcy nodded curtly, before shooing those gathered around to step back. He whispered Elizabeth's orders to a woman standing off his shoulder, and she scurried away to bring the girl something to soothe her throat. Then he knelt beside Elizabeth. "What do you think we should do?" he asked softly for her ears only. "I would dislike bringing more censure upon Annie's head by insisting that Bradburn permit her to remain until she is well enough to return to work."

Elizabeth shifted her weight to lean closer to him. "Mr. Bradburn may have no choice."

"How so?"

She smiled knowingly. "Have you had measles, Mr. Darcy?"

His eyes shot to the flushed face of the girl lying upon the ground. "Bradburn shan't be happy."

"He must separate those who have had the disease previously from those who have not. Someone should fetch the doctor or an apothecary to confirm what I believe to be true. I suspect, as the workers sleep in close quarters, others have been exposed to the disease."

"I will see to the necessary preparations," he assured her.

She shifted closer still. "You did not answer me, Mr. Darcy. If you have not known measles, you must leave the area immediately." She blushed prettily, but she said what was sensible, rather than what propriety would require. "I had heard it said that if a man contracts measles late in his life, such could prevent him from siring a child. You still require an heir for your estate."

A twitch of amusement touched his lips. "I had a mild case of the measles when I was but seven and a more severe case at age ten."

She smiled sweetly. "Then I would be pleased to claim your assistance."

Chapter 11

BRADBURN HAD NOT been happy when Darcy had sent for Allard. Elizabeth had spent nearly two hours reorganizing the men's and women's shelters to house those who had previously known the disease and those who had not, assigning Bradburn's workers to a complete cleaning of the existing shelters, and assisting the physician with Annie. The doctor had agreed it would be best to isolate Annie from the other workers. "Don't want no epidemic," he had declared, and so Bradburn had had no choice but to remove the lock from one of the empty buildings, in anticipation of additional cases.

"I did not expect such high-handedness upon your part," Allard complained when he and Darcy stepped away from the cleaning efforts.

"I would prefer to think my actions were based upon Christian charity, rather than conceit. Would you have preferred my ignoring the girl's illness and permitted all your workers to claim their beds?"

Allard's color deepened. "Bradburn would have seen to the girl's care," he insisted.

"Would he?" Darcy asked skeptically.

"Most assuredly," Allard declared boldly. "Bradburn is my wife's brother. I trust him to regulate what goes on here."

Darcy quickly disguised his surprise at learning of Bradburn's familial connection to Allard. Such went a long way in explaining why Mrs. Allard had called upon the man to mete out punishment to the maid. "The only thing I have observed Bradburn 'regulating' was the girl in the blue dress I spotted sneaking into one of the empty buildings," Darcy said with a snarl. "And as to the others, I do not consider the threat of a whip as tender concern."

"I object to your insinuations, Darcy!"

Darcy edged closer. "And I object to your condescending tone," he warned. "I witnessed Bradburn's threat to Annie. It was only set aside when Mr. Hill offered to complete his duties, as well as the girl's."

"Then why did you not speak your concerns to me when the incident occurred?" Allard accused.

"I thought the matter settled."

Allard's gaze fell heavily upon Darcy. "And when did you decide it *unsettled*? Was it *Mrs. Darcy's*, if that is truly her name, influence?"

Darcy swore a silent, unsatisfying oath, for Allard had crossed the line. "I will not revisit my conversation from yesterday." One corner of his mouth curled in anger. "If you speak another word against Elizabeth, we will be meeting at dawn to settle your disparagements."

Allard's lip curled into a sneer. "I believe it best that you and the lady leave my home today."

"Gladly." Darcy's features hardened. "But before I leave, I would like to know if you are simply ignorant of what is executed in your name or whether you willfully participate in Bradburn's many schemes."

Darcy's accusation had the desired effect: Allard flinched. The man sputtered, "What foolishness do you speak?"

Ill-conceived annoyance laced Darcy's tone. "Your man of business thoroughly described in several lengthy letters a well-thought-out plan for the future of Webster Hall, but I arrived only to discover a plan that adds extra coins in your pocket, and I assume in that of Bradburn, at the expense of those you employ. You herd workers from one task to another, willy-nilly, depending upon the season, but what I find most offensive is the fact that you charge your cottagers a fee for the services that they once received for free. When did they become more than simple tenant farmers? Being employed in these sheds places them further in debt.

"And where are the villagers, who would customarily depend upon the estate's continued good health? Why must those employed in your name be from a distance far removed from ordinary practices? Where are the road improvements? The expanded markets? Can the workers leave their positions for better opportunities or are they compelled to stay because of their debts? Where is the benevolent master described in the correspondence I received?"

Allard scowled. "You speak an untruth. I treat my tenants with more respect than you do yours!"

"Believe as you wish," Darcy pronounced in dismissal. He presented the man a tilt of his head rather than a bow of respect. "I pray you find peace before your world tumbles to a halt. Farewell, Allard. This has been truly enlightening."

Darcy handed her down from the let carriage before a small inn. They were a little less than three hours removed from Allard's estate, but he had noticed how with each mile of the journey, Elizabeth's shoulders had relaxed a bit more.

Their return to the manor house had been executed in relative silence. As he walked beside her, Darcy's mind had reviewed all his interactions with Allard and how he had failed to notice the weaknesses in the man's business aplomb before arriving on the man's threshold. Thankfully, Elizabeth had not attempted to tease or cajole him from his self-chastisements. She was not that kind of woman, one who chattered on, filling the air with nonsense. No. Elizabeth Bennet was a woman who used language as she did every other facet of her life, with a combination of intelligence and economy.

It was only when the manor came into view that she offered, "I must beg your pardon, Mr. Darcy, for I have again interfered in your well-structured life."

He halted their progress and turned her to him. "I consider your presence in my life a blessing, and you are not to think otherwise. You have prevented me from making two monumental mistakes. How can you think me from sorts?"

She searched for the sincerity in his expression for several elongated seconds before the worry set her features transformed into a smile that had Darcy's heart skipping a beat. "Shall that be my role in your life, Mr. Darcy? Savior?" Good humor filled her tease, and he found himself smiling in return.

"My personal guardian angel," he said softly as he brought her gloved hand to his lips, where he kissed the inside of her wrist.

A flush of color raced to her cheeks, but she did not rip her hand from his grasp. Instead, with a delightful laugh, one that had a rush of warmth filling his abdomen, she taunted, "Mrs. Bennet will testify that I am more devil than angel, and you, sir, would do well to remember as such."

"May I be of assistance, sir?" The innkeeper rushed forward to greet them.

Darcy tucked Elizabeth closer to his side. "My cousin and I require rooms," he announced. They had agreed that as they traveled in the direction of the Flynns' estate that it was probable that they would encounter others from Flynn's household, who might recognize Elizabeth, and so she was now *Darcy's relation* instead of *his wife*. He would go to extremes to protect Elizabeth's reputation, for he had grown truly fond of her.

The innkeeper eyed them suspiciously. "Not many of your ilk come this way."

Darcy understood the man's insinuation. "My cousin and I were guests at the Allard estate outside of Edinburgh, but measles have struck some of those employed upon the estate. We thought it best to depart early before the illness spreads to those in the main house." He told the truth—just not the complete truth.

"Measles, heh?" the man asked as he turned the register so Darcy might sign it. "That be a bad business." He handed Darcy the pen, but did not place the ink well upon the table. "Before ye be signing, sir, ye shud know there be a weddin' occurrin' here this evening. Not exactly the weddin', more along the lines of the celebration. There be no assembly hall or meeting place large enough to hold the sizable family gathering. Most in the area call in here regularly. Might'n be a bit loud."

Darcy did not wish to climb back into the crowded let carriage with Sheffield and Hannah observing his every interaction with Elizabeth, but he dutifully asked, "And the next decent inn?"

"For the likes of you, sir, some twelve miles along the main road south."

Darcy leaned down to ask, "What say you, Elizabeth?"

"In truth," she said softly, "I could sleep through the roughest storm God chose to deliver. A few partiers will not disturb me. A good meal and a bath are all I require for the evening."

"Then we will stay." He grinned at her. "You heard the lady. Two rooms as far removed from the jubilation as possible."

Within a quarter hour, they dined in the common room of the inn. Only three others occupied the room, so they were relatively alone and could speak freely. "I wish to extend my apologies," he said in serious tones. "I thought myself in charge of what has occurred between us since you ran from the church, but I fear I have done you irreparable harm. I have placed you in a abrasive surrounding and opened you to further accusations. You must permit me to do more than present your sisters with a larger dowry."

She looked up in alarm. "Such as?"

"I would not be opposed to our joining," he stated honestly.

Since taking her acquaintance, Darcy had often considered the possibility of calling her *wife.*

Elizabeth shook off the idea. "I could not entertain your address, Mr. Darcy. Even if you had not brought me aboard your yacht, my actions at the church discredited my name. It was foolish of me to think such cheekiness could be ignored. Even if I had simply thwarted Mr. Collins's plans, I named my fate. I doubt either the gentleman or your aunt would have remained silent regarding my purposeful slight. And I find it hard to believe that my father will be capable of controlling Mrs. Bennet's aspersions. He has failed miserably in the past when Mrs. Bennet sets her mind to such misery. Most certainly, all in the neighborhood know something of my ill-advised bravado by now."

He did not approve of her decision, but Darcy nodded his agreement. "I must abide by your choice."

Silence settled between them, and it was not the kind of silence that caused distress. It was more of the manner in which two friends can sit together, even when they disagree upon something important. He searched for a means to change her mind, but he knew Elizabeth adamant in her opinions. Before he could form an argument to persuade her, the wedding party, literally, carried the newly-wed couple into the inn. The bride and the groom were perched on the shoulders of four bulky Scotsmen, who proudly hefted the pair higher, to the cheers of all those trailing behind them.

"Oh," Elizabeth sighed heavily as she looked on. "Is she not beautiful? Such joy upon her countenance. Do you suppose they are in love?"

Darcy studied the pair as their escorts set them upon the floor. "The groom appears enthralled with his bride." He noted the look of longing upon Elizabeth's face, and he felt a bit sad that because of him, she would never know such happiness. "Is that your desire? To marry for love?" Such would go a long way in explaining why she had refused him, for Darcy knew her affections had not been stirred by their acquaintance.

She shrugged off his questions. "Do you find it odd, Mr.

Darcy, that I am as susceptible to the idea of discovering a man who holds me in deep regard as are my sisters? Is it not foolish for a woman of my years to carry the wish of the Cinder Maid buried deep in her heart?"

"My parents married for love," he admitted. "Together, they were a force with which to be reckoned." Darcy chuckled in remembrance. "They were quite remarkable. I always believed if I could replicate their devotion to each other in my own marriage that Pemberley could survive and prosper."

"Then when did you have a change of heart?" she challenged. "From your own lips, Miss De Bourgh did not claim your heart."

"I do not know exactly how to define that particular moment." He sat staring out the window over her shoulder. "I thought I had several years before I must choose a wife. Thought myself above entering the marriage mart. But..." He closed his eyes to drive away the taste of bile rising to his throat whenever he considered the betrayal practiced at George Wickham's hands.

"But?" Elizabeth prompted, as she slipped her hand into his. "Know that I can serve as your confidante, Mr. Darcy."

He opened his eyes to study her beautiful countenance. How was it possible that they had known each other less than a fortnight; yet, she was essential to all that he held most dear? "But a former friend used our relationship to attempt a seduction of my sister." He had said the words aloud, and all his fears of the world swinging away from its axis had proved false. "I blundered — not giving her the attention she required," he explained, "and Georgiana is so broken that I am desperate to restore her good humor. I thought that Anne might prove a comforting force for Miss Darcy. Mayhap even lead my sister to a better understanding of Georgiana's lack of fault in the matter."

Tears pooled in Elizabeth's eyes. "And who is to lead you to a better understanding of your role in the matter, Mr. Darcy?" she asked in sympathetic tones.

He squeezed her hand. "My fault will never be obliterated. It is Georgiana's heart that requires protection. She is not yet sixteen and was easily misled by a man she recognized as part of our family's legacy. Miss Darcy trusted him, but all Mr. Wickham, who was my childhood chum and the son of my father's steward, wished was my sister's substantial dowry."

"Oh, William," she whispered. "You cannot take the blame for some blackguard's disposition. You can only execute your life with honor." She smiled weakly. "I know young girls. I was one very recently." A bit of a tease entered her tone. "We give our hearts away many times before we discover a man worth knowing."

"Pardon, friends," the innkeeper said as he set two steaming plates before them. "Wanted to get yer meal out before the celebration became too rowdy." He chuckled good-naturedly as he glanced over his shoulder at the wedding party. "The bride be the daughter of Sir James Metts, a knight who earned his title via our local bishop. She be a good girl. Don't know much of the groom. He be Greek. And Catholic. Never knew a Greek before. Some sort of diplomat, I hears. They met in London at a musicale, whatever that may be." He set two tea cups upon the table without saucers. "Don't know 'bout the spirits, but the young man claims this a traditional drink for those of his kind. Says it tastes of aniseed or fennel. Wishes you to join him in a toast to his bride." The innkeeper poured two fingers full in the cups.

Elizabeth eyed the drink suspiciously. "And what does the gentleman call these spirits?"

"Ouzo."

She glanced to Darcy. "Are you familiar with the drink?"

"It may surprise you, my dear," he said with a genuine smile, "but I never experienced a grand tour nor do I associate with high rollers."

Her mouth formed a teasing pout. "Then I suppose it falls to me to taste the brew first. I would not wish to stain your immaculate reputation by demanding that you imbibe first."

Darcy's smile widened. "We will partake of the brew together." He lifted his cup to tap it gently against hers. "To life."

"To love," she added.

Then they turned as one toward the happy couple, and with the others gathered in the room, they declared, "To a happy marriage."

Chapter 12

HE JERKED AWAKE with the jolt of the carriage wheel hitting another rut in the road. Darcy hated to leave behind the dream, for it was one that greatly perplexed him. He knew the dream was likely part of his foggy memory of what had occurred at the inn overnight, but he could not name the events with any certainty. He could count on one hand the number of times he had imbibed too much, for he was a man who prided himself on control; however, all he could recall of the previous evening was the happy smile upon Elizabeth Bennet's lips as she spun around him during a Scottish reel. The men had cleared the center of the room for a bit of dancing, and somehow—although the details of his participation were blurry—he and Elizabeth had joined in. She had glowed under his close attention, and his heart had swollen with affection for her. At least, he thought that was what had occurred. Surely, he had not dreamed the heat of her body close to his.

What he could not recall was what had occurred after the dancing, but he knew it had something to do with the paper slid under his room door early this morning. He had yet to share it with her or with anyone. Even Sheffield had not seen the certificate, for his valet had been in the inn's kitchen fetching warm water, so Darcy could complete his morning ablutions.

We are married. The words ricocheted through his dulled senses. *But how could that be possible? Is our joining legal or did someone play a misplaced joke upon them?* Had he again married Elizabeth Bennet? Irony. For if he had pronounced his vows to the lady, they were truly binding. He personally knew of two chaps who had eloped to Scotland rather than waiting for the banns to be read and who had not achieved the permission of their intendeds' fathers.

"What do you find so amusing, Mr. Darcy?" she asked through tight lips. She eyed him suspiciously, as if she pondered what had occurred between them last evening as much as he did. Did Elizabeth remember something of an exchange of vows between them? He certainly could not ask her with Hannah and Sheffield sharing the coach. And would she believe him if he declared it to be so, especially after he had indicated that he would welcome her as his wife? She would likely think he had arranged a fake certificate of marriage.

But he had reasons to believe the document legitimate, for it carried her given name. He had not called her "Elizabeth Bennet" before any in attendance at the inn's celebration. At least, he was relatively certain that he had not done so. And her full name appeared on the paper rolled up and tied with a ribbon and buried in his luggage.

"I was just wondering if the ouzo affected your appetite, my dear?" He heard Hannah's muffled snicker, and he knew for certain that Elizabeth had suffered from over indulgence. "We will stop soon for a change of horses. If you wish, we might claim refreshments. The innkeeper said you ate very little breakfast before we departed."

She appeared a bit green about the corners of her mouth, but she kept an easy smile upon her lips. Only when she flinched with each jostling of the coach did Elizabeth betray how poorly her head must be after so much alcoholic consumption. "Do you suppose we might stretch our legs instead? I would take pleasure in a short walk before we resume our journey."

"We will do both," he assured her. "Although we experienced a late start, we will turn onto the main road soon, and then we will make better time. We should be in England by late afternoon."

"And how many days do you anticipate before we reach Pemberley?"

"Not long. Two days. Perhaps three. Depends upon the weather. I sent my own coach north from London when we departed. I had hoped it would have arrived at Webster Hall before we left the Allards, but we should be able to change into a more comfortable conveyance by tomorrow, at the latest."

She glanced to the two servants sharing their carriage before she spoke. "May I make an observation regarding what we viewed of the Allards' venture?"

"I hold no objections," he assured her.

"I have been thinking upon what you shared of the work at the shearing pens. If I am correct, you found the operation efficient, and you are considering replicating the idea at Pemberley."

"I am."

She nodded her understanding. "I plan to make a similar suggestion to Mr. Bennet. Centralizing the shearing of wool could prove beneficial for all concerned. I am ashamed to say that several of Mr. Bennet's tenants do not take proper care of the sheep prior to claiming the wool nor do they take the wool as a complete pelt, thus lowering the price of the product. Having those trained in removing the wool quickly and cleanly would improve profits."

Darcy smiled knowingly. When had he ever met a woman who could discuss the running of an estate in such astute terms? He suspected that Mr. Bennet had "trained" Elizabeth in the everyday duties of a land owner. "Agreed. There were other parts of Allard's concept that showed promise; yet, I could not countenance the idea of charging my cottagers for the privilege of each service the man envisioned. I already collect rents on the farms. I believe that if the cottagers know success, they will stay at

Pemberley, and they will treat the land with the same reverence as I do."

"I find that honorable," she said. "I was also thinking of other services that could improve the lots of those upon my father's farms, and, therefore, perhaps, on yours. I doubt if any society can survive without those willing to toil the land, but, even so, the lure of the cities must surely be tempting to those struggling to eke out a living. It seems to me that you and Mr. Bennet must discover a product that is specific to your part of Derbyshire, or in my father's case, to Hertfordshire. It should not be found in any other part of England. Create your own markets by being the best at one thing, rather than being one of many vying for the customer's coins."

"Do you mean something similar to the Loaghtan sheep found on the Isle of Man?" Darcy asked, his interest piqued.

"Although I have never seen the brown wool produced by those herds, my Uncle Gardiner says the product earns those involved a plump purse," she explained.

Darcy's features screwed up in concentration. "I doubt I could convert many of the locals to the Loaghtan herds, but the idea is worth exploring."

He liked the way Elizabeth's eyes lit up when he complimented her intelligence. "Why not concentrate on traditional methods of raising the sheep?" she said with renewed enthusiasm. "One of my father's tenants refuses to graze his herd on the improved land or to feed them anything but locally grown grain. His sheep are always superior to the other herds."

"Interesting," he mused aloud. "Create a product customers would seek for its quality."

"The factory towns will grow and products will be made quickly and cheaply for the masses, but where will the best households shop? There will always be those who will tolerate only quality products. Moreover, the *nouveau riche*, of which many aristocrats disclaim, will likely follow suit. My Uncle Gardiner is an excellent example of those in trade who have earned the respect of society and who surrounds himself with the pleasures of good living. Although Mr. Gardiner does not go about in the same society as does your uncle, he lives equally as well, perhaps better, than many with titles."

"From what I know of the gentleman, I would agree," Darcy assured her.

Sheffield cleared his throat. "Pardon, sir, but Miss Elizabeth's suggestions had me thinking of the black pudding made upon the Isle of Lewis. Nothing finer. Mayhap you should consider multiple products."

"Dovedale has its cheeses," Hannah added.

"As does Swaledale in Yorkshire," Sheffield observed. His servants appeared as excited by Elizabeth's idea as was he.

"I dearly love the clotted cream from Cornwall," she declared. "There must be something you could cultivate that could provide Pemberley a distinct role in your family's history."

Darcy spoke with enthusiasm, "We could attempt to develop a better potato or a better apple by cross cultivation. One that would taste as sweet, but last longer in the root cellars." He rubbed his hands together in satisfaction. "Your ideas provide me much to consider. Thank you, Elizabeth."

She was quick to say, "And do not forget the womenfolk upon the farms when you are considering changes. They can contribute also. Perhaps handmade lace. Or brandy butter." Such happiness filled her features that Darcy could not help but smile widely. Elizabeth Bennet was absolutely incomparable.

"Mr. Darcy, it is magnificent." He delighted in watching Elizabeth's eager enjoyment at her first sight of Pemberley. Secretly, he never tired of the myriad of emotions prancing across her features. It was all quite mysterious to him, but he delighted in them, nonetheless. She undoubtedly possessed more life in her smallest finger than any of the society ladies who were regularly paraded before him for his approval did in their whole bodies. Darcy had decided that Elizabeth Bennet was exactly what he required to drive away the loneliness of his world. "I have never viewed a house as perfectly situated as is Pemberley."

"Needless to say, I think it beyond compare," he said politely. It was midafternoon of the third day of their journey, and he was gladdened by the prospects of sleeping in his own bed, not that he thought his doing so would drive away the tempting dreams of Elizabeth that welcomed him each evening. However, her allurements were almost too much to keep him from her room at the various inns in which they stayed. At least, at Pemberley, he knew he could not seduce her before his servants or his sister.

They had met Mr. Farrin and Jasper on the English side of the border, and he had welcomed the sight of his well-sprung coach. With his carriage as their chosen transportation, Sheffield occasionally chose to ride on top, which permitted them all a bit more leg room.

Darcy had yet to broach the subject of their marrying in Scotland. He did not wish to upset the delicate truce they had achieved over the past week. They conversed often, and he found that Elizabeth Bennet could speak to a variety of subjects. He read to her and she to him. They walked together. He shared more of his dreams for Pemberley's future, and she told him the stories of her family. He was a coward, for he did not want to argue with her again. Occasionally, he noted that she looked at him oddly, and he wondered if she, too, had memories of the night they drank too much ouzo.

He convinced himself that he would send his solicitor to Scotland to confirm the legitimacy of their marriage and then approach her.

"You appear to have company, Mr. Darcy," she said in what sounded of anxiousness.

Darcy glanced out the coach's window. "Bingley," he groaned. "What is he doing here?"

"Was he at the wedding?" she asked after shooting a glance to the snoring Hannah.

"No. Aunt Catherine omitted him from the guest list, for Bingley is from trade. Needless to say, he could have made an appearance. Churches are required to have open doors during such an event, in case someone not expected wishes to lodge an objection to the couple's joining, but Bingley's manners would keep him from the nuptials. We have been chums since Cambridge."

"Is he likely to keep your confidences?" she asked as they rolled to a halt.

"Bingley would, but if his sisters travel with him, your presence will be harder to explain in a manner where I might still protect your reputation," he confessed.

The coach shifted as Jasper climbed down from his seat on top. He shot another worried glance to Elizabeth as the footman swung open the door and put down the steps. He wished he had a few extra minutes to concoct a reasonable explanation, but there was little either of them could say as Hannah sat up to claim her duties. Darcy could just imagine the tales that would entertain his staff this evening.

Reluctantly, he stepped from the coach and turned to assist Elizabeth down. "Your sister?" she whispered.

"Yes, Georgiana," he confirmed an instant before Elizabeth stepped around him.

"Miss Darcy," she said as she rushed forward to catch Georgiana up in a hug. "Thank you for asking your brother to fetch me from my relations' home and for sending Hannah with Mr. Farrin to accompany me. Aunt Flynn could not spare a servant."

Georgiana appeared bewildered, but, thankfully, his sister held her tongue.

Meanwhile, he had greeted Bingley and had turned his friend so Darcy might perform the introductions. "Bingley, with the lady's permission, allow me to give you the acquaintance of Miss Darcy's particular friend, Miss Elizabeth Bennet."

Bingley looked as confused as did Georgiana, but his friend's natural amiability had him greeting Elizabeth with open admiration. "I am so pleased that Miss Darcy has such a lovely friend."

"I am the fortunate one," Elizabeth corrected. "The Darcys

have been most generous. I was in Scotland with my father's cousin when Mr. Bennet took a fall from his horse, and the family coach was not to be spared so I could return home. When Miss Darcy learned of my situation, she contacted her brother, and Mr. Darcy graciously agreed to escort me to Derbyshire, where I shall reunite with my eldest sister and then travel on to Hertfordshire."

Bingley remarked to Darcy, "I thought you were at Allards. Did you leave early to aid Miss Bennet?"

Darcy slapped Bingley good-naturedly upon the back. "Suffice it to say, Allard was not what he claimed. I was pleased to have the excuse to expedite Miss Elizabeth's reunion with her family. Come inside, and I will tell you what I discovered upon Allard's property." He turned Bingley toward the open door. "Georgiana, mayhap you could show Miss Elizabeth to her quarters. I imagine she wishes to freshen her clothing before we take tea. Hannah, please report to Mrs. Reynolds, and tell her that I wish for you to remain in service to Miss Elizabeth until she must leave us."

Elizabeth locked arms with Miss Darcy. "I apologize for involving you in this farce," she whispered.

The girl finally found her voice. "You are the woman from the church," she accused.

Elizabeth glanced around to note the presence of Hannah and several footmen. "We can discuss this in private. For now, follow your brother's instructions. Defaming me before others also defames Mr. Darcy. I am here at his insistence."

The girl stiffened, but she nodded her agreement. Silently, they followed the waiting butler to a lovely suite in what was obviously the family wing. "Mr. Darcy sent a message ahead yesterday. His orders were to prepare the green suite for you, miss." He opened the door to a room twice the size of her quarters at Longbourn. "Everything should be as the master instructed, but if you require anything else, please ring the bell. Hannah will assist the footmen with your bags." He bowed properly. "I am

Mr. Nathan. Do not hesitate to seek me out if all is not to your liking."

"Thank you, Mr. Nathan. I have no doubt all is in order. Please tell the housekeeper that the room is lovely. I appreciate the personal touches, especially the fresh flowers."

"Mrs. Reynolds will be pleased to hear you say so, miss."

"That will be all, Mr. Nathan," Miss Darcy instructed. When the butler closed the door behind him, Miss Darcy crossed her arms over her chest in a defensive stance; yet, the girl took the offense. "Now, perhaps you might explain why my brother has brought you to our family home."

Elizabeth fought the urge to roll her eyes. Why was it the young thought they deserved answers to questions that did not apply to them? "Perhaps questions regarding Mr. Darcy's reasons should be directed to the gentleman himself. He originally claimed he wished to protect me from Lady Catherine De Bourgh and to verify whether the vows we exchanged were legal."

The girl's features screwed up in a manner that was reminiscent of her brother. "That makes little sense. Darcy could have sent you to a secure place to wait out Lady Catherine's ire while he learned of the ceremony's authenticity."

Elizabeth removed her bonnet and placed it upon the bed. "Such were my thoughts, but as I was unconscious for several days, decisions were made for me. Surely you must know that your brother is a hard man to persuade to an opposing position once he has set his mind to a task."

"Unconscious?" the girl asked in bewilderment.

Elizabeth sighed heavily. It was an excellent idea that her mother had not sent her off to school, for she had little patience with the poor innocents that the English school system produced. "Do the men in your family think you too fragile to know what goes on in their worlds?"

Miss Darcy's eyes grew wider. "They mean to protect me," she insisted.

Elizabeth removed her gloves and unbuttoned her spencer. "Do you require protection?"

"Does not every woman?" the girl countered.

"I suppose we do, but only because men write the rules." She removed several pins from her hair to release her simple braid. "Perhaps it might be best if I speak honestly." Elizabeth did not wait for the girl's permission.

"Mr. Darcy rescued me from the street where I was struck by a coach following my escape from St. George. He took me to Darcy House where I was attended by Dr. Nott for both a head injury and a dislocated shoulder. I was given more laudanum than I am accustomed to consuming. Therefore, when your brother learned that Lady Catherine meant to send a magistrate for me, he removed me to his yacht. I have been with him since I awoke aboard his ship. I thought to demand a return to my home, but as my reputation is likely beyond repair, I chose to bargain with the man. He required a 'wife' to conduct business with Mr. Allard, and my sisters require a larger dowry in order to attract proper husbands after my downfall. We came to an agreement. Over the past fortnight, we have shared conversations and meals and leisurely walks, as well as a carriage. Although Hannah was at my side the entire time, and nothing untoward has happened between us, I will still be counted as a fallen woman. I am truly grieved that you have been made a part of this madness, but my eldest sister will be joining me here in two days, and my dearest Jane does not deserve your censure. She has done nothing but be the best of sisters. I would ask you to treat her with proper respect, even if you cannot in your heart think to extend a like response to me.

"While I am at Pemberley, I would rejoice in learning more of you, for your brother speaks so glowingly of your charms that I possess a great desire to know you better. However, if you prefer to remain unattached, I shall understand and keep my distance."

Chapter 13

HE HAD EXPECTED Georgiana's questions, but Darcy had not thought she would call upon him as quickly as she did. After sending his sister off with a woman Georgiana did not know, he had spent less than a quarter hour with Bingley, providing his friend with an abbreviated report on what Darcy had discovered at Allard's estate.

"My goodness," Bingley had observed. "I thought the man had more sense than to turn over his holdings to another's oversight. He deserves to be proved a fool."

Darcy had finished off his brandy. "You will stay with us for a few days, will you not, Bingley? I have been pondering several ideas of my own on which I would wish your opinion."

"Gladly, Darcy," his friend said. "I meant to join my Brother Hurst in Staffordshire, but nothing there requires my immediate attention. I called in today only to check upon your recovery. Your message to me after your botched nuptials caught up with me in York when I was visiting with Lord Swenton. I had thought you would retreat to Pemberley to avoid the Society gossips. It was only when I arrived on your doorstep today that I learned that you had called upon Allard. Miss Darcy informed me that yesterday the staff had a message announcing your return to Pemberley. I stayed to greet you in case you required a gentleman's perspective on your recent difficulties. I assumed you would not wish to discuss the matter of a failed marriage with Miss Darcy."

Bingley had been correct: Darcy did not wish to explain to Georgiana how he had come to depend upon Elizabeth Bennet's presence in his life, for it made no sense to him either. Yet, as his sister requested to speak to him, Darcy would not turn her away. She would insist upon answers that, in truth, he did not possess.

"How could you, William?" she demanded as soon as Sheffield closed the door behind him.

"How could I what?"

"Bring that woman into this house," she declared.

He took her by the hand and led Georgiana to a chair. "Sit," he instructed. Once she was settled, he pulled another chair before hers and set his gaze upon her. "That woman has a name: Miss Elizabeth Bennet. She is a gentleman's daughter from Hertfordshire, and, therefore, she deserves your respect."

Georgiana's eyes widened in surprise, for he rarely spoke to her in a stern tone. "But she has obviously been traveling with you since the church service in London."

Darcy sighed heavily. "Did the colonel not provide you an explanation of what occurred at Saint George?"

"Our cousin offered no insights in my presence. He summoned Mrs. Annesley to return with me to Pemberley. Fitzwilliam said such was your wish."

"It was my wish to return you to Derbyshire," Darcy assured her. "And I suppose if I asked Fitzwilliam why he did not present you an understanding of what has passed between me and Miss Elizabeth that he would say you are too young to know such things." Georgiana frowned her disapproval. "Yet, I think otherwise," he was quick to say. "Only recently you thought yourself old enough to choose a husband."

Georgiana caught his hand. "I cannot explain how grieved I am at disappointing you. But how is your traveling with a lady anything like what I intended?"

He brought her palm to his lips and placed a kiss in its center. "I do not mean to chastise you, dearest one, but I have reached my majority, and you have not. I remain your guardian. Moreover, Mr. Wickham possessed nefarious motives. Miss Elizabeth does not."

"Are you certain?" she argued.

"I am relatively certain the lady held no knowledge of my wealth until today when she viewed Pemberley." He closed his eyes to compose his response. "I simply wished to make a point: The colonel and I have neglected you too long. We have seen to your education, but not to your self worth. We meant to protect you, but we did you a disservice by keeping the world's derision from your door. If we had been more open with you regarding Mr. Wickham's true character, the scoundrel could not have persuaded you to act upon your own."

Confusion marked his sister's features. "How is what you say connected to Miss Elizabeth?"

He cleared his throat before he replied. "Georgiana, I wish I could explain why I chose to keep Miss Elizabeth close. Initially, I told myself that I wished to protect her from Lady Catherine's retributions, but I no longer believe it so."

"The lady ruined your nuptials, William," Georgiana protested.

"For which I will be eternally grateful," he countered. "You know I hold Anne in familial affection, but my reasons for considering her were selfish. I failed you, and I thought if I married someone familiar that you would no longer appear so down in the countenance. That a confidante would provide you the solace you sought."

"You meant to sacrifice your happiness for me?" she gasped.

"You are my family. My only family. How could I not do otherwise?" He stroked the back of her hand. "Such is one of the reasons I so admire Miss Elizabeth, for you see, when she executed her guise upon my wedding, it was to prevent her eldest sister from being forced into a marriage with a man any sensible woman would reject. Miss Elizabeth meant to pronounce the vows using her sister's name, thus voiding the marriage."

"She meant to execute a fraud?" Georgiana questioned. "Then how did she come to be at your nuptials instead of her sister's planned wedding? And what of your name being used during the ceremony?"

"The lady is not familiar with London. The hackney delivered her to the wrong church, for she was to be at a different 'saint' church that was near the Thames, and with the heavy veil, she did not realize her mistake until afterwards," he explained. "As to the names, the man who thought to claim her sister is a 'William' and Miss Elizabeth's middle name is 'Anne.'" Darcy chuckled at the irony of all that had occurred. Only in a novel could one expect the listener to believe such a story. "Miss Elizabeth was willing to risk her reputation to save her sister from a lifetime of drudgery. In Scotland, she stood up to Allard's wife when the woman ordered a maid whipped for a simple misstep."

"Is that the reason you departed from Scotland earlier than you expected?"

"That and a little matter of dealings under the table to which I might have remained ignorant if not for Miss Elizabeth's suspicions. She alerted me to the evils practiced by Allard's overseer, a man called Bradburn."

"You sound as if you are quite taken with Miss Elizabeth," Georgiana observed in cautious tones.

Darcy found himself smiling. "I fear I cannot conceal my growing regard for the lady." He caught his sister's hand again. "I realize this situation is unorthodox, Georgiana, but I would consider it a great favor if you would befriend Miss Elizabeth while she is at Pemberley. Just provide her the opportunity to learn to love you as much as I do."

"Do you mean to marry the lady?" His sister's expression turned to uncertainty.

"If she will have me, I would marry her again."

Elizabeth smiled easily at Mr. Bingley as the gentleman related a tale of his and Mr. Darcy's days at Cambridge. The gentleman was everything that was excellent company, but she preferred the long periods of silence she had shared with Mr. Darcy, where the two of them were left to ponder what was said previously, over the constant need to fill the air with conversation that Mr. Bingley displayed. The idea that she had become dependent on Mr. Darcy's company frightened her more than she could say. She supposed this new realization had something to do with the foolish dreams she had experienced since she had met the man, and especially since that night at the Scottish inn. Even when she laid down for a restorative sleep this afternoon, she had imagined the heat in Mr. Darcy's eyes when he had looked upon her.

"Why do you not share with Mr. Bingley something of your family, Miss Elizabeth?" Miss Darcy asked in all politeness.

The girl had yet to pronounce an apology for her earlier accusations, but her tone had softened since Miss Darcy had spoken to her brother, and Elizabeth had no doubt that Mr. Darcy had *ordered* the girl to be civil to Elizabeth.

"I am certain the gentleman would not care to hear of a house full of females. I know my poor father would not wish me to advertise the foolishness of his daughters," Elizabeth said in the tone she employed when she feared being found wanting.

Mr. Darcy laughed at her protest, but she thought she noted something of his protective nature when he said, "Miss Elizabeth is the second of five daughters, Bingley. I have not had the pleasure of the acquaintance of the others, but I am certain they are as delightful as she."

"With that," she said as a flush of color rushed to her cheeks, "mayhap we should leave the gentlemen to their port, Miss Darcy; that is, unless you wish to tarry."

The girl's cheeks also reddened, but she managed, "We

shall await you in the yellow drawing room, Darcy." She stood regally to lead the way from the room.

When they reached the drawing room, Elizabeth said to the girl's back, "I apologize, Miss Darcy. It was not my place to announce our exit."

The girl spun around to face Elizabeth. "I do not know what to make of you, Miss Elizabeth. Everything I view of you says you are a lady whose actions and speech are correct and refined, but how do I justify what I see with the idea of your traveling alone with my brother?"

Elizabeth did not think there was a means to answer the girl. First, she was never alone with Mr. Darcy, but she supposed that did not matter in the greater scheme of things. "Must you justify it?"

"I do not know," the girl confessed. "Do you plan to marry my brother? Is that your purpose?"

Elizabeth hid her disappointment, for she had hoped that Miss Darcy's ire had waned. "If there is some legal statute that proves us to be legally wed based on what occurred at St. George, then I will have no recourse but to remain with Mr. Darcy and he with me. Although it is not my wish for such an outcome, I believe your brother and I would do well together. However, I know of no precedence that would name us as husband and wife."

"What if my brother acted upon his honor and made you a proposal?" Miss Darcy pressed.

Elizabeth eyed the girl sadly. All Miss Darcy knew of marriage and of the world was what drivel society had taught her. "Mr. Darcy has suggested that he would hold no objection to our joining, but I did not entertain his proposal. You may find it odd, Miss Darcy, especially in light of what you know of me, but I would wish to marry for affection."

"You would refuse the wealth you see before you?" the girl asked in incredulity.

"Although on some level, from the beginning, I knew your brother must be a wealthy man, but I did not realize the extent of his prosperity until I viewed Pemberley upon our arrival today. And though you are not likely to believe me, I would still refuse him, for affection is not part of our relationship. Mayhap it is because my sisters and I cannot aspire to the wealth you have known every day of your life, but I warrant that each Bennet sister wishes to marry a man she respects and loves. Duty is not part of the equation."

"Do you think because I know the privileges Pemberley provides that I will settle for a marriage without love?" Miss Darcy accused.

Elizabeth shook off the idea. "I think you are a young lady searching for what to value in your life. I suspect all that has gone before appears foolish when you look back upon your actions, but you cannot claim that misstep, for if you do, others will think you a simpleton. Your family has told you that if you perform as they demand all will be well. Yet, even so, you are adrift. That is my opinion of you, Miss Darcy. A young girl on the cusp of womanhood, but still adrift." She curtsied to the girl. "Please deliver my regrets to your brother and Mr. Bingley. I fear I have developed a headache." With that, Elizabeth turned on her heels to depart.

However, a sob halted Elizabeth's steps. She turned slowly to the girl, whose countenance had screwed up in desperation. "I do not wish to be adrift," she said as the tears flowed freely down her cheeks.

"Most assuredly you do not," Elizabeth announced as she crossed to the girl to catch Miss Darcy up in a comforting embrace. "No one wishes to find his way alone. We all need to surround ourselves with people who understand and support us."

"I have no right to criticize you," the girl said on a hiccupped sob.

"You have every right to wish the best for your brother," Elizabeth corrected. "And he for you. You were frightened that I meant to replace you in Mr. Darcy's heart. I understand. Truly I do."

Miss Darcy raised her head in distress. "William cannot observe me in tears!"

Elizabeth agreed, for she knew Mr. Darcy would demand to know what had transpired between her and his sister. "Come." She tugged Miss Darcy along behind her.

"Where to?" The girl balked at Elizabeth's haste.

"Just come," Elizabeth insisted. When they reached the hall, she laced her arm through Miss Darcy's. "Mr. Nathan, would you please inform the gentlemen that Miss Darcy and I decided to walk the gallery. I have a great desire to view the family portraits, and Miss Darcy has promised me a tour."

"As you wish, miss."

Elizabeth had spent an hour in the gallery before answering the call of the evening's supper bell. She had been drawn to one particular portrait when she had stumbled upon the gallery after taking a wrong turn while attempting to find her way to the lovely garden she could view from the window in her suite. Having encountered the estate's housekeeper in the long hall, she had permitted the woman to regale her with tales of Mr. Darcy's ancestors, while she had studied the gentleman's image, captured upon canvas. He was certainly a devastatingly handsome man.

When they reached the gallery, she directed Miss Darcy to a bench along the wall. "Do we discuss what has occurred or do we go about our lives in silence?"

Miss Darcy looked about, as if she expected someone to be listening in upon their conversation. "Darcy would be displeased with my actions. I should keep my own counsel."

Elizabeth nodded her understanding. "My mother always says it is easier to pronounce our grievances to strangers, for they hold no stake in the situation, and they speak with clear reasoning. Yet, I can commiserate with your hesitation. How can you think to share yourself with a woman you do not respect?"

"But you are not truly a stranger," Miss Darcy countered.

Elizabeth smiled knowingly. "No. I do not suppose we remain unknown to each other, but you know something of my secrets. It seems only fair that I be made known to yours. Only then might we become friends."

"Why must we become friends?" the girl argued.

"It is not necessary." She frowned at the girl's stubbornness, but she told herself not to be offended. She knew Mr. Darcy to be very closed-mouthed, and she supposed his sister had learned to be the same. It certainly was not a characteristic with which she could find fault in the pair. Elizabeth stood to brush the wrinkles from her gown. "Please relay my apologies to your brother and Mr. Bingley. The headache I mentioned earlier has returned with a vengeance."

With a brief curtsy, she turned to leave, but Miss Darcy caught Elizabeth's hand to stay her departure. "Please. Do not go. Darcy will worry for your health, and my actions have brought him enough heartache."

Elizabeth reluctantly sat beside the girl a second time. After several minutes of silence, she caught Miss Darcy's hand in hers before turning the girl's chin where she might look upon Miss Darcy's features. "With my youngest sisters," she began, "when I wish to learn something of one of their secrets, we *play* a game of sorts where I ask questions, and they respond with a simple affirmative or negative. Should we attempt to play?" Miss Darcy nodded her agreement.

Elizabeth had a good idea of the girl's *secret*, so she asked, "With Lydia or Kitty, the secret usually involves a gentleman. Am I correct?"

The girl's eyes widened in horror. "How did you know? Is it so obvious? Will William realize my mind is elsewhere?"

Elizabeth assured her, "Not at all, but you said you possessed no right to criticize me. Naturally, I assumed you knew an indiscretion of your own."

Miss Darcy studied Elizabeth's countenance before she presented Elizabeth a slight nod of understanding. As tears pooled in her eyes, the girl said, "His name is George Wickham, and he made me promises that he had no intention of keeping."

Chapter 14

DARCY HAD NO doubt that Elizabeth knew of his presence in the shadows. From his position beside a full suit of armor, reportedly belonging to a long-lost ancestor, he watched the woman who stirred his desires rock Georgiana in a sisterly embrace. Although he had not heard their entire conversation, Darcy had heard Georgiana sob, "All he wanted was my dowry. He never loved me, for I am not the type of woman any man could love."

He wished to go to Georgiana and offer his own comfort, but Elizabeth nudged his sister to her feet. "The man is a fool if he could not recognize your tender heart, and no woman should suffer a fool." She wrapped her arm about Georgiana's waist to guide his sister's steps. "Come. You will stay in my room tonight."

"I could not," Georgiana protested, but she permitted Elizabeth to lead her toward the sleeping quarters. Darcy knew in his heart that despite her words to the contrary, his sister's heart wished for the comfort only another woman could provide. He had been correct in the aspect that Georgiana required a woman's guidance, but he had erred in thinking Anne De Bourgh could have filled the role. Looking upon the pair, he knew without a doubt that only Elizabeth Bennet had the good sense to place Georgiana's needs first.

"Nonsense," she told his sister. "At Longbourn, there is always a sister to tend a bruised heart. It is the quickest means to a new resolve. As you possess no sister, permit me the role on this night. I promise you will not regret it. We will brush each other's hair and send Hannah to the kitchen for tea and a small tray of Cook's apple tarts. We will eat too much, laugh at our foibles, and be stronger because we did so together."

Darcy felt the tug of affection blossom more fully as he watched the pair walk away. In his dealings with her in Scotland, he had secretly thought that Elizabeth might become a steadying influence on Georgiana, but now he had proof of it. Elizabeth had spoken of *fools*, and the word described him perfectly. To have even considered that any other woman, especially his Cousin Anne, who possessed no sisters of her own, could welcome a girl so uncertain of her worth had been *foolish* beyond belief. Just as he had learned to trust Elizabeth Bennet, it seemed Georgiana was also to learn several valuable lessons at the woman's hand.

She fidgeted in anticipation. They waited before the house for the coach carrying her sister to appear. The previous two days had been the most fulfilling ones he had experienced since the passing of his beloved mother. Life had returned to Pemberley in the form of a spritely maid from Hertfordshire. It could be his imagination, but he thought his staff stepped lighter—that they eyed Miss Elizabeth as a possible mistress of the house. He knew for certain they had not done so with Caroline Bingley, and they had found the woman wanting in every way. The thought reminded him of how he had "permitted" Caroline to think of herself in that role and how he must now dissuade her without offending Bingley.

He had witnessed how his staff rushed to do Elizabeth's bidding. Only yesterday, he and she had walked the nature trail together, but they had been caught in the rain. Upon their return to the house, Elizabeth had insisted that they enter through the kitchen, rather than the main foyer. "The maids scrubbed the floor in preparation for Jane's arrival. I shan't create more work for them," she had protested when he balked at the idea. In the end, he sat upon a bench in the kitchen while Sheffield wrestled wet boots from Darcy's feet.

While he watched in contented amusement, Elizabeth had made her apologies and then scampered up the servants' stairs to her quarters. Behind him several of his staff whispered their approval of her actions. The smile upon his lips appeared again and again with the remembrance of the image of her slim ankles beneath her skirt tail as she scurried away from him.

As the coach rolled to a stop before the house, he nudged her. "Go greet your sister," he encouraged in quiet tones. "I shan't punish you by insisting that you remain one minute more from Miss Bennet's embrace. There is no need to stand upon propriety when it comes to family."

She gifted him with a happy smile before hastening across the graveled drive to reach the woman alighting from the carriage. Immediately, the pair were in each other's arms. Something like relief marked each woman's features. Suddenly, he was jealous of the familial connection so easily displayed. He adored Georgiana, but the twelve years between them often kept them from sharing true moments of affection, like the one he self-consciously observed between Elizabeth and Miss Bennet.

"You should close your mouth, Mr. Bingley," his sister said with an uncharacteristic tease. Darcy noted she blushed with the words, but her shoulders held a rigid defiance he had often noted in Elizabeth's bearing. "That is unless you wish to capture the flies circling the horses' rumps." A girlish giggle followed, and Darcy could not wipe the smile from his lips. He did not approve of his sister's familiarity, but he did approve of her newfound voice.

He turned at the unexpected boldness of his sister's words to discover Bingley standing mouth agape. Darcy's eyes followed the line of his friend's gaze. It rested purposely upon

Miss Bennet. To his discerning eye, Darcy would agree that the lady was a classic beauty: golden blonde curls in an upsweep, fair, creamy skin, and slender build. There was a time such a countenance would have caught his attention immediately, but he found he much preferred Elizabeth Bennet's features to all others. "I believe my sister has the right of it, Bingley," Darcy said with a chuckle. "If I did not know you to be a gentleman, I might liken your expression to a freshly caught trout."

Bingley noisily clamped his teeth together, but his friend's eyes never left Miss Bennet's countenance. "She is an angel, Darcy," Bingley murmured.

In preparation for the introductions, Darcy caught Georgiana's hand to place it upon his arm. "Then I pray the lady does not possess the devilish tongue of a shrew." Darcy was accustomed to Bingley regularly giving his heart away on a passing fancy, and he assumed this was a like circumstance.

"How could she be such?" Bingley argued.

Arm-in-arm, the Bennet sisters approached. They stopped before him to curtsy as Elizabeth prepared for the introductions. "Mr. Darcy, with your permission, I would make you and your household known to my elder sister, Miss Bennet."

Darcy bowed in respect. He did not want Elizabeth to think he would not welcome her family to Pemberley. "I have heard several tales from Miss Elizabeth regarding her sister's excellence. I am pleased finally to place a face to the name. Welcome to Pemberley, Miss Bennet."

The young woman appeared awestruck by his house, but she managed to say, "Elizabeth's description falls grossly short in relating your manor's splendor, Mr. Darcy. I am humbled by your warm welcome."

Elizabeth smiled brightly at Georgiana. "And this is my particular friend, Miss Darcy."

Georgiana exchanged curtsies with Miss Bennet before saying, "I thank you for sharing your sister with me. I have enjoyed Miss Elizabeth's company." And Darcy knew his sister's words were true. Since the evening in the gallery, Georgiana had sought out Elizabeth repeatedly for advice and company. It did his heart good to view the attachment.

"I have no doubt," Miss Bennet responded. "If Lizzy cannot entertain a soul, then the person does not possess a sense of the absurd."

Elizabeth continued her duties. "And this is Mr. Darcy's close associate, Mr. Bingley."

It was odd to watch Bingley and the lady. Miss Bennet's expression displayed the same raw intensity, as did his friend's, but the lady recovered her composure faster than did Bingley. "It is my honor, Miss Bennet," Bingley murmured as he bowed over the woman's hand.

Although the way the Darcys and Mr. Bingley had welcomed Jane gladdened Elizabeth's heart, she knew relief when she and her favorite sister were able to escape to their rooms. When Elizabeth closed the door behind them, she turned to find consolation written upon Jane's face. "I was so worried," Jane expelled as she gathered Elizabeth into another sisterly embrace. "When I received Aunt Gardiner's letter that you had suffered a head injury, all I could think was that you could have died, and it would be my fault—my punishment for being a disobedient daughter—the loss of my dearest sister."

"It grieves me that you suffered," Elizabeth said as she directed Jane to the chairs arranged before the open window. Mrs. Reynolds had graciously placed Jane in the room across from Elizabeth, the one that overlooked the garden maze. The housekeeper had the room aired out yesterday so everything smelled fresh and inviting. "I wish Aunt Gardiner had included more assurances of my likely survival."

"In truth, on hindsight, I doubt she had time to construct a properly worded letter what with Mama's aspersions regarding my behavior. I understood Aunt and Uncle Gardiner chose not to mention your involvement in the end of Mr. Collins's wedding hopes." Her sister wrung her hands in agitation.

Elizabeth explained, "That was part of the decision that Uncle and Mr. Darcy made. As no one in Hertfordshire knew of Mama's desperate plans to save Longbourn other than you, Mary, and I, the gentlemen assumed it would be best to contact Papa and permit him to control Mrs. Bennet's loose tongue. Our mother will be instructed to say that with Papa's illness, our parents thought it best to place their eldest daughters in situations where they might encounter eligible gentlemen outside the neighborhood. Mama reportedly took you to London to reconnect with Aunt Gardiner's relatives in Derbyshire. Meanwhile, Papa sent me to his cousin in Scotland."

"What if someone learns the truth?" Jane pleaded.

"No one will learn if we all play our parts," Elizabeth insisted. "We do speak the truth, just not all the details: Mama escorted you to London, where you were then taken by coach to Derbyshire. Did you meet a gentleman or two in Derby who took a liking to your beauty?"

Jane blushed heavily. "Yes, but..."

"No 'buts,' Jane. You must return to Longbourn and repeat what has been agreed upon. You will speak openly of the gentlemen you encountered in Derbyshire."

"But I have no hopes of Sir David or Mr. Walker extending a proposal," Jane protested.

Elizabeth loved Jane more than any of her sisters, but upon occasion she wished Jane possessed something of Lydia's bravado and was not so guarded in her interactions with others. If so, they might not have been in this predicament. Jane should have stood firm against their mother's manipulations. "You do not need to return to Longbourn as an engaged woman — only with the illusion of a well-sought after female. All Mama needs to know is something of each gentleman's countenance and an estimation of his annual income. Do not mention debts or encumbrances. Just provide Mrs. Bennet a distraction and a reason for her to forgive you for ruining her plans.

"Will she forgive me, Lizzy?"

Elizabeth knew this was the real reason Jane worried over

their return journey to Hertfordshire. "Mama will forgive her most beautiful and most obedient daughter's faults. Have you not heard her effusions over the years? I guarantee that Mary, Kitty, and I have Mrs. Bennet's words etched on our hearts. You and Lydia are the prizes of the Bennet family," Elizabeth argued. "And we both know that she will make certain that any fault of yours was at my hands. Our mother will add your disobedience to a long list of complaints that she has against me."

Jane looked on in complete shamefacedness. "It was not my wish to sound so mean-spirited, Lizzy."

"And I did not mean to speak in chastising tones." She shrugged in resignation. "Our mother is what she is. I recognize her desperation, but I cannot approve of her methods to find us eligible matches." A heavy sigh escaped Elizabeth's lips. "You could also mention taking the acquaintance of Mr. Bingley and Mr. Darcy. You did meet them while in Derbyshire. Just do not relate our time at Pemberley."

Jane smiled weakly. "Obviously Mr. Darcy's income should impress Mrs. Bennet, but I know little of the gentlemen. It is not as if I can simply ask of their incomes, and we shall not be at Pemberley long enough to learn of their situations."

Elizabeth squeezed the back of her sister's hand. She had not missed Jane's initial reaction to Mr. Bingley. Privately, she was pleased that Jane had not turned her beauty and sweet personality upon Mr. Darcy, for Elizabeth would surely miss the gentleman's most excellent conversation and the way he did simple things to please her. The gesture of fresh flowers in her room each day had wormed its way into her heart to the point that she had begun to press the flowers between the pages of one of the books he had purchased for her. She planned to make a sachet when she returned to her Longbourn. It would be a forever remembrance of her days with Mr. Darcy.

"Fortunately for you, I possess a particular friend at Pemberley, who has kindly spoken of each gentleman's individual wealth," she teased.

Jane gasped, "Surely Miss Darcy does not speak so

intimately of either her brother or Mr. Bingley!"

Elizabeth chuckled. "Most assuredly, she would not act from propriety, but the servants can always be prevailed upon to share a *well-known* secret. Mr. Bingley's income is estimated to be somewhere around five thousand per year, but like Uncle Gardiner, Mr. Bingley is in trade."

"That would not bother me," Jane said in undisguised honesty. "And what of Mr. Darcy?"

Elizabeth whispered conspiratorially, "A mere ten thousand." She laughed when Jane's eyes grew twice their normal size.

"Ten...ten thousand," she stammered. "Oh, Lizzy, marrying such a man would be something, would it not?"

Elizabeth could not conceal her frown of disapproval. "Do you fancy him, Jane?"

Her sister shook her head in denial. "What little I observed of the man, I found him amiable, and the fact that he considers Mr. Bingley a close associate speaks well of his nature. We have both witnessed those of society who turned their backs on Uncle Gardiner despite the wealth he has accumulated. In truth, though, I would forever be intimidated by such a man. He rules his world. It would take a woman with a strong and confident disposition not to be swallowed up by his familial pride and his position. I could never be that person."

Elizabeth did not think she could be the woman her sister described, but a secret part of her wished it were so. "Even if we must return to Longbourn as Mama's most recalcitrant daughters, we shall not be empty-handed. I promised to remain with Mr. Darcy while he conducted business in Scotland if he would advance my sisters' marriage prospects. Each of you will receive an additional five hundred pounds as part of your dowries."

For the second time in as many hours, Jane's mouth stood agape. "You did what?" Her voice rose in incredulity. "That is two thousand pounds! My opinion of Mr. Darcy has changed dramatically! How dare he? You are a gentleman's daughter! Your reputation will be ruined if word of what has occurred between you two becomes common knowledge."

Elizabeth slipped from her chair to kneel before her sister. Claiming Jane's hands, she said, "It was not Mr. Darcy's fault that I ended up at the wrong church. If I had not interfered with his nuptials, the gentleman would now be married to his cousin, Miss De Bourgh. He has attempted to make the best of an ill-timed situation. He has protected my health by hiring an excellent physician to oversee my recovery and my safety by removing me from the reach of his aunt, Lady Catherine De Bourgh, who dispatched a magistrate to arrest me for committing fraud."

"Oh, my!" Jane's fingers trembled.

"Mr. Darcy has purchased clothes and books for me. Fed and housed me for more than a fortnight. Accepted the presence of my most beloved sister in his household. Demanded that his sister understand a situation well beyond her years. More importantly, he presented me a purse filled with coins that I could have used to return to Hertfordshire on my own and the promise of a maid to accompany me on my journey." She placed Jane's hands in her sister's lap before standing. "It was my choice to remain with the gentleman. Despite Mr. Darcy's best efforts, I do not expect that my indiscretion will long be kept secret, for the gentleman's aunt is Lady Catherine De Bourgh, Mr. Collins's patroness. Her ladyship will not long be thwarted by her nephew's efforts to keep my identity a secret, especially as Mr. Darcy has refused any future efforts upon his aunt's part to reschedule the wedding to her daughter. In truth, I doubt it will escape Lady Catherine's notice that two country upstarts dared to rebuke both her cleric and her efforts for an endogamous marriage. I have no future, but as an eccentric aunt to my sisters' children. As such, I bargained for a better situation for you, Mary, Kitty, and Lydia."

Chapter 15

DARCY HAD NO doubt that Miss Bennet had questioned Elizabeth regarding his and the lady's situation. She did not present either of them a look of disdain, more one of disbelief, not of the facts but of the unusual circumstances that had brought them together. In many ways, what had occurred was Miss Bennet's fault. If the lady had simply agreed to marry Mr. Collins, none of this would have happened. Darcy was certain that particular fact had not slipped Jane Bennet's notice. Even so, Darcy did not object to the lady's reticence in marrying Collins, for if she had accepted the man, he would never have met Elizabeth Bennet, and that would have been the greatest fault of his life.

Yet, Miss Bennet should not worry for her sister's future, for Darcy had come to the decision that only Elizabeth would serve as his wife. Now, all he had to do was to convince the lady. Before she departed Pemberley, he would share their Scottish marriage certificate and learn something of her preferences. Tonight, he held a different sort of request.

"I thought that after supper, that instead of cards, Bingley and I might stand up with you ladies for a bit of impromptu dancing."

"You wish to dance, William?" Georgiana asked in astonishment.

He chuckled lightly. "I know you would expect me to choose intelligent conversation over dance, but who says I cannot have both. Our drawing room is not an overcrowded ballroom full of self-possessed popinjays. I will do quite well with the activity."

Bingley laughed easily. "I am well acquainted with a few London popinjays."

"As am I," Darcy assured their party. "But tonight, Bingley, we will enjoy the company of delightfully intelligent females, an anomaly in much of society."

"Most gentlemen prefer their female companions lacking in opinions," Elizabeth challenged as he knew she would.

"If the conversations I often overhear at my club are indicative of the opinions of much of society, I would pronounce your assertion true. However, I would like to think I am not counted among the uncultivated savages spouting such nonsense."

Elizabeth's eyebrow arched higher. "You would not censure your wife, Mr. Darcy?"

"Not unless she placed herself or our children in danger," he countered. "I mayhap will not always agree with her, but I would seek her opinions."

He waited for her response, but was disappointed when Bingley said, "Then it is agreed. We will dance this evening." His friend eyed Miss Bennet with a look of longing. "I can think of nothing more pleasurable."

"I shall play," Georgiana offered in concession.

"Absolutely not," Darcy and Elizabeth said in unison.

"You will dance with both me and Bingley. If you are to make your Come Out soon, it is imperative that you become more comfortable in social situations. You must learn to comport yourself upon the dance floor and to converse while doing so. Dancing with Bingley and me will provide you the opportunity to practice your skills."

Elizabeth nodded her agreement. "Most assuredly, Miss Darcy. I shall play while you stand up with your brother and Mr. Bingley."

"I had hoped that you and Georgiana might take turns," Darcy explained. "I would not wish for my guest to miss out on the dancing. I imagine you enjoy the exercise," he said with a twinkle in his eyes, while Elizabeth responded with a like look. It was as if she could read his mind.

"Jane plays tolerably well," Elizabeth explained. "We can share the duties with Miss Darcy."

"Excellent," Darcy declared. "Bingley, what say you to abandoning our customary port and cigars this evening?"

His friend nodded about the table. "I am agreeable."

As one, they stood and escorted the ladies to the drawing room. Bingley naturally claimed Miss Bennet's hand on his arm, which suited Darcy very well. He placed Georgiana on one arm before extending the other to Elizabeth. What was it that made him so aware of the lady's presence? The feel of Elizabeth's fingers upon his arm? Was it her indomitable spirit? Her willingness to sacrifice all to protect her sister? The scent of a passionate woman?

"I shall play first," Elizabeth announced upon their entrance into the room. She left his side to make her way to the instrument, and it was all Darcy could do not to reach for her. "Miss Darcy and my sister play so well," she explained as she sorted the sheet music, "I would be ashamed to follow either your sister or Jane. My fingers are not so faithful as theirs."

While she separated the music, he and Bingley made quick work of moving the furniture and rolling up the smaller carpet. With a space cleared, Darcy claimed Georgiana's hand. "Precedence means you will not always be at the head of the line," he explained as he set her before him. "It will depend upon your dance partner's place in society. But as this is our house, we will fill the role as the lead couple."

"I know, William," she said shyly. "Mrs. Annesley already has me studying Debrett's."

He smiled lovingly upon her, for he recognized how hard

it was for her to speak against whatever he said. "I am the one performing poorly. I simply wish for you to understand that you may ask me any question regarding protocol, who is related to whom, whom to avoid, and whom to encourage. I will endeavor to answer all questions honestly."

"And without judgment?" she ventured with a shy smile.

Darcy laughed easily. Georgiana had made progress under her short time with Elizabeth Bennet. The lady was good for both him and his sister. "I cannot promise not to know concern for you," he said as they passed each other in a tight turn, "but I do promise always to place your feelings first."

After four tunes, Elizabeth finally relinquished the instrument to her sister, whose performance was perfection, but in his opinion, it lacked the liveliness of Elizabeth's playing. While he partnered Elizabeth for a minuet, he asked, "I know you plan to leave us the day after tomorrow, and so I pray you will permit me another indulgence. Is it too much to ask that you accompany me tomorrow? I wish to claim your opinion of the changes my steward has executed in the shearing pens."

He noted how Elizabeth discreetly considered him. "Do you think we should remind the others that we traveled together beyond your care of your sister's friend before I arrived at Pemberley?" she asked softly.

"I understand your concern," he said with a formal bow required by the dance. "Among those gathered here, only Bingley does not know of our true connection, and I imagine he will be too fascinated with Miss Bennet to note our conversations."

"He does appear to like her very much." Elizabeth sighed heavily.

"Then you will accompany me?" Darcy prompted.

"I would be honored," she assured him. "If Jane asks, I shall tell her I hope to encourage our father to institute a like operation at Longbourn, which is the truth."

They had broken for tea after Miss Bennet's efforts, and although they all agreed they had known enough dancing for one evening, Georgiana insisted upon playing for everyone. The fact that his sister was willing to perform before others was reason enough for Darcy to remain on the makeshift dance floor, but the prospects of dancing again with Elizabeth was equally as great an incentive.

"What shall I play?" Georgiana asked as she perched upon the bench before the instrument.

"A waltz?" Bingley called.

"A Scottish reel," Darcy requested at the same time.

Georgiana looked up in surprise at his response, for a Scottish reel would never be his first choice of dances, but she nodded her agreement. "A reel for Darcy and then a waltz for Mr. Bingley." She placed her fingers upon the keys.

Darcy turned to bow to Elizabeth. "May I claim this dance, Miss Elizabeth?" he teased.

She presented him a long, slow look. "A Scottish reel, sir?" Her eyebrow arched in challenge. "You never cease to amaze me, and just when I thought to know something of your nature."

"In remembrance of our time together in the fair country," he announced with a self-satisfied smile.

"You treasure those days, sir?" she asked as they executed a series of quick steps before he turned her in a backward circle, his forearm bracing her waist.

"Most assuredly," he breathed into the hair above her ear.

Then he watched her—their gazes locked in intimate memories, and Darcy knew the exact second their shared experiences arrived. She twirled around him, just as she did in his favorite dream of her. While he had nourished the dream each night since they had departed Scotland, permitting it to wind its way to a blissful end, he held no doubt that Elizabeth had willed it from her memory. Yet, it had returned. She stumbled, and he caught her arm to prevent her fall.

"I apologize, Mr. Darcy," she murmured as she resumed the energetic steps.

"No harm, Miss Elizabeth."

They continued the prescribed dance, but he doubted Elizabeth could recall it. Her mind was elsewhere, and so, when he caught Georgiana's attentions, he motioned for her to bring the tune to a close. In his dream, the dance ended with a kiss. Needless to say, he could not kiss Elizabeth before their families and Bingley, but he did the next best thing. He turned her to stand before him. Behind them, Miss Bennet fanned her face following the exertion, but he and Elizabeth stood connected by an incident of which neither of them had spoken previously.

"One more dance," Georgiana announced before changing out the sheet music.

Elizabeth's gaze darted to his face. "Perhaps we should change partners," she suggested nervously.

Darcy had expected her reaction. For him, it was satisfying to know his *dream* was rooted in reality. "And deny Bingley the opportunity to waltz with Miss Bennet? I fear my friend would call me out if I suggest he abandon your sister."

"Then I shall play, and Georgiana can take my place," she insisted.

"Georgiana is not yet out in society. She does not know the steps." He extended his hand to her. "Waltz with me, Elizabeth."

Her gaze flittered to his face before settling on his outstretched hand. It was obvious that she wished to escape to her quarters, rather than to place her fingers upon his open palm, but she bravely set her fears aside.

As Georgiana played the first strain of introductory notes, Darcy directed Elizabeth into his embrace. They were closer than propriety suggested, but no one made note of the sizzle of awareness that gripped them in its hold. Silence cropped up to claim the space between them. Nervously, she wet her lips to say, "Is there to be no conversation, Mr. Darcy?"

"Tell me of what you desire to speak," he instructed, as he carefully maneuvered her around the tea cart. "And I will claim my share of the subject."

She giggled self-consciously. "I can think of no subject we have not previously broached, sir."

"Then permit us to enjoy the music and the beauty of the dance," he suggested. "I, for one, can think of nothing more perfect: a well-played piece, the joyful freedom of the movement, and the most compelling woman of my acquaintance in my arms."

Why had Mr. Darcy not said something previously? she wondered for the umpteenth time in the last hour. *And why did I possess no knowledge of the kiss we shared until this evening?* Yet, even as the accusations passed through her mind, Elizabeth knew the answer: Admitting that she had permitted Mr. Darcy to kiss her would be admitting that her feelings regarding the gentleman were deeper than they should be.

She thought back upon her acquaintance with the man. Here, at Pemberley, there was nothing in his manner that suggested anything but his amiability, but that was not so in their other social encounters. He had held himself aloof with the Allards, but perhaps that had been his sense of the forbidding personalities of Mr. and Mrs. Allard. She certainly had not been herself under the couple's roof.

Slowly, Elizabeth closed her eyes to bring forth the man's image to determine his character, but a hundred or more images swirled through her memory before she settled upon the one from the Scottish inn. His jaw held the shadow of his beard. Eyes of heated silver. Dark lashes. Garbed in the clothes of a country gentleman while providing any who cared to look upon him the assurance of his noble ancestral lines. He was quite the most handsome man of her acquaintance. Not *polished* handsome, as was Mr. Bingley, but ruggedly so.

She had always thought herself an astute observer of human nature, but Mr. Darcy perplexed her prodigiously. He had flirted with her this evening. Of that, she was certain. "But for what purpose?" she whispered into the darkness.

Frustrated, she punched the pillow and attempted to find a comfortable place to rest her head. "Dratted man!" she grumbled.

She had attempted to despise him, especially after waking

upon his yacht. "You need not hide your disdain for me," he had accused when they had argued over their arrangement.

"I do not know you well enough to express an opinion, sir. If I agree, you will consider me most impolite. If I disagree, you will label me a liar." That was the beginning of their relationship moving from confrontation to an alliance of sort.

Suddenly her mind returned to the argument they had had at the Scottish inn. "How did things become so complicated between us?" Mr. Darcy had offered to make her his wife, and although she was not set against marriage, in general, her heart still wished to know affection, and so she had refused him.

"Then we drank the ouzo," she whispered. Her mind strained to recall how many sips of the drink she had consumed. All she could recall was a dozen or more toasts to the married couple. She had barely sipped the drink after her first tasting of it, and she had not asked for a second cup. "But my cup was always filled," she moaned in remembrance. "Either the innkeeper or one of the wedding party was always at our table with the decanter. No wonder my head felt as if someone used a hammer to strike it soundly the next morning," she reasoned aloud.

At length, the images of that evening settled heavier in her mind. Somehow, she was dancing with Mr. Darcy. A Scottish reel. Just like this evening. They smiled at each other, and he had stopped suddenly to catch her waist in his large hands. She had nervously wet her lips, and she found herself swaying closer to him. She caught at his forearms for her balance. He was so near that she could see the faint lines that would one day mark his eyes. She had attempted to swallow, but a moan had marked her lips instead.

His smile remained soft while still formidable, as he edged her closer still. They were on the edge of a makeshift dance floor and surrounded by strangers. His eyes settled upon her lips. "If you do not want this, Elizabeth, leave now," he had instructed.

She should have responded as he had suggested, but she had wanted to know what would come next. She was determined never to know a husband, but she had desired her moment with

Mr. Darcy, so she had remained standing before him, as desire skittered up her spine.

As it was then, a warmth gathered low in her belly, but she had continued to study Mr. Darcy's dear countenance, unable to step away from him. His hands edged her closer to him, before he lowered his head to claim her lips. It was her first kiss — likely the only kiss she would ever experience — and it was all for which she had ever desired. Her fingers burrowed into his coat, and she held on for what felt to be an eternity, but it was was, in reality, mere seconds.

As the image faded, Elizabeth found herself frowning internally, and tears pooled in her eyes. No man had ever dared to touch her — to kiss her. To make her wish for something she could not have. She had always kept everyone at arm's length; yet, with one kiss, Mr. Darcy had upset the best of her plans.

Chapter 16

"THIS IS BRILLIANT," Elizabeth praised Mr. Burton, Mr. Darcy's land steward. The man presented her an explanation of what his employer intended as part of the extension of the estate's shearing facility. Jane was less enthused by the prospects Mr. Burton shared, but her sister stood by Elizabeth's side throughout the man's demonstration. "You have taken a simple idea and created what appears to be an excellent solution to the woes of Mr. Darcy's cottagers."

Mr. Burton beamed with pride. "It was the master's doing, miss." He said sheepishly, "Mr. Darcy credits you and his valet with suggesting that he look beyond the obvious."

Elizabeth blushed thoroughly as she shot a glance to where Mr. Darcy and Mr. Bingley were deep in conversation. After her numerous dreams last evening regarding what she now knew was a very real kiss shared with the gentleman, she had dreaded this excursion, but as was customary with the man, Mr. Darcy had anticipated her confusion. He performed the role of perfect gentleman, with the barest of interactions between them beyond what was necessary. A fact that was as frustrating as the knowledge that she had actively participated in their kiss—at least she had if her dreams were an indication of the ardor she had displayed. "I am pleased that a man of Mr. Darcy's experience thought such a scheme worthy of his efforts."

Before the steward could respond, Mr. Bingley returned to Jane's side. "Did you assist Mr. Darcy?" her sister inquired as she slipped her hand about Bingley's proffered arm.

"It is all quite fascinating," Bingley admitted. "Darcy has been most generous in instructing me on some of the intricacies of running an estate. My sisters believe it is time I claim my place in society—our family's place, I should say."

"That is admirable of you," Jane observed.

"Perhaps we should return to the house," Mr. Darcy suggested. "As this is your last day in Derbyshire, I have asked Cook to prepare a special meal for this evening, and I am certain Miss Darcy will wish the opportunity to bid you both a proper farewell."

Within a half hour, the gentlemen escorted them into Pemberley, where Jane immediately accepted Mr. Bingley's offer to walk in the garden.

Elizabeth had hoped her sister might provide her some "protection" against Mr. Darcy's commanding presence, for she was not prepared to speak of the familiarity they had shared, nor address the necessity for their parting, but such was not to be. With her sister and Bingley's departure, Mr. Darcy said, "Would you join me in my study, Miss Elizabeth? I have a matter of import to share with you."

Despite her best efforts, she stiffened, every pore on alert. "Certainly," she murmured.

Mr. Darcy gestured for her to precede him, and after swallowing her dread, Elizabeth set her steps in motion. In less than a minute, she stood within his private sanctum. A quick look about the room said the study suited Mr. Darcy perfectly. Dark wood framed the pale green walls and a bay of windows. Sunlight leading to his desk marched a trail across the Persian carpet. A slight scent of cheroots hung in the air. The furnishings spoke of the gentleman's style and his excellent taste.

"Should I send for tea?" His voice came from behind her, and Elizabeth jumped as the door clicked closed.

She turned quickly. "That is not necessary, sir." She said a silent prayer for guidance. "I am certain Miss Darcy will be down for tea soon, and I should freshen my clothing before I join her. Mayhap, whatever brought us here might be addressed."

"Would you care to sit?" he asked dutifully.

Elizabeth attempted to keep the irritation from her tone, but it was difficult, for the memory of their kiss had placed an uncomfortable wedge of awkwardness between them. She would admit, if only to herself, that she yearned for the natural companionship she had experienced with the man up to this point. "Do you think it necessary?"

He crossed to stand behind the desk. "I believe it would be best."

With a snit of disapproval, she seated herself before his desk. "You have my attention, Mr. Darcy."

"So I noticed," he said as he sat. "In truth, Miss Elizabeth, this was not how I thought this conversation might go."

Elizabeth despised sounding shrewish, but she could not keep her dismay from her words. "And what conversation might that be, Mr. Darcy? I believe our conversations have naturally wound their way to an end to our relationship. We have little left to say to each other."

He hesitated before responding. "What if I do not agree?"

"Agree to what? Our ability to converse freely? Or an end to our relationship?" she countered.

His mouth tilted upward in a dry smile. "I see you have finally recalled the kiss we shared while still in Scotland."

Elizabeth wished to deny his easy taunt, but she could not. "Was that not your purpose in asking Miss Darcy to play a Scottish air last evening?"

He shot her a grim smile. "I had hoped your recall would consider the event more memorable," he admitted. "I found knowledge of our indiscretion most enjoyable, for it proved what I knew to be true." He tilted his head to the side as if he meant to study her.

With a heavy sigh, she demanded in abject frustration, "Why?"

"Why did I find kissing a beautiful and intelligent woman enjoyable?" he mocked with a twinkle in his eyes.

"In my defense," she said with a flush of color claiming her cheeks, "I was unaccustomed to the power of such a sweet liqueur."

"I hold no doubt," he said with a smile of understanding.

Elizabeth spared him a look of helpless contrition. "Forgive me. I am acting foolish. It was only a kiss between friends. As with much of our time together, no one but the two of us needs to know of our indiscretion."

"One would think so," he said as he opened the drawer to his desk before pulling out a rolled sheath that he placed before her. "Yet, we have another matter to discuss."

"What is...?" she began before she broke off, at a loss for how to describe the paper she unrolled. "Oh no! No! No. No!" she exclaimed as her eyes scanned the paper. "What perfidy do you practice, Mr. Darcy?"

"Me? I assure you, Miss Elizabeth, this is not of my doing. My first knowledge of this paper was when it was slipped under my inn door on the morning of our departure from Scotland."

"Is that not convenient?" she snapped as she shoved the document to the side and stood. "I refuse to entertain the idea of our joining on the same evening I was plied with a strong drink. Do you think to convince me that we married against my wishes?"

Mr. Darcy spared her a sharp glance. "You place the full blame of this matter on my shoulders?"

"Was it not you who questioned my reaction to the ouzo?" she charged. "Did you see me in my cups so that you might have your way in this matter? I told you over supper that I would not entertain an engagement between us."

He stood to circle the desk to stand before her. "It is not necessary for a man of my station to trap a woman into marriage," he chided. "I could have my pick of Society's beauties. It would be rare to discover a woman not willing to accept my hand!"

"Then I am the oddity, Mr. Darcy, for I have no desire to marry you!" She struggled against the fury scurrying through her veins.

Sarcasm laced the gentleman's response. "Are you the odd bird out, Miss Elizabeth? Some parts of my memory of that particular evening remain unclear, but I recall our kiss in vivid detail, and I assure you, madam, that no one forced you into my arms. You came willingly."

Elizabeth had spent her entire life claiming to be a woman of decision and never permitting any one to hold complete control over her. It was her "role" in the Bennet household, and she would permit no one to upset her well-ordered life. "Mayhap I wished to know something of a life of leisure," she challenged. "I do not know how you accomplished this...this..." She waved her hand in dismissal. "But your ploy will not work. I will return to Longbourn, and you will remain in Derbyshire. You will burn this attempt at bringing me under your protection. Someday, perhaps, we will meet again, and we will laugh at this foolish escapade, but not today. I find nothing humorous in this matter."

Mr. Darcy's jaw tightened. He caught her shoulders to hold her in place, so she could not escape him. "Listen to me, Elizabeth Bennet. I *did not* make arrangements for this marriage certificate, for if I had, I would have claimed my husbandly privileges before now. Moreover, you should know that I have sent my solicitor, Mr. Harvey, to Scotland to learn whether our marriage is legal or not. For now, you may return to Hertfordshire, but if we are joined, I will be coming for you. If you are my wife, I will insist that you take up your position as Mrs. Darcy."

"Did you and Mr. Darcy argue?" Jane asked as Mr. Darcy's smaller coach rolled away from Pemberley.

Elizabeth schooled her features to blandness. "Certainly not," she assured her sister. "What makes you think so?"

"You barely spoke to each other last evening," her sister declared. "I thought perhaps you exchanged words of discord, especially after he made no appearance to bid you farewell this morning."

Despite her best efforts to conceal her emotions, Elizabeth frowned. She despised parting from the gentleman without a moment to speak her gratitude for all he had done for her. She owed him that much. "There was a fire in one of the tenant's cottages. Mr. Darcy was called to the scene early, for his men thought it might spread to a large barn where grain was stored. I do not imagine that the gentleman meant purposely to snub us." She did not explain how she had come by the information of the fire nor how the gentleman in question had slipped a hastily-written note under her door before he departed Pemberley. She had already read it at least a dozen times.

My dearest, loveliest Elizabeth,

Forgive me for taking liberties with my salutation, but it is true that in my heart, you will always be my Elizabeth. It grieves me that I wasted our last evening together worrying over something as insignificant as a piece of paper. In the scheme of life's troubles, what truly matters is the delight I experience when you walk in a room and the brief happiness I have known in your presence. Pressing matters — a fire in one of the cottages that could spread to a grain storage facility — will prevent me from claiming your hand in parting, but know that you will forever remain in my thoughts.

FD

"Not us," Jane corrected. "It is you that Mr. Darcy watches carefully."

Elizabeth snatched a quick breath to dispel the flicker of hope budding in her chest. "The gentleman worries that his aunt's ire has not abated and that the grand lady will send the magistrate after me. That is the duty you have observed upon Mr. Darcy's countenance. Nothing more."

He might have made it back to Pemberley in time to bid the ladies farewell, but Darcy had chosen to watch their coach depart Pemberley's drive from a nearby hill rather than from the steps of his manor house. If the lady held any knowledge of how attached he was to her, surely she would not have abandoned him without so much as a backward glance at the home he loved with every breath of his life. He studied Elizabeth Bennet's profile as the coach turned toward the main road.

"God willing," he murmured as her familiar image disappeared behind the tree line. With a sigh, he added, "I should follow her, but until I possess irrefutable proof of our joining, no means to change the lady's mind exists." He turned his horse toward Pemberley. Setting his heels to the gelding's side, he chuckled in irony. "Who do I expect to fool? Even if the law says she is my wife, Elizabeth will balk at the idea of a forced marriage. What I need to do is to court her properly, but I am not certain that is possible with our history."

Those thoughts carried him to his sister's favorite drawing room where he encountered a puppy-faced Bingley thumbing through a book. "Did you see the ladies off safely?" Darcy asked as he shed the long coat he wore and handed it off to Mr. Nathan to be aired properly to remove the smell of smoke from the fabric.

"I did," Bingley admitted half-heartedly. "And I am already feeling bereft of the Miss Bennets' company."

Darcy smiled knowingly. "Meet me in my study in a quarter hour. I must remove these soiled clothing before I can be good company. I will admit that I could use a strong drink, and I imagine you could use one also."

"Indeed, I could."

"Then I will meet you as quickly as Sheffield can help me from these things."

Within twenty minutes, Darcy appeared in his study where Bingley stood looking longingly upon the gardens beyond the patio door. "Permit me to pour you a brandy," Darcy announced, although Bingley appeared reluctant to give up his post. "I appreciate the kindness you showed both ladies. Your attentions were generous."

"It was not kindness," Bingley protested as he crossed to Darcy to claim the drink. "I thoroughly enjoyed the company of both Miss Bennets, but I was exceptionally fond of the elder Miss Bennet's company. She possesses the sweetest of natures."

Darcy would not have been half as amused if Bingley had professed an interest in Mr. Bennet's second daughter. "Are you certain, Bingley? It is not as if I doubt your sincerity, but I have witnessed your regard easily won in the past."

"I swear, Darcy. This is different."

Darcy cautioned, "You have known Miss Bennet but a matter of days."

"How long is necessary for the heart to engage?" Bingley questioned. "Who says a man and a woman must know each other for a year or even a lifetime before they can experience deep affection in marriage? Is that not what marriage means? A joining of two individuals who learn to become one? None of us can know how long it should take for that singularity to form. Should not each joining be different? As different as the two people who claim affection?"

Darcy thought of the smile upon Elizabeth's lips when she circled him in their pivotal dance at the inn. "No one can know for certain when love makes an attachment," he murmured. "But you must know your sisters will not approve of Miss Bennet. Mr. Bennet is a landed gentleman, but his wife is from trade. Mrs. Bennet is the sister of Mr. Edward Gardiner. Are you familiar with the man?"

"Of Mayo's Imports and Exports?"

"The very one," Darcy confirmed. "Miss Bingley would prefer that your wealth opened more doors into society than Miss Bennet can provide. You hold an obligation to your family."

Bingley set his brandy aside and began to pace the floor. "I am aware of Caroline's opinions; I have heard them often enough, but she has yet to hear mine," Bingley declared. "I wish above all else to marry for affection. I do not think I can live a life where I did not honor and respect my wife. What if Miss Bennet is my one opportunity for happiness?" He turned his full attention on Darcy. "How do I resolve this dilemma? How am I to know for certain that Miss Bennet would welcome my courting her?"

Darcy had asked himself the same questions in the last hour. How could he court Elizabeth and make her understand that he was her husband? "I would say you must discover a means to be in the lady's company again so you might determine if she returns your interest."

"As Miss Bennet has returned to her family in Hertfordshire, and I am late in arriving in Staffordshire, it is not likely we will meet again," Bingley said in serious tones.

"And it is your wish to encounter Miss Bennet again?" Darcy asked with a lift of his eyebrow.

"Have you not been listening to me, Darcy?" Bingley growled. "Yes, I would be happy to claim a means of being in Miss Bennet's company again. But it is impossible!"

Darcy sat heavily in his chair. He hesitated only a moment. "Bingley, by luck, Miss Elizabeth shared something of the neighborhood in which Longbourn sits. Ironically, an estate nearby is available to let, and you have expressed the need of an estate for society to view you as a gentleman. I have heard Miss Bingley express such an opinion on multiple occasions. Mayhap it is time that your man of business pays a call upon Netherfield Park in Hertfordshire to determine its worthiness."

Bingley's eyes widened. "Would that not be too obvious? Would my doing so not indicate a declaration for Miss Bennet?"

"As I see it, Bingley, you have two choices: follow proprieties' strictures and forget about your growing interest in Miss Bennet, or bend proprieties' rules and seek out the woman that sets your heart in flight," Darcy challenged.

"You will come with me, Darcy? To advise me on the soundness of the estate if my man of business thinks it is a wise choice," Bingley pleaded.

"Let the estate for a year. A few months will provide you time to learn if the house is sound in winter and whether Miss Bennet returns your interest. Who knows? Perhaps after a few months you will discover that neither the estate nor the lady is worth your time."

"I doubt that to be true," Bingley observed.

Darcy leaned forward to press his point. "You should not inform Miss Bingley of your intention to let the estate until after you have made a visit to Hertfordshire to view it for yourself. Only after you plan to stay should you ask Miss Bingley to serve as your hostess; until that time, concentrate on coming to an understanding with Miss Bennet."

"You have the right of it, Darcy. I would not wish my sister's lofty airs to influence Miss Bennet's opinion of our future happiness."

Chapter 17

IT SHOULD HAVE surprised Elizabeth that Mr. Darcy had planned her and Jane's retreat to Hertfordshire, but it did not. The man was built for protection, and she owed him another debt for his tender care of her and her sister. Mr. Farrin and Jasper, the gentleman's most experienced coachman and footman, had set them down each evening before the best of inns and had placed a basket of food inside the carriage each morning for her and her sister's enjoyment. Fresh horses had been sent ahead to assure their ride was not interrupted. Moreover, it had not been necessary for her to use even one coin from the purse the gentleman had given her in Scotland. Mr. Darcy had charged Jasper with presenting payments and gratuities and paying tolls during their journey.

"Thank you, Jasper," she whispered as the footman set her down before Longbourn. Because they did not travel a full day on the Sabbath, it had taken them four days to reach her home, but somehow when she turned to look upon it, the manor house had lost some of its appeal. It was not that she compared her father's country estate with the grandeur of Pemberley, but rather she thought herself changed by the experience of taking Mr. Darcy's acquaintance. Elizabeth had always felt a bit from step within her family, and now she wondered how she would ever fit in again.

"You are most welcome, miss," Jasper whispered in turn. "Mr. Farrin and I be wishing to see you again soon in Derbyshire. We'll leave your trunks here."

He started to step away to assist Jane down, but Elizabeth stayed him with a touch of his sleeve. "Convey my gratitude to Mr. Darcy."

That was all the time she had before her family burst forth from the house. Lydia and Kitty rushed by her to spy inside the carriage and to greet Jane, while Mary caught Elizabeth up in an uncustomary display of emotions, which Elizabeth thoroughly welcomed. She had been uneasy about leaving Mary to explain things to her father, and it did her good to know her sister held no animosity toward her. At length, she released Mary to greet Jane, while her eyes landed upon the sweet, familiar countenance of her father. His eyes held the sheen of tears, which filled her throat with emotion. He had lost some weight, but it was a prayer answered to view his standing before the house. She dropped all pretext and scurried into his open arms.

"Oh, Papa," she murmured as he caught her to him. "I was so worried."

He kissed her temple. "A little cough cannot take your old papa away from you." He set her from him to look upon her. "How are you, my Lizzy?"

"Healed now that I can stand before my father."

From beside her, Elizabeth heard the snit of disapproval, and she turned to greet her mother with a restrained hug. "I have missed you, Mama."

Her mother tutted her denial. "Such a fine carriage. I doubt such luxury brought forth thoughts of your parents and the anxiety your absence created."

"Mrs. Bennet," her father said in firm tones. "If you have a concern with either Jane's or Elizabeth's behavior, you will address them first to me, for I extended my permission to each to be from home."

Her mother glared at her father, but eventually Mrs. Bennet dropped her eyes in submission. Elizabeth had never observed the like.

Her father nodded his approval before addressing his daughters. "Lizzy. Jane. I would welcome hearing of your journey. Perhaps you will join me in my study. Let us say in an hour."

"Yes, Papa," she and Jane chorused.

Everyone turned to enter the house, but Elizabeth took a moment to wave a farewell to Mr. Darcy's servants and to speak privately with Mr. Hill, as he gathered her and Jane's trunks together.

"Mr. Hill," she said softly. "I wanted you and Mrs. Hill to know that I recently encountered Josie and Lachlan when I was in Scotland. I wish to report they were both in health a fortnight prior." She would not mention the punishment Josie had endured at Bradburn's hands nor the measles spreading through the work camp. There was no need to worry her father's long-time servant.

"Did you, Miss Elizabeth?" he asked in familiar tones. "The last I heard from me sister in marriage the two were at an estate thirty miles removed from the Flynns. It be good to know they've returned home."

Elizabeth blushed. She had been so intent on reporting on Lachlan and Josie that she had forgotten she supposedly spent time with the Flynns. "They have not returned. The brother of my particular friend does business with a Mr. Allard. As his was the carriage that delivered Jane and me to Longbourn, it was by accident that I encountered your niece and nephew." She would not explain further, for she knew Mr. Hill would not question her on the matter, and the less said the better.

"That be good to know just the same," he said as he shifted a hat box in his grasp. "Next time Mrs. Hill writes to me late brother's wife, I'll ask Mrs. Hill to include your news. It'll please my sister-in-marriage that you recognized her children so far from home."

Elizabeth eyed Jane and then her father before asking, "How did you convince Mama not to speak openly of this debacle?"

Her father sighed deeply. "I do not fool myself into thinking that my tactics will last forever, for Mrs. Bennet's *enthusiasm* is difficult to contain for long. Both my Brother and Sister Gardiner lectured her upon the foolishness of her actions, but I find withholding my lady's pin money has a more profound effect upon her hearing."

"I apologize for causing you more grief, especially as you were very ill," Jane said dutifully.

"It was Mrs. Bennet who brought on your intolerance, and so I deem it justified. She knew I would never agree to her manipulations. To match any of my daughters with a man for whom I hold little respect is not to be considered.

"Unfortunately, Gardiner has advised that I attempt to smooth the man's feathers by offering your rejected groom a visit to Longbourn. Although, in my opinion, this goes against all that is holy, I will do what is required to protect you and Lizzy from gossip. Therefore, Mr. Collins will arrive at Longbourn at the beginning of next week. I have warned your sisters that he will likely offer marriage to one of them, as, thanks to your mother, he has it in his mind that doing so guarantees my acceptance of him as a son and relieves him of any bitterness I might hold against his side of the family. If it were my choice, I would never set eyes on the man who is my heir presumptive. I would meet my Maker and never think upon him. However, Mrs. Bennet has convinced the man, who can only be a nitwit, for his late father was the biggest fool I ever encountered, that each of my daughters is prepared to save Longbourn and this family. I will extend my warning of his intent to you two, as well." He hesitated before adding. "This house means nothing to me. What matters is the happiness of my daughters. I should have prepared for your futures with more diligence. Mayhap if I had, Mrs. Bennet would not have acted so irrationally. But there was always the promise of a son—an heir, and by the time that prescription to our woes was no longer a possibility, I was too set in my ways to change."

"All any of us want is the opportunity to discover a man who will respect us," Jane assured him.

"Thank you, Jane. Now if you will pardon us, I should speak to Elizabeth privately." Jane nodded her understanding. As she rose, she gave Elizabeth's shoulder a gentle squeeze. When the door clicked behind her sister, her father asked, "Tell me what occurred between you and Mr. Darcy."

Elizabeth sat straighter. "If you ask if the gentleman placed unreasonable demands upon me, he did not. Mr. Darcy treated me as a valuable member of his household, and he did all he could to protect my reputation. Mr. Darcy is truly the most honorable man of my acquaintance."

"Viscount Lindale, sir."

Darcy looked up from the chessboard he shared with Bingley to find his cousin Roland entering the room. He stood quickly and crossed the room to greet the man. "What brings you to this side of Derbyshire, Lindale?" He shook his cousin's hand enthusiastically.

Lindale paused before responding, and Bingley took the hint. "We can finish our game later, Darcy." His friend bowed to the viscount. "It is good to see you again, Lindale." With that, Bingley exited the room, closing the door behind him.

"Come." Darcy gestured to the chairs gathered before the open window. "Would you care for a brandy?"

"That would be excellent." Lindale moved his coattails to the side before sitting. As youths upon the estate, he and the colonel were constantly tearing their breeches and snagging their shirt sleeves, but Roland had always been the most fastidious of youths—never a smudge of dirt on his person. Darcy had always assumed that his eldest cousin mimicked the earl, and the actions were instilled in Roland at a young age. The only other person of Darcy's close acquaintance growing up more fastidious in his appearance than Roland Fitzwilliam had been George Wickham. That being said, he knew Wickham could never match the viscount in consequence or social ties, and so his former friend had turned his frustration against the injustices of the world, as Wickham saw them, to his current occupation: swindling all who befriended him.

Darcy handed Roland the drink and assumed the seat across from the viscount. "Although I am always glad to see you, Lindale. It is not often you venture into this part of Derbyshire. Therefore, I assume Matlock sent you to speak to me."

Lindale sipped his brandy. "I suppose you know Father is fit to be tied. He escaped London and all the drama therein only to have the dragon lady follow him to Derbyshire."

Darcy weighed his words carefully. "Actually, I was unaware of Matlock's return to the neighborhood. I have been at Pemberley less than a week." He sipped his own drink. "What is Lady Catherine's current plan to force me to marry Anne?"

Lindale sighed heavily. "As we anticipated our aunt will persuade Anne to sue Miss Bennet for criminal conversation if you do not agree to her demands."

Darcy's hackles were on alert. "Does her ladyship know Miss Elizabeth's identity?"

"I do not think she is in possession of all the details, but it is only a matter of time before she learns the woman's name. She has a man investigating who might have seen the woman who ran from your nuptials. The fact that her rector was left at the altar upon the same morning as your disastrous exchange of vows has not slipped her notice. She has begun to wonder if there was a connection. But to answer your question, Lady Catherine has not learned of Miss Bennet's identity from your Fitzwilliam family."

"How does our aunt think to prove criminal conversation?" Darcy reasoned. "Criminal conversation involves a marriage and an affair outside of the marriage vows. As Anne and I never spoke our vows, no marriage occurred, and when I lifted Miss Elizabeth's veil, it was the first time I laid eyes upon the lady."

Lindale confirmed, "Lady Catherine is no fool. She realizes no case exists, but she will have Miss Elizabeth tried in the court of public opinion. Her ladyship believes you will bend to her wishes, rather than place yourself or the lady in a bad light. Lady Catherine's threat is not an idle one, Darcy. She means to see you with Anne, even if she must ruin you and our family."

Darcy stated in firm tones. "Have the earl assure her ladyship that her taking revenge on Miss Elizabeth will not win my favor. Matlock should also remind Lady Catherine that although I do not hold a title, I am not without influence. I could refuse Anne and then ruin my cousin's chances of another offer for her hand."

Lindale protested, "You would not punish Anne because of her mother's vile temper!"

"I would not," Darcy assured his cousin. "But her ladyship needs to consider the consequences of her actions."

"Have no doubt that Lady Catherine means to force your hand. I am not certain Father can reason with her," Lindale warned. "However, I will forward your message to both the earl and our aunt."

"Her ladyship can threaten all she wants. I will not change my mind. Rather I will end all connections to the De Bourgh family. I will present her the direct cut in public. It would grieve me to do so to my mother's sister, but I will act against her if she pursues this madness. Tell Matlock such is my resolve." Darcy set his glass upon the table with a hard *thunk*. "Remind her ladyship that it was Anne who abandoned me at the altar. It would be my prerogative for a breach of promise suit."

"All of which Father has said to his sister upon multiple occasions," Lindale assured Darcy.

Darcy shook his head in disappointment. "I cannot believe that Lady Catherine wishes to share the family's internal shame with the *ton*. What is there to gain? What says Anne of this disaster?"

"When I discovered Lady Catherine's presence at Maitland Hall, I sent my viscountess and Anne to the Fitzwilliam property in Scotland." His cousin hesitated before continuing. "I should tell you that Lady Lindale has insisted that we wean Anne from the copious doses of our cousin's *special* tonic prescribed by that quack Lady Catherine employs as Anne's physician. Lady Lindale believes the doctor uses laudanum too liberally. My wife cuts the dosage in half every few days."

"How has Anne performed?"

"Remarkably well," Lindale confided. "The first few days were rough—the effects of the laudanum were prevalent when my lady started cutting the tonic with some berry juice for the color, but I am pleased to say that each day, Anne is stronger and more active. Father has reprimanded Lady Catherine for her lack of care in Anne's stead; however, her ladyship blames any of Lady Lindale's concerns on Anne's physician. Our aunt denies her role in Anne's condition and says the physician had reassured her ladyship over the years of Anne's poor health. Even so, Lady Catherine will not warrant that she would not again see Anne using the tonic prescribed for our cousin's excessive exhaustion. Lady Lindale is encouraging Anne, upon her upcoming birthday, to claim her inheritance, but Anne still fears deposing her mother. We pray she will come around or all my lady's efforts will be for naught."

"I am glad Anne has been removed from Lady Catherine's care. Such was one of the reasons I thought a marriage between us possible, but now I know Anne is not the type of mistress that Pemberley requires. An estate as large as this one requires a mistress who will not only actively tend to her personal needs, but who will tend to my cottagers' problems, as well as assist me in planning for the estate's future. The Pemberley of today was my father's dream; now I must execute my dream to secure its future. Each generation of Darcys must adapt to the changing times. Anne, unfortunately, is too indecisive to serve as my mate. If she will not claim what is rightfully hers, how can I depend upon her to protect what is ours?"

His cousin studied Darcy with a serious gaze. "It sounds as if you have already located the woman you describe as your future wife."

Darcy cleared his throat and resisted tugging at his cravat, which suddenly felt excessively tight. "Would the Fitzwilliam faction of the family accept such a woman?"

"If the lady is who I assume you mean, I know several who would be pleased to view the look upon your face when you describe the new Mistress of Pemberley. We have waited for years for you to claim happiness."

Chapter 18

HER FATHER HAD received a second letter from Mr. Collins. The man's missive indicated he would arrive at Longbourn by four of the clock on Tuesday. Mr. Bennet had read part of his cousin's letter to the family over supper on Sunday. From the contents of the letter, her father's suspicions regarding the man's nature had proved true. "Mr. Collins seems to be a most conscientious and polite man, upon my word; and I doubt not, he will prove a valuable acquaintance," Mr. Bennet said with his customary tone of amusement.

Mrs. Bennet preened with pride. "There is some sense in what he says of our girls, Mr. Bennet, and if Mr. Collins is disposed to make any amends for being your heir, I shall not be the person to discourage him."

"I hold no doubt, my dear, that you would welcome the opportunity for one of our girls to be Longbourn's future mistress, but I will only give my permission if one of our said daughters wishes said opportunity," her father warned in serious tones.

Elizabeth observed, "I suppose there is something to be said for Mr. Collins's extraordinary deference for his patroness and his kind intention of christening, marrying, and burying his parishioners whenever it was required." Elizabeth attempted to keep the strain from her voice when she referred to Lady Catherine De Bourgh. She still did not know what to make of the woman who screeched at her at St. George. Her father obviously noted her unease, and he winked at her, and so she had presented him a small smile. He understood her qualms about Mr. Collins's visit. She continued, "He must be an oddity, I think. I cannot make him out. There is something very pompous in his style of writing. And why should he apologize for being next in line for the entail? It is not as if he had a choice of being born. Can he be termed sensible, sir?"

Her father chuckled. It was the way with him: They fulfilled each other's needs for the absurd. No one else in the family stood witness to the ridiculous, as did they. "No, my dear. I think not. In truth, I have great hopes of finding him quite the reverse, despite Mrs. Bennet's hopes to the contrary. I find there is a mixture of servility and self-importance in his letter which promises well. I am impatient to take his acquaintance."

As stated in his letter, Mr. Collins proved punctual to his time and was received with great politeness by her parents. Elizabeth made a point of sitting beside Jane during this first meeting, but her concerns were unnecessary. She and Jane had sat rigidly, aware of an impending disaster that did not arrive. Earlier in the day, when she had spoken to her father about whether or not Mrs. Bennet had actually met Mr. Collins after the end of his disastrous wedding in London and whether that would prove awkward upon the man's arrival, she had not thought to ask what Mr. Collins knew of Jane's defection. "Mrs. Bennet reportedly collapsed in a faint when their party realized Jane was not to arrive at the church. As Mr. Collins had chosen to wait in quiet study in the anteroom for the ceremony to commence, he and your mother never spoke before or after the event. Your Aunt Gardiner says that he stormed from the church when the vicar at All Saints at Kingston informed him of the situation," her father had explained.

"Mrs. Bennet, may I compliment you on having so fine a family of daughters," he said with an air of superiority. "I have heard much of their beauty." Mr. Collins pointedly looked to Jane, and her sister dropped her eyes in embarrassment. "But, in this instance, fame has fallen short of the truth. I hold no doubt that you will see them all, in due time, disposed of in marriage."

Elizabeth frowned her disapproval of the man's inane speech, while Lydia and Kitty giggled behind their fans. To her youngest sisters, their cousin was in no means interesting. It was next to impossible that Mr. Collins would ever wear the scarlet coat of the militia that had arrived in Meryton during Elizabeth's absence, and if her sisters' chatter proved accurate, it was now some weeks since they had received pleasure from the society of a man in any other coat.

Mr. Collins's gallantry was not much to the tastes of Mr. Bennet's daughters, but their mother, who quarreled with no compliments, answered most readily: "Under the circumstances, you are very kind, sir, I am sure: and I wish with all my heart that an appropriate marriage for all my daughters may prove so." She looked pointedly at Jane. "For else they will be destitute—as will we all be. Things are settled so oddly in these matters."

"I am very sensible, madam, of the hardship the entail causes my fair cousins, and I could say much on the subject, but I am cautious of appearing forward and precipitate. But I can assure the young ladies that I come prepared to admire them. At the present, I will not say more, but perhaps, when we are better acquainted—"

Finally, her father interceded. "It sounds, Mr. Collins, that you arrive today with the expectations of knowing more of my daughters. I pray that is not your only purpose in paying us a visit, and here I thought you meant to examine, and likely praise, Longbourn's furnishings and its silver plate."

Collins shot a questioning glance to Mrs. Bennet, as if he expected her to speak to his reasons for arriving at Longbourn. Elizabeth wondered if her mother had gone behind Mr. Bennet's back and contacted the man a second time. She would not put it past Mrs. Bennet to do so, for once her mother had an idea in her head, she was not easily turned aside. Elizabeth held no doubt that Collins's arrival on Longbourn's threshold was as her father suspected: It was all about the promises Mrs. Bennet had made the man. Had her mother written to Collins and promised that a marriage would still be desirable between him and one of her daughters? The man appeared to think he had only to play his "heir" card, and either she or one of her sisters would sacrifice herself to become the future mistress of Longbourn. Elizabeth doubted that the gentleman cared which one of Mr. Bennet's daughters would be his, only that one would prove he was more than a pompous twit. "I...I beg your...your pardon, sir," Collins stammered, as a flush of embarrassment crept up his pudgy cheeks. "I meant no offense."

"You should know, sir," Mr. Bennet said in reprimanding tones, "that I cherish my daughters' opinions, even the silly ones." He presented Kitty and Lydia a pointed look of disapproval before continuing. "I would never force any of them to marry simply to thwart the strictures of the entail."

"Mr. Darcy?" Mr. Nathan tapped on the door to Darcy's study. "Pardon the interruption, sir, but your aunt, Lady Catherine De Bourgh, wishes to speak to you. She is most adamant that she knows you are at home and says she will not leave until you two speak on a matter of import."

Darcy had expected his relation's call since Lindale's departure two days prior. "Permit her ladyship to wait five minutes before you escort her up. But first, take the back stairs and locate Mr. Bingley in the billiard room. Make my excuses to the gentleman and tell him business will keep me from joining him. Then tell Mr. Bingley that I require him to escort Miss Darcy when my sister calls upon the vicar. Relay a similar message to Miss Darcy. Be certain to explain that Lady Catherine has made an unexpected call, and I think it best that my sister is not in the house with my aunt. I would prefer both my friend and Miss Darcy are removed from Pemberley until I can finish my business with Lady Catherine."

Nathan's expression did not change, but his words held elements of dread. "I understand, sir." Darcy was certain that Lady Catherine did not appreciate Mr. Nathan's not permitting her free reign over Darcy's household.

With his servant's exit, Darcy braced his composure with several gulps of his finest brandy. Even so, the sound of his aunt's footsteps in the hall had him stiffening his spine.

"Lady Catherine, sir." His servant barely had time to open the door before his aunt strode into the room.

"Mr. Nathan, have my bags placed in my usual room," his aunt instructed without so much as a by-your-leave.

Darcy's ire grew quickly. He despised such presumptuousness. "Mr. Nathan, you will leave her ladyship's bags upon her coach. And instruct my aunt's coachman to remain nearby with her carriage. Lady Catherine will *not* be staying at Pemberley."

Mr. Nathan nodded his understanding and rushed from the room, closing the door behind him.

"So, this is the welcome I am to receive," her ladyship harrumphed. "Your mother would be ashamed of you, Darcy." She sat heavily in an armed chair.

Darcy remained standing beside his desk. He spoke in clipped tones. "I was considering something similar as to Lady Anne's reaction to your poor manners, Aunt. I can guarantee that George Darcy would never have tolerated your ordering his servants about, and neither will I. This is Pemberley, madam, not Rosings Park. I am the master here."

His aunt snarled, "I see your insolence continues."

"And I see you still think that the world will bend to your whims," he countered.

Rather than fuel their standoff with more inflammatory accusations, Lady Catherine switched tactics, a device he had observed her employ previously. Darcy had always thought her doing so was an intelligent means for a woman to earn agreement over business matters in a man's world, but her diversion would not work on him. "Is that girl in this house?" she demanded.

Darcy propped a hip on the corner of his desk and attempted to appear casual when he responded, "I fear Georgiana is not at home at this time. My sister will be sorry to have missed your call."

Lady Catherine's chin rose in stubbornness. "So that is the way you wish to discuss this matter. Very well. Then I shall be more direct. Did you bring Miss Elizabeth Bennet to Pemberley when you left Matthew Allard's estate in Scotland?"

Darcy schooled his features. Someone would pay dearly for sharing his business with Lady Catherine. "I am not in the habit of discussing my personal life with anyone, and you of all people should realize I am more Darcy than Fitzwilliam. Your line of questions will not win you my favor."

"I see you mean to protect this upstart! Are you so enthralled with the woman's arts and allurements that you cannot see reason? If you fancy her, Darcy, then make her your mistress. Anne will ignore your indiscretions. I will instruct my daughter in the ways of men. Anne can be your wife while this strumpet can suffer your lust."

His aunt's description of aristocratic life sickened Darcy. "I have no intention of marrying Anne. You may beg. You may threaten. You may cajole. You may bargain. But I will never change my mind. I permitted you to use the memory of my dear mother to coerce me into agreeing to marry Anne, but Fate had other ideas. Anne was late, and I spoke my vows to another."

"We both know those vows are not legal," she drawled in warning tones.

Darcy had heard from his solicitor regarding those first vows exchanged with Elizabeth, and as expected, his first marriage to the woman had proved void. Mr. Jaffray had filed the papers to have the ceremony declared null. "Such knowledge does not change my resolve. I will not marry Anne."

"Would you prefer that I instruct Anne in suing Miss

Bennet for criminal conversation?" she challenged.

"Although neither Anne nor I could officially testify in such a suit, the truth would win out. A skilled barrister can make certain all the facts are relayed to the judge. The lady in question could not have claimed my affections away from your daughter, for beyond a fondness between cousins, I never loved Anne." He would not say that Elizabeth Bennet held his heart in her delicate hands. "Moreover, as I did not hold the lady's acquaintance until several hours after that morning at St. George, it would be impossible for her to draw me away with her arts and allurements. All such a suit would do would be to bring ruin upon Anne's head and mar my family name. You would have your vengeance and little else to keep you warm in the winter. No man would ever claim Anne after such a public display, but I suppose that is what you wish. You wish Anne forever to remain under your control."

"Anne's dowry of thirty thousand pounds can cover any flaw you name," Lady Catherine argued.

"Yes, I suppose her dowry and the promise of Rosings Park can conceal all but one of my cousin's failings: that of possessing an overbearing and controlling mother. Only the most desperate of men would consider aligning his name with Sir Lewis's daughter. You would turn over Anne's future to a man of no principles. That fact should surprise me, but it does not," he said in sad tones. "Such a man would run through every penny of Anne's inheritance, leaving you and your daughter as Matlock's poor relations. I suppose that must be my justice."

"You think me so cold-hearted?" his aunt demanded. "Everything I do, I do for Anne."

"You may tell yourself these lies," Darcy cautioned, "but your family, and soon society, will recognize you as a bitter, vindictive woman." He sighed heavily. "If you persist in this madness, I will sue Anne for breach of promise. Her fortune will be greatly reduced, for I will win my suit. There were at least two dozen witnesses that can swear to the fact that she left me at the altar. If not for the false exchange of vows, I would have been long gone from the church by the time Anne arrived. You, too, would have been gone, likely looking for your wayward daughter to strangle her, as you attempted to do when she did arrive. Are you willing to tarnish your daughter's name twice in the court of public notice? Poor Anne who has never had a Season. Who has never been permitted the freedom to form a friendship. Who is poorly educated beyond what her governess provided her. That Anne will be irretrievably ruined." His tone held the warning of winter's embrace. "I do not wish to see Anne suffer, but I will not permit you to injure an innocent just to puff up your consequence."

"An innocent?" his aunt accused in her most implacable voice. "The woman traveled with you to Scotland where she passed herself off as Mrs. Darcy. You see, Mr. and Mrs. Allard were quite pleased to tell my man of your indiscretions. Allard was most displeased that you withdrew your financial support of his latest venture."

Allard's financial future would be nonexistent when Darcy finished with the man. He would permit no one to bandy about Elizabeth's name in a vile manner. "We could debate this matter all afternoon," he announced as he stood. "I believe somewhere within your hard resolve you want what is best for Anne, and I am flattered that you think me a suitable match for my cousin, but I wish to marry in affection, and my feelings for Anne are more brotherly than those of a potential husband." A profound sadness crept into his tone when Darcy spoke of his cousin's situation. He should have done more to assist Anne before things had reached this turning point. Like most in the family, he had thought all would change when Anne inherited Sir Lewis's properties and fortune. He had never considered the fact that Lady Catherine would do all she could to shove Anne out Rosings Park's door in order to maintain control of all of Sir Lewis's holdings. "Do you not wish something more for your daughter and your dearest sister's only son than a marriage of convenience?"

"I wish to see Anne well settled," she declared in undisguised contempt.

Darcy hesitated briefly before accepting the gauntlet. His aunt would force him to be ruthless. "Then you leave me no choice, madam. If you force me into marrying Anne, I will leave you with little more than a humble cottage and a pair of servants to tend you for the remainder of your days. Anne will be five and twenty in two months. I will postpone the wedding until your daughter inherits Rosings Park per Sir Lewis's will. All of it will belong to her, and as the estate and the fortune are entailed upon the female line, when we marry, as Anne's husband, I will have control of it all. I have no intention of bringing Anne to child, so all your manipulations will be for naught. As you say, I will take my lust elsewhere. At Anne's death, I will sell Rosings Park and all it holds piece by piece, until nothing remains of Sir Lewis De Bourgh's legacy. All you hold most dear will be scattered among the households of those with the funds to purchase it. I will destroy everything you have ever loved: Rosings Park and Anne. And each day of your miserable life you will know that I did these things in retribution for your foolish sense of consequence." Needing to be away from his aunt, Darcy started for the door. "Good day, your ladyship. I will have Mr. Nathan see you out." With that, he was gone, never looking back to view the look of astonishment upon his aunt's features.

Lydia and Kitty led their contingency into Meryton. Every sister, except Mary, had agreed to walk into the village. To their dismay, Mr. Bennet had requested that Mr. Collins attend them. Elizabeth fully understood, for Mr. Collins was forever underfoot. This morning, the annoying man had followed Mr. Bennet into the library. There Collins had pretended nominally to be engaged with one of the largest folios in the collection, but really, he talked to Mr. Bennet, with little cessation, of his house and garden at Hunsford.

Such doings certainly discomposed Mr. Bennet exceedingly. In his library, her father had been always sure of leisure and tranquility, and though prepared, as he had told

Elizabeth upon more than one occasion, to meet with folly and conceit in every other room of the house, he was accustomed to being free from them there; his civility, therefore, was most prompt in saying, "Mr. Collins, you should join my daughters in their walk. The exercise will be restoring."

Elizabeth assumed it was her father's peace of mind that required *restoring*; therefore, she offered no objections to his cousin accompanying them. Mr. Collins being, in fact, much better fitted for a walker than a reader, was extremely well pleased to close his large book and join them. In pompous nothings on Collins's side and civil assents from her and her sisters, their time passed until they entered Meryton.

From that point forward, Lydia and Kitty ignored Mr. Collins completely. "Lyddie and Kitty are on the hunt for officers," Jane whispered conspiratorially. "Since the militia has come to Meryton, such is all of which they speak."

Elizabeth chuckled as Mr. Collins prattled on beside her, completely oblivious to her younger sisters' desertion. "Nothing less than a very smart bonnet or a new muslin in a shop window will be able to compete for their attentions," she teased.

However, it was not simply her sisters' gazes, but that of every lady upon the street, that silenced Elizabeth's next remarks. It was a young man, whose appearance was greatly in his favor: He had all the best part of beauty—a fine countenance and a good figure, and every female eye, including hers, was riveted upon him.

"There's Mr. Denny," Lydia squealed and darted away, dragging Kitty behind her. Reluctantly, Elizabeth, Jane, and Mr. Collins followed at a more sedate pace. She could hear Mr. Collins's tut of disapproval, and for once, she was in agreement with the man.

Her youngest sisters pretended to be looking at hats in a window display, but it was obvious they were spying on the young man and what must have been the Mr. Denny, of whom Elizabeth had heard much over the past week. Lydia and Kitty purposely stood back away from the window, so they were blocking the walkway when the gentlemen approached. Naturally, Mr. Denny and the stranger stopped to speak to her sisters.

"Ladies." Mr. Denny bowed, and his friend followed suit. "What brings you to Meryton on this fine afternoon?"

"We mean to call upon our Aunt Philips," Lydia shared with a silly fluttering of her eyelids. Elizabeth smothered her smile of amusement behind a cough.

The man in uniform looked in her direction. "Might you perform the introductions, Miss Lydia," Captain Denny instructed.

Mr. Denny's request appeared to fluster Lydia, but her youngest sister managed to give the captain her, Jane's and Mr. Collins's acquaintances.

After the officer greeted each of them, he turned to his companion. "Now permit me to introduce my friend, a fine gentleman who returned with me from London on this very day. I am happy to say George here has accepted a commission in the corps." Every eye was on the newcomer, who wanted only regimentals to make him completely charming. "Ladies. Mr. Collins. Permit me to present my friend Mr. Wickham."

Chapter 19

INSTINCTIVELY, SHE DROPPED a curtsy, but Elizabeth could not remove her eyes from the gentleman. Certainly, there could be more than one *Mr. Wickham* in the world, but she held no doubt this was the same man Miss Darcy had described. While she organized her thoughts, the others enjoyed a happy readiness for conversation—a readiness, she noted, to be perfectly correct and unassuming. At length, her curiosity could no longer withstand the suspense. "Are you from Derbyshire, Mr. Wickham?" she asked in what she hoped were innocent-sounding tones.

The gentleman eyed her in interest. "Why do you ask, Miss Elizabeth?"

"Simply, according to my youngest sisters, most of the men of the Meryton militia are from Derbyshire."

Mr. Wickham nodded his acceptance of her explanation with a simple inclination of his head. "Do you know Derbyshire, ma'am?"

"Not well," Elizabeth admitted with congenial intentions. "Miss Bennet stayed with relatives near Derby recently, and we met each other in the shire upon my return from Scotland."

Mr. Wickham smiled at her, and Elizabeth understood

how a woman might be easily distracted by the man. Both Lydia and Kitty stood in awe of his fine countenance. "Then you passed very near to the house where I numbered my youthful days. Did you perchance learn anything of Pemberley?"

She noted Jane's anxious glance, but Elizabeth ignored her sister for the moment. Her desire to learn more of Mr. Wickham had taken precedence. "I learned that it is a fine estate, and I heard several speak of its splendor. Someday soon, promise me that you will speak more of it to me, Mr. Wickham. I would be most pleased to hear of an area my sister and I recently visited and compare it to my aunt's accolades for her home shire."

"I would take enjoyment in the exercise also, Miss Elizabeth," he assured her.

"We should call upon our aunt," Jane reminded the group. Mr. Denny and Mr. Wickham walked with their party to the door of Mr. Philips's house and then made their bows to leave in spite of Lydia's pressing entreaties that they come in and in spite of Mrs. Philips's throwing up the parlor window and loudly seconding the invitation.

Mrs. Philips was glad to see her nieces, especially the two eldest, whose recent absence from Longbourn had kept them from her parlor. "How is Mr. Bennet's health?" she asked as she busily rushed to the bell cord to ring for tea.

"His recovery continues," Jane answered while Elizabeth's mind replayed her brief encounter with Mr. Wickham. She had no reason to encourage the man, other than her loyalty to Mr. Darcy. She wished to know if Mr. Wickham spoke poorly of the gentleman. She prayed he did not, for if Mr. Darcy learned of Mr. Wickham's disparagements, the gentleman would likely call his former friend out, and dueling was illegal in England.

Reluctantly, her thoughts returned to the situation before her. Her elder sister introduced Mr. Collins to their aunt. Odd. Until that moment, Elizabeth had forgotten that Mr. Collins had accompanied them. Her thoughts were full of Mr. Darcy and Mr. Wickham.

Aunt Philips received Mr. Collins with her very best

politeness, which he returned with as much and more. "I apologize, ma'am, for my intrusion, especially as I claim no previous acquaintance with your personage," he said as he bowed twice again. "Although I count myself justified in doing so by my immediate relationship to my dear cousins."

Lydia ignored Mr. Collins's effusions to say, "Tell us, Aunt, what you know of Mr. Wickham."

"I fear I cannot add to what you likely already know. Mr. Denny brought him from London. Mr. Wickham is to have a lieutenant's commission. I have been watching him this last hour as he walked up and down the street."

Parading for all of us to see, Elizabeth thought. *I wonder who paid for his commission. Did he possess the funds to claim the role of a junior officer?* She had assumed from what the Darcys had confided that Mr. Wickham was often short of funds, but when she thought back upon the conversations, neither of the Darcys spoke of the man being destitute.

"You girls will come to dine tomorrow evening, will you not?" their Aunt Philips pressed. "I shall send an invitation around with Mr. Philips for Mr. Wickham. You will come also, Mr. Collins." Elizabeth noted how her younger sisters rolled their eyes in disgust at their aunt's gesture of kindness. "We shall have a nice comfortable noisy game of lottery tickets and a little bit of hot supper afterwards."

Lydia and Kitty clapped their hands in excited acceptance. Soon their party departed in mutual good spirits. Needlessly, Mr. Collins repeated his apologies in quitting the room and was assured, with unvarying civility, that his excuses were not necessary.

"What did you mean by mentioning Derbyshire?" Jane questioned in quiet tones, as they lagged behind the others.

Elizabeth spoke with equal softness. "Mr. Darcy confided a story of a former friend who betrayed him. A man called Mr. Wickham."

"It cannot be," Jane gasped.

"I am certainly glad that neither of us spoke of our time at

Pemberley or the taking of the acquaintance of the Darcys or Mr. Bingley. Only Papa and the Gardiners hold knowledge of our true travel destinations."

As no objection was made to the young people's engagement with their aunt, and all Mr. Collins's scruples of leaving Mr. and Mrs. Bennet for a single evening during his visit were most steadily resisted, the coach conveyed him and his five cousins at a suitable hour to Meryton; and the girls had the pleasure of hearing, as they entered the drawing room, that Mr. Wickham had accepted their uncle's invitation and was then in the house.

When this information was given, and they had all taken their seats, Elizabeth looked on as Mr. Collins was at leisure to study the Philips's furnishings and such around him and admire his surroundings. Needless to say, he was so much struck with the size and furniture of the apartment that he declared he *might almost have supposed himself in the small summer breakfast parlor at Rosings.* This was a comparison that did not at first convey much gratification; but when Mrs. Philips understood from him what Rosings was, and who was its proprietor — when she had listened to the description of only one of Lady Catherine's drawing rooms, and found that the chimney-piece alone had cost eight hundred pounds, she felt all the force of the compliment, and no longer resented a comparison with the housekeeper's room.

In describing to her all the grandeur of Lady Catherine and her mansion, with occasional digressions in praise of his own humble abode, and the improvements it was receiving, he was happily employed until the gentlemen joined them. To the girls, who could not listen to their cousin, and who had nothing to do but to wish for an instrument, and examine their own indifferent imitations of china on the mantlepiece, the interval of waiting appeared very long. It was over at last, however. The gentlemen did approach, and when Mr. Wickham walked into the room, Elizabeth felt that she had neither been seeing him before, nor thinking of him since, with the smallest degree of unreasonable admiration. The officers of the —shire were in general a very creditable, gentlemanlike set, and the best of them were of the present party; but Mr. Wickham was as far beyond them all in person, countenance, air, and walk, as *they* were superior to her broad-faced, stuffy Uncle Philips, who was breathing port wine when he followed them into the room.

Elizabeth was more than anxious to view whether Mr. Wickham would accept the invitation to dine with her aunt or not. Thoughts of the gentleman had not left her overnight, and she had yet to decide whether to pursue learning more of the lieutenant.

Mr. Wickham was the happy man towards whom almost every female eye turned, and Elizabeth knew satisfaction when he finally seated himself beside her and with the agreeable manner in which he immediately fell into conversation, though it was only on its being a wet night, and on the probability of a rainy season. Although the subjects were tedious, she held no doubt that Mr. Wickham could make the commonest, dullest, most threadbare topic interesting by his skill as a speaker.

With such rivals for the notice of the fair as Mr. Wickham and the officers, Mr. Collins, unfortunately, sank into insignificance; to the young ladies he certainly was nothing; but Elizabeth noted that he had still at intervals a kind listener in her Aunt Philips, and was, by her aunt's watchfulness, most abundantly supplied with coffee and muffins. Although she held no allegiance to the man, neither did Elizabeth wish him to think poorly of her family's hospitality and report it back to Mr. Darcy's aunt.

When the card-tables were placed, Mr. Collins had an opportunity of obliging Aunt Philips in return, by sitting down to whist. "I know little of the game at present," said he, "but I shall be glad to improve myself, for in my situation of life—" Mrs. Philips was very thankful for his compliance, but did not wait for his reason, for one of her other guests required an armed chair rather than a straight-backed one, and so she rushed off to find a servant to comply with the request.

Mr. Wickham did play at whist, and with ready delight, he was received at the second table, seated between Elizabeth and Lydia. At first there seemed danger of Lydia's engaging him entirely, for she was a most determined talker; but being likewise extremely fond of lottery tickets, she soon grew too much interested in the game, too eager in making bets and exclaiming after prizes, to have attention for any one in particular. Allowing for the common demands of the game, Mr. Wickham was therefore at leisure to talk to Elizabeth, and she was very willing to hear him, though what she chiefly wished to hear she could not hope to be told—the history of his acquaintance with Mr. Darcy. She dared not even mention that gentleman. Her curiosity, however, was unexpectedly relieved as Mr. Wickham began the subject himself.

"How long were you in Derbyshire?" he inquired.

"Miss Bennet was with our relations for nearly a month. As I explained previously, I joined her on my return from Scotland. I fear I spent less than a week in your home shire." She paused before adding, "My sister confirms that we were very close to Pemberley in our travels. Is that not the estate you mentioned yesterday?"

"Most assuredly." He adjusted the cards in his hands. "I have been connected to the estate and the Darcy family, in a particular manner, from my infancy." He lowered his voice, "Did you encounter the current Master of Pemberley during your stay in Derby?"

Elizabeth did not enjoy lying to the man, but she could not share news of her relationship with Mr. Darcy with anyone. "I certainly would remember such a meeting," she said enigmatically.

"I hold no doubt," Mr. Wickham spoke in conspiratorial tones. "Most women find the current Mr. Darcy handsome. I imagine they also find his estate a noble one and his income of ten thousand per annum tempting."

Although she had not expected to hear Mr. Wickham speak so freely of Mr. Darcy, Elizabeth smiled at the man. "It does not sound as if you find the gentleman agreeable."

"I have no right to give my opinion," said Wickham, "as to his being agreeable or otherwise. I am not qualified to form one. I have known him too long and too well to be a fair judge. It is impossible for me to be impartial."

"Upon my word," she exclaimed, "you appear quite set against the gentleman."

Mr. Wickham paused to study his cards, but after a short interruption, he continued. "I cannot pretend to be sorry that he or any man should not be estimated beyond his desserts; but with him, I believe it does not often happen. The world is blinded by Mr. Darcy's fortune and consequence, or frightened by his high and imposing manners, and sees him only as he chooses to be seen."

Mr. Wickham's description of Mr. Darcy certainly set in sharp contrast to the man Elizabeth knew. Certainly, she realized he could be highhanded, for she had accused him of that fact herself, but she did not think him worse than any other man in his position. "My, I would not wish to take the acquaintance of the man you describe."

Mr. Wickham sympathetically patted the back of Elizabeth's ungloved hand, where it rested upon the table, an act she found disconcerting and too forward for such a short acquaintance. However, she swallowed her objection in order to learn more of Mr. Wickham. She found his account of Mr. Darcy troublesome, while fully understanding how others might believe Mr. Wickham's tone of sincerity. She wondered how often Mr. Wickham wove his tale of woe and for what nefarious purposes.

"Most who meet Mr. Darcy take him, even on slight acquaintance, to be an ill-tempered man," he confided. "As to my relationship with the man, it always gives me pain to meet him, but I refuse to avoid him. Yet, I must proclaim to all the world a sense of very great ill-usage and most painful regrets at his being what he is. His father, Miss Elizabeth, the late Mr. Darcy, was one of the best men that ever breathed, and the truest friend I ever had, and I can never be in company with the current Mr.

Darcy without being grieved to the soul by a thousand tender recollections. His behavior to me has been scandalous, but I verily believe I could forgive him anything and everything rather than his disappointing the hopes and disgracing the memory of his father."

Although she had visited Pemberley but a few days, Elizabeth knew Mr. Wickham bent the truth to his liking, for all she encountered praised the current Mr. Darcy as the best of masters. No one who knew him had a bad word for Fitzwilliam Darcy. Wickham's obvious manipulation fascinated her, and she found her interest in the subject increase. She listened with all her heart. Part of her wished openly to deny Mr. Wickham's accusations against Mr. Darcy, but she could not defend the man she held with tenderness in her heart, for doing so would bring shame upon her family. "I cannot imagine such a disagreeable creature," she declared.

Mr. Wickham began to speak on more general topics—Meryton, the neighborhood, the society—appearing highly pleased with all that he had yet seen and speaking of the latter, especially, with gentle, but very intelligible, gallantry.

"It was the prospect of constant society, and good society," he added, "which was my chief inducement to enter the —shire. I knew it to be a most respectable, agreeable corps, and my friend Denny tempted me further by his account of their present quarters and the very great attentions and excellent acquaintances Meryton had procured for them. Society, I own, is necessary to me. I have been a disappointed man, and my spirits will not bear solitude. I *must* have employment and society. A military life is not what I was intended for, but circumstances have now made it eligible. The church *ought* to have been my profession—I was brought up for the church, and I should, at this time, have been in possession of a most valuable living, had it pleased the gentleman we were speaking of just now."

"Indeed!"

"Yes—the late Mr. Darcy bequeathed me the next presentation of the best living in his gift. He was my godfather and excessively attached to me. I cannot do justice to his kindness. He meant to provide for me amply and thought he had done it; but when the living fell, it was given elsewhere."

"Good heavens!" cried Elizabeth; "but how could *that* be? How could his will be disregarded? Why did not you seek legal redress?" Even though she knew Mr. Wickham's tale could not be accurate, for a moment, she found herself caught up in the impact of lies. She now fully understood how Miss Darcy could believe such a skilled conniver.

"There was just such an informality in the terms of the bequest as to give me no hope from the law. A man of honor could not have doubted the intention, but Mr. Darcy chose to doubt it—or to treat it as merely a conditional recommendation and to assert that I had forfeited all claim to it by extravagance, imprudence—in short, anything or nothing. Certain it is, that the living became vacant two years ago, exactly as I was of an age to hold it, and that it was given to another man; and no less certain is it, that I cannot accuse myself of having really done anything to deserve to lose it. I have a warm, unguarded temper, and I may perhaps have sometimes spoken my opinion *of* him, and *to* him, too freely. I can recall nothing worse. But the fact is, that we are very different sorts of men and that he hates me."

"How can it be so?" Elizabeth strained to keep the anger from her tone. The man Mr. Wickham described could not be the same man who presented her fresh flowers each morning. "Did you think to make his sins known publicly?"

"Some time or other he *will* be duly chastised—but it shall not be by *me*. Till I can forget his father, I can never defy or expose *him*."

Elizabeth began to understand something of Mr. Wickham's character. He was a man envious of Mr. Darcy's influence and his wealth. Therefore, Mr. Wickham meant to chip away at Mr. Darcy's honor with lies that few would speak to Mr. Darcy's face, but which would hurt him, nevertheless.

"But what," said she, after a pause, "can have been his motive? What can have induced him to behave so cruelly?"

"A thorough, determined dislike of me—a dislike which I cannot but attribute in some measure to jealousy. Had the late Mr. Darcy liked me less, his son might have borne with me better; but his father's uncommon attachment to me irritated him, I believe, very early in life. He had not a temper to bear the sort of competition in which we stood—the sort of preference which was often given me."

So that will be his tale, she thought. *Many will believe him if they encounter Mr. Darcy's arbitrary manner of business before they know his mercy.* "I cannot think that any man would act so despicably," she prompted.

"I will not trust myself on the subject," replied Wickham, "*I* can hardly be just to him, for we were born in the same parish, within the same park, the greatest part of our youth was passed together as inmates of the same house, sharing the same amusements, objects of the same parental care. *My* father began life in the profession which your uncle, Mr. Philips, appears to do so much credit to—but my father gave up everything to be of use to the late Mr. Darcy and devoted all his time to the care of the Pemberley property. He was most highly esteemed by Mr. Darcy, a most intimate, confidential friend. Mr. Darcy often acknowledged himself to be under the greatest obligations to my father's active superintendence, and when, immediately before my father's death, Mr. Darcy gave him a voluntary promise of providing for me, I am convinced that he felt it to be as much a debt of gratitude to *him* as of affection to myself."

"How abominable must be the man you describe!" Again, Elizabeth kept her comments vague, but encouraging to Mr. Wickham's tale.

"Almost all his actions may be traced to pride; and pride has often been his best friend. It has connected him nearer with virtue than any other feeling. But we are none of us consistent, and in his behavior to me there were stronger impulses even than pride. Misplaced pride in his noble name has often led him to be liberal and generous—to give his money freely, to display hospitality, to assist his tenants, and relieve the poor. Family pride, and *filial* pride—for he is very proud of what his father was—have done this. Not to appear to disgrace his family, to degenerate from the popular qualities, or lose the influence of the Pemberley House is a powerful motive. He has also *brotherly* pride, which, with *some* brotherly affection, makes him a very kind and careful guardian of his sister, and you will hear him generally cried up as the most attentive and best of brothers."

For a split second, Elizabeth wondered if Mr. Wickham's words explained the difference between the Mr. Darcy she knew and the creature of the lieutenant's accusations. To learn the truth, she asked, "What sort of a girl is Miss Darcy?"

Mr. Wickham shook his head. "I wish I could call her amiable. It gives me pain to speak ill of a Darcy. But she is too much like her brother—very, very proud. As a child, she was affectionate and pleasing, and extremely fond of me; and I have devoted hours and hours to her amusement. But she is nothing to me now. She is a handsome girl, about fifteen or sixteen, and, I understand, highly accomplished. Since her father's death, her home has been London, where a lady lives with her and superintends her education."

It was then that Elizabeth knew Mr. Wickham spoke with the proverbial forked tongue. Her feelings for Mr. Darcy were a mix of fear and need, but she knew Miss Darcy as well as she knew her own sisters. Georgiana Darcy was of a sweet nature— kind and thoughtful. The girl's only faults were her shyness and her lack of confidence in her unique abilities.

Uncertain how to respond to the lieutenant's blatant misrepresentations, she was thankful to see that the whist party was breaking up. "I believe our talk must wait for another day to know a conclusion," she said with a well-placed smile. "My aunt has a supper planned for the remainder of the evening."

The players gathered round the other table to watch the accounting of the last hand of the players still at it. Elizabeth found herself between Mr. Collins and Mr. Wickham. Her aunt, who stood on the other side of Collins, made the usual inquiries as to his success at the game. According to Collins, it had not been very great: he had lost every point; but when Aunt Philips began to express her concern thereupon, her father's cousin assured her with much earnest gravity that it was not of the least importance, that he considered the money as a mere trifle, and begged that Aunt Philips would not make herself uneasy.

"I know very well, madam," said he, "that when persons sit down to a card-table, they must take their chance of these things—and happily I am not in such circumstances as to make five shillings any object. There are undoubtedly many who could not say the same, but thanks to Lady Catherine de Bourgh, I am removed far beyond the necessity of regarding little matters."

Mr. Wickham's attention was caught and after observing Mr. Collins for a few moments, he asked Elizabeth in a low voice whether her relation were very intimately acquainted with the family of De Bourgh.

"Lady Catherine De Bourgh," Elizabeth replied, "has very lately presented Mr. Collins a living. I hardly know how my father's cousin was first introduced to her notice, but he certainly has not known her long." She attempted to keep her tones all that was innocent, but the mention of her ladyship had Elizabeth's nerves skittering up her spine in a dramatic shiver she was hard pressed to disguise.

"You know, of course, that Lady Catherine De Bourgh and Lady Anne Darcy were sisters; consequently, her ladyship is aunt to the present Mr. Darcy."

Elizabeth swallowed hard against the panic rising in her chest. "No, indeed, I did not. I knew nothing at all of Lady Catherine until recently. Mr. Collins sings her ladyship's praises."

"Her daughter, Miss De Bourgh," Mr. Wickham continued to confide, "will have a very large fortune, and it is believed that she and her Pemberley cousin will soon unite the two estates."

"Vain must be the attentions of the women you described earlier to set their caps for Mr. Darcy's proposal if he means to marry another," she observed. "Mr. Collins speaks highly both of Lady Catherine and her daughter; but from some particulars that he has related of her ladyship, I suspect his gratitude misleads him, and despite her being his patroness, she is an arrogant, conceited woman." *And I pray the lady never discovers my identity, for if her ladyship has her way, a magistrate will remove me from Longbourn in chains.*

"I believe her to be both in a great degree," replied Wickham. "I have not seen her for many years, but I very well remember that I never liked her and that her manners were dictatorial and insolent. She has the reputation of being remarkably sensible and clever; but I rather believe she derives part of her abilities from her rank and fortune, part from her authoritative manner, and the rest from the pride of her nephew, who chooses that every person connected with him should have an understanding of the first tier of society."

Elizabeth allowed that Mr. Wickham had provided a very rational account of the Darcys and the De Bourghs, and they continued talking together with mutual satisfaction until supper put an end to cards. The break provided the rest of the ladies their share of Mr. Wickham's attentions. Ironically, she was glad to be free of the lieutenant's company. Handsome, he may be, but he was everything Mr. Darcy said of him and more. Silly as it would sound if she said the words aloud, she felt "dirty" simply having been in the man's company.

Thankfully, there could be no conversation in the noise of Mrs. Philips's supper party, but as she watched him with a feeling of disgust, she noted how Mr. Wickham's manners recommended him to everybody. Whatever he said was said well; and whatever he did, done gracefully. It was no wonder that Georgiana Darcy believed herself in love with the scoundrel.

Elizabeth went away with her head full of him, but not in a good way. She could think of nothing but of Mr. Wickham, and of what he had told her, all the way home; but there was not time for her even to mention his name as they went, for neither Lydia nor Mr. Collins were once silent. Lydia talked incessantly of lottery tickets, of the fish she had lost and the fish she had won; Mr. Collins, in describing the civility of Mr. and Mrs. Philips, protesting that he did not in the least regard his losses at whist, enumerating all the dishes at supper, and repeatedly fearing that he crowded his cousins, had more to say than he could well manage before the carriage stopped at Longbourn House.

Chapter 20

"MR. DARCY?" HIS butler interrupted Darcy's meeting with Mr. Burton.

"Yes, Mr. Nathan?" Darcy attempted to keep his irritation from his voice, but it had been eleven days since Elizabeth had departed Pemberley, and with each passing day, he had grown more impatient to see her again.

"You said to inform you when Mr. Harvey arrived."

Actually, Darcy had ordered his servant to send Mr. Harvey up to see him, whether it be day or night. He had been anticipating Harvey's return from Scotland since the day the man departed. Lionel Harvey had served as Darcy's man of business in Derbyshire, while the man's cousin, Luther Watson, addressed Darcy's needs in London. Both men also served Lord Matlock in a similar manner, and Darcy's late father had sworn by the men's trustworthiness.

"Excellent," he declared. "See Mr. Harvey up." To Burton, he said, "Remain for a few extra minutes. Hopefully, Harvey has news of the man from Scotland of whom we spoke previously."

Within minutes, Mr. Nathan escorted Harvey into the room. Darcy rose to shake the man's hand and to offer him a drink. When they were all settled together, he explained, "I asked Mr. Burton to remain, for he is the one who will oversee Mr. Hill's work if the man agreed to my offer."

Harvey nodded his understanding. He reached into a leather satchel to remove several pieces of paper. "As you instructed, sir, I made contact with Mr. Hill. I must say, Mr. Darcy, it was no easy task to speak to Hill privately. Mr. Bradburn refused my entreaties to meet with the man; however, without Bradburn's knowledge, Doctor Wilton managed to set up a meeting between me and Mr. Hill."

Darcy was not surprised by Harvey's report. "Mr. Bradburn is a cruel one. It is probably best, for Hill's sake, that Bradburn thought his refusal prevented you from meeting with Hill. How did the Scot receive my offer?"

Harvey consulted his notes. "Hill was enthusiastic, to say the least."

"Then he will join us at Pemberley soon?"

Harvey chuckled. "By *enthusiastic* I mean to say that Hill, his sister Josephine, and his new wife will be at Pemberley within the next fortnight."

"Wife? Annie? I thought perhaps the man had eyes for the girl," Darcy observed.

Harvey cleared his throat nervously. "I assured Mr. Hill that his wife would be welcomed at Pemberley. I pray I did not misspeak."

"I am a firm believer that a wife makes a man a better tenant. All is well in that respect, but I do not anticipate being at Pemberley when Hill arrives. Mr. Bingley and I have business in the southern shires." On that very morning, he had heard from Bingley regarding Netherfield Park in Hertfordshire. They could view the estate anytime they chose. Bingley had traveled on to Staffordshire the day after Lady Catherine's call upon Pemberley. His friend was to make the necessary inquiries regarding the property, and if it proved to be all they had hoped, Bingley would let the estate for the first year. They had agreed to tell no one of their destination until Bingley could settle his intentions upon

Miss Bennet. Darcy could not be so obvious, but he had sworn a private oath not to leave Hertfordshire without Elizabeth Bennet by his side. He turned to Burton. "Can I count on you to see the man settled and his duties assigned in my absence?"

"Yes, sir," Burton agreed. "As we discussed previously, I have identified a small cottage for Mr. Hill's occupancy."

Darcy nodded his approval. "I will meet with you again before I depart; in that manner, we can define Hill's role upon the estate. Meanwhile, I will speak to Mrs. Reynolds regarding Josephine's employment within the household. Burton, I will leave it to you and Hill to decide whether Mrs. Hill will tend Hill's household or join her new husband in the shearing yard."

"I will see to it. Is there anything else, sir?" Darcy shook his head in the negative. "If not, I will leave you to settle business with Mr. Harvey." His steward stood. "Send for me when you are prepared to discuss more of Hill's duties at Pemberley."

Darcy nodded his dismissal. When Burton quit the room, Darcy instructed, "Tell me how those on the list I provided you took to the news of Allard's operation."

"Very much as you expected, sir," Harvey assured Darcy. "I have compiled copious notes that you may peruse at your leisure, but each man asked proof of your assertions. When I explained what you had discovered in your interactions with Allard, they asked that I extend their gratitude to you for keeping them from making a disastrous investment. Although I possess no direct knowledge of their transactions, I am certain each made moves to eliminate their financial support of Allard." Darcy had not yet finished with Allard, but Harvey's efforts were an excellent beginning. The men Harvey contacted were those with whom Darcy regularly did business. He had simply expressed his desire that his good name not be associated with Allard. Darcy had a reputation to maintain among his colleagues. However, as to the Allards' offense to Elizabeth, Darcy would see the man brought to his knees in a most satisfying retribution.

"You performed well. I appreciate your diligence," Darcy assured Harvey. "And now to my personal matter."

Mr. Harvey blushed, before clearing his throat, as he dug deeper into his satchel for additional paperwork. "As I assumed the legitimacy of your claim to have married Miss Elizabeth Bennet was in question, I asked several of those who witnessed the ceremony to provide a written testimony to the event."

Darcy purposely released the breath he did not realize that he held. Although he possessed only fragments of memories of that evening at the Scottish inn, the truth had taken up residence in his chest. "Then the marriage is legal?" he asked in what could only be called satisfaction.

"It is, sir. Sanctioned by the Church of Scotland. As legal as those Mr. Robert Elliot offers to couples eloping to Gretna Green." Mr. Harvey's eyes had yet to meet Darcy's. "I did not mean to imply, sir, that you and the lady eloped."

"No harm," Darcy assured the man. "I am simply glad the certificate is legal. The lady was most insistent that I seek the truth of the matter." He sat back in his chair, savoring the idea of his taking Elizabeth Bennet to wife. "Is there anything else of which I should be made aware, Harvey?"

Mr. Harvey blushed again. "The innkeeper and the others who were willing to speak of the event said both you and Miss Bennet were deep in your cups. I pray you are not disappointed to find yourself a married man."

"Nothing of the sort," Darcy explained. "I have been considering making the lady my wife for some time now. The situation is not unpleasant."

Harvey nodded his head in the affirmative. "Good. I am glad to hear it. The papers I have provided you should be all you will require to settle the matter."

Darcy stood to end their meeting. He wished to spend the afternoon reliving his marriage through the eyes of those who had witnessed it "I must ask you to keep knowledge of my marriage a secret until I bring my wife to Pemberley."

Harvey followed Darcy to his feet. "I understand, sir. This is a delicate negotiation."

Darcy chuckled. "Delicate. Confounding. Enthralling. Pick

your adjective, Harvey, and you will describe Miss Elizabeth." He shook the man's hand in parting. "I will contact your cousin regarding the settlement papers after I meet with Mr. Bennet. I will ask Mr. Watson to send you copies. It seems I have placed the carriage before the horse, and I pray Mr. Bennet is not offended."

Mr. Harvey frowned his misunderstanding. "How could any man, or woman, for that matter, not wish to align his household with yours, sir?"

Darcy wagged his head in amusement. "That is just it, Harvey. Miss Elizabeth is not just *any* woman. She is the answer to my heart's questions, but, as of yet, I am not certain that I am the answer to hers. However, someday, I mean to be."

Elizabeth set her letter to her aunt upon the tray to be franked by her father. For the past two afternoons, Mr. Wickham had been with the officers that had called upon Longbourn, and it was all she could do not to call him out when she overheard his repeating his lies to his friends as well as to her family and the Lucases. It was one thing for the lieutenant to share his tale of woe with her, but it was quite another for him to prejudice others against a man they did not know. It was not as if anyone from Meryton were ever likely to encounter Mr. Darcy, but she did not want Mr. Collins to carry such tales to Lady Catherine. Imagine if her ladyship arrived in the neighborhood to thwart the tales Mr. Wickham shared, and while in residence, likely at her father's house, for there was not a decent inn in the village where a woman of Lady Catherine's consequence could stay, she recognized Elizabeth's countenance as the very one that had ruined her daughter's wedding. Elizabeth shivered with dread just thinking upon a confrontation with the woman.

Reconsidering her letter, she retrieved it from the tray. In hindsight, she doubted that Aunt Gardiner would hold more information on Mr. Darcy and Mr. Wickham's relationship than did she. Both Mr. Darcy and his sister had confided a tale of Lieutenant Wickham's perfidy, and no matter how often

Elizabeth attempted to ignore their story, she could not, for each had described a situation in which Miss Darcy had known ruination. Neither Mr. Darcy nor his sister would have spoken so freely of an event that could smear Miss Darcy's name and destroy her chance of a good marriage if what they had shared were untruths.

Settled upon what must be done, she tapped on the closed door to her father's sanctuary. She heard the groan of frustration in his "Come." Mr. Bennet thought she might be Mr. Collins coming to interrupt her father's peace again.

She opened the door to announce, "It is I, Papa. Might I claim a bit of conversation?"

He smiled at her. "I always have time for my Lizzy. But hurry and close the door before Collins realizes I have risen from my nap."

"I believe you are safe for now. Our cousin has accompanied Mary and Kitty to Lucas Lodge," she confided.

"I suppose the idiot thinks I will be more receptive to his pleas for my permission to marry Mary or Kitty than I was to his request to seek both yours and Jane's agreement."

Elizabeth closed the door behind her. "Both?" she teased as she crossed to her favorite chair.

"Not at the same time," he explained. Her father carefully marked the page in his book before setting it aside. "On Sunday, Mr. Collins pledged his devotion to Jane and asked my permission to court your sister. He offered all the assurances of his ability to provide for her."

"But?" Elizabeth's eyebrow rose in amusement.

"But I choked on my coffee and had to return to my room to rest so I would not again succumb to lung fever. Needless to say, under the circumstances, I could not present my cousin a proper response," he said with a twinkle in his eyes.

"And what of me?" she asked as she stifled her giggle. "*Needless to say*," she emphasized her father's words, "Mr. Collins could not also profess to adore me."

Her father's smile widened. "You err, Lizzy. The fool

took my coughing fit as a sign of my disapproval of his offer for Jane, for which Mr. Collins apologized repeatedly for offending me. He had *aspired to rob the Bennet family of its diamond*, and he understood that the life of a country rector's wife was not one which *would nurture Jane's delicate nature*."

Elizabeth rolled her eyes heavenward. "I pray the dear Lord will protect us from bumbling men of the cloth."

"Do not permit your mother to hear you disparage Mr. Collins. She means to see one of you girls as the mistress of Longbourn, and even my withholding her pin money will not keep her from her machinations."

"So, did Mr. Collins promise his undying devotion to me?" Elizabeth fanned her face with her handkerchief in the manner often employed by her mother during a fit of nerves.

"Mr. Collins swears Lady Catherine will adore you," her father said with a large grin. "When her ladyship returns to Rosings Park, Collins means to write to her of your *amiable* qualities."

"Yes, I am certain Lady Catherine would welcome to Rosings Park the woman who set crossways her ladyship's plans to marry her daughter to Mr. Darcy," Elizabeth said in sarcastic tones.

"Which is why I suddenly claimed that a bee attempted to sting my cheek." Her father laughed aloud. "Mr. Collins did not consider the fact that all the windows were closed, and no bee could enter the room. As Collins swells up like a fat squash when stung by a bee, he hightailed it from the room before I could deny his request. That is what he deserves for boring me with his tiresome tales and for aspiring to the *true* diamond of the Bennet family."

Elizabeth was always glad to hear his praise of her worth, but she had to ask, "Then you simply postponed Mr. Collins's proposal to me. What if he insists upon pledging his plight?"

"I will tell him that no mere man is good enough for my Elizabeth," her father said in serious tones. "I will only permit you to marry if you desire it."

Elizabeth thought of Mr. Darcy, but quickly buried her hopes. "How will you put Mr. Collins off of Mary, Kitty, and Lydia?"

"I have considered presenting Collins permission to marry Lydia. That would remove your youngest sister's silly conversations to Kent until I can place my spoon in the wall. Moreover, Lydia's becoming the next mistress of Longbourn would be most satisfying to Mrs. Bennet," he underpinned logically.

Elizabeth was glad for the opportunity to return to her purpose in calling upon her father. "Lydia is one of the reasons I wished to speak to you."

Her father sobered. "What has the foolish chit done now? Speak your concerns, Lizzy."

She squared her shoulders before beginning. "I have noted of late the extent of Lydia's obsession with the militia officers and specifically her interest in Mr. Wickham."

"The new lieutenant?" her father asked.

"Yes, sir. I have reason to believe that Mr. Wickham is not the type of gentleman you would wish to welcome into your wife's drawing room."

Chapter 21

WHEN THE NEWS arrived from the gate house of the return of Bingley's carriage, Darcy was on his feet immediately. He would admit, but only to himself, that he had worn a path upon the rug in his study as he had paced in frustration. He would never be able to claim patience as one of his virtues. At length, Bingley's coach came into view, and Darcy breathed easier, for only his friend could be seen through the coach's window. Darcy had feared that Bingley would permit Miss Bingley to accompany him to Pemberley. Along with Lady Catherine, Caroline Bingley was one of those he did not currently wish to welcome to his home.

Bingley scrambled from the coach. A wide grin marked his friend's features. As he crossed to where Darcy waited, he announced, "Congratulate me, Darcy. I am the new master of Netherfield Park."

"You did it!" Darcy's smile expanded as he shook Bingley's hand. "Then your man of business thought the estate a good investment?"

"Says it is in excellent shape. Only sat empty this last year. The owner has no remaining family, and the estate is not entailed, so he moved into smaller quarters in London. He is willing to sell me the house and land if I find it agreeable."

Darcy leaned in to say privately, "Meaning it brings you into closer proximity to the lovely Miss Bennet." Surprisingly, his friend blushed. "Perhaps we should take our conversation inside." To his butler he said, "Place Mr. Bingley's things in his usual room." He turned Bingley's steps toward the house. "I am excited to hear of the estate."

When they were settled in Darcy's study, he said, "I am all ears, Bingley."

His friend laughed, and the emotion was such a contrast to the mood Bingley had expressed upon his departure from Pemberley a fortnight past that Darcy could not help but to smile along with his friend. "I believe Mr. Connick and I tipped the express riders enough in the last week to pay their salary for the year." He laughed again. "The hardest part was keeping the negotiations from my sisters."

"I imagine it so," Darcy said in sympathy. "But you would not wish to raise Miss Bingley and Mrs. Hurst's hopes until you are certain the estate is in 'livable' condition."

Darcy knew Bingley's protest regarding his sisters' welfares was secondary to his friend's desire to reclaim Miss Bennet's attentions, but he kept his thoughts to himself, for his deep need to look again upon Elizabeth's countenance was equal to Bingley's wish to see Miss Bennet.

"As I indicated, Mr. Connick contacted Mr. Morris, the man overseeing the estate in the owner's absence. Connick traveled to Hertfordshire and viewed the manor house. He deemed it in fine repair. The property hosts several hundred acres, and, in truth, the idea of taking command of such an endeavor would frighten me if I did not claim your friendship, Darcy. I pray you still willing to travel to Hertfordshire with me."

"Most assuredly." Darcy again swallowed his desire to leave for Longbourn at once. "When do you plan to travel to Hertfordshire?"

"Mr. Morris has made arrangements for the servants to

open the house this week. I thought you and I could leave in two days, if that is acceptable to you. We could be in Hertfordshire in time for Sunday services. Do you not think it a capital idea to surprise Miss Bennet after church?"

Actually, Darcy had thought a social call upon the Bennet household more appropriate, but as long as Elizabeth was part of the Meryton congregation, he would be satisfied. "Needless to say, Miss Bennet will not expect you among the parishioners."

"Do you think it a poor idea?" Bingley asked in concern.

Darcy chose his words carefully. "Initially, I was thinking a social call best, but after closer consideration of your suggestion, the church service would better serve your purpose. If you simply take up residence at Netherfield Park, then you must wait for Mr. Bennet to call upon you first, before you could return the call. You might spend a week or more waiting for Mr. Bennet's call. The man has been in poor health of late. He may not be able to make an appearance, and then where would you be? Encountering Miss Bennet at church would eliminate the protocol of waiting for an invitation to Longbourn."

Bingley's features took a downward turn. "Do you think many of the neighborhood will call at Netherfield?"

"I imagine quite a few will want to greet the man who has assumed control of one of the larger estates in the area," Darcy explained. "Likely news will quickly spread of your wealth and more than one family will parade their unmarried daughters before you."

Panic crossed Bingley's countenance. "I never thought of others counting my fortune before my character. Somehow I thought country society was less demanding than the strictures one encounters in Town society."

Darcy chuckled. "Said the man who spends the majority of his days in London. Do you not recall the women at the various country parties we have attended? It will be the same in Hertfordshire unless early on you make it known that you intend to court Miss Bennet. You need to secure Mr. Bennet's permission within a few days of your arrival or prepare to be beset upon by country society. You should remember, my friend, all those ladies of the *ton* are country girls come up to Town."

Bingley laid his head back against the chair's cushion and closed his eyes. "If people are to call at Netherfield, I will require a hostess, and here I thought not to have Caroline's waspish tongue spewing warnings in my ear against my courtship with Miss Bennet."

Darcy kept his opinions to himself, other than to suggest, "The majority of those calling upon you will be the other land owners and a few men of esteem from the town. Your housekeeper could sit with you if ladies call. Mrs. Reynolds often acts in that capacity when Georgiana is still in Town."

Bingley's eyes sprang open, while hope crossed his expression. "Why do we not ask Miss Darcy to accompany us?"

Darcy argued, "My sister is just sixteen. When she joins me to greet my neighbors, it is because she knows them and they, her."

"But she would have Mrs. Annesley to assist her. It would provide Miss Darcy the opportunity to practice her skills as a hostess without any unreasonable expectations, and you will be there if the situation becomes too much for her. I imagine Miss Elizabeth would also sit with Miss Darcy upon occasion if we asked it of her."

Darcy would not mind having Elizabeth to himself alone at Netherfield, but he said, "My sister is excessively shy in such situations, but I will permit you to ask Georgiana to fill the role as hostess. It will be up to you to convince her. If I ask, she will agree to what I suggest simply to please me. And I insist that you express both the advantages of her spending time in Hertfordshire, along with what she should expect if she agrees to be pressed into your service."

"I promise simply to ask and not to plead for your sister's company," Bingley swore.

Soon after breakfast on Monday, Mr. Collins set about doing what he had come to Longbourn to do. Elizabeth should have noted the man's nervous preparations, but she still fretted over what she had disclosed to her father regarding Mr. Wickham and Mr. Darcy. Their conversation returned often to *when* and *how* Mr. Darcy had shared the information. She knew her father was still not convinced that Mr. Darcy had treated her kindly and respectfully, and that fact was upmost in her mind when Mr. Collins decided to act.

If only she had considered the fact that Mr. Collins's leave of absence from Kent must soon come to an end or the fact that the man would act without her father's permission, then she would have known to run to her room and bar the door until the "danger" passed.

Collins discovered her, Kitty, and Mrs. Bennet in the front parlor mending socks and unmentionables. A clearing of his throat was Elizabeth's first indication of his presence in the room, for she concentrated on her stitches and on her thoughts of Mr. Darcy. She was not a great sewer, and she knew Mrs. Bennet would make her tear out the ill stitches and begin again if the thread knotted. "May I hope, madam," he said, and Elizabeth flinched with the interruption, sticking her finger with the needle instead of the cloth, "for your interest with your fair daughter Elizabeth when I solicit for the honor of a private audience with her in the course of the morning?"

Before Elizabeth had time for anything beyond a blush of surprise and a sucking of the wounded finger, Mrs. Bennet instantly answered: "Oh, dear! Yes, certainly. I am certain Lizzy will be very happy — I am sure she can have no objections. Come, Kitty, I want you upstairs." And gathering her work together, she hastened away.

Elizabeth called after her, "Dear, ma'am, do not go. I beg you will not go. Mr. Collins must excuse me. He can have nothing to say to me that anybody need not hear. I am going away myself."

"No, no, nonsense, Lizzy! I desire you will stay where you are." And upon Elizabeth's seeming , with vexed and embarrassed looks, actually about to escape, she added, "Lizzy, I insist on your staying and hearing Mr. Collins!"

With a heavy sigh, Elizabeth thought it wisest to get it over as quickly and as quietly as possible, and so she sat down again and attempted to conceal both her distress and her diversion.

As Mr. Collins possessed no feelings of diffidence to make the situation discomforting for himself, he set about his proposal in a very orderly manner with all the observances which he supposed a regular part of the business. "Believe me, my dear Miss Elizabeth, that your modesty, so far from doing you any disservice, rather adds to your other perfections. You would have been less amiable in my eyes had there not been this little unwillingness; but allow me to assure you that I have your respected mother's permission for this address."

"But you do not have Mr. Bennet's permission," she countered.

As if she had not spoken, Mr. Collins continued, "Almost as soon as I entered the house, I singled you out as the companion of my future wife."

Elizabeth mumbled, "How so? When I was your second choice?" but when she looked to Mr. Collins, the man was gesturing like a great actor upon the stage. He had no idea she had even spoken.

"My reasons for marrying are, first, that I think it a right thing for every clergyman in my circumstances to set the example of matrimony in his parish; secondly, I am convinced that it will add greatly to my happiness to have a steady companion; and thirdly, which perhaps I ought to have mentioned earlier; that it is the particular advice and recommendation of the very noble lady whom I have the honor of calling patroness."

Elizabeth barked a nervous laugh. The absurdity of the idea that the woman who had threatened to have her arrested would welcome her at Hunsford could not be held inside. "I assure you, Mr. Collins, I could never please Lady Catherine De Bourgh. My temperament is not one easily subdued." Moreover, the idea of regularly viewing Mr. Darcy with his cousin was not something Elizabeth thought she could sensibly tolerate. "Therefore, accept my thanks for the compliment you are paying me. I am very aware of the honor of your proposals, but it is impossible for me to do otherwise than decline them."

"Utter nonsense," Mr. Collins replied with a formal wave of his hand. "I suppose I am now to learn that it is usual with young ladies to reject the addresses of the man whom they secretly mean to accept. I am therefore by no means discouraged by what you have just said, and I shall hope to lead you to the altar ere long. Also, as to your lack of fortune, as I explained to her ladyship, I am perfectly indifferent and shall make no demand of that nature on your father since I am well aware that it could not be complied with, and that one thousand pounds in the four percent, which will not be yours until after your mother's decease, is all to which you may ever be entitled. On that head, therefore, I shall be uniformly silent."

"Upon my word, sir," cried Elizabeth, "I am perfectly serious in my refusal. You could not make me happy, and I am convinced that I am the last woman in the world who would make you so. Nay, were your friend, Lady Catherine, to know me, I am perfectly persuaded she would find me in every respect ill-qualified for the situation."

"Were it certain that Lady Catherine would think so," said Mr. Collins very gravely, "it would be my duty to think otherwise, but I cannot imagine that her ladyship would at all disapprove of you. And you may be certain when I have the honor of seeing her again, I shall speak in the highest terms of your modesty, economy, and other amiable qualifications."

She knew without a doubt that Lady Catherine would never term Elizabeth as modest or amiable or without faults. Rather her ladyship would call her a *doxy* and other colorful and disparaging nouns and adjectives. "Indeed, Mr. Collins, all praise of me will be unnecessary. You must give me leave to judge for myself and pay me the compliment of believing what I say. I wish you very happy and very rich, and by refusing your hand, do all in my power to prevent you from being otherwise. In making me the offer, you must have satisfied the delicacy of your feelings with regard to my family and may take possession of Longbourn estate whenever it falls, without any self-reproach. This matter may be considered, therefore, as finally settled." She rose as she spoke.

When he continued to speak of her charms, Elizabeth withdrew in silence, determined that, if Mr. Collins persisted in considering her repeated refusals as flattering encouragement, to apply to her father, whose negative response might be uttered in such a manner as to make it decisive, and whose behavior, at least, could not be mistaken for the affectation and coquetry of an elegant female.

Chapter 22

THE DAYS FOLLOWING her refusal of Mr. Collins's proposal were miserable for Elizabeth, for Mrs. Bennet was slow to abandon the point. She talked to Elizabeth again and again, coaxed and threatened by turns. Her mother even endeavored to secure Jane in her interest, citing Jane's blame in the matter, but Jane with all possible mildness, declined interfering, and Elizabeth, sometimes with real earnestness and sometimes with playful gaiety, replied to Mrs. Bennet's attacks. Though Elizabeth's manner of response varied, her determination never did.

Mr. Collins's stiffness of manner and his resentful silence marked their lack of interactions until the day her friend Charlotte Lucas announced her engagement to Collins. It stunned Elizabeth to view Charlotte's agreement to such a marriage, but there was little she could do. That Charlotte could encourage Mr. Collins seemed almost as far from possible as that she could encourage him herself, but she had learned much about people and change since she had taken Mr. Darcy's acquaintance, and although her opinion of Mr. Collins never altered, she did consider Charlotte's desperation at finding a proper husband. Her friend was well on the shelf at seven and twenty years, and there were very few eligible young men in the neighborhood. Such was the reason Mrs. Bennet was willing to pledge one of her daughters to the man. In reality, Elizabeth's prospects were as few as Charlotte's, and mayhap in seven years she would make the same choice.

The news of Collins's engagement only exasperated Mrs. Bennet's lamentations, especially when Mr. Collins recounted what he knew would be Lady Catherine's hearty approval of his marriage to Charlotte. With interest, Elizabeth noted that Collins spoke as if his patroness remained from Rosings Park, and she wondered if Lady Catherine was still in London. Did the woman continue to search for her? Or had Mr. Darcy accepted his cousin once again and the family was planning for a new ceremony? When Collins announced his return to Kent, she privately celebrated his removal from Longbourn, but he followed that announcement with the news he would return at month's end to exchange his vows with Charlotte, and he would *again* be staying at Longbourn. Lydia's audible groan of disbelief mimicked Elizabeth's internal one.

The only thing that saved Elizabeth from banishment from the family was the news carried to Longbourn by one of their neighbors. As quickly as Mrs. Long departed Mrs. Bennet's sitting room, Elizabeth's mother rushed into the drawing room, where the family had gathered. "My dear Mr. Bennet, have you heard that Netherfield Park is let at last?"

"I have not your resources, my dear, for just such information," he replied without looking up from the newspaper he read.

"But it is," she insisted. "Mrs. Long has told me all about it. She says Netherfield has been taken by a young man of large fortune from the north of England. He has let the house for a mere three months, but he has accepted the option for longer if he approves of it, which we know he will, for it is one of the finest houses in the neighborhood. The servants are to open the house this week to air it out, and he should arrive within a fortnight. And, most fortuitous of all, he is single."

"And the gentleman's name?" her father inquired as he reluctantly set the newspaper aside.

"Mrs. Long was not certain. Barton. Butler. A name that begins with a *B*."

"Like *Bennet*?" her father asked with a lift of an eyebrow, and Elizabeth hid her smile of amusement.

"The man is not another Bennet," her mother protested. "I would remember such a coincidence. Moreover, what do I care of his name? He is said to possess four or five thousand per year. You must know that I am thinking of his marrying one of our girls."

"Is that his design in settling here?"

"Design? Nonsense. How can you talk so? But it is very likely that he may fall in love with one of them."

Elizabeth was but three miles removed. Darcy had specifically asked one of Bingley's new servants of Longbourn's directions. He was half-tempted to order his horse saddled so he could call upon her. If he were at Netherfield alone, he would storm Longbourn and demand that she accept him as her husband, but society's strictures kept him in his seat—for now.

"The house is quite comfortable," Mrs. Annesley remarked over supper. "You will do well here, Mr. Bingley."

Georgiana eyed Mr. Bingley in amused bewilderment. "I agree with Mrs. Annesley," she said in what sounded of innocence, but Darcy doubted her purpose. Elizabeth's effect on Georgiana remained. She grew more confident each day. "But I do not understand why you chose Hertfordshire for your new home. There were several fine houses available within thirty miles of Pemberley. I am certain my brother would have enjoyed having you as part of the neighborhood."

Bingley's eyebrow rose in consideration. "Darcy, I think I enjoyed your sister's company better before she took to teasing me shamelessly."

"I fear I must agree," Darcy said with a smile. "But what is

221

a man to do? The women in our lives set the tone of our days, and I, for one, would prefer to suffer a loving tease than a shrewish tongue any day."

"You make an excellent point, Darcy. Women are more adept at mastering the nature of things," Bingley stated.

"That is because they will take the time to tease out a man's secrets," Darcy declared.

Mrs. Annesley good-naturedly patted the back of Bingley's hand, but the lady spoke to his sister. "Mr. Bingley means to follow his dreams, Miss Darcy. Personally, I am delighted to see a man who is willing to admit he requires a special woman in his life."

Georgiana's features tightened. "And what of you, William? Do you someday soon mean to follow a dream?"

"No, my dear," Darcy said smartly. "When the time comes, I plan to lead my present life into my future."

Elizabeth glanced about the church yard. Clusters of people gathered upon the green. As quickly as her family departed their coach, Lydia and Kitty had darted off to join Maria Lucas and Miss Emily King. The young ladies conversed with several of the officers. The latest gossip was that the militia would withdraw to Brighton for several weeks of maneuvers in preparation for a longer stay in the port city next spring. The news of the officers' withdrawal had Lydia nearly in tears.

"Who is that?" Jane asked from beside her, and Elizabeth turned to view a beautifully polished black coach come to a halt beside a farm wagon.

Her heart lurched in anticipation. She would know that particular coach anywhere. She had ridden in it previously and had enjoyed the company of its owner. *He has come for you*, her heart announced, while her head reasoned that Mr. Darcy likely required her signature upon some sort of document before he could begin his new life with his cousin or a lady of the *ton*. His threat of "*If we are joined, I will be coming for you*," was simply that:

a threat. Words spoken in anger.

"Come, Jane." She reached for her sister's hand. "I think we have discovered the identity of our new Netherfield neighbor."

She realized everyone in the churchyard had turned toward the unknown carriage, but Elizabeth continued to pick her way along the graveled path with Jane in tow behind her. Without looking at him, she knew the second Mr. Darcy had stepped from the coach from the gasp escaping Jane's lips and her sister's stumbling steps. Elizabeth dropped Jane's hand and continued upon her way. She had to reach him before the others demanded to take his acquaintance. At length, she looked up, and Mr. Darcy turned to smile at her. Unfortunately, his smile had the habit of sending her heart beating at the pace of a thoroughbred horse in full gallop, and she paused to suck in a steadying breath.

In that moment, Miss Darcy appeared in the opening. "Miss Elizabeth," she called in joyful tones. "We have come for a visit."

While Mr. Darcy assisted his sister to the ground, Elizabeth discovered her courage. She rushed forward to greet the girl with a welcoming embrace. "Have you grown since I last saw you?" she teased as the girl beamed with pride. "You look exceptionally lovely today."

"It has only been a month, Lizzy," Miss Darcy said as she smiled widely.

"But it feels a year or more," Elizabeth was quick to say, as she caught the girl's hand and turned to the gentleman and his waiting coach mates. Nervously, she greeted the others first. "Good morning, Mr. Farrin. Jasper," she called to Mr. Darcy's servants.

"Morning, miss." The coachman acknowledged her with a tip of his hat.

She was uncertain her mouth could form the words to welcome Mr. Darcy. What if his purpose in Hertfordshire was a farewell? Elizabeth did not think she could bear his denial.

She glanced over her shoulder to where Jane remained upon the path to view the astonished delight upon her sister's face when Mr. Bingley climbed down from the coach. *Barton. Butler. Bingley,* she thought. *A name which starts with the letter 'B.'* "Mr. Bingley," Elizabeth murmured. "Mrs. Annesley." Bingley briefly acknowledged her before crossing to where Jane stood proudly waiting for him.

"Perhaps we should join Mr. Bingley," Mrs. Annesley suggested to Miss Darcy. "I should very much like to renew my acquaintance with Miss Bennet."

When they stepped away, Mr. Darcy asked, "No greeting for me, Miss Elizabeth?" A scowl marked his features.

"Why are you here?" she asked on a breathy exhale.

He studied her face for a brief moment before his shoulders visibly relaxed. "You know why I am here, Elizabeth."

Despite her best efforts, tears filled her eyes. "That is just it, Mr. Darcy. You see, I possess a very active imagination. I can think of a hundred reasons you would follow me to Hertfordshire, but I only require the truth. Please tell me your reasons,; therefore, I might know how to proceed."

He stepped before her to say softly, "I have arrived in Hertfordshire to court my wife."

The sound of those gathered behind her reminded Elizabeth that they were not alone. There was no time to discuss his meaning of "courtship" or the legality of their marriage. She noted her father and Sir William Lucas crossing the green and coming in their direction. "Mr. Darcy, you cannot stay!" she whispered in a panic.

He tilted his head to look hard upon her features. "Is not the church large enough to accommodate four more?"

She shot another quick glance to her father's steady gaze upon her and Mr. Darcy. Mr. Bennet did not look pleased by her approaching the gentleman. "Do not be obtuse!" she ordered. "You cannot remain in Meryton," she said on a rush, "because Mr. Wickham is here."

"What? Where? When did he arrive in Hertfordshire?" Mr. Darcy's gaze searched the crowd for Wickham's personage.

"I have not yet seen him this morning," she quickly

explained, "but Mr. Wickham is part of the Meryton militia. He has secured a lieutenancy. Miss Darcy cannot encounter him."

"My sister and I cannot simply leave," he insisted.

"But he has told everyone of the supposed injustices inflicted upon his person by you," she protested. "Moreover, Mr. Collins is staying with us at Longbourn. If he learns you are here, my father's cousin will inform Lady Catherine of your presence in Hertfordshire, and she will make the connection to your botched nuptials."

"Her ladyship already knows your name," he explained. "The Allards gladly provided the information. I suspect Josie was made to tell Lady Catherine's investigator your true name."

That was all they could share before her father said in disapproving tones, "Jane has made the introductions of the others. Mayhap you would care to introduce us to the man I assume is Miss Darcy's brother."

Their reuniting had not gone as Darcy imagined, but, at least, Elizabeth was before him, and he could look his fill. Needless to say, he would have preferred the dream where she rushed into his arms and kissed him with ardor.

A sharp elbow well-placed into his side shook Darcy from his fantasies. "I will thank you kindly to cease staring at my daughter as if she were the Holy Grail," Mr. Bennet hissed from his place along the pew beside Darcy. As Georgiana had insisted, after learning the news of Wickham's presence in Meryton, upon joining Elizabeth on the Bennet family pew, Mr. Bennet and Sir William had joined Darcy and Bingley in the pew belonging to the owner of Netherfield. Mrs. Annesley had graciously joined Lady Lucas at the suggestion of Sir William.

"Did you offer the same advice to Mr. Bingley?" Darcy whispered from his mouth's corner.

Bennet waited until Mr. Williamson's, the Meryton rector, voice rose again in volume before he spoke. "I recognize a lap dog when I see it. I also recognize a lion."

Darcy could not help but smile. Evidently, Elizabeth's father was the source of her sharp wit. "Mayhap I am watching over my sister. I am a very protective brother."

"I am no fool, Mr. Darcy," Bennet growled.

"I am glad to hear it," Darcy said in steely tones. "I generally excel with a challenge."

When the service ended, a woman identified previously as Mrs. Bennet elbowed her way through those gathered around Mr. Bingley. Darcy had purposely avoided too many introductions, permitting Bingley time to greet his new neighbors and to claim center stage. "Mr. Bingley," she said so emphatically that the woman beside her flinched. "I pray you and your party will join us for nuncheon at Longbourn. We Bennets are your nearest neighbors."

Bingley glanced to Darcy, who readily nodded his agreement. "As the staff at Netherfield is still learning its way about the house, I would appreciate the hospitality."

"Excellent!" she declared with a small hop of excitement. "We will expect you at one. The meal will be served at two."

"Mr. Darcy?" He turned to find Elizabeth beside him. "Although Mrs. Bennet suggested one of the clock for your arrival at Longbourn, by the time Mr. Bingley greets the community, it will be near that time. I must assist my mother; therefore, I have asked Miss Darcy to walk back to the estate with me. Mr. Bennet's coach could not hold eight. Jane, Mary and I walked to services this morning to leave room for the others. Your sister suggested that you may wish to join us. In that manner, Miss Bennet and my sister Mary can join Mr. Bingley and Mrs. Annesley in your coach, leaving only four for Mr. Bennet's carriage. I am a very good walker, and Miss Darcy claims to be one also. I know you to be hardy enough for the mile to Longbourn."

He bowed to them. "It would be my pleasure."

Darcy took a moment to whisper the arrangements in Bingley's ear before following Elizabeth to where her father stood watching them. When Elizabeth explained her need to speak to him and Georgiana alone, Mr. Bennet declared, "I do not like this sudden interruption in our day, Lizzy."

"Papa," she soothed. Darcy watched as Elizabeth reasoned with her father. "We knew we could not keep the rest of the world in ignorance of my daring. It cannot be long until Mr. Collins realizes Mr. Darcy's identity. He will report Mr. Darcy's presence in the neighborhood to Lady Catherine. It is imperative that Mr. Darcy and I discuss how best to proceed before Mr. Collins is made known of the facts. Your cousin dines with the Lucases this afternoon. Surely Sir William will have something to say of Mr. Bingley's and Mr. Darcy's sudden appearance at Netherfield."

Mr. Bennet glared at Darcy. "I do not welcome having someone force my hand."

"At least," Darcy said in uncompromising tones, "you can be assured a *lion* will do all within his power to protect his *pride*."

Chapter 23

"A LION, MR. Darcy?" Elizabeth asked as they turned their steps toward the road leading to Longbourn.

He chuckled as he assumed his place at her side. He thought to place her hand on his arm, but Elizabeth kept her hands clasped behind her as she strolled along, and so he accepted his role as her escort. "It is a better moniker than *the lap dog* your father determined Bingley to be."

Elizabeth smiled widely, and he enjoyed viewing the happy thoughts upon her face. "It is good to know Mr. Bennet's health has returned. There were many weeks when he made no witty comments." She squinted up at Darcy. "*A lap dog* would be considered a compliment to what my father calls Mr. Collins, when he thinks no one is listening. Mr. Bennet has been especially caustic in his interactions with his cousin since your aunt's rector proposed marriage to me."

Darcy stumbled to a halt. "He did what?"

"Proposed," Elizabeth said with a teasing lift of her brow. "You understand, do you not, Mr. Darcy. Proposals lead to nuptials which lead to 'I, William, take thee, Elizabeth.'" Her smile spread across her features when she noted his lack of humor. "As you pointed out to me, Mr. Collins Christian name is 'William.'"

Georgiana giggled, and both he and Elizabeth turned to stare at his sister as if they had forgotten she accompanied them. "Lady Catherine would have Miss Elizabeth arrested if Mr. Collins delivered Lizzy to Hunsford. It would not surprise me if that was not her purpose in permitting him to come to Hertfordshire."

Darcy warned, "You should not speak so disparagingly of our aunt."

"Should I lie?" his sister questioned.

Elizabeth caught Georgiana's hand. "I am honored that you meant to defend me with your speech, but I believe your brother does not wish you only to look at a person's negative qualities. Is that not correct, Mr. Darcy?"

"Elizabeth speaks sense," he said, but he made no further comment, for his mind could not release the idea of another man taking Elizabeth to his bed. The idea was intolerable to him!

"Moreover," Elizabeth said on a rush when Darcy remained silent, "I refused Mr. Collins, and he is now engaged to my friend, Charlotte Lucas. If her ladyship meant to employ Mr. Collins deviously, he would not have turned his attentions so readily from me to Miss Lucas. He has written to Lady Catherine to ask for her ladyship's approval, but to the best of my knowledge, your aunt is not in Kent."

Georgiana looked to him. "Do you think her ladyship learned something of Anne's presence in Scotland?"

Darcy's expression tightened. "I pray not, but it would take little effort for our aunt to discover that Anne and Lady Lindale traveled to the Fitzwilliam property in Scotland. A few coins to a servant would bring her the necessary information. Lady Catherine thought to bring a criminal conversation suit against you," he told Elizabeth. "But such would be Anne's dominion, not our aunt's, for my cousin is well past her majority. Mayhap her ladyship means to force Anne to pursue a breach of promise suit against me. Both would require Anne's cooperation."

"Crim...criminal conversation?" Elizabeth stammered. "That would mean she would charge that an affair occurred between us. A public accounting of our relationship would be spread in every newspaper in the land."

Darcy did not think a judge would accept such a case, for the evidence was too sparse, but he would not guarantee that his aunt was not vindictive enough to pursue a public chastisement for his stubbornness. "I will not permit her ladyship to torment you. If she persists, I will bring a breach of promise suit against Anne. She was the one who left me at the altar. I will claim a large portion of Anne's inheritance if that be the case."

Tears pooled in Elizabeth's eyes. "But your cousin is not at fault in this matter. I am. You may say you would have left the church before Miss De Bourgh appeared, but I know your nature, Mr. Darcy. You would have waited to learn of your cousin's fate. If you bring a breach of promise suit against Miss De Bourgh, she will be termed a *jilt*. Her reputation will be more problematic than mine. Surely there must be another means from this debacle."

"There is," he said. "Marry me again. If we marry quickly, Anne will not be marked by negative gossip—just a bit of sympathy."

She smiled weakly. "I have already married you twice, sir."

He winked at her. "And the second time stuck." Darcy watched as realization crawled across Elizabeth's features. "I could claim you as my wife and return you to Pemberley, and there would be nothing anyone could do. However, such was not my purpose in coming to Longbourn. It is my wish to court you properly, so we might have time to learn more of each other. You would also have time to come to accept our situation. Afterwards, we could marry again before your family and friends. You would like that, would you not, Elizabeth?"

"I would, sir. What a generous gesture," she said wistfully. "It would be wonderful to have others see me as valued."

He smiled upon the look of longing marking her features. "I mean to please you, Elizabeth."

"But if her ladyship has returned Miss De Bourgh to London, we do not have the luxury of a proper courtship," she reasoned.

"I could promise you a few weeks," Darcy suggested.

Georgiana cleared her throat, and again Darcy had forgotten about her listening to his conversation with Elizabeth. "I think I have a means to make the others think your courtship began weeks ago."

"It did," Elizabeth and Darcy said together.

"Exactly," Georgiana spoke in triumphant. "Could we not say that when Elizabeth visited with me that William found her beguiling and proposed to her, but you, Miss Elizabeth, did not accept Darcy because you worried for your father's recovery from lung fever. If Mr. Bennet had passed, you would have been obligated to be in mourning for a year, and you did not think it appropriate to make my brother wait. But now that Mr. Bennet claims health..."

Darcy scowled. "I am not certain I approve of how efficiently you devised that story."

"It is your fault," his sister countered. "You are the one who sent me to a girls' school. Nothing is more conniving than a gaggle of young girls trying to outsmart the headmistress."

He said sarcastically, "I am pleased my patronage proved beneficial to your education."

"Do not berate your sister," Elizabeth warned. "Miss Darcy has the right of the situation, but we must discuss our story with Mr. Bennet."

"I suspect I will require my dueling pistols when we meet with your father," he drawled in irony.

"I suspect you will," Elizabeth agreed.

While her father and Mr. Darcy examined several of Mr. Bennet's "first editions" in the library, Elizabeth made Georgiana known to her family.

"When did you meet Miss Darcy?" Kitty asked

suspiciously.

"Last spring when I stayed with Aunt and Uncle Gardiner," Elizabeth explained.

"In Green Park," Miss Darcy chimed in. "A man grabbed my reticule, but Miss Elizabeth noted his escape and tripped him up. My brother and my Cousin Colonel Fitzwilliam apprehended the man." Elizabeth was amazed by the girl's ability to weave a story. Perhaps Mr. Darcy was correct: They should beware of Miss Darcy's dramatics.

"Why did you not tell us of your heroics?" Kitty continued to eye Elizabeth in disbelief.

Elizabeth shrugged her indifference. "It was nothing. I simply stuck out my foot as the man raced past me. It was Mr. Darcy and the colonel who captured the thief. All I received was a severely bruised ankle."

"Needless to say, my brother wished to extend our family's appreciation, but Elizabeth, being Elizabeth, refused, but she did accept my offer of friendship. We have corresponded over the last year." Georgiana appeared happy with the attention of the room, while Elizabeth tried not to fidget. She expected that any second one of her family would break out in laughter, thinking she and Miss Darcy practiced an elaborate witticism. Elizabeth wondered what had happened to the shy girl she had met at Pemberley. Mayhap it was because Georgiana was among strangers. Just as Elizabeth had told the girl at Pemberley: It is always easier to perform before strangers than it is before those who hold expectations. "Until recently I was at school."

"I never noticed letters going out with Miss Darcy's directions upon them," Lydia declared.

"I did not know I required your permission to write to an acquaintance, Lydia." Elizabeth attempted to turn the conversation. "I met Miss Darcy on two other occasions when I was in London: once at a lending library and another in a tea room. Mr. Darcy escorted us each time." It would be necessary to establish a connection with the man prior to her being at Pemberley. "When our Scottish relations could not spare a coach to deliver me to Derbyshire to meet Jane, I contacted Miss Darcy. Her brother was good enough to send a coach for me. It was the same coach that returned us to Longbourn. Jane and I were fortunate to spend a few days at Pemberley before we returned to Hertfordshire. Is that not correct, Jane?"

Although Elizabeth had not discussed the story she repeated, she knew Jane would not betray her. Elizabeth was in this hot water because she had protected Jane. "It is a lovely estate, Miss Darcy. And the hospitality was impeccable."

Mr. Bingley added, "I was greatly pleased to take the acquaintance of both your daughters, Mrs. Bennet. Needless to say, it was serendipitous that Miss Elizabeth told Darcy something of Netherfield Park, for I have been considering the letting of an estate for some time. And I thought it necessary to find one close to London, for my business interests often demand my presence in the City. My sisters have insisted upon our claiming our part of society."

"You are very good to speak so kindly of both Jane and Elizabeth, Mr. Bingley. You do our family a great service with your words of appreciation. And taking Netherfield was an excellent idea, for the society in Hertfordshire is superb. It is close enough to London to make business convenient, and we dine regularly with one and twenty families."

Mr. Bingley smiled easily. "I am glad to hear it. Moreover, I will require no introduction, for I possess the acquaintance of your family to guide me."

"Most certainly," her mother declared with a smug glance to Jane.

Darcy thought Mr. Bennet would have an apoplexy when he showed the man the Scottish marriage certificate. "As you can observe, the certificate holds Miss Elizabeth's signature."

"Have you touched my daughter?" her father growled.

The question held the unspoken slap of a challenge. "I have not. I respect Miss Elizabeth too much to claim husbandly privileges she did not want."

"What if Elizabeth never accepts you as her husband?" Bennet argued.

"As there are no grounds for an annulment, we would have but one choice: We would be forced to pretend this document does not exist. We would go our separate ways," Darcy assured the man. "But if we choose to marry elsewhere, our marriages will be a sham and our children marked as bastards. All it would take would be one person to make our marriage known to others and we would be ruined. Although the wedding party at the inn were strangers before that night, they were not without connections to London society. The bride was the daughter of Sir James Metts and the groom a Greek diplomat to England. We would risk more scandal raining upon our heads."

Sarcasm overran Bennet's response. "You would prefer not to walk away from Longbourn without Elizabeth as your bride?"

Darcy found himself admitting, "I hold your daughter in tender regard, sir. I wish her to be my wife. I would count myself blessed to claim her."

Bennet closed his eyes and sighed heavily. "What do you propose?" he rasped through strong emotions.

Darcy smiled in genuine amusement: He had won. "I thought to court your daughter while I am at Netherfield."

"Court her?" Bennet questioned.

"Family is everything to Elizabeth. She would walk through the fires of Purgatory to save any one of you. Although we are legally married, and I could demand that she leave with me at once, I am intelligent enough to know our life will be better if this period of awkwardness is met on Elizabeth's terms. Her wish is to marry before her friends and family, and I mean to give her that memory and that respectability. Unfortunately, I must warn you that my aunt's continuing need for revenge may cause me to shorten our courtship, but I promise to mitigate the situation if it is in my powers. I simply require your permission to make Elizabeth happy."

"Do you wish to tell me what is going on between you and Miss Elizabeth?" Bingley asked when they returned to Netherfield. "I thought your suggestion of my letting Netherfield Park was for my benefit—to permit me to court Miss Bennet. Now I am not so certain I have not been played a fool."

Darcy had expected the conversation after Mr. Bennet made the announcement over the midday meal that he had granted Darcy permission to court Elizabeth. The shock on Bingley's features had warned Darcy of a difficult discussion.

"I did think that your letting Netherfield would bring you again into Miss Bennet's company," Darcy admitted. "I thought you required more than two days of acquaintance to determine if the lady is the 'angel' you declare her to be."

"Then do you not also require more than an acquaintance of a few days to decide whether to court Miss Elizabeth? I heard the tale your sister shared with the Bennets of her first taking Miss Elizabeth's acquaintance, and none of it makes sense. If you and Colonel Fitzwilliam caught a pickpocket in Green Park, I would know of it. Moreover, Miss Darcy left school more than a year ago. You had her with that lady's companion Mrs. Younge," Bingley charged. "Please tell me you have not compromised your sister's friend."

"I made a grave error in judging Mrs. Younge's character," Darcy said in distraction, "but that does not address your concerns." He paused to level a steady gaze upon his friend. "I require your complete circumspection regarding what I share, Bingley."

His friend's brow puckered in a frown, but he said, "Absolutely."

Darcy squared his shoulders. "Miss Elizabeth is the woman who interrupted my nuptials."

"What?" Bingley nearly came out of his chair. "When did you meet her? Have you held her in affection for a long time? Was she jealous? What was her motive? I would never suspect her to be so bold!"

"If she were not bold," Darcy said enigmatically, "your Miss Bennet would now be Mrs. Collins."

"I do not understand," Bingley admitted.

For the next several minutes, Darcy explained how Elizabeth meant to thwart her mother's plans, but had destroyed Lady Catherine's instead, how she was injured in her escape from the church, how he had placed her on his yacht so they might avoid the magistrate, how although he offered to send her to Hertfordshire, that she had remained with him in exchange for his agreement to protect her sisters, how Elizabeth's intuition had saved him a small fortune, and how he had escorted her to Derbyshire to reunite with Miss Bennet.

"You mean to save Miss Elizabeth's reputation by marrying her," Bingley summarized.

"I mean to marry the lady because I have fallen in love with her," Darcy corrected. "In truth, we are already married. During a wedding celebration held at a Scottish inn, Miss Elizabeth and I chose to marry. Unfortunately, we both had had too much to drink, and it took several sworn statements before Miss Elizabeth accepted the reality of our joining. But I fear our 'history' will color Elizabeth's personal image of her true worth. I do not wish her to think our joining is a matter of necessity. I choose to woo her properly to show her my affection, and mayhap earn a bit more of hers."

"My word! Not even Shakespeare could concoct this charade, but does not your aunt still disapprove of your refusal to marry Miss De Bourgh? As I assume you and Miss Elizabeth have not already consummated the marriage, will Lady Catherine press for an annulment?"

"An annulment cannot be achieved by a lack of consummation of the marriage," Darcy explained. "Only if it could be proved that one or both of us cannot perform our marital duties. As long as there is the potential of a future consummation, an annulment cannot be earned."

Darcy presented his friend a shrug of resignation. "There

is little either Lady Catherine or my cousin Anne can do beyond financial compensation, but my aunt's squawking could cloud Elizabeth's reputation. The problem will be how long I can publicly court Elizabeth before my aunt makes her next move. Needless to say, I can simply announce we married in Scotland and be done with it, but there remains a stigma in English society that follows those who escape to the Scottish shires, as if not marrying in the Church of England is a sin against God. And your previous assumption of Elizabeth's being compromised will be a common one. Although there is no possibility of 'an eight month baby' to blight her reputation further, gossips will speak of Elizabeth's connections to trade and how her father's circumstances are greatly below mine. I do not know how much of the gossip I can misdirect by professing my love for her before we marry again in her family church, but I mean to lessen any damage to her reputation. I wish those in society to accept Elizabeth, not only because she is Mrs. Darcy, but because they find her as fascinating as do I."

"Mr. Bennet, I must object to your daughter Elizabeth's acceptance of Mr. Darcy's attentions." Mr. Collins had returned to Longbourn for the evening meal, and as Elizabeth had predicted, Sir William had informed Mr. Collins of the identity of the strangers at this morning's services. The rector had thought to greet the nephew and niece of his patroness properly upon his return to Longbourn, but her father's cousin was barely through the door when Mrs. Bennet had told him of Elizabeth's impending engagement. In truth, Elizabeth could not find fault with her mother's desire to permit Mr. Collins to know that her second daughter had earned the respect of a man greater than he, but Elizabeth wished not to have the man spoil their supper with his ranting.

"I am to dissuade my daughter from accepting a man said to be worth ten thousand a year?" her father said in acerbic tones. "I think not, Cousin." Elizabeth knew it had cost her father greatly to accept Mr. Darcy's suggestion, and she was honored by both men's desire to protect her.

"But the gentleman cannot marry my fair cousin, for Mr. Darcy is engaged to marry the daughter of my esteemed patroness, Lady Catherine De Bourgh," Collins protested.

"You are still angry because Lizzy refused you," Lydia taunted. "Although I cannot see the man's attraction, for in my opinion, Mr. Darcy cannot hold a light to the likes of Captain Denny or to Mr. Wickham, but if my sister will be a rich, fine lady, who am I to complain?"

"Mayhap Lizzy will be able to introduce each of you to fine gentlemen who seek a wife," Mrs. Bennet mused aloud.

Mr. Bennet silenced both his wife and youngest daughter with a purposeful gaze of warning. "Mr. Collins, you are not yet master of Longbourn, and my daughters' futures still remain in my hands. As I am not prepared to place my spoon in the wall for many years, I will make the decisions in this household. You have no say in this matter."

"You leave me no other recourse!" Collins said as he rose, tossing his serviette upon the table. "I shall report this travesty to Lady Catherine, and she will demand that Mr. Darcy withdraw the offer of his hand."

Her father smiled sadly upon Elizabeth, but it was not a look of anger, but more one of longing. "I fear," he said in crisp tones, "Lady Catherine De Bourgh has no control over Mr. Darcy's heart. From what I hear, it was the great lady's daughter who brought an end to the gentleman's engagement to Miss De Bourgh by not making an appearance at their wedding. Thus, Mr. Darcy is permitted to give his heart to our Lizzy. Her ladyship cannot command the gentleman to change his mind. What God has joined together, let no man, or woman, for that matter, put asunder."

Chapter 24

JANE TAPPED ON Elizabeth's door late in the evening. "May we speak privately?"

Elizabeth set aside the documents Mr. Darcy had provided her father regarding their Scottish wedding. She had read the various accounts of how they had come to be married. Elizabeth found it odd that they matched the fragments of memories she had of that night. How when another couple among the wedding party had declared their desire to marry, and how Mr. Darcy had again suggested that they might be joined, and how she had permitted her good sense to take a rear-facing seat to her heart. Even though it lacked her customarily smooth stroke of the pen, she could not deny that it was her signature on the paper. "Certainly."

Jane shut the door behind her, but her sister did not cross to the chairs or even to the bed to sit. "I do not wish you to marry Mr. Darcy," Jane announced without preamble. "You did enough in protecting me from a marriage to Mr. Collins, and after taking our cousin's acquaintance, I am doubly thankful, but you should marry a man you affect, Lizzy. I will not permit you to sacrifice yourself for this family's reputation. I will speak to our father regarding his permission."

Elizabeth marveled at her sister's unaccustomed daring. Jane was the most gentle in nature of all the Bennet sisters, and Elizabeth suspected her sister had rehearsed her speech before calling at Elizabeth's quarters. "So you think living at Pemberley would be a sacrifice?"

"You know my intention, Lizzy," Jane said in irritation.

"Then you mean living with a man who has treated me with nothing but kindness is too much to ask of me? A man whose relations include those of an earldom? Or perhaps it would be a sacrifice to have my children inherit all that the Darcys' noble name provides?"

"But you do not love him!" Jane argued.

"How do you know my feelings?" Elizabeth countered. "You know how I came to be in Mr. Darcy's debt, but you know nothing of how I sought his comfort and reassurance when I discovered that Mr. Bradburn had used a whip on Josie Hill. Or how much I admire Mr. Darcy's intelligence and his willingness to hear my opinions and put my suggestions into action at Pemberley. All you know is that I stumbled upon Mr. Darcy's wedding and made a shamble of it. Although you have never spoken the words, you suspect Mr. Darcy has abused the trust I place in him. But I swear, Jane, you are mistaken. Mr. Darcy and I began as foes and became friends. We were in each other's company for hours upon end, and we were forced to learn the best and the worst of each other. I would say that most couples of the gentry rarely are as well acquainted as we two, for their interactions are set within the parameters of what society demands. Although our acquaintance is of short duration, I suspect we are more aware of each other's foibles than are those who courted for a year or more. You hold no knowledge of how much I miss his sharp wit and astute opinions when we are apart for mere hours, rather than days and weeks. And you know nothing of how much I miss his smile, for it is not freely displayed for all the world to see, but saved for those special moments he shares with those he affects. Some believe love is a spark that explodes into fireworks of desire, but I am of the persuasion that love is a gentle nudge that leads a person down a path he did not know was there until he looked upon his beloved's countenance."

"You are declaring your love for the man?" Jane questioned.

"I do not know the measure of love or what defines it," Elizabeth replied, relief marking her features, "but I believe that if it is not love that fills my heart, it soon will be. In Mr. Darcy's eyes I view genuine sincerity. I believe he is as wounded as I, keeping people at arm's length, fearing betrayal, but we have learned to trust each other. Despite those who would keep us apart, we have reached out to each other to wipe away the disillusionment — to lessen the wariness. We each could remain in this world where we build walls to keep others out, or we can abandon our safe harbors and set to sea together. Despite its uncertainty of the occasional storm, I choose the second option."

Her talk with Jane had done more than to allay her sister's concerns: it had permitted Elizabeth to accept the idea of being married to Mr. Darcy. She rested her hand upon his arm as they walked toward Oakham Mount. Mr. Bingley and Jane had joined them, while Georgiana had remained behind at Longbourn. Miss Darcy and Mary had agreed to practice a duet that they could share upon the pianoforte to entertain them upon their return.

"Mr. Collins departed Longbourn early this morning," Elizabeth shared. "My father's cousin was most adamant that the relationship between you and me could not exist."

Mr. Darcy pretended to consider the severity of the situation. "Upon my word, what should we do? We do require Mr. Collins's approval, do we not?" One corner of his mouth turned up in irony.

"Be serious, Mr. Darcy," she warned.

"I will be serious when you call me by my Christian name. Like it or not, you are my wife, Elizabeth."

She said softly, almost shyly, "Who said I object." Odd as it may seem to others, Elizabeth could not withhold her smile when she looked upon the change in the gentleman's features.

He brought them to a halt, and the gaze he presented her was perfectly wicked. "I pray you speak the truth, Elizabeth."

"We cannot undo what God and man deemed legal, and it is my opinion, that we will do well together."

"We argue," he pointedly said.

She shrugged in resignation. "But we do so in a reasonable manner."

"That we do." He set their steps in motion again. "I suppose your purpose in mentioning Mr. Collins is that my aunt's rector means to report our courtship to Lady Catherine."

"He does," she said honestly.

"And you assume that Mr. Collins's actions will change our plans to marry before your family," he summarized.

"Your promise of weeks must surely be changed to days," she reasoned.

His free hand engulfed hers where it rested upon his arm. His warmth invaded the cotton gloves she wore and slipped up her arm. Something she could not define leapt between them as if an exceptionally strong string tied them together in a manner she had never expected. Awareness stabbed her. Without his saying so, Elizabeth knew that Mr. Darcy would do all within his power to protect her. It had been too long since she thought to depend anyone but herself, and the idea pleased her immensely.

"What do you suggest we do?" he asked in husky tones. It was good to view her emotions reflected upon the gentleman's countenance.

They had stopped walking again, and as she gazed upon his now familiar face, the silver of his eyes appeared to be liquid heat. A simmering gaze. *Desire*, she thought. *The lion*. The idea stunned Elizabeth. She had experienced several flirtations over the years, but no one had ever looked upon her thusly — no one had ever courted her. She studied his countenance. He discomfited her completely, but Elizabeth knew true satisfaction, for Mr. Darcy, *her husband*, appeared as shocked by this new revelation as she.

"Who is to say a man cannot court his wife?" she stated primly.

"Indeed!" he chuckled easily. "I will 'court' you for the remainder of our days together. I do not expect a dull day ever again, my dearest Elizabeth, and I will go to my grave praising your excellence." They walked on in silence for several minutes, each considering their future together.

"I shall endeavor to make you a good wife, William." Everything in her seemed to melt when she permitted herself the familiarity of his Christian name. Her whole life changed in a blink of her eyes.

As was typical with Mr. Darcy, he took what they had decided and planned how to proceed. "Later today, I will call upon Mr. Williamson and secure an ordinary license as well as to name a day this week when we can pronounce our vows."

Elizabeth exhaled a breathy giggle of anticipation. "Mrs. Bennet's nerves may never recover."

His smile faded. "I doubt Mr. Bennet will be joyous with our news. And to think only yesterday I promised him a long courtship."

They had both been correct. The announcement's effect upon her mother had been most extraordinary; for, on first hearing it, Mrs. Bennet sat quite still and unable to utter a syllable. Nor was it under many, many minutes that she could comprehend what she had heard, though not, in general, backward to credit what was for the advantage to her family or that it came in the shape of a lover to any of them. She began, at length, to recover, to fidget about in her chair, get up, sit down again, wonder, and bless herself.

"Good gracious! Lord bless me! I do not know how you managed it! How you convinced Mr. Darcy to marry you so quickly! I pray you have not sacrificed your virtue to him! Such a great man! And who could blame you if you had! But you've always been the smart one! Imagine stopping a thief and winning a husband! Only think upon it! Dear me! Mr. Darcy! And to think you spoke not a word of his first proposal and your refusal. Who would have thought that a man of Mr. Darcy's consequence would take a liking to your sharp tongue. Can it really be true? Oh, my sweetest Lizzy! How rich and how great you will be! What pin-money, what jewels, what carriages you will have! I am so pleased—so happy! Such a charming man! So handsome! So tall! And just think! Your connection can lead his friend to Jane! Oh Lord! What will become of me! I shall go distracted!"

That had been several hours prior, and now a glance to where her mother held court in Lady Lucas's drawing room meant soon the entire neighborhood would know that Elizabeth had won the heart of a man with a substantial fortune.

Her father, on the other hand, scowled at each of Mrs. Bennet's twittering giggles of excitement. To say he was less than *joyous* with her and Mr. Darcy's decision would be an understatement. He had demanded to speak to Elizabeth privately after hearing Mr. Darcy's explanation. "Lizzy, there must be another means from this situation. I think it admirable that Mr. Darcy wishes to demonstrate to your family and friends that he freely chooses you and there is no stain upon your reputation, but your relationship with the man has spelled nothing but disaster. Woe is the day that my Brother Gardiner left you at Darcy House."

"Odd that, sir," she retorted. "Although I wish our first meeting did not bring grief to others, I count taking Mr. Darcy's acquaintance a godsend. How could I ever find another who would offer me such respect and such caring devotion? I have given Mr. Darcy my heart, Papa. Please do not make this difficult. Permit Mrs. Bennet and the others to think ours is a speedy courtship for all the right reasons. Such is not a lie. We have known each other but six weeks; yet, my heart has known his forever."

Elizabeth looked up from her musings at the sound of bodies shifting to make room for others in the room, hoping to view Mr. Darcy's entrance at the gathering. Instead, Mr. Wickham strolled in, his confident smile never leaving his lips, but she noted how his eyes scanned the room looking for someone in particular. She had no doubt that one of his fellow officers had informed him of Mr. Darcy's presence in Hertfordshire, as well as of her betrothal.

Fortunately, her two younger sisters had waylaid Lieutenant Wickham and Captain Denny before the officers made their way across the room. Elizabeth anxiously glanced to the door again. In many ways, she wished Mr. Darcy and his sister would shun this evening's entertainment, but she knew the gentleman would not abandon her when all within a ten-mile radius of Longbourn must now be acquainted with her engagement announcement.

Earlier in the day, she and Mr. Darcy had taken his sister aside not only to explain the change in their plans, but also to speak to Georgiana of Mr. Wickham and the possibility of crossing his path while in Meryton. "You must understand that Mr. Wickham will likely insult you or will say something misleading that will tarnish your reputation," Elizabeth warned.

"William has said that my being here for a few days will help thwart Mr. Wickham's lies," Miss Darcy countered.

Elizabeth nodded her head in the affirmative. "Yet, just as many will believe that I married your brother because I am ruined, some will still choose to believe the gentleman's lies. I do not wish to alarm you, but you must be prepared for some whispers and rumors."

Miss Darcy glanced to her and Mr. Darcy. "As long as you are near, I will draw my strength from your love."

"As you wish then," she said. Elizabeth was less certain of the girl's performance than was her brother. "Just remember that Mr. Wickham claimed you to be excessively proud," Elizabeth explained. "All you must do to prove him in error is to be yourself. Be welcoming and helpful."

"Mary," Elizabeth whispered when there was a break in the conversation swirling about her, "might I implore you to greet Mr. Darcy and Miss Darcy in the front foyer and warn my betrothed of Mr. Wickham's presence in Lady Lucas's drawing room?" Miss Darcy and Mary had formed a quick friendship over a love of music and playing the pianoforte. "Miss Darcy will require your closeness."

"I do not understand," Mary said in hushed tones, "but I will do as you ask, for I would not wish Georgiana to know distress of any kind." Mary made her excuses and slipped from the room. Meanwhile, Elizabeth prepared for Mr. Wickham's approach. She noted how he freed himself from Lydia's hands upon his arm, how he bent to whisper something in Lydia's ear that made her sister blush, and how he set his steps in her direction. Within seconds, he stood before her. "Miss Elizabeth," he said in tones she could imagine employed by the serpent in the Garden of Eden, "I am to understand that I must wish you happy with your recent betrothal."

She noted her father had placed himself in a position to overhear her conversation and to intervene, if necessary. She had not seen Mr. Wickham since the day Mr. Bennet had quietly instructed Mr. and Mrs. Hill to refuse the calls of all the officers except Colonel Forster.

"Thank you, Mr. Wickham," Elizabeth said, attempting to sound ignorant of the man's intent. "I am quite satisfied with the arrangement."

"I can imagine," he said. "Darcy's pockets are deep. As I said previously, most women can overlook Darcy's faults because of his family's consequence, but I did not expect you to be counted among them."

"Mayhap it is not Mr. Darcy's fortune that attracts me," she countered.

"His pride, perhaps?" Mr. Wickham challenged. "I thought you disdained Mr. Darcy's pride."

"You are in error, sir," she said with a lift of her chin. "It was you who termed the gentleman prideful. Not I."

Although he reined it in quickly, it was satisfying to note the slight break in Mr. Wickham's composure. "You led me to believe you were unfamiliar with Darcy and Pemberley."

Elizabeth shrugged in what she hoped appeared to be nonchalance. "I admit I did not mention that Miss Bennet and I spent two days at Pemberley while arrangements were made for our return to Longbourn. Although Mr. Darcy extended a kindness by providing us transportation, my father was still ill and knew nothing of the arrangements. My Uncle Gardiner knew of Mr. Darcy's assistance, but he cautioned that we should not openly speak of it, for others might view our actions as unseemly. Beyond my father, nothing was said within my family. Surely, I could not confide the details of my travels to a stranger. As to when we spoke of Pemberley, we were of an acquaintance of only a little over four and twenty hours. Therefore, I chose not to disclose the arrangement between my family and Mr. Darcy."

Mr. Wickham waved off her explanation. "But you said you wished no connection to Darcy, and now I discover you are engaged to the man."

Elizabeth's ire simmered below the surface, but she hid much of her contempt. "I have admitted that I was not forthcoming on our first acquaintance, but I object to your accusations of my misleading you. If you would concentrate your recall upon our conversation, I never spoke against Mr. Darcy. I said I would not wish the acquaintance of the man you described. And that is certainly the truth: I would not seek out such a man."

"I am pleased you found me more agreeable than Mr. Wickham's tales would lead you to believe," Mr. Darcy said as he stepped from behind Wickham to capture Elizabeth's hand and to plant a kiss upon her knuckles to demonstrate his possessiveness. There was no other explanation for it, for Elizabeth knew that an English gentlemen might offer an kiss of the air above the hand of royalty, but few actually kissed a lady's glove; yet, she found that she enjoyed Mr. Darcy's hot breath seeping through her evening gloves. It did odd things to her heart. "I apologize for being tardy, love."

"You were sorely missed, sir," Elizabeth cooed with a teasing lift of her lips. "But I forgive you, for I much prefer the sharp criticism of a single intelligent man to the thoughtless approval of the masses."

Mr. Darcy's eyebrow rose in what she assumed was inspiration. "Johannes Kepler. I did not know you had read Kepler."

She stroked his cheek with the tip of her finger in what could only be called a flirtation. "Several times. We shall debate the man's laws of planetary motion upon another evening, William."

"As you wish, love," he whispered before turning to face Wickham. "You should know, Mr. Wickham, that Miss Elizabeth is brutally honest. Deception is not part of my lady's repertoire."

"But you think it part of mine," Wickham accused.

Elizabeth heard Mr. Darcy's jaw tighten, but his expression did not change. "I think you are a man who chooses to abuse his friends." He tucked her closer to his side. "Did I explain, Elizabeth, that Mr. Wickham's tale of my refusing him the living at Kympton is true to an extent? I refused his second request for the living. Mr. Wickham refused the living the first time we met on the matter and demanded three thousand pounds in compensation for the tenets of my father's will, which I granted. It was only after he had wasted his inheritance that I refused his second request that I grant him the living." She noticed that many others in the room had ceased their conversations to listen in on Mr. Darcy's explanations.

"And as to my father loving Mr. Wickham best, jealousy, on my part, does not exist. My fault lies in the fact that I hid many of Mr. Wickham's sins from my father, who held an obligation to the late Mr. Wickham and who attempted to treat his godson kindly. I did not have it in me to tell my father what I had observed of Mr. Wickham's dissipation over the years. I could not bear to view the disappointment on my revered father's countenance, especially after his health began to decline. I permitted George Darcy to pass to his glory in ignorance of his godson's true nature."

"We should depart," Captain Denny cautioned from beside Mr. Wickham.

The lieutenant shot a deathly glare in Mr. Darcy's direction, but he said, "As you wish, Denny."

Elizabeth watched as Mr. Wickham turned on his heels to depart, but he paused when he saw Georgiana behind him. Thankfully, Mary had interlaced her arm through Miss Darcy's to offer her support. "Georgiana," Mr. Wickham inclined his head in Miss Darcy's direction. "How very good to encounter you again. I believe we last saw each other at Ramsgate."

Before Mr. Darcy could catch the scoundrel up and thump him soundly, Elizabeth stepped past Wickham to stand between the lieutenant and Miss Darcy. "Ramsgate?" she declared in wonder while addressing Miss Darcy. "We were just speaking of the resort the other day, were we not, Mary, and, you naughty girl, mentioned nothing of visiting the area. When were you at Ramsgate, Miss Darcy?"

"Some three months past," Mr. Wickham said with a smirk.

Elizabeth turned a look of puzzlement upon him. She noted how Mr. Darcy had come to stand off Wickham's shoulder and how the gentleman's hands clenched and unclenched at his side. "Three months?" Elizabeth asked in questioning tones. "Are you certain?" She turned to Georgiana and willed the girl to follow her lead. "Was that before or after you stayed with me at my Uncle Gardiner's home in Cheapside?"

"Cheapside?" Wickham snorted. "Darcy would never permit his sister to stay in Cheapside. I doubt he has ever crossed into Cheapside even when he leaves London by carriage."

"As is the way with you, Mr. Wickham, *you assume to know me, but you do not.* Georgiana was without a lady's companion after I dispensed with Mrs. Younge's services, but I was required elsewhere for business. Naturally, I accepted Miss Elizabeth's offer for Miss Darcy to reside with her at the Gardiners' Town house. My dearest Elizabeth resolved both my and Miss Darcy's dilemmas. And as to Miss Darcy's being in Ramsgate, I can attest that such is impossible, for my sister was under the protection of the Gardiners at the time. Mayhap you encountered another young woman that you thought to be Miss Darcy. After all, it has been many years since you were in her presence. She was not much more than an infant when my family sent the two of us off to school. I was in my second year at Eton when my mother passed. You were rarely at Pemberley after that. As the Gardiners are Miss Elizabeth's relations, they have showed my sister the same tender care as they do their nieces. And you must know that I will permit only those who will protect Miss Darcy to claim my sister's attentions."

Chapter 25

ELIZABETH HAD THOUGHT the whispers following Mr. Wickham's exit the worst she and Mr. Darcy would endure, but Fate, it seemed, meant to test their resolve. "Miss Elizabeth," Mrs. Hill said anxiously. "Your mother desires that you join her in the drawing room."

"What is amiss now?" Elizabeth said as she released the laces on her half boots. "I meant to try on my dress for the wedding."

"I be sorry, miss, but Mrs. Bennet was most insistent. Lady Catherine De Bourgh has called."

Elizabeth's heart stuttered to a halt. A cascade of opposing emotions washed over her and caught her breath, ripping it from her chest. Guilt. Shame. Longing for what might have been. Lost hope.

"Miss Elizabeth, are you unwell?" Mrs. Hill asked in concern.

Elizabeth moistened her excessively dry lips. She reached for the boot to lace it again. "Mrs. Hill, please inform my father of Lady Catherine's arrival and ask him to send one of the grooms to Netherfield to inform Mr. Darcy of his aunt's presence at

Longbourn."

"Yes, miss."

Elizabeth pressed the wrinkles from her dress as she crossed the room. "Hurry, Mrs. Hill," she instructed. "I require Mr. Darcy here posthaste."

Scurrying down the steps, she anxiously entered the room only to hear her ladyship say, "This must be a most inconvenient room for the evening in summer; the windows are full west."

Her mother appeared relieved when she noted Elizabeth's entrance. "Here is our Lizzy. See, Elizabeth. Lady Catherine has come to bestow her blessings upon you and Mr. Darcy."

Elizabeth straightened her shoulders as Lady Catherine glared at her. Darcy's aunt studied Elizabeth from head to toe, and she knew the grand lady found nothing of merit in Elizabeth's appearance. "That is excessively kind of her ladyship. May I ring for tea, Lady Catherine?"

"Your mother has offered refreshments." Lady Catherine, very resolutely and not very politely, declined eating anything. "I thought perhaps we might have a private talk, Miss Elizabeth. Mayhap the little wilderness I noted on one side of your lawn will serve us well. I should be glad to take a turn in it, if you will favor me with your company." Lady Catherine rose to place an end to the conversation with Mrs. Bennet.

"Go, my dear," cried her mother, "and show her ladyship about the different walks. I think she will be pleased with the hermitage."

Elizabeth glanced to Mr. Darcy's aunt. "I should fetch my parasol. The sun is full on." She would not provide the woman an opportunity to criticize Elizabeth's lack of sense by walking out without a bonnet or something to shade her complexion from the sun. "I shan't be more than a minute, your ladyship." She scampered away before Lady Catherine could object.

She was more than a minute, but not so many minutes as to irritate Lady Catherine further, just enough time to gulp several steadying breaths before her return. When she descended the stairs for a second time within ten minutes, she discovered

Mr. Darcy's aunt examining the dining-parlor, but Elizabeth ignored the woman's affront. Instead, she said, "This way, your ladyship."

Outside, a waiting woman sat stiff-backed in her ladyship's coach, and Elizabeth pitied the woman who must suffer not only the heat, but also Lady Catherine's insolence and her disagreeable nature. As they entered the copse, Lady Catherine began in the following manner:

"You can be at no loss, Miss Bennet, to understand the reason of my journey hither."

"I suppose I do," Elizabeth said in what she hoped were calm tones.

"You are about to discover that I am not to be trifled with. My character has ever been celebrated for its sincerity and frankness; and in such a moment as this, I shall certainly not depart from it. Your cheekiness is beyond belief. Not only did you waltz into my daughter's nuptials and destroy her exchange of vows with my nephew, but now you think to marry my sister's only son—my own nephew, Mr. Darcy. This is not to be borne!"

"Mr. Darcy!" He turned at the sound of his name. After the incident the previous evening with Mr. Wickham, Darcy possessed too much anger to sit around making polite conversation with his sister and her companion, and so he begged to be excused to ride out. Cerberus appeared equally distraught by being cooped up in the stables, and so he had ridden the animal hard, unconsciously charging the rise that overlooked Longbourn, where he had reined in the animal. He enjoyed the idea that somewhere within the house below, Elizabeth was making her way through her day, and that he would be with her before long. He pointedly frowned when he heard the youth call his name, for he disliked being distracted from one of the few things that brought him pleasure. Even so, he kicked Cerberus's sides to ride in the direction of a young groom sitting astride a farm horse without a saddle.

"What ho!" he called when he reached the boy.

"Mornin', sir." The boy tugged upon his forelock. "I've a message from Mr. Bennet."

Darcy's brow puckered in disappointment. "Mr. Bennet?" He had hoped whatever the note said it would be from Elizabeth.

"Yes, sir." The youth fetched a piece of paper from inside his shirt and handed it to Darcy.

Darcy unfolded the single sheet to read: *Lady Catherine is at Longbourn. Elizabeth requires your assistance.*

Darcy did not pause to thank the boy or even to toss him a coin for his troubles. "Good God!" he groaned as he sent Cerberus into a full gallop.

"What would you have me do, Lady Catherine?" Elizabeth replied testily. "I cannot undo what has been done. Perhaps if you had been less intent upon having me arrested, we could have resolved this issue by now."

"So what occurred at St. George was my fault? You shoulder no blame in this matter?"

Elizabeth protested, "The fault of what occurred can be placed at the feet of many, but I am the culprit who interrupted your daughter's vows, or should I say, lack of vows, for Miss De Bourgh was not present at her own wedding. I did not act from purposeful malice, but I am grieved by the anguish my actions caused your daughter. If I could correct my mistake I would do so."

"But you can correct your mistake, Miss Bennet," Lady Catherine replied. "You can tell my nephew that you will not have him. Explain to Darcy that you employed your arts and allurements to make him forget what he owes to himself and all his family."

"I beg your pardon, your ladyship, but how do I confess to feminine wiles I do not possess?" Elizabeth reasoned, "In fact, if I did practice such manipulations, Mr. Darcy would never have looked at me twice. Your nephew has had his fill of ladies of the *ton.*"

"You think you know Darcy better than his dear family!" her ladyship hissed. "But you are nothing more than an obstinate, headstrong girl."

"I know that Mr. Darcy desires a woman who will stand beside him while he fights for Pemberley's future. He requires no china figure upon the shelf that he must coddle."

Lady Catherine turned a sharp gaze upon Elizabeth. "Miss Bennet, do you know who I am? I have not been accustomed to such conniving behavior as this. I am almost the nearest relation that Darcy has in the world. I am entitled to know all his dearest concerns, especially as they apply to my daughter."

"But you are not entitled to know mine, nor will such behavior as this ever induce me to be explicit," Elizabeth declared in prickly defiance.

"Let me be rightly understood, Miss Bennet. This match, to which you have the presumption to aspire, can never take place—no never. Darcy is engaged to my daughter, and I mean to see a wedding between them. Now what have you to say?"

"Only this—that if he is so, you can have no reason to suppose he will claim me to wife," Elizabeth countered.

Darcy reined in his horse before Longbourn, slid to the ground, and started for the door, but halted when he heard a familiar voice say, "Your Miss Elizabeth is not inside, Cousin."

He turned to his aunt's waiting coach. "Anne! Where is she?" He wondered if Lady Catherine had arrived with a magistrate, and Elizabeth was, even now, being transported to London. If so, he would strangle his aunt and enjoy each second of her suffering.

"She and my mother walked off in the direction of the hermitage. Your lady is quite fetching, Darcy," she said softly.

"I am sorry, Anne," he said in true devotion to his cousin, but Darcy was not sorry to have taken Elizabeth Bennet's acquaintance. Despite all they had been through, he looked forward to spending the remainder of his days with her.

"As am I," Anne added. "I should never have permitted my mother to press for our alliance, but I did not know how to avoid the future she set for me."

This was the most coherent conversation that he and Anne had shared in years.

Darcy glanced toward the enclosed garden. "Then come with me," he suggested. "Assist me in convincing Lady Catherine that to persist in her way of thinking is madness."

Anne shook her head in denial. "I persuaded her ladyship that I would not tolerate her bringing charges against your Miss Bennet. I doubt she will accept more of my protests at this time."

"Anne," he said softly, "if you require my assistance in claiming your inheritance, you need only to send a note around. I am forever your dutiful cousin."

Anne smiled kindly upon him. "Will you marry Miss Elizabeth, Darcy?"

He squeezed the back of Anne's hand where it rested upon the coach's lowered window. "I have already made Miss Elizabeth my wife. Her ladyship's protests will not change my future."

"Then you should hurry after your wife. I do not image that my mother will treat her with respect."

Darcy nodded his departure and set off with long strides in the direction of an arched arbor, only to find Mr. Bennet on the other side of an oak tree. "I see Tobie found you," Bennet whispered.

"Why do you wait her?" Darcy demanded.

"If Lizzy required my assistance, I would have stepped in, but my daughter is quite adept at foiling the best laid plans."

"She is bloody magnificent," Darcy declared. "But..."

Mr. Bennet's heavy sigh cut off Darcy's objection. "You will likely require this to convince your aunt that her protests are futile." He handed Darcy the rolled certificate. "If her ladyship complains, tell her she has my sympathies, for I am equally as unhappy to lose Elizabeth to you as she is to lose you to my daughter. You are claiming the best of the Bennet family, and

I warn you that if Elizabeth knows one day of sorrow, you will incur my anger."

Darcy took the certificate, nodded to his father-in-marriage, and strode toward the place where he could view the tips of the feathers bobbing upon his aunt's turban. He heard his aunt say, "Darcy is engaged to my daughter, and I mean to see a wedding between them. Now what have you to say?"

Before he could reach the pair, Elizabeth declared, "Only this—that if he is so, you can have no reason to assume he will claim me to wife."

"But I have already claimed you, love," he said as he strode into the clearing. He stopped beside Elizabeth, placing an arm about her waist. "How many times must a man marry the woman he affects?"

Elizabeth edged closer to him, as if she appreciated his appearance, and he noted the slight tremble in her spine. "I was thinking a minimum of three times for good measure," she said in what one would think were light-hearted tones, but he heard relief in her words.

"Darcy," his aunt snarled. "I expected you of all people to be reasonable. But do not deceive yourself into a belief that I will ever recede. I shall not go away until you have given me the assurance I require."

"Did you not understand, Aunt?" Darcy said slowly, as Lady Catherine was dimwitted. "I cannot marry Anne, for I married Miss Elizabeth Bennet a month ago. You would not have me commit bigamy would you?"

"A...a month?" Lady Catherine stammered. "It was but six weeks since your promise to Anne."

Darcy knew her ladyship was wondering if Elizabeth could, even now, be with child. "Yes," he said with a smile. "We were married after only an acquaintance of eleven days. Would you care to view the marriage certificate? Mr. Bennet had it among the marriage settlement papers in his study." He lifted Elizabeth's chin so he might look upon her countenance. "Elizabeth, your father awaits you at the rose arbor. Return this to his care." He handed her the record of their marriage. "I will finish allaying Lady Catherine's concerns and join you in a few minutes."

Elizabeth appeared hesitant to leave him, but she followed his instructions after he gave her hand a squeeze of reassurance.

With Elizabeth's leave taking, he stepped close to force Lady Catherine to look up at him when he spoke to her. "You are to leave Elizabeth alone," he said in warning tones. "All your complaints are to be directed to me, but know this, your ladyship, neither duty, nor honor, nor gratitude has any possible claim on me in the present instance. No principle will be violated by my marriage to Elizabeth. And with regard to your charges of family resentment and the indignation of the world, if Elizabeth knows contentment in marrying me, your pronouncements of doom would provide me not one moment's concern. I strongly believe the world, in general, will have too much sense to join in such petty scorn."

He caught his aunt's arm to direct her steps toward her coach. "Anne is of age. If she wishes to pursue a breach of promise suit, she may, but this is no longer your concern. You have forgotten that society and law and justice are domains of a man's world. You may have run Rosings Park to your liking, but you have no say in whom your daughter chooses to marry, when Anne will inherit Rosings, or the decision of a judge, if Anne feels it necessary to claim redress for my choosing another so soon after our aborted nuptials. Sir Lewis De Bourgh, your late husband, decided Anne would be his beneficiary, not you, and a judge would look upon Anne's reluctance in arriving at the church on time as an indication of her wish to marry another. You know what I say is true, but you still wish to bend the world to your liking."

She balked at the length of his steps, but Darcy held tight to her arm, half lifting and half dragging his aunt along the well-worn path. "You cannot break the bonds of marriage, and so I will advise you instead to prepare Anne for time in society. My cousin's dowry will be inducement enough to attract a bevy of suitors. Keep quiet regarding what has occurred between me and Anne, and my cousin will do well with Matlock's blessing. Better yet, permit Lady Matlock to introduce Anne to society. Her ladyship's connections are deeper than yours."

When they reached the coach, he jerked open the door and unceremoniously boosted his aunt to the coach's bench. "And no more of Anne's special tonic. If I hear of your abusing my cousin again, I will storm Rosings and remove you as its mistress."

Lady Catherine sputtered, but Darcy's glare silenced her for the moment. To Anne, he said, "I must apologize again, Cousin, for I imagine Lady Catherine will have much to say regarding our conversation in the Bennets' garden upon your return to Kent."

Anne smiled genuinely upon him. "I wish you happy, Darcy."

"And you, too, Anne. As for me, I can be nothing less with Elizabeth by my side."

"I thought we might find you here," Georgiana charged when she joined him and Elizabeth in the Bennets' drawing room. "I told Mr. Bingley that you could not remain long from Longbourn," she teased.

Darcy shrugged his resignation. "I had intended to escort you on your social call, but Mr. Bennet's servant found me on the road between Netherfield and Longbourn. Our aunt made an unexpected call upon Elizabeth this morning."

Georgiana collapsed into the chair beside the settee he and Elizabeth occupied. "Oh, Lizzy! Are you well?"

Elizabeth laughed in irony. "Her ladyship did not do me physical harm, Georgiana."

"No," his sister said, "but my aunt is capable of ripping a hole in one's soul with her sharp criticisms."

"Georgiana!" Darcy warned.

"But it is true, Brother," she protested. "Lady Catherine complains that I do not practice my music faithfully while declaring music the source of her delight, as well as declaring herself superior to all of England in true enjoyment of music. And that is not counting her claims of possessing natural tastes in music. Although she never learned to play, her ladyship claims she would have been lauded as proficient, as would have been Anne if our cousin's health would have permitted Anne time to practice."

"I am glad Lady Catherine never suffered through my playing. Her ladyship would find another reason to despise me," Elizabeth observed.

Darcy caught her hand where it rested upon the settee between them. "None of that. Lady Catherine rarely approves of any person that she cannot rule autocratically. I imagine even if I had not arrived to stave off her attacks, you would have dealt with her ladyship quite thoroughly. I hold no doubt in your ability to win an argument. And if you doubt my evaluation of my aunt's stubbornness, think about how afeared Mr. Collins is of her. Do you wish to fawn excessively?"

"Of course not," Elizabeth assured him.

"Then place this episode behind you. We will marry in fewer than two days, and I mean to see you happy. Lady Catherine has no say in the matter, as you well know."

"But..." she began.

"No contradictions, Elizabeth," he ordered. "Permit me to show you how much I wish you to know the magic of Pemberley as your home."

With a sigh of resignation, she said, "I am your student, Mr. Darcy."

"Excellent," he declared. "But first you must ring for either Mr. or Mrs. Hill."

"There is fresh tea upon the tray," Elizabeth objected.

"Please do as I ask," he insisted. "You will not be sorry."

"Very well." He watched in amusement as his wife reluctantly crossed the room to the bell cord to give it a pull. "Are you satisfied, sir?"

Darcy simply nodded his acceptance of her testy

disposition. He suspected that Elizabeth regretted all that she should have said to Lady Catherine. It was his lovely wife's nature to question her actions after the incident.

"You rang, Miss Elizabeth?" Mrs. Hill said as she stepped through the open door.

"Mr. Darcy asked that I summon you." Elizabeth crossed her arms over her chest and waited impatiently for him to speak.

He smiled knowingly at his wife. "Mrs. Hill, I suppose Miss Elizabeth mentioned her recent encounter with your niece and nephew."

Mrs. Hill nodded her head in affirmation. "Mr. Hill was most pleased to learn they be safe, sir. It was good of Miss Elizabeth to trouble herself in delivering the news, but she has always treated me husband and me most kindly."

Darcy kept his eyes upon Elizabeth, but he spoke to the Bennets' housekeeper. "Then you will be pleased to know that Miss Elizabeth will be your relations' new mistress. Lachlan Hill will be employed upon my estate as an assistant to my land steward, Mr. Burton. Josephine will join my household staff."

"William," Elizabeth gasped. "You did this for me?"

"Most assuredly. It distressed you to leave the Hills behind under Mr. Bradburn's care, and I required a man with knowledge of the shearing pens Mr. Burton has seen remodeled. Mr. Hill and Annie will have a cottage upon the estate."

"Annie?" Elizabeth asked in excitement.

"Yes, it appears that young Mr. Hill would not leave Scotland without his new wife."

"My nephew has married?" Mrs. Hill asked in surprise.

Elizabeth turned to her father's long-time servant. "Oh, you will like her! I will come to the kitchen later and tell you and Mr. Hill what I know of Scotland, the Allards, Annie, and Mr. Darcy's vision for Pemberley and Lachlan's role in making that dream come true."

"Mr. Hill would like that very much, Miss Elizabeth. He worries so over his kin." She curtsied to Darcy. "Thank you, sir."

"My pleasure," Darcy assured the woman. "And would

you see that the young groom who came to fetch me earlier is presented this coin? I was in such a hurry to answer Mr. Bennet's summons that I neglected the boy."

The housekeeper looked pleased by Darcy's actions when she stepped from the room.

Elizabeth turned to Georgiana. "Miss Darcy, would you and Mrs. Annesley please enjoy the view of the garden from that far window?"

"I do not understand," his sister said.

"It is simple," Elizabeth stated. "I plan to share my gratitude for the kindnesses practiced by your brother, and I do not wish my exuberance to embarrass either of you."

His sister smiled mischievously. "I promised Miss Mary that I would meet her in the small sitting room where we might practice our music together. Come, Mrs. Annesley. I would not wish to keep Elizabeth's sister waiting."

As quickly as the door closed behind his sister, Elizabeth rushed across the room. Darcy stood in time to catch her to him.

"Oh, William," she sighed and buried her face in his shirt. "You are too good to me."

"Mr. Hill will be an asset to Pemberley. I would have employed him even if you refused to be my wife, but I am glad your gratitude has driven you into my arms," he whispered. He lifted her chin. "I mean to kiss you, Elizabeth."

She nodded her agreement. Darcy had thought their kiss would be a simple one, but as soon as their lips touched, passion gripped him, and he gathered Elizabeth closer to meld her to him. Heat sank into his bones, and it was all he could do not to place her on the floor and follow her down. It took every ounce of his well-honed discipline not to lock the door and to claim his husbandly rights. With effort, he loosened his hold and lifted his lips from hers.

"Oh, my," Elizabeth whispered in wonder.

"Oh, my indeed," he groaned.

Chapter 26

"YOU SENT FOR me, Papa?"

"Yes, come in my girl." He motioned to where Mr. Darcy sat before her father's desk. The two men in her life had finally agreed to discuss the marriage settlements.

"I see you are both alive," she said with a nervous giggle, as she closed the door behind her. "I hope you are making progress."

Mr. Darcy rose to extend his hand to her. "Mr. Bennet and I agreed we needed to rescue you from the preparations for the wedding breakfast."

She crossed the room to place her hand in Mr. Darcy's. "I thank you both for the consideration. I am sorry my wedding has Mrs. Bennet in a dither."

Her father shrugged his acceptance. "If there is one thing Mrs. Bennet does well, it is to organize an entertainment. Even though this is her first wedding breakfast, I imagine my lady has been planning for it for years."

Elizabeth was amazed to hear her father speak kindly of his wife. Usually, his comments were only a step removed from caustic. She had often wondered how two people so different in nature could come to together long enough to create five children. "I am certain Mrs. Bennet would appreciate hearing you say so."

"I will think upon it," he said stubbornly. "Mr. Darcy has explained something of the improvements he plans for Pemberley, but he suggested that you possessed ideas specific to Longbourn."

She glanced to Mr. Darcy to offer a smile of gratitude for his encouraging her father to listen to her ideas. "I do, sir. I was thinking that if several measures could be put in place that you might put something more aside for my sisters, the way you always planned."

"Mr. Darcy has generously agreed to keep the bargain you negotiated with him," her father explained. "Do you think I require more invested into your sisters' futures?"

"William, that agreement is no longer necessary," she protested.

"It is necessary," her husband insisted. "It was your negotiation to save your sisters that convinced me that you were the woman I required in my life. The funds will be part of a discretionary allotment set aside as part of your pin-money. You may spend it as you wish. If you wish to make it a gift to one or each of your sisters or spend it upon fripperies, it will be your choice, Elizabeth."

Her eyebrow rose in challenge. "Fripperies?"

Mr. Darcy smiled upon her, and her heart took flight. "Yes, something such as five hundred pairs of gloves delivered in a trunk with a gold lock and key. I never asked if you had any such eccentricities, my dear."

She shook her head in disbelief. "I shall save the funds for those who require my assistance," she stated primly.

Mr. Darcy chuckled. "How very stodgy of you, love."

Mr. Bennet cleared his throat to capture their attention. "Might we discuss the ideas for Longbourn before Mrs. Bennet realizes you are missing from her gathered workers, Lizzy?"

Elizabeth blushed thoroughly. "Certainly, Papa."

"Lizzy?" Someone shook her shoulder, pulling her from her dream of speaking her vows to Mr. Darcy, and Elizabeth was slow to leave the dream behind. "Lizzy, please."

Reluctantly, Elizabeth cracked open her eyes. Her room remained draped in darkness except for the flame of one candle upon the bedside table. She focused her vision on her sister's face, expecting to see Jane. "Mary, what are you doing here? What is amiss?" She elbowed her way to a seated position. "Has something happened to Papa? Or Mama? Or Mr. Darcy?" Heaven forbid that her husband had fallen from his horse and broken his neck.

Mary shook off Elizabeth's concerns. "It is nothing of the sort."

Elizabeth scooted over in the bed and pulled Mary down beside her. It was not like Mary to have nightmares or even to have a restless night. Elizabeth assumed that was because the middle Bennet sister was the type to handle disappointment well, to set realistic expectations, and to be the most independent of them. When Mary came along, it was odd to watch her take up her place in the family. Jane, as the oldest, was the parent-pleaser, while Elizabeth was the one most likely to upset their mother, but was exceedingly close to her father. Mary chose a role in the family most opposite of her two older sisters. Although she had a kind heart, sometimes Mary was downright stand-offish. "Then explain to me what has brought you to my room."

"Lydia has eloped," Mary stated in a matter-of-fact manner. That caught Elizabeth's attentions completely, but Mary continued with her report. "That is to say, she means to elope if we do not stop her."

Elizabeth threw back the blanket. "Tell me what you know." She rushed about the room donning clothes as she went.

Mary sighed heavily. "You should know by now, Lizzy, that people assume just because I wear spectacles that I am also deaf and dumb."

That remark brought Elizabeth up short. "Oh, dear one, do not say such things. You are perfectly lovely just the way you are."

"But it is true," Mary argued. "People regularly speak secrets before me and assume I cannot hear them. If I wished, I could blackmail half of Meryton. Kitty and Lydia share secrets before me all the time, pretending I am not in the room."

Elizabeth would have a very serious talk with Kitty before she departed Longbourn with Mr. Darcy. "As I dress, tell me what you overheard."

"After your and Mr. Darcy's confrontation with Mr. Wickham, I remained close to the lieutenant, pretending to be buried in the pages of a book, until he and Captain Denny departed the party. I did not want Mr. Wickham to upset Miss Darcy again. Mr. Wickham spoke privately to Lydia and earned our sister's agreement to meet him in Meryton on the following day. Although they attempted to leave me behind, I insisted upon walking to the village with Lydia and Kitty. There they met with Mr. Wickham in Sampson's Mercantile. While Kitty kept an eye on the street for Aunt Philips or Maria Lucas to interrupt them, Mr. Wickham and Lydia stepped behind a curtain leading to Mr. Sampson's office and the storekeeper's rooms above the shop. Lydia and the lieutenant had forgotten I was in the store, but I listened in. Mr. Wickham swore his devotion to Lydia and encouraged her to elope to Gretna Green this very night. I sat awake for hours to listen for her attempted escape from the house, for I meant to foil her plan, but I fell asleep. I am grieved to have failed the family. I fear she has been gone for an hour or more. She and the lieutenant are to catch the public coach at half past four."

"There is no public coach at that time leaving Meryton," Elizabeth argued.

"That is why Lydia left so early. She talked Tobie into driving her to Sutter's Bend in the dog cart. It will take her a couple of hours to cover the less than five miles."

Elizabeth rushed to her desk and retrieved a piece of foolscap. "Bring the candle closer." She grabbed a pen that required sharpening, but she did not have the time to complete the task properly. Although her finished note held blotches of ink, it was readable. "Wake Mr. Hill. Tell him this note must be delivered to Mr. Darcy and tell him to have Papa's curricle prepared immediately."

"And what will you be doing?"

"Waking our father and convincing him to give chase."

Mary caught Elizabeth's arm. "Do you think Mr. Darcy will cancel the wedding if Lydia is ruined?"

Elizabeth instantly ignored the possibility. "I am certain such is Mr. Wickham's hope: to destroy Mr. Darcy's wedding day — to continue to plague William's days. The scoundrel will use Lydia and then abandon her, which will ruin us all, or he will marry our sister, so he might claim a relationship with the Darcys and profit by it. But know this, he will not ruin Mr. Darcy's wedding plans, for the gentleman and I have been married for over a month. Tomorrow's ceremony is meant to prove to other people that Mr. Darcy and I freely chose each other, and there is no scandal associated with our joining."

"That certainly explains Miss Darcy's comment of her surprise at viewing you and her brother departing Mr. Darcy's coach together," Mary said in irony.

Elizabeth kissed her sister's cheek. "Too often we all forget what a remarkable young woman you are. I shan't make that mistake again. Now hurry, dear one. We must prevent our youngest sister from again proving she lacks sound judgment."

"I will check the inn," her father growled as he stepped down from the curricle. "You stay with the carriage, Lizzy." Although they had made good time thanks to a bright moon marking the road, Elizabeth worried that they would miss the pair or that Lydia and Mr. Wickham chose a different route.

"I will check the stable," Mr. Darcy announced. How her

husband had caught up with them, Elizabeth would never know for certain, but from the froth covering his horse, she suspected he had ridden hard. She had been ecstatic when she heard his voice call out her name when he overtook them. He wore only his breeches, a shirt tucked in at the waist, boots, and a loose coat he would wear when inspecting his fields at Pemberley. His hair was not combed, and she liked the way a few curls draped over his forehead. She would be viewing him thusly very soon, and the idea sent warmth skittering through her veins.

"Be careful," she warned each man as she accepted the reins from her father.

"I have Cerberus tied to your carriage," Darcy said as he paused to squeeze her hand in comfort. "We will find them in time."

He kept walking before she could respond, but Elizabeth noted the weariness in his shoulders. Even though they had had no time to discuss what had occurred, Elizabeth knew Mr. Darcy blamed himself for Mr. Wickham's continued dissipation. Despite none of this madness being his fault, he would know shame at bringing ruin to her father's door.

For the next quarter hour, she split her vigil, first looking toward the inn and then toward the stables. After many agonizing minutes, her father stepped to the inn door to motion her inside, but before she could scramble down from the seat, the stable door split in the middle and what could only be a man's body flew through the air and crashed upon the broken wood. Ignoring her father, Elizabeth hiked her skirts and broke into a run to reach Darcy.

When Sheffield had delivered Elizabeth's note, it was all Darcy could do not to bring down Netherfield with a string of curses rushing to his lips, but he had no time to nurse his misery. Instead, he turned his energies into reaching Elizabeth. *I must protect Elizabeth.* His brain tapped out the familiar tattoo. *And I must put an end to Mr. Wickham's manipulations.* After sending

Sheffield to the stables to wake a groom to saddle Cerberus, Darcy had jerked on a shirt, breeches, and his boots. He had strapped his pistol over his shoulder and had donned his field coat to disguise the gun's presence. After securing directions from the sleepy-eyed groom, he set Cerberus at full gallop to reach Elizabeth and her father, who were somewhere on the road ahead of him.

Only when he could make out Elizabeth and Mr. Bennet's silhouettes against the moonlit road did Darcy slow his mount. When he came alongside the curricle, Elizabeth smiled at him. Only then did Darcy realize that he feared that Wickham's duplicity would have her turning from him.

There was no conversation, but he was satisfied to have her near. It was odd, but when Elizabeth was close, he assumed all was possible—that they would discover a means to triumph over every obstacle placed before them. Only when Mr. Bennet reined in his horse before a small posting inn did anxiousness again claim a place in Darcy's chest.

"I will check the inn." Mr. Bennet sounded angry. "You stay with the curricle, Lizzy."

Darcy wished to accompany Mr. Bennet—to be the one who dragged Wickham, kicking and screaming for dear life, from the inn, but as Mr. Bennet made no request for Darcy's company, he did the next best thing, he dismounted. "I will check the stable."

"Be careful," she warned.

Unable not to touch her, he squeezed her hand. "I have tied Cerberus to your carriage." He attempted to study her features, so precious to him, but the moon slid behind a cloud. "We will find them in time," he said to reassure her, but as he walked away, Darcy wondered if he would ever be free of Mr. Wickham.

Reaching the stable, he eased the door open and slipped inside. He did not wish to spook any of the animals nor the inn's grooms, who likely slept in the hayloft. He waited until his eyes adjusted to the muted moonlight coming through some of the cracks between the wood before he stepped further into the darkness. Eventually, he could make out the stalls and a few horses within. Slowly and methodically he made his way along the line of wooden pens, carefully placing one foot before the other, fearing stepping upon a discarded pitch fork or broom that would smack him in the face.

At the last stall, he had thought his time wasted, but then the horse within shifted to the right to reveal a man stretched out upon an improvised mattress of hay covered by a blanket. Even though he could not view the man's features, Darcy knew without a doubt that the figure was Wickham. He hoped the fool had not also hidden Lydia Bennet in the stable. Surely even Mr. Wickham would not place a child in danger by hiding a girl in a man's world.

With guise in mind, Darcy unlatched the stall's gate. "Easy, boy," he whispered when the horse whinnied. He ran his gloved hand along the animal's neck to calm it. "I mean you no harm." He edged into the stall, nudging the horse's side to move it out of the way so he could bend down beside the sleeping figure.

Removing the gun from its holster, he pressed it to the man's temple. "Tell me why I should not send your sorry arse to hell," he growled.

It did not surprise him that Wickham answered with his customary confidence. Darcy could never understand how a man possessing such ease of speech could not bluff the other players in a card game, but George Wickham reportedly was one of the world's worst card players. The scoundrel always lost more than he won. If Wickham simply practiced his ability to persuade others, Darcy's former chum could be rich from cards or investments or even politics. Match the man's easy manner of speaking of what sounded of the truth with Wickham's fine countenance and there was no end to the possibilities. "Because George Darcy would not approve of his son killing his godson."

"I beg to differ, Mr. Wickham. I believe my revered father would pull the trigger himself."

Wickham shifted uncomfortably, but Darcy kept the gun at his enemy's head and a knee braced upon Wickham's chest.

"Why do you never refer to me as *Wickham*, Darcy? Why am I always *Mr. Wickham* to you? We were once great friends."

"Great friends do not turn upon one another," Darcy argued. "And as to your name, the answer is quite simple. If I called you *Wickham*, it would indicate we hold a familiarity, but the last *Wickham* I knew was your worthy father. The *mister* means you are nothing more to me than a distant acquaintance. Like my tenants and my men of business and my solicitors and such, you are simply a *mister*, a person with whom I occasionally interact, but one who knows little of the man I am beyond being the Master of Pemberley. It will sound prideful to say this, but our bloodlines are not equal. Yet, that is not the full extent of the difference, for Bingley and I do not hold the same noble ancestry, but I count him among my closest associates and am thankful each day for his gracious acceptance of my friendship. The real reason behind my lack of recognition of your place in my life is the George Wickham of my youth, a man I would have been proud to recognize with the familiar name of *Wickham*, died when you took over his life — when you chose dissipation over loyalty. We have nothing in common other than we were both born on Pemberley estate."

The moonlight between the boards forming the barn displayed Wickham's smile. "What now, Darcy?"

"We will first determine if you have taken advantage of Miss Lydia." He nudged Wickham with the toe of his boot, indicating for the scoundrel to stand. Darcy rose to his feet, but Wickham did not move.

Instead, he said, "I have no desire *to take advantage of Miss Lydia*. She is but a silly girl and my lust is not so deep as to seduce a child. However, I would be open to a negotiation to insure my silence on the matter."

"You must negotiate with Mr. Bennet," Darcy countered. "But I should warn you that my future father-in-marriage does not possess deep pockets. You will likely discover the exercise futile."

Wickham pushed himself up on his elbows to look up

at Darcy. "But are you not willing to protect the family of your bride-to-be?"

"Is that your ploy, Wickham? If so, you have greatly erred. I would rather throw more money at the Bennet sisters' dowries to assure their marriages than to present you even one pence." He gestured again with the gun. "Stand."

He should have expected Wickham's desperation, but Darcy was weary from all the drama of late, so when Wickham swept Darcy's legs from beneath him, Darcy tumbled backward into the horse's hindquarters. The animal spooked and darted from his stall with Wickham quick on the horse's tail. Meanwhile, Darcy slammed hard into the packed dirt and straw. The impact jarred him solidly, but he managed to right himself quickly. He scrambled to his feet and gave pursuit.

Darcy easily caught up to Wickham, for his former friend had encountered a stubborn stallion who meant to escape through the closed barn door. Wickham attempted to shoo the horse from his way to make his escape, but Darcy caught the dastard's shoulder and spun the no-good around to plant the man a facer. He fumbled for his gun in their tussle, but he lost it in the hay.

"This is for Miss Lydia," he growled. He followed his first assault with a series of jabs and punches that would have made Gentleman John Jackson proud of his student. "And this is for Georgiana." An upper cut to the chin. "This is for abusing my father's trust." A punch to the midsection that doubled Wickham over. "And this is for all the lies you have spoken against me." He stood Wickham up and hit the man squarely in the nose, sending Wickham windmilling backward through the closed barn door; the wood split with the impact of Wickham's body.

Blind with fury, Darcy scooped up his gun and followed Wickham through the jagged opening and out into the night. He caught up with his enemy only a few feet removed from the opening; Wickham was rolled in a tight ball and he cradled the end of his nose in his open palm. As the scoundrel sputtered and spit blood, Darcy again knelt over him and rested his knee upon Wickham's chest—his weight holding the dastard in place.

"Now, again, I ask why I should not send you to your Maker on this night?"

"Bloody hell, Darcy!" Wickham cursed in venomous tones. "You broke my nose!"

"Answer me," Darcy ordered. "Why should you not count this as your last night upon this earth?" All the years of dealing with Wickham's manipulations boiled down to this moment, and Darcy meant to be done with the man.

From where she came, Darcy would never know, but Elizabeth's arms encircled his neck and chest—latching onto him, and she kissed his cheek and temple. "Do not do this, William," she pleaded. "He is not worth your spending the remainder of your days regretting Mr. Wickham's death."

"No one would notice his leave-taking," he argued as his anger subsided with each of her administrations to his soul.

"True. But many would grieve deeply for your absence. Your family and your tenants and your friends and your wife. I want the dream of you and our children," she insisted. "Do not permit Mr. Wickham to win with his death."

His chest rose and fell with each breath, but, at length, with a heavy exhale of exhaustion, Darcy nodded his agreement and made to stand to release Wickham, but as he stepped back, the heel of his boot caught the hem of her dress as she also stood. She started to fall, and Darcy reached for Elizabeth to keep them both from stumbling backwards into a heap of arms and legs. He did not realize he had pulled the trigger until the sound of the gun split the night air.

Chapter 27

ELIZABETH SMILED AS her mother exited the anteroom to check one last detail before the ceremony began. It felt good to have a moment alone to compose her thoughts. She was exhausted. They had arrived home at three of the clock, and, not unexpectedly, sleep had been hard to come by even after she knew her bed.

Once it was determined that Mr. Darcy had not accidentally killed Mr. Wickham, the innkeeper roused out his man-of-all-works to fetch the physician who lived upon the other side of Sutter's Bend. It was not charitable of her to think, but Mr. Wickham would not soon forget Mr. Darcy's retribution: The lieutenant not only sported a large bump upon his broken nose, but the bullet had blown off the top of Mr. Wickham's left ear — missing his head, but removing a chunk of the cartilage that created the curve of his ear. His perfection would no longer open doors for him.

As the men sorted out what was what, it had been Elizabeth's task to keep Lydia in the let room. "I wish to see Wickham," Lydia demanded in between bouts of tears.

"Mr. Wickham is with the physician," Elizabeth said

calmly. "Now you must dress. Our father means to leave as quickly as accounts are settled."

"But I wished to be the first of my sisters to be married," Lydia whined.

"Oh, my darling," Elizabeth gathered Lydia into a comforting embrace. "Mr. Wickham has admitted to father he had no intention of taking you further than London. His sudden suggestion of an elopement was retribution for the set down Mr. Wickham received at Lucas Lodge."

"Then this is all Mr. Darcy's fault," Lydia accused.

Elizabeth set Lydia from her. "This is *not* Mr. Darcy's fault," she emphasized, "and I will not have you place blame on William's shoulders. The blame belongs to a man who permits bitterness and jealousy to rule his days and to a girl too young and too stubborn to understand the ramifications of her actions. You cared *nothing* for what your elopement would have done to each of your sisters nor for the shame our parents would have been required to shoulder. You and Mr. Wickham acted selfishly and irresponsibly. By his own words, the man cared nothing for you, Lydia! You were just a means to his revenge, yet you foolishly cling to the idea of being married first. Would that have made you happy for more than a few minutes? Would being married before your sisters place food in your stomach or a roof over your head? Would it have permitted you a place in society or would you even now be attempting to find a means home from an area of London where men abuse young women without a thought to their care? I do not believe I can stomach your naiveté one minute longer! Now get dressed. I have had enough of your willfulness for one evening!"

The next morning, over a sober and awkward breaking of their fast before the wedding ceremony claimed all their attention, the whole family, but especially Lydia, was surprised not to earn their mother's support when Mr. Bennet announced that Lydia and Kitty would not be permitted to go out in company again until they reached the age of eighteen. "You will spend your time in study. Mrs. Bennet will hire a tutor for you. Even when you think to call upon Meryton or the neighbors, you will be escorted by one of your sisters or by your parents. Neither of you has proven yourself to be trustworthy."

"Reason with him, Mama," Lydia had pleaded. "Kitty and I cannot return to the schoolroom now that we have been out in society. What will the gentlemen think of us?"

"They will think what they should have thought all along," Mr. Bennet snapped. "That neither of you has the good sense the dear Lord presented a goose. That you are immature and not worthy of their attentions!"

"I am in agreement with Mr. Bennet," their mother had said in her harshest tone. "Your impetuous journey not only placed you in physical danger, but your actions threatened Elizabeth's wedding to Mr. Darcy, not to mention my hope of Mr. Bingley's pursuit of Jane and Mr. Grange's interest in Mary. And that is not to mention what it would have done to the standing of Mr. Bennet and me in the neighborhood. Despite what you think, we do hold a responsibility to your father's position in society."

Elizabeth could not believe her ears and from the expression on her other sisters' faces, neither could they. Mayhap Mr. Bennet took her advice and offered his wife a compliment. In reality, all her mother's *nerves* were designed for no other purpose than to have the attention of her family, a characteristic she now saw displayed, much to Mrs. Bennet's obvious chagrin, in her youngest daughter.

"I did not know that Mr. Grange was interested in Mary," Jane said softly.

Her mother preened as if the matter was settled. "Mr. Grange has spoken to your Uncle Philips of Mary's excellent character."

"Would you be interested in Mr. Grange?" Elizabeth had asked her sister.

Mary shrugged her response. "Who can say? I have barely exchanged more than a dozen words with the man. However, now that someone cares to ask, I am more of Charlotte Lucas's nature. If he had asked, I might have accepted Mr. Collins, for like Charlotte, I am not a romantic. A kind, sensible man would serve me well."

Although she not believe all her sister purported, Elizabeth knew pride in Mary's finding her voice, for she suspected her sister's newfound opinions had something to do with the newly formed friendship with Miss Darcy, who also of late had learned to express her perspective to others and not worry if she would be found wanting.

Mr. Bennet stated, "The word 'sensible' can never be applied to Collins."

Elizabeth recalled a time, not so long removed, when she spoke of being hopeful only for a "kind and sensible" man, and that was followed by her hopes of a man who would respect and honor her. Now she would have both, as well as a man who had proved time and time again that he affected her. "Well, I pray by the time you decide to marry that your betrothed has set a spark of romance in your heart."

Mary smiled at Elizabeth. "I doubt any of us can compete with Mr. Darcy's devotion to you."

"I am blessed by the gentleman's attentions," Elizabeth admitted with a blush. "But you, my dear, will continue to benefit from Miss Darcy's company," Elizabeth declared. Georgiana had invited Mary to return to London with her on the morrow. Darcy's sister could not remain in a bachelor household, and so it was decided that Mrs. Annesley would escort Georgiana and Mary to London. Mr. Darcy had ordered his small coach to retrieve the girls and Mrs. Annesley early Saturday morning. "And while you are in London, I have made arrangements with Miss Darcy's modiste for you to have a fitting for several gowns appropriate for the entertainments you will attend. I am glad you will have the opportunity to enjoy the culture of the City with someone who enjoys music and literature as much as you."

"New gowns?" Mary asked in awe.

Elizabeth laughed. "Yes, Mr. Darcy has provided me a large sum of discretionary funds as part of my pin-money. I promised William to use the funds for those who require my assistance, and I can think of no better recipient than my sister."

"What of Kitty and me?" Lydia asked with a pout.

"When you have earned father's reprieve, we will discuss it," she countered.

Georgiana's tap on the anteroom's door drew Elizabeth from her memories of the last twelve hours. "Oh my, Elizabeth," her new sister to be said with a sigh. "You are so beautiful. Your dress is perfection — simple and stylish. You shall send my brother to distraction."

"How is he?" Elizabeth asked. "No repercussions from last evening?"

Georgiana giggled. "Mr. Sheffield says Darcy has a few bruises and a bit of stiffness from his fight with Mr. Wickham, but I understand Wickham suffered from William's hours in Gentleman Jackson's salon."

"It was a sight I shall never forget," Elizabeth assured the girl. "Although I should not know satisfaction with the outcome, I felt your brother vindicated."

Georgiana perked up. "I have been sent to deliver these." She extended a velvet box in Elizabeth's direction.

Elizabeth accepted the item with a questioning glance to Miss Darcy. "Your brother should not have," she murmured as she cracked the lid open. A gasp caught in her throat.

"They are morganite. Known as emeralds when they are green, beryl occurs less often as pink stones. They are rare and one of my favorite stones."

"I can see why," Elizabeth mumbled as she studied the pair of earrings made from the pink stones Miss Darcy had described and surrounded by small diamonds. "They are exquisite."

"Darcy thought they would go with this." From behind her back, Miss Darcy produced a floral arrangement for Elizabeth. The bouquet held roses and ivy and dahlias and carnations.

"I have missed the fresh flowers Mrs. Reynolds placed in my room daily at Pemberley," she admitted.

Georgiana sighed heavily. "I pray someday that I know a man who loves me equal to what William loves you." She backed away from Elizabeth as if she had recalled a last minute detail. "I must go. Thank you for being my new sister."

Before Elizabeth could respond, Miss Darcy had scurried from the room. Elizabeth stood in puzzlement for a moment before she removed the earrings from the box and fastened them securely to her lobes. She wished she had a mirror to admire the jewels her husband had chosen for her, but she would have to wait until she reached Longbourn before she could give them her full approval. Retrieving the bouquet, she lovingly fingered the ribbon and the rose petals, but was surprised when she noticed a piece of paper hidden within. Delicately, she removed the half sheet of foolscap, folded over several times. Unfolding it, she read:

My dearest Elizabeth,

As I sit at this desk, I remain in awe of the miracle of you, and my heart overflows with love. From the beginning, you destroyed my hard-earned peace, and many times I found myself spiraling from control, but it was always you who served as my anchor. With you, the loneliness has dissipated. I cannot give credence to how often I rush to be in your company. I am only content when you are near — only satisfied when I hear your voice. Despite our madcap beginning, I would suffer all our trials and more to know you but one day — one hour, even. You are my everything: firmly planted are my hopes. You are the coming chapters of my life.

Your William

"My word," Elizabeth sighed as tears of emotion pooled in her eyes. "And to think it all began with a foolish mistake."

"Are you prepared, Lizzy?" her father asked from the open door.

She quickly turned her back to him to refold the note and return it to its hiding place in the bouquet. "I am." She gestured to the flowers. "From Mr. Darcy. Would it be from place if I carried my flowers during the ceremony?"

"It is your celebration, my dear one," he said sadly. "Make

this day yours." He gathered her close to kiss her forehead. "I could not have parted with you, my Lizzy, to anyone less worthy. May you know the happiness of this day forever, my child."

The church bell rang; it was a joyful notice to those gathered in the Meryton church that today was his wedding day. Darcy did not recall whether the bells at St. George had done so or not, but he was glad Mr. Williamson took the trouble on this particular day, for he wished all the world to know of his good fortune in discovering a remarkable woman. He turned to the arched entrance just as Elizabeth appeared in the opening. Her hand rested upon her father's arm, but Darcy knew that even though they had not yet shared the intimacies of marriage, that she was no longer Elizabeth Bennet, but rather Elizabeth Darcy. She looked only to him and did not hesitate to make her journey to his side. She smiled and all was right in his world.

She wore a pale green gown and carried the bouquet Georgiana and Mrs. Annesley had designed from the flowers he had chosen especially for Elizabeth from Bingley's garden and conservatory. He wondered if she had read his note, but her steady gaze said she had.

Their eyes met and held, and that invisible connection he had known from the beginning of their acquaintance—yes, that zing of recognition that had shot up his arm when he spoke his vows to the veiled Elizabeth at St. George—remained and grew stronger. The reality of their closeness stretched out its fingers to her, and Darcy mimicked the emotion. He reached out his arm in her direction, extending his hand to her. Sweetly, as if they meant to dance another waltz—this one a dance of life— Elizabeth paused in her procession down the short aisle to dip a deep curtsy to him in acceptance.

Where in his dreams of their Scottish wedding there was a hint of tarnished resolution in her features, today there was only what could be termed as love. She moved forward to accept his outstretched hand without hesitation.

In awe of the beautiful woman at his side, Darcy recalled very little of the ceremony except when Mr. Williamson asked: "Into this holy union Fitzwilliam and Elizabeth now come to be joined. If any of you can show just cause why they may not lawfully be married, speak now; or else, forever, hold your peace."

Together, he and Elizabeth turned to face those gathered to witness their joining. Gloriously, when no one stepped forward to protest, they broke into laughter, saying, "Finally!" together.

Epilogue

FIFTEEN MONTHS LATER

"WHERE IS SHE?" he asked anxiously as he handed Mr. Nathan his hat and coat.

"The mistress is in her quarters with the midwife, sir."

Darcy nodded his thanks before darting up the stairs and turning toward their adjoining quarters. Without notice, he burst into his wife's room to find Hannah pressing Elizabeth forward into a half-seated position. A sheet covered his wife's legs, but from the obvious pain contorting her face, Elizabeth suffered greatly.

"Mr. Darcy, you should not be here," the midwife chastised. "You've done your part. Now it be your wife's domain."

Darcy silently cursed his lust, for it had brought Elizabeth to this moment. *Please do not take her from me, God,* he murmured before telling Mrs. Neuwirth that he meant to stay.

As the pain subsided, Elizabeth collapsed back against the pillows. Her beautiful hair was wet and matted, but he thought her never lovelier.

"I see Mr. Sheffield sent for you even though I specifically instructed him that it was not necessary," his wife said in a breathy exhale of irritation.

Darcy crossed the room to claim her hand. "You promised you would wait until I returned from Maitland Hall," he argued gently.

"Such was my intention," she spoke in weary tones, as Hannah wiped her mistress's face with a cool cloth. "Yet, like its father, this child possesses no patience."

"It is a Darcy trait, one of which you are well aware," he said in dutiful acceptance. He knew his wife was not angry with him. When Hannah stepped away from the bed to provide them a semblance of privacy, he leaned closer to say, "It grieves me to see you suffer, my love."

"None of that, Mr. Darcy," his wife demanded with a tight grip of his hand. "When we married, I told you I wanted the dream of you and *children*. That is plural. If my mother could endure this five times, I plan to be equal to the task. Set your mind to it, sir."

In truth, Darcy did not think he could remain from Elizabeth's bed even if he made a silent vow never to place her in danger again. "My mind is set, Lizzy." He leaned forward to brush a kiss across her lips, but she caught him about the neck to hold him in an intimate exchange.

"Now be off with you, Mr. Darcy," she said against his lips when she released him. "As Mrs. Neuwirth said, this is woman's work."

"I love you, Elizabeth," he said as he stood.

"And I you, William."

"There you are, sir."

Darcy looked up to see Sheffield in the door of the small chapel built in the 1700s as a place for the estate workers to come for prayers in time of need. In Darcy's opinion, the chapel was one of the most remarkable structures upon the estate grounds. Darcy had retreated to this sanctuary when he could no longer tolerate the cries of pain emanating from Elizabeth's room. This is where he had come to pray when his mother was dying—to ask God to spare Lady Anne's life, and despite the futility of that day, he had returned again to ask God to show mercy upon the most important woman in his life. The noise of Elizabeth's screams had gone on for hours, and he could not be near when she suffered and not respond.

"I understand why Mrs. Darcy did not wish you to send for me," he said lamely. "I came here to say a prayer for my wife's safety."

"And what of your child?" Sheffield asked.

"I pray for the infant also," Darcy admitted. "But, in truth, I could live without an heir, but I do not think I could tolerate another day on this earth if God chose to claim Elizabeth."

"Such was the way with your parents," Sheffield observed. "From the day of Lady Anne passing, your revered father marked his days until he could be with her again. She made him promise not to abandon you before you were ready. Did you know that? If not for seeing you to your maturity, I imagine he would have been happy to permit the least cold or sniffle to claim him."

Until today, Darcy would not have understood his father's doing so. "Is there news from Mrs. Neuwirth? Does Elizabeth still suffer? Is that why you sought me out?"

Sheffield smiled at last. "The midwife thought it time that you meet your child, Mr. Darcy."

"But is Elizabeth safe?" Darcy demanded.

"Hannah says the mistress is exhausted, but well."

Darcy sank to his knees. "Dear God, thank you."

Sheffield knelt beside him. "Let us say a proper prayer for the continued health of both your wife and the child, and then as I am as anxious as you to have a look at your son, we will return to the manor together."

"A son?" Darcy said in awe.

"Aye, sir. An heir for Pemberley. When you finish holding and kissing the lad, we should send someone to ring the chapel bell. Your cottagers will wish to know the glad tidings."

Darcy chuckled. "You are more aware of my role as master than am I."

"No, sir." Sheffield said seriously. "You are the Master of Pemberley. It is a role you were born to, as will be your son. I am merely your valet and a friend when you require one. Today is such a day, for your mind is not on your duty, but upon the woman you love."

"Then let us pray for God's guidance in both my duty to this land and to the woman that stirs my soul."

Later, as he stood in wonderment looking upon the perfect countenance of his son, Darcy held very still to savor the moment. "Do you hear the bells, my boy?" He drew a finger across the child's chin. "Those are for you. They tell all of Pemberley that their future is now in these tiny hands." His son's fingers wrapped around Darcy's finger, and he knew a different kind of contentment than he knew with Elizabeth, but the bond was as deep and as strong.

"You should call Josie to take him to the nursery," his wife said in amusement.

"Later." Darcy cuddled the child closer as the boy's eyes slowly drifted downward. "He is the best of us, Lizzy."

Elizabeth yawned loudly. "Heaven help us, if he were the worst of us. We would both be candidates for Bedlam."

"What name have you chosen?"

She sighed as her eyes, too, slid closed. "Bennet George Thomas Edward Darcy." Another deep yawn nearly smothered her words as she said, "*Bennet* and *Thomas* for my father. *George* for yours. And *Edward* for both the good colonel and my Uncle Gardiner. All the men, beyond his father, who define our son."

"Quite a mouthful for a babe this small." Darcy could not draw his eyes from the sleeping child. "Excellent choice, love. Your father will be ecstatic. As will be my cousin and your uncle, and I imagine even the late George Darcy smiles down from Heaven upon your thoughtfulness." He turned to the bed where she rested, but his wife was already asleep. He lifted the child where he could kiss the boy's head. "That magnificent woman asleep on the bed is your mother, Bennet George Thomas Edward Darcy. And like me, you are blessed among men, for she loves you more than is reasonable." He leaned down to kiss the top of Elizabeth's head, but she was in deep slumber. "Now, although you will not remember this day, I plan to show you off to those who call Pemberley home, and some day they will relate the story of your birth to you, just as they related the story of my birth to me. You will be embarrassed by all the attention, but you will know pride in your birthright—pride in the love that makes you a Darcy." He eased the door open to slip into the hallway. "First, we will meet Mr. Sheffield and then Mr. Nathan and Mrs. Reynolds. They have been with Pemberley since before your dear Papa was born, and they know more about it than even he does." He made his way to Mrs. Reynolds's sitting room where all the upper servants had gathered to be introduced properly to his son. "Everyone," Darcy said with great emotion coursing through him, "this is Bennet Darcy, the future Master of Pemberley."

~ *Finis* ~

Excerpt from
Pride and Prejudice
and a Shakespearean Scholar

Arriving December 2017

"I AM NOT made for Mama's aspirations," she sniffed. "I've no head for strutting about like a peacock." With the toe of her boot, Elizabeth Bennet nudged the loose pebbles on the well-worn path leading down the slope of Oakham Mount. Her mother would be furious if she knew that Elizabeth had snuck off to claim a few moments of peace, but to save her own sanity, Elizabeth had dared to risk her mother's wrath.

Longbourn had been in a tizzy since Mr. Bingley, the Bennets' newest neighbor, had accepted the family's invitation for supper. The prospects of an eligible young man with a reported five thousand pounds per year as income dining at Longbourn had Mrs. Bennet with visions of marriage proposals dancing in her head, for the lady was certain the gentleman would choose one of her daughters to be "Mrs. Bingley."

"Mama has always been insistent upon putting us forward," Elizabeth grumbled. Although she enjoyed socializing with a variety of neighbors, until today, Elizabeth had never really considered the prospects of marriage, especially a marriage with someone she could not respect and admire, or worse, that particular someone not respecting and honoring her—someone she might know little of before the nuptials.

She paused to study the scenery below her from her favorite vantage point. The land was soft and rolling, nothing like the mountains her Aunt Gardiner described as part of Derbyshire's landscape. *"Derbyshire offers the most magnificent views in all of England,"* her aunt was often fondly saying of her home shire. According to her aunt, Oakham Mount was not really much of a mountain, but this path and this "rising hillside" was Elizabeth's sanctuary.

With a sigh of resignation, she tucked a stray strand of auburn colored hair beneath the band circling her "work" bonnet. It was made of straw, and she wore the headwear whenever she assisted Mr. Hill in the garden or called upon her father's tenants. As she jammed the wisp of hair into her pinned braid, she wished, not for the first time, that she possessed Jane's golden curls or Lydia's deep brown locks. "Instead, I am *blessed* with hair too red to be considered brown and too brown to claim the term 'strawberry,'" she groused.

When she reached the lowest point of the path coming off the mount, she chose to sit upon a downed tree, a place she often claimed as her seat while writing in her diary. Her father called her scribblings a "journal," but Elizabeth preferred the word *diary* because it sounded more literary in nature, although, in truth, what she wrote in the book each day was anything but literary — just the ramblings of a girl coming into her womanhood. She had been writing each day since she was sixteen, after receiving her first "diary" from her Aunt Gardiner as part of a celebration of Elizabeth's coming into society. That original book held gold embossed lettering and she treasured it more than any other gift she had every received, other than the single pearl she wore on a chain about her neck that had once belonged to her great-grandmother. Now, she wrote in the blank books her father kept in a drawer of his desk for her. They were plain, nothing like that first diary, but Elizabeth maintained the exercise because she thought it kept her sane in a house full of female twittering and ribbons and constant talk of which gentleman was the most handsome among the eligible young men in the neighborhood. She was certain that before the evening was over that Mr. Bingley would claim that particular title, even if he had a large wart on the end of his nose and crossed eyes. "After all," she murmured, "he has a fortune of five thousand a year."

Before sitting, Elizabeth removed the hard covered book from the pocket in the smock she wore over her day dress. She should have removed the outer garment before she left Longbourn, but when her mother had taken to her bed for a restorative nap, Elizabeth claimed the advantage of the reprieve and set out for her favorite walking path.

Plopping down upon the log, she kicked off her half boots, undid her ribbon garters, and removed her stockings. "Wonderful," she sighed as she rubbed the soles of her feet against the cool grass, which was still quite green, even thought autumn had made its presence known in the last week. She was well aware that her actions were extremely improper, and if her mother learned of them, Elizabeth would have a high toll to pay for the liberties she had taken but she rarely denied herself such pleasures. "Moreover, when was the last time I met anyone along this turn of the road?"

She dug a pencil from her pocket and opened her diary. "Mayhap, I should write what Mama's lecture would be if she caught me in such a state." The idea brought a smile of amusement to her lips as she mimicked Mrs. Bennet's overly stern tone: *Running about the countryside like some sort of hoyden! Not a servant or a sister to keep you company! Sitting upon a fallen tree as if it were a throne! Your ankles and feet exposed to any who pass by!*

Subconsciously, she tucked her bare feet under the hem of her dress, but that was the only concession Elizabeth made to her mother's sense of propriety. "I am a hopeless case, Mama," she whispered before she took up the pencil to write. Some days she wrote only a paragraph. On other days, she filled several pages.

Today, she began by recording the Shakespearian lines that her father had assigned her for the day's reading. They had spent a good hour or more digging into the truth of the lines. She thought it odd though that he had been insistent on her dwelling on the advantages and the disadvantages of being persuaded to marry. "Mayhap, Mama's silliness is wearing off on him after all these years," she murmured aloud.

Her dear Papa had always favored her over her sisters — perhaps because, like Mr. Thomas Bennet, she truly found the magic in the written page — and they had spent countless hours over her lifetime discussing his life-long obsession with William Shakespeare, beginning as early as when she was a small child sitting on his lap. He read Shakespeare to her daily, and she could recite many of the Bard's plays from heart. Over the last seven years, their discussions specifically dealt with her father's attempt to discredit the papers of James Cowell, whose work was supposedly the basis of the research of one James Wilmot, who professed that it was Francis Bacon who wrote the plays and the poetry attributed to William Shakespeare. It always amazed Elizabeth that her father, a simple country squire, was considered one of the most renowned Shakespearean scholars in England. Moreover, with Bacon's home of Gorhambury House in Hertfordshire being nearby, Mr. Bennet's fellow scholars often called upon Longbourn to participate in a never-ending debate.

As her mind wandered over all these things, her pencil flew across the page. She attempted to compose her own poem, patterned after Shakespeare's lines, but she termed herself sorely lacking. "The above poem proves I am not gifted with the ability to express myself in such a succinct form," she wrote beneath her feeble efforts at greatness. In deep concentration, she took no notice of the crunch of newly fallen leaves until a shadow fell over her shoulder to steal away the sunlight.

Excerpt from
The Earl Claims His Comfort
Book 2 of the Twins' Trilogy

Arriving September 2017

AUGUST 1820, YORKSHIRE

"CANNOT RECALL THE last time I slept in my own bed," he murmured to no one in particular as he stood to claim his bearings. The room swirled before his eyes, but Rem shook off the feeling. Of late, it was common for him to know fuzziness marking his thinking.

Levison Davids, the 17th Earl of Remmington, set the glass down harder than he intended. He had consumed more alcohol than he should, but as his home shire often brought on a case of maudlin, he drowned his memories. He turned toward the door attempting to walk with the confidence his late father always demanded of his sons. Lev was not trained to be the earl. His father had groomed Rem's older brother Robinson for the role, but Fate had a way of spitting in a man's eye when he least expected it.

Outside, the chilly air removed the edge from the numbness the heavy drink provided him, and for a brief moment Rem thought to return to the common room to reinforce the black mood the drink had induced. A special form of "regret" plagued his days and nights since receiving word of his ascension to the earldom some four years prior, and he did not think ever to be comfortable again.

"Storm comin'," the groom warned when he brought Rem's horse around.

"We're in Yorkshire," Remmington replied. "We are known for the unpredictable."

Customarily, he would not permit the groom to offer him a leg up, but Rem's resolve to reach his country estate had waned. He had received a note via Sir Alexander Chandler that Rem's presence was required at the Remmington home seat, and so he had set out from France, where he had spent the last year, to answer a different call of duty.

Sir Alexander offered little information on why someone summoned Rem home, only that the message had come from the estate's housekeeper. Not that it mattered who had sent for him. Tegen Castle was his responsibility. The journey from France had required that Rem leave an ongoing investigation behind, a fact that did not please him, even though he knew the others in service to Sir Alexander were excellent at their occupations. Moreover, the baronet had assured Rem that several missions on English shores required Remmington's "special" skills, and he could return to service as quickly as his business knew an end.

He caught the reins to turn the stallion in a tight circle. Tossing the groom a coin, he kicked Draco's sides to set the horse into a gallop.

As the dark swallowed them up, Rem enjoyed the feel of power the rhythm of the horse's gait provided. He raced across the valley before emerging onto the craggy moors. At length, he skirted the rocky headland.

He slowed Draco as the cliff tops came into view. When he reached Davids' Point, he urged the stallion into a trot. Rem could no longer see the trail, but his body knew it as well as it knew the sun would rise on the morrow. After some time, he jerked Draco's reins hard to the left, and as a pair they plunged onto the long-forgotten trail. He leaned low over the stallion's neck to avoid the tree limbs before he directed Draco to an adjacent path that led upward toward the family estate, which sat high upon a hill overlooking the breakwaters.

When he reached the main road again, he pulled up on the reins to bring the animal to a halt. Rem patted Draco's neck as he stared through the night at his childhood home, which was framed against the rising moonlight. It often made him sad to realize how much he once loved the estate as a child and how much he now despised it.

"No love left in the bricks," he said through a thick throat. "Even the dowager countess no longer wishes to reside here. How can I?"

It was not always so. Although he was a minor son, Rem always thought to share Tegen Castle with his wife and children–to live nearby and to relate tales of happier days.

"But after Lady Delia's betrayal and then, likewise, that of Miss Lovelace, I possess no heart to begin again."

In truth, of the two ladies, Rem had only loved Lady Delia.

"Fell in love with the girl when I was but fourteen and she, ten."

Rem crossed his arms over the rise of the saddle to study the distant manor house.

"Perhaps Delia could find no solace here," he murmured aloud.

Even today, it bothered him that Delia had not cared enough for him to send him a letter denying their understanding. He learned of Delia's marrying Baron Kavanagh from Sir Alexander, with whom Rem served upon the Spanish front. Sir Alexander's younger brother delivered the news in a cheeky letter.

"I suppose Lady Delia thought being a baroness was superior to being Mrs. Davids. Little did she know I would claim the earldom. More is the pity for her." A large raindrop plopped upon the back of his hand. "If we do not speed our return to the castle, my friend, we will arrive with a wet seat."

He caught up the loose reins, but before he could set his heels into Draco's sides, a shot rang out. By instinct, Rem thought to dive for the nearby ditch. Yet, the heavy drink slowed his response, and before he could act, he knew the sharp sting of the bullet in his thigh.

Draco bolted forward before Rem had control of the stallion's reins. He felt himself slipping from the saddle, but there was little he could do to prevent the impact. He slammed hard into the packed earth just as the heavens opened with a drenching rain. The back of his head bounced against a paving stone, and a shooting pain claimed his forehead. Even so, Rem thought to sit up so he might take cover, but the effort was short coming. The piercing pain in his leg and the sharp sting claiming his vision fought for control. The blow to his head won, and Rem screwed his eyes closed to welcome the darkness.

Other Novels by Regina Jeffers

Jane Austen-Inspired Novels:

Darcy's Passions: Pride and Prejudice Retold Through His Eyes

Darcy's Temptation: A Pride and Prejudice Sequel

Captain Wentworth's Persuasion: Jane Austen's Classic Retold Through His Eyes

Vampire Darcy's Desire: A Pride and Prejudice Paranormal Adventure

The Phantom of Pemberley: A Pride and Prejudice Mystery

Christmas at Pemberley: A Pride and Prejudice Holiday Sequel

The Disappearance of Georgiana Darcy: A Pride and Prejudice Mystery

The Mysterious Death of Mr. Darcy: A Pride and Prejudice Mystery

The Prosecution of Mr. Darcy's Cousin: A Pride and Prejudice Mystery

Mr. Darcy's Fault: A Pride and Prejudice Vagary

Elizabeth Bennet's Excellent Adventure: A Pride and Prejudice Vagary

Elizabeth Bennet's Deception: A Pride and Prejudice Vagary

Mr. Darcy's Bargain: A Pride and Prejudice Vagary

Mr. Darcy's Present: A Pride and Prejudice Vagary

The Pemberley Ball: A Pride and Prejudice Vagary Novella

The Road to Understanding: A Pride and Prejudice Vagary

A Dance with Mr. Darcy: A Pride and Prejudice Vagary

Honor and Hope: A Contemporary Pride and Prejudice

The Road to Pemberley (which contains "The Pemberley Ball" as a short story)

Regency and Contemporary Romances:
Angel Comes to the Devil's Keep - Book 1 of the Twins' Trilogy
A Touch of Scandal – Book 1 of the Realm Series (aka The Scandal of Lady Eleanor)
A Touch of Velvet – Book 2 of the Realm Series
A Touch of Cashémere – Book 3 of the Realm Series
A Touch of Grace – Book 4 of the Realm Series
A Touch of Mercy – Book 5 of the Realm Series
A Touch of Love – Book 6 of the Realm Series
A Touch of Honor – Book 7 of the Realm Series
A Touch of Emerald - The Conclusion of the Realm Series
His American Heartsong - A Companion Novel to the Realm Series
His Irish Eve
The First Wives' Club – Book 1 of the First Wives' Trilogy
Second Chances: The Courtship Wars
One Minute Past Christmas (a contemporary short story of an extraordinary Christmas)

Coming Soon...
The Earl Finds His Comfort: Book 2 of the Twins' Trilogy (arriving September 2017)
Pride and Prejudice and a Shakespearean Scholar (arriving December 2017)
Indentured Love: A Persuasion Vagary
Lady Chandler's Sister - Book 3 of the Twins' Trilogy

Meet the Author

Writing passionately comes easily to Regina Jeffers. A master teacher, for thirty-nine years, she passionately taught thousands of students English in the public schools of West Virginia, Ohio, and North Carolina. Yet, "teacher" does not define her as a person. Ask any of her students or her family, and they will tell you Regina is passionate about so many things: her son, her grandchildren, truth, children in need, our country's veterans, responsibility, the value of a good education, words, music, dance, the theatre, pro football, classic movies, the BBC, track and field, books, books, and more books. Holding multiple degrees, Jeffers often serves as a Language Arts or Media Literacy consultant to school districts and has served on several state and national educational commissions.

Regina's writing career began when a former student challenged her to do what she so "righteously" told her class should be accomplished in writing. On a whim, she self-published her first book *Darcy's Passions*. "I never thought anything would happen with it. Then one day, a publishing company contacted me. They watched the sales of the book on Amazon, and they offered to print it."

Since that time, Jeffers continues to write. "Writing is just my latest release of the creative side of my brain. I taught theatre, even participated in professional and community-based productions when I was younger. I trained dance teams, flag lines, majorettes, and field commanders. My dancers were both state and national champions. I simply require time each day to let the possibilities flow. When I write, I write as I used to choreograph routines for my dance teams; I write the scenes in my head as if they are a movie. Usually, it plays there for several days being tweaked and *rewritten*, but, eventually, I put it to paper. From that point, things do not change much because I completed several mental rewrites."

Every Woman Dreams Blog
https://reginajeffers.wordpress.com

Website
www.rjeffers.com

Austen Authors
http://austenauthors.net

English Historical Fiction Authors
http://englishhistoryauthors.blogspot.com

Join Regina on Twitter, Facebook, Pinterest, Google+, and LinkedIn.